THE HOUSE OF SACRIFICE

ANNA SMITH SPARK lives in London, UK. She has a BA in Classics, an MA in History and a PhD in English Literature. Besides her novels, she has also been published in *Fortean Times*, *Hansard* and the poetry website, www.greatworks.org

Previous jobs include fetish model, English teacher and petty bureaucrat. Anna can often be spotted SFF conventions wearing very unusual shoes.

www.courtofbrokenknives.org
@queenofgrimdark
Anna Smith-Spark

Praise for The Empires of Dust

'Fierce, gripping fantasy, exquisitely written; bitter, funny and heart-rending by turns' Adrian Tchaikovsky

'A blood-spattered tapestry. There's rough humour, high drama and a love of story-telling that shines through every page'
Daily Mail

'Anna Smith Spark is a dynamic new voice in the field of grimly baroque fantasy, a knowing and witty provisioner of the Grand Guignol, a cheerful undertaker strolling across the graveyard and beckoning you to admire her newest additions.'
Scott Lynch

'A bold experiment and feels like something new'
Mark Lawrence

'Spark's world is gritty and vivid, populated at every turn with richly drawn characters. With a plot that twists through serpentine intrigues, Spark's series f... ...ns'
...ly

'Holy cr... ...gs

'A mast... ...gs

Also by Anna Smith Spark

The Empires of Dust
The Court of Broken Knives
The Tower of Living and Dying
The House of Sacrifice

ANNA SMITH SPARK

The House of
Sacrifice

Book Three of The Empires of Dust

HARPER
Voyager

HarperCollins*Publishers*
1 London Bridge Street,
London SE1 9GF

www.harpercollins.co.uk

Published by Harper*Voyager*
An imprint of HarperCollins*Publishers* 2020
1

Map by Sophie E. Tallis

A catalogue record for this book
is available from the British Library

ISBN: 978-0-00-820415-0

Set in Sabon by Palimpsest Book Production Ltd, Falkirk, Stirlingshire

Printed and bound in the UK by CPI Group (UK) Ltd, Croydon CR0 4YY

This book is dedicated to my mother.

The Continent of Irlast

Illyr
Ethalden
River Nimenest

SEA of TEARS

Neir Forest
Ander

Tarboran

SEA of GRIEF

Balkash L.

Arunmen

Kara Kol Desert

River Alph

Cen Elora

CLOSED SEA

Tereen

Mountains of the Heart

Samarnath

Gaeth

Theme

Calchas

SMALL SEA

River Ekat

Chathe

Rose Forest

Issykol

Eralad

Forest of Khotan

Elarne

Mountains of Pain

Sekemleth Empire

River Essern

Turain

Nor Desert

SEA of TEARS

Mar

Pen Amrean

PART ONE

THE JOY OF THE WORLD

Chapter One

Hail Him. Behold Him.
Wolf lord, lord of carrion,
Joy to the sword that is girt with blood.
Man-killer, life-stealer, death-bringer, life's thief.
King-throned, glorious His rule:
The sea-eaten shore, the stones of the mountains,
The eagles, the fleet deer, the wild beasts,
Men in their cities, rich in wisdom,
All are bound to Him,
His word is law.
With bloody hands He governs,
Sets His rule and His measure,
A strong tree, a storm at evening,
The sea rising up to swallow a ship.
The night coming, the sudden light that makes the eyes blind,
The floodtide, the famine, the harrowing, the pestilence.
King and Warrior.
Golden one, shining, glorious.
Life's judgement, life's pleasure, grave of hope.

The city of Ethalden, that is the most beautiful place on all the black earth of Irlast. Its towers are made of pearl and silver. Its walls are solid gold. It stands on a great plain of rich grassland, on the banks of the river Jaxertane that flows wild down to the cold dark endless sea. It is a jewel beyond comparing. The glory of all the world. Wondrous thing! Look upon it and be blinded, dazed by its magnificence, fall upon your knees, worship, marvel, worship. Oh you who are nothing, you who are but maggots, crawling pitifully in the bitter dust. Kneel and give thanks, rejoice that you have lived to see it, that such brilliance was raised in this blessed era of the world's end.

Perfection is built here! Kneel, kneel, cry out in terror, turn away your eyes from its radiance! Its streets are paved with marble. Its palaces are ivory and white glass. Its bells ring out in music, the air is filled with perfumes, the river runs clear, the corn grows golden, the trees are heavy with sweet fruit. Treasure houses stacked with riches. Wealth beyond mortal ken. Numberless are its herds, its flocks, its swift horses; its people dress in silks and satins, its women beautiful as goddesses, its men strong as giants, in their eyes is the light of knowledge and power over all things.

Its foundations are living bodies, flesh putrefying, bones cracking beneath its weight. Its mortar is tears and blood. At its heart there stands a palace of desolation, built in honour of a mighty king.

Such a king . . .

You think, do you, that he would have died somewhere, in the desert, on the shores of the White Isles, in the ruins of Ethalden, if I had not saved him? That none of this would have been? You think, do you, that without him the world would be at peace? If he died, do you think that there would be no war, no cruelty no murder, no pain, the world would be a good and loving place? 'Why do we do this?' I asked him once. And he looked out across the world that we have made, and did not speak. 'If not me,' he said at last, 'then perhaps someone else.'

My own city of Sorlost they say has been brought low by killing violence. We did not do that. 'The people of Sorlost deserved it,' you will say. 'Child killers. Blood-sodden. Their city is based on murder, go there, Thalia, send Marith your husband there to punish them.'

The people of Sorlost are wise. They merely make visible what all the world is based on.

Take the bread your children are eating, send them to bed hungry, give the bread instead to the starving poor.

No?

In Sorlost, at least, they do not lie. In Ethalden, our tower built on human suffering, we do not lie.

Osen Fiolt is a bad man, for following him, for doing as he orders, for being his friend. Osen wants power and wealth, does not care where it comes from. Oh, yes. I wish Osen was not his friend. But I am worse, because I married him? Because I live my life? Because I do not stick a knife into his throat? To me, he has always been kind and loving. To me, he is a good man. As for the rest – I turn my eyes away from it, as we all do. Refugees and beggars stagger across the world, men, women, children, their tears are a drowning flood: what do you do? What more can be expected of me? Should I be better than anyone else is?

It grieves me, yes, I weep over it, what we have come to, what the world is.

In a different life . . .

In a different place . . .

There is no different life. There is no different place. There is here and now, there is what I have, what I can be, what I can do.

Kill him? Oh, it is rather too late for that, is it not? Leave him? Why should I do that? Because it would be a better thing than staying with him? Because I should suffer, for marrying him? Because he has done harm to others, and thus I should not find pleasure in his love? Because he is a bad man and so I should not love him, because you do not want me to love a bad man because I am – what? Because I should be better than that? If I ran away to the other side of Irlast, dressed myself in sackcloth and ashes, did penance with aching hands, tended the starving, kissed the wounds of the sick – so what? So what?

You do not expect Osen to leave him, renounce all of this. You do not expect this of any of his friends.

You will still say, perhaps, that I am a fool, lovestruck, blinded, his victim, that I would flee from him if I could, because . . .

We sit together, talk, laugh, argue, hold great feasts and parties, walk in the gardens, ride in the fields, sit quietly to read. I am trying to improve his taste in poetry. He is introducing me to the Pernish stories of his childhood. But I should not love him, because . . .?

We march onwards, an army like a storm, like the clouds rushing over the sun. The world trembles. The men in their bronze armour sing the paean, hold their heads high, smile as they march. The world bows before us. Every soldier here in our army, they are as mighty as kings. Life is good, life is joyous for them.

That is not a good thing, no. It would be better indeed if we were all to be men of peace.

But we are not men of peace.

I will not be blamed for living my life.

Chapter Two

Marith Altrersyr, King of the White Isles and Ith and Illyr and Immier and the Wastes and the Bitter Sea, King of All Irlast, Ansikanderakesis Amrakane, Amrath Returned to Us, King Ruin, King of Shadows, King of Dust, King of Death
His Empire

Marith Altrersyr the King of All Irlast stood on the brow of a hill looking across towards the city of Arunmen.

It was still early morning. Soft pale light, pink and golden. In the valley the scent of wood smoke, the smoke rising to blur the light. Birds wheeled in the sky, turning, twisting like outstretched fingers. Reminded him of Thalia's hair. They called harsh and lonely. Hungry, cold, fragile things. Moved in the sky turning and turning. Their cries muffled by the ringing of a blacksmith's hammer. Wheeled and called, flew off to the east.

The sun caught their wing beats. Black and white in the sky. The hammer rang out loudly. Then silence. Waiting.

Waiting.

'Marith!'

Marith turned. Looked down the hillside. Osen Fiolt, the Lord of Third Isle, the Lord of the Calien Mal, Death's Lieutenant, Captain of the Army of Amrath. His best friend. Osen rode up towards him. A young man, dark and handsome but for the scar on his face.

'Marith! They're waiting for you!'

Marith rubbed his eyes. From across towards the city came a distant rumble. A flash of white fire against the city walls. The birds rushed back overhead, black and silver. Singing. He took a long drink from the bottle at his belt. Watched the course of the birds across the sky.

Ah, gods.

Osen pulled up his horse beside him. 'Beautiful morning for it.'

'I think it might snow.'

'Do you? A bit early in the year for snow?'

'Thalia would like it.'

'The men wouldn't.'

'No. No, I suppose not. But it would be beautiful. Snowfall. Don't you think?'

Osen said, 'Are you ready, then?'

Looked back over the morning landscape. The hammer rang again. Smell of wood smoke. Another distant flash of light against the city's walls. Dark cloud twist of birds, rising afraid.

He drank from the bottle. 'I suppose I'll have to be.'

Swung himself up onto his horse. A white stallion, saddled in red and silver, red ribbons plaited in its tail, gold on its hooves, sharp bronze horns decorating its head. Osen brought his own horse to fall in beside him. Reached out and their hands touched.

'Third time lucky?'

'Third time lucky.'

They kicked their horses into a gallop.

'Amrath!' Marith shouted. 'Amrath and the Altrersyr! Death! Death!'

Before him, on the plain, the Army of Amrath stood to attention. Bronze armour. Bronze swords. Long iron-tipped ash-wood sarris spears. Their helmets plumed in red horse-hair. Dark-tempered bronze over staring eyes. Horses armoured and masked, heads like skulls, blinkered, blind to everything. Red standards fluttering.

Raw and bloodied. Dripping screaming weeping over the army's lines. In the sky above, two dragons circled. Red and black. Green and silver. Huge. Shadowbeasts danced around the dragons, formless faceless long-clawed.

The Army of Amrath.

Waiting.

All of them.

Waiting for him.

Marith rode along the front of his army, Osen at his side. He drew his sword. Raised it, shining, the morning sun flashing on the blade. White metal, engraved with rune signs. The rune letters burned in the sunlight. The ruby in the sword's hilt glowed scarlet. Blue fire flickered down the length of the blade.

Henket. Mai. Eth. Ri.

Death. Grief. Ruin. Hate.

He shouted to the men, his voice loud as the sword's light. 'Soldiers of Amrath! My soldiers! Twice now, this city has resisted us! Resisted us and betrayed us! Now, today, it will fall!'

An explosion shattering against the black walls of the city. White fire, silent as maggots. White fire, silent, and then screams. The wind caught his cloak and sent it billowing out behind him. Dark red, scab-coloured, tattered into a thousand shreds of lace. Dried blood flaked off it. Fresh blood oozed off it. It stank of blood and shit and rot and smoke. He wore his silver crown but was otherwise bareheaded, the morning sun bright on his black-red hair. His skin like new-spun silk, smooth and perfect, gleaming. His grey eyes soft like a child's eyes. Soft pale grey like moths.

'Destroy it!' Marith shouted to his army. 'Destroy it! Tear it down! Let nothing be left alive!'

'Amrath!' the army screamed back at him. 'Amrath and the Altrersyr! Death and all demons! Death! Death! Death!'

Columns of soldiers began to move forward. Siege engines hurled rocks running with banefire. Mage fire, white and silent. Dragon fire, glowing red. The beat of war drums. Clamour of trumpets.

Voices chanting out the death song. Slowly slowly moving forward. Slow and steady, the drums beating, fire washing over them, rocks and banefire loosed from war engines on the city's walls. Falling dying, trampled by those behind them. Slowly steadily marching on. Slow long ranks marching towards the city. Destroy it! Destroy it! The only thought in all the world in all their minds. The dead zone between the city and the encircling army. Broken bones and ruin and dead men. Banefire. Mage fire. Dragon fire. War drums and war trumpets. And now, loud and urgent, the thump of battering rams against the city's gates. War ships in the harbour, grappling. A storm rising. Towering huge dark waves.

'Amrath! Amrath! Death!'

Waves of men breaking against the city. Waves of water. Waves of fire. Waves of death and pain.

Snow began to fall.

White flakes caught in Marith's shining hair.

'Break it! Break it! Down! Down!'

The ram smashed into the Tereen Gateway. Again. Again. Again. A tree trunk thicker than a man's armspan, carved at its end into a dragon-head snarl. Covered with bloody ox-hides, to keep it from catching fire. Obscene. Comic. Pumping away in out, in out, in out, steaming dripping bloody battering pounding raping iron wood meat. Three huge siege engines hurling rocks and banefire. Machines on the walls hurling rocks and banefire back at them.

Marith circled his horse, making it rear up. Gilded hooves sharp like knives.

'Break it down! Now!'

A shower of boiling sand poured down from the battlements. Soldiers collapsed screaming, clawing at their skin. Inside their armour, burning. In their hair. In their mouths and eyes. The bloody hides on the ram hissed. Cheers from the Arunmenese defenders above.

The ram swung again. Off to the left, a blinding white flash and a dragon's roar. The gate groaned. Splintering. Shadowbeasts gathered, a clot in the air. Shapes twisting, forming, dissolving, huge shapeless dark beating shrieking wings. They dived together, claws and wing beats, jaws opening faceless, clawed limbs tearing down the stones of the wall.

'Now! Now! Break it down!' Marith's horse reared, trampling snow. Red-hot sand showered down around him. His horse screamed in pain. Fire arrows thudding into the battering ram. His soldiers' bodies piling on the ground.

The sky roared at him. A thousand screaming raging mouths. Another flash. The dragon howled. The men fell back shrieking in fear. White light rising up before him. Spear-shape. Cloud-shape. Shining. Grass-green eyes opening, staring; hands reaching for him, numberless beyond counting, and in every hand a sword with a blade of silver light.

God thing. Life thing. A demon conjured up to protect the city. The great high holy god of Arunmen whose temple was gold and green bronze.

Bastard thing. Twice now, it had beaten him off.

'Get the gate open! Now! Now! The ram!'

His sword was shrieking in his hand. Red jewel at the hilt winking at him. Glittering. Red light like the red light of the Fire Star. The King's Star. His star. *There's your star, Marith, and there's mine. Look!* A red jewel, the sword forged for him in the Tower of the Eagle, back before he was truly king, forged in blood and ashes, forged to look like the sword the first Amrath had owned. He'd had a sword before, once, with a red jewel in its hilt, he had named it Sorrow, and this sword he had named Joy.

Marith charged his enemy. So tiny, a man shape on horseback, throwing himself headlong towards this towering raging maelstrom of light. Behind him the ram started. Drumming on the gateway. Break it down! Break it down! His siege engines loosed all together. The machines on the walls showering sand and rocks and banefire back at his men. Mage fire. Dragon fire. Dying.

Marith King Ruin met the light god with a crash.

* * *

All his vision was silver.

Slurred. Like being underwater. All the movements just a moment too slow. Cool and soft around him. It felt like Thalia's skin. A hundred sword blades meeting his sword stroke. A hundred sword blades cutting at him. Grass-green eyes closed and opened. All staring. Sad sad eyes: they looked like the eyes of an old man. Marith fought it. Cut at it. A sword and a hand fell away and another grew up in their place. He cut it again, again a hand falling, again another hand growing up. Swords struck back at him. Glanced off him. Warded them off, didn't feel them, and then a blade got down into the meat of his shoulder, and a wound opened up dry and ashy, and he hurt. He lunged deep into its body. The centre of it, white silver light swallowing him. His horse was screaming. His horse was dead. It reared and kicked at the light surrounding it. Gilded hooves coming down. The grass-green eyes closed and opened. Countless silver swords stabbed at him.

Bastard stupid thing. Twice now, it had beaten him.

The battering ram thudded against the Tereen Gateway. Trumpets rang for an assault on the walls. Voices shouting: 'Ladders! Ladders! Up there! Get moving!' Soldiers rushing up them. Fast with knives clutched in their teeth. A ladder falling backwards, soldiers falling from it dying. Spiralling down off the ladders screaming in a cloud of red-hot sand.

Snow, falling over everything. White snow, black ash, silver fire, red blood. Snowflakes silent and soft as feathers. Muting the sound.

Memory of snow falling, the day he killed his father. White blossom, falling like snowflakes, as they cheered him entering the cities of half the world.

Thalia would like the snow, he thought.

The light god wounded him. Hard, raw pain in his arm, making him almost drop his sword Joy. He cut off hands and swords and they grew up stronger, swords stabbing. Grass-green eyes staring at him. Twice, this damned thing had defeated him. Twice, his soldiers had been forced back. Fire hissed on the bloody ox-hides. The ram beginning to burn. Men dying. Men rushing up to replace them pounding it hard at the gate. The ladders trembling, swaying like bird-legs, another going over, soldiers falling, one soldier falling was burning, fell like a star. Soldiers stumbling blinded by red-hot sand.

Osen's voice shouting furiously, 'Break it! Break it! Destroy it! Now!'

'Amrath! Amrath!'

White fire washing over the battering ram. The ox-hides smoking, burning, men dying, men rushing up wounded and bloody to take their place. The dead horse reared and kicked at the light god. Knife-sharp gilded hooves. Marith cut and hacked at the light god. Swords falling. Swords cutting him. Grass-green eyes opened and closed.

The gate shattered open beneath the beating of the ram. The Army of Amrath surged forward. Trampling their dead and dying. Fighting each other to be first through the gate. A trumpet rang out triumphant. Cheering. Screaming.

'Breech! Breech!'

'Amrath!'

'Breech! Breech!'

The light god roared in fury. Swords and hands ripping at Marith. Marith smashed back at it.

Shouts and cheering turning to screams as the machine on the walls showered down burning sand. The shadows rose up to destroy it. A bright white flash of mage fire sent them burning back. The machine loosed more sand, shimmering as it came down.

'Breach! Breach!'

'In! Now!'

'In! In!'

The Army of Amrath surging in through the gateway. Through the shower of sand falling. Through blasts of white and silver mage fire. Through shuddering falling walls. Soldiers rushing up the ladders. Up onto the battlements. Trying to get to the war engines. Mage fire crashed over them. Burning. More and more rushing up behind.

Voices shouting the war song: 'Death! Death! Death!'

Marith hacked at the light god. Grass-green eyes staring at him. Numberless hands and sword blades. Swirling silver all around him, washing him, cool and soft. He hacked like hacking at a tree trunk. Ignored the swords cutting him. Nothing could harm him. Remember that! They cut him and they hurt him but there was nothing. Dry ash wounds, blood like rust, nothing to bleed, nothing to die. Like a dried-up river. Dry dead dust. A famine. He slashed at the thing's shining light, cut it into pieces, over and over, all the hands and the swords cutting him. Grass-green eyes staring at him. He cut them. Destroying them. Hammering down his sword blade. Over and over and over and over. The dead horse reared and kicked at it. Bit at it with yellow teeth. Cut and cut and cut.

A burst of light. White and silver. Brighter than sunlight. The snow shining with every colour of the rainbow. Light reflected in every soldier's eyes.

Scream like glass and bells ringing. A thousand rushing shooting stars.

White light. Burning. White shining blazing sparks of fire. Cut and cut and cut and cut.

Screamed.

Screamed.

Gone.

Twice, it had defeated him.

Third time lucky, indeed.

Marith drew his breath. Patted his horse to thank it.

Charged after his soldiers through the ruins of the gate.

King Ruin. King Death. Such joy and such wonder. The one true perfect thing.

Inside the Tereen Gateway was a killing ground. Rubble, rotting corpses, barricades, fires. A crude wall, too high for his soldiers to climb over, thrown up behind.

'Hold!' a voice was screaming. 'Whatever comes at us! Hold! Hold!' Gritted lines gritted teeth gritted spears, grey hopeless dead men. The last defenders of Arunmen. Marith felt almost sorry for them. Their swords and spears trembled in their hands. They knew. When he first crossed the river Alph, Arunmen had surrendered unconditionally, thrown open its gates, feasted and crowned him king. Hanged its last king from the gates of the palace as a welcome gift. Two months after they crowned him, the people of Arunmen had declared themselves a free city, massacred the garrison he'd left. Ungrateful bastards! Just because he'd been a bit tied-up in Samarnath city of towers and wretchedly difficult suicidal 'freedom or death we shall not yield' maniacs, they thought they could turn around and thumb their noses at him?

He charged into the line of defenders, hacking at them. An arrow thudded into his back; he felt the heat of its fires, shrugged it off, killed someone. The dead horse screamed. Its mane was burning. Delightful smell of burning hair. There were spears in his face, jabbing at him hitting out with his sword. The ruby on the hilt shining. White light rainbows on the blade. His face flushed, bloodied. Blood and dust in his hair. Beautiful. Shining like diamonds. Shining like all the stars in the heavens, like sunlight on water, beautiful perfect shining with rainbows, moon-white skin and red-black shining hair, killing them. White-silver blood-red scab rot filth death ruin screaming his men on in through the rubble of the gate. The men coming on behind him, grappling with the defenders, climbing and tearing at the inner wall.

He killed someone else. A third. A fourth. Shouts from the walls: they'd got a bridgehead up there on the battlements. A body crashed down in front of him. Helpfully took out an Arunmenese soldier rushing forward with a nasty big sword. A crash and a cheer off from the Salen Gateway. That gate too was breached. Osen and his men would be in.

'Amrath!'

'Amrath and the Altrersyr!'

'Death!'

A horseman came riding at him, the horse already maddened by the screaming stink of blood. He struck the horse with his sword and it shattered, flew apart all these dark shapes. It was just a shadow. The rider came crashing down, the hilt of a sword in its hands, crumbled metal, crumbling away into dust, its hands were eaten away by the eaten metal. You see now, you see, even my touch is corruption, I am ruin, I am a god and after me is only death. He killed his enemies. Five, ten, twenty to a stroke. A hundred dead. A thousand. They crumbled before him, they were nothing, he is death and ruin, he cannot be harmed. Alone, he could kill them all, on and on, killing, he could stand here and kill for all eternity, every man and woman and child who walks the earth, he could kill. This is all that I am, he thought. All that I could ever be and do.

His hand moved, holding the sword. He closed his eyes. He felt things die beneath his sword strokes. Cut through them, cut the world open, they were ragged and torn apart, they looked like clouds torn ragged by the wind and the moonlight shines through them and the sky behind them is both darker and bright with light.

Smoke was rising over the city. Marith raised his face in joy as the red dragon flew overhead. A great warm wash of dragon fire. Warm soft flames caressing his face. He could feel the battering ram pounding against the Sea Gate, the storm waves smashing against the harbour. Crash as the siege engines loosed. More and more of his men coming in around him, fanning out, pushing the defenders back. The city before them burning. Dragon fire. Mage fire. Banefire. Falling from the heavens. A roar of triumph off to his left from the walls: voices shouting, hailing him. Fighting. Killing. Pressing onwards. His men pouring in. Flowing into the city, fighting, killing, tearing it down. The red dragon came down to land. Crushed bodies: soldiers, women, children; children throwing roof tiles, firewood, fighting trying to defend the city with ragged bare hands. The dragon breathed out flames and consumed them. Children throwing roof tiles. Women with kitchen knives. Smashed the buildings of the city down over them. Burned them. Cut them open in its jaws. The shadowbeasts lifted them, dismembered them, dropped them falling in pieces spiralling to the ground. Snow falling around the bodies. Red blood. White ash. White snow. Soldiers in at every breach, fighting. Pressing forward. Over and over. Endless. Rolling climax building. Wave after wave after wave. His soldiers ripping everything apart. Dismembering everything. Opening the city up like a body. Battering it like waves on rock. Marith fighting, killing, the whole city spread before him, watching it fighting, watching it falling, watching it burn and break and yield and fall into dust. On and on his men running through the city, killing everything. The storm beating against the harbour. The siege engines loosing banefire and rock.

The defenders retreating. Their city burning. Blood running in torrents. Pulling back to their own houses. Hoping without hope that their own families might somehow be saved. The snow coming thicker. Muting sound and vision. Cold sweet silent white air. The Army of Amrath spilling over everything. Wading through the city's dying. Soaked and mired in death. That smell it had! Heavy, sweet, honeyed tang. Breathe it in, it never goes stale. The smell of the butcher's block that is the smell of power and the illusion of living. Every death to be treasured. Hoarded. I did this. I made this.

Blood and filth and human ruin: that is the face of god. Arunmen is taken! Arunmen is fallen! And here now he is king.

Osen Fiolt and Valim Erith met him at the gates of the palace of Arunmen. Onyx towers like the city walls, high as cliffs, black as storm clouds, its roofs gold tiles but they'd stripped off the tiles to pay for their pointless futile war. Osen had a squad of men guarding it. They can have the city, Marith had told his captains, but the palace is to be kept intact for me.

'It's clear,' said Valim. 'We've been through it.' Lord Valim of Fealene Isle; a companion of Marith's father, older therefore than Marith and Osen, too cautious in his thinking but a good leader

17

of men, as many older men are. He had been with them since the beginning of everything, had fought in every battle, had lost his son and his brother in battle, but still Marith felt something like shame around him, who had seen him as a child, been a young man armed and shining when Marith was a child staring up in awe.

Valim got down on his knees before Marith. '*Ansikanderakesis Amrakane*. My Lord King of Arunmen.'

'I was already King of Arunmen.' So unnecessary. All of this.

'Come on, then,' said Osen. 'Let's go and have a look, see what they've left us.'

'Tell the men three days,' said Marith. He looked at the snow falling. 'Try and make sure they don't burn absolutely every building down.'

Valim nodded.

'Have they found the ringleaders?' asked Marith.

A look of irritation. 'We will.'

'You hope,' said Osen. Marith gave him a look.

They went into the palace together, Marith and Osen. Marith's footsteps rang very loud on the tiled floor.

Hated this part, somehow. Walking through halls and corridors, walls closing around him, on and in and in. Smell of smoke. Servants' faces. Dead faces. Dying faces. So many times, we've done this, he thought. But always so strange.

'I thought Valim said it was clear,' said Osen. He kicked a slumped body, one of their soldiers. It groaned. 'This isn't clear.'

They came to the throne room. Servants and nobodies in grand rich clothing, faces grey with terror, trying to protest with every fibre of their being that they'd always worshipped Marith Altrersyr as their true king. More bodies. Marith's soldiers and the Arunmenese soldiers who had tried to fight them off.

Why? Marith thought. Why did they try to fight them off? It's an old wooden chair.

The walls of the throne room were made of amber. Thick and drowning: Marith stared at the walls, looked through the amber like looking through water, there were flowers trapped in it, insects, encased in the walls. He put his hand on the amber and it was almost warm. It felt like skin. Not cold, like stone. The throne on its dais: wood, twisting patterns in the grain, red canopy old and cracked and dusty, that was said to be the skin of a sea beast that a king of Arunmen had once killed. The steps of the dais were thick with gold paint.

Tasteless. Like every single bloody one of them. Power awe glory power wealth! Bloodstains on the wood that nothing could scrub out. Marith climbed the dais. Sat down on the throne.

'The King of Arunmen!' Everyone kneeling, Osen, the soldiers, the servants and officials of the palace who had surrendered to them, all kneeling with their faces pressed on the stone floor. Gold-coloured skin in the amber light. Like they were all yellow and sick.

Yellow light and smoky, bloody chambers. Marith closed his eyes. Panicked fear he was going to throw up.

Arunmen had surrendered to him. Made him sit here once already, king and master, all enthroned in yellow light. Filthy poxy place in the middle of sodding nowhere. No desire in him then ever to come back.

'Marith?'

Marith opened his eyes. Osen was staring at him, everyone else still prostrate heads down, crouched beetled staring at the floor. Pile of dead bodies. Dying bodies. Valim Erith had said the place was clear. Here I am seating myself on my throne in a room full of corpses. We don't even try to pretend it's anything else any more.

'Get up,' he said. Creak of armour. Creak of old men's bones. Some of these servants must have turned their coats three times now, from the dead king Androinidas to Marith Altrersyr to the pretender who'd rebelled against him to Marith Altrersyr again.

He said, 'Kill these people. All of them.'

Osen tried to smile at him. 'You need a drink and a hot bath, Marith.'

Marith took the flask from his belt, discovered it was empty. 'I do.'

'I sent riders. Thalia will be here in a few days, I should think, unless the snow gets much worse. So cheer up. Look, let's go and get you clean.' '*Don't kill them*,' he saw Osen mouth over his shoulder at his soldiers.

They went up to the king's private rooms, up in a tower above the throne room. The bedchamber had windows of green glass, the light cool like the light beneath trees. Marith felt easier here, breathing in the green. The walls were hung with leaves and flowers, preserved by magecraft fresh and perfect as the day they were first picked. The bed had curtains of silver tissue. The ceiling was set with fragments of mage glass to mimic the stars. Three weeks, he had spent here before, when he first came to Arunmen. Kept Sun's Height and the feast of Amrath's birthday. Days of peace and sweet, joyous nights.

He went over to the window, pressed his face against it. His face felt so hot. Through the window he could see trees, distorted by the ripples in the glass. A hot wind rattled the window, bringing the stink of smoke. Turned back to the room and there were bloody smear marks on the green glass window. Bloody footprints on the floor.

I remember the Summer Palace in Sorlost, burning. The smell of it. The heat of it. A column of fire, the walls were running with fire, I've never seen fire move like that, before or since. Not dragon fire, not banefire, nothing. It was like all the gods of the world were in that palace, consuming it. It moved like breath. I remember the people dying, the Emperor's guards, the servants, I have no idea how many we must have killed. The Emperor on his gold throne, with a yellow rag around his head, soiling himself. A servant girl with her face opened up like a flower, throwing herself through a window to escape. Old men pleading for mercy, cowering behind piles of tattered books. The palace walls flowed with fire, my sword was red with blood, my hands ached from killing. My whole self stripped down to killing and death.

'They're getting a bath prepared for you,' said Osen. A girl came running, offered wine in gold cups. She bowed her head to Marith. Her body leaning forward so that he could see down her dress. Sweat, running down inside her dress. Reached out and took the cup and his hand shook and the cup fell. Wine stain over the blood. The cup rolled on the floor. He stared at it. The girl stood very still.

Marith opened his mouth. Felt himself about to scream. A choked dry shriek came out of him.

'Get out,' said Osen. 'Everyone. Out. Now.'

A man who was perhaps a senior servant, the master of the bedchamber, dripping in silk and jewels, fat face fat hands, fussing about, 'The mess, My Lord, My Lord King, the mess, I'll have the girl whipped, I—'

Osen said, 'Get out. Now. Everyone.'

'You're not injured, somehow?' Osen asked when they were alone.

'Of course I'm not injured. Don't be absurd. I'm just tired.' Marith rubbed his eyes. 'Three assaults in four days. Tiring.'

A strange look on Osen's face. Osen said, 'Good.'

'Of course I'm not injured. How could I be injured?'

'I said, good. How could you be injured? I was just concerned.'

Osen knelt down, began to peel Marith's armour off him. Blood spatter, blood and gore streaming down him, flaking off him, whole bits of what had once been people, congealing in lumps, running off his skin.

'Gods, this stinks,' said Osen. He was as filthy as Marith was. Marith reached down and fumbled with the straps of Osen's armour in turn.

'Leave it. I'll do it later. The important thing is you.' Osen took his hand. 'You're shaking.'

'I'm fine.'

'This carpet is bloody ruined,' said Osen. Still struggling with Marith's armour that was stuck to him with blood. 'It'll have to be burned.'

The last time he'd been here, at Sun's Height. Kneeling on the carpet at Thalia's feet, Thalia's face shining bronze like candles, looking down at him. Love and joy and peace.

Osen said, 'There! Gods, wretched thing.' Clatter of metal. The armour lying in blood and spilled wine. 'Let's get you next door to the bath, then. I'll get you a drink for when you're in there.'

Blink of hope. 'Hatha?'

'A bit early in the day, don't you think?'

Marith blinked. 'Please?'

'You're the king. I do as you say. But, look, maybe try to go a bit easy. Maybe?'

Marith rubbed his eyes. 'I'm fine.'

'You said. But, look: go easy. Alleen's choosing the drinks tonight. We tossed for it, who got to storm the Salen Gateway, who wussed out with the Sea Gate but got to choose the victory drinks. And you do look . . . tired. So go easy beforehand, maybe? Yes? No?'

Marith rubbed his eyes. 'I'm fine.'

His legs were shaking. Osen had to help him into the bath. Voices of the servants fussing cleaning up his bedchamber. His head was aching. His whole body was aching. The bath chamber had windows of blue glass. Made his skin look blue and dead. Could hear screams. Smell of smoke, sound of fire. The girl sobbing, where she was being whipped.

Chapter Three

Four years, since Marith Altrersyr destroyed the palace of the Asekemlene Emperor of the Sekemleth Empire of the Eternal Golden City of Sorlost, carried off the High Priestess Thalia the Chosen of the Great God Tanis to be his bride, bested first his father and then his uncle in battle to claim both their kingdoms, avenged the betrayal of his ancestor Amrath in the ruins of Ethalden to be crowned King of Illyr, Amrath Returned, called all the fighting men of Irlast to his banner, set out to conquer the world.

Four years.

And most of Irlast was indeed now conquered. Cities razed. Armies broken. Kings and princes and magelords grovelling in the dust. Immier, Cen Andae, Cen Elora, Chathe with its rose trees all uprooted, the Nairn Forest a thousand miles of grey ash. The sky had been red from sunrise to sunset to sunrise, when he burned the Nairn Forest. The smoke had blocked out the sun. From the Bitter Sea to the Sea of Tears, he was king and master. Always, his power was growing. His shadow lengthening. His fortress of Ethalden was built of gold and gems and human flesh. He held court crowned in mage light and emissaries came to praise him from every corner of the world. His armies were uncountable like the grains of sand in the desert. Undefeated like the sea rising in winter. Feared like a famine when the rains fail. Over the face of the world they ran like water and the world was drowning. Over the face of the world they ran and their coming was like night.

Marith the World Conqueror. God of war and ruin and grief and hate and vengeance. Dragonlord. Dragon kin. Demon born. Lord of Shadows. Death made manifest. Great king.

Four glorious, wonderful, perfect, joy-filled years.

Chapter Four

He was slumped in bed the next day when Osen came to tell him that the Arunmenese rebel leader had been captured.

'Oh. Wonderful.' Sat up. Lay down again. Oh gods. 'He couldn't have stayed uncaptured for another few hours? Just until my hangover went away?'

'What did I tell you?'

'What did you tell me?'

'I—' Osen shook his head. 'Never mind. I can deal with it, if you want.'

'No, no. I should. I want to see him.' Bastard. Ungrateful stupid bastard. Marith thought: I left Arunmen untouched. I. Left. Arunmen. Un. Touched. And this ungrateful idiot decided to rebel against me. Which part of 'untouched' was so difficult for people to understand?

Managed to get up and dressed, just about. With Osen's help. But, look, three assaults in four days. Tiring. And it was all Alleen Durith's fault really, he had chosen last night's drinks. Marith gulped watered wine, his hands shaking, fighting down nausea. The girl holding his cup stared at him trying not to look at him, like she was watching a man's death. The palace staff kept sending servant girls to attend him, thin tight dresses and big whispering eyes. Send them away. One of them had almost touched his hand, carrying

25

in his clothes. His hand tingled, like he'd touched something dirty, couldn't wash it off. Sweat, running inside her thin silk dress.

He came back into the throne room. They'd spent all day scrubbing it clean. Sat here last night and the bodies had still been piled here, he'd seen them, his soldiers and the enemy soldiers, piled up in mounds at his feet while he feasted, he thought again: why? It's a stupid tasteless wooden chair. Mounted the steps of the dais, sat down, his legs were shaking. Curse Alleen Durith. He'd put on his red cloak, all bloody, it stank like his head hurt, it left trails of slime like slug trails on the chair. The crown of Arunmen on his head, and it was irritatingly heavy, and the previous King of Arunmen must have had a really weirdly shaped head.

All very formal. The High Lords of his empire knelt in fealty before him, kissed his hands, offered him praise and gratitude as their king and as their god. Osen Fiolt. Alleen Durith. Lord Erith. Lord Nymen. Lord Meerak of Raen. Lady Dansa Arual of Balkash. Lord Cimer the Magelord. Lord Ranene the weather hand. Lord Ryn Mathen the King of Chathe's cousin who led the allied Chathean troops. All his great High Lords, his captains, his friends, his trusted companions, the men and women upon whom he had bestowed the glory of his reign.

All nine of them.

No. That wasn't exactly fair on himself. Yanis Stansel was back in Illyr acting as regent, raising fresh troops and overseeing the final construction of Amrath's tomb. Kiana Sabryya was on her way to join them, escorting Thalia from Tereen.

Ten. Eleven. And perhaps once he'd have been astonished to think he might count his companions as high as that. More even than the fingers of both hands! Look, look, father, look, Ti, look at me! Eleven friends!

Valim Erith said, 'Bring him in.'

Stirring, voices calling outside the doorway. 'Bring him!' A troop of guardsmen entered. A tall man chained and bound in their midst. He was naked. Dripping blood. Stinking of excrement. Hate and rage and terror on the man's face.

'My Lord King,' Valim said. 'The prisoner.'

Well, yes, obviously.

The guards dropped the man at Marith's feet.

So.

Marith looked down at him. Pale dying eyes. Refused to meet Marith's gaze.

Marith said slowly, 'I left Arunmen untouched. I granted you freedom under my suzerainty. I left you unharmed. Yet you defied me. Usurped my crown. Claimed you could destroy me. Why?'

The prisoner spat at him. A great gobbet of yellow phlegm on the gold-painted dais.

'Why?'

Clatter of iron chains. The prisoner looked up straight at Marith. Stared at him. A wild man's eyes. Pale and dying. Filled with hate. Empty croaking voice like a fucking frog: 'Filth. Pestilence. Poison. Better all the world died in torment, than lived under your rule.'

That's why? That's all? Marith stared at the phlegm oozing slowly down the steps of the dais. I call myself King Ruin, King of Death, King of Shadows. You think I don't know what I am?

'I am your king,' Marith said. 'The Lord of All Irlast.'

The prisoner lowered his eyes again. 'You are my king. The Lord of All Irlast. So better that I die.'

'You let a lot of your men die for you first,' said Alleen. 'And a lot of mine.' He looked at Marith. 'This is pointless. Just get it over with and kill him.'

'Better that every living thing in Irlast dies than submits to you.' Spat more phlegm. Opened his bowels and shat himself at Marith's feet. 'My soldiers were lucky, that they died before they had to look at your face.'

'They looked at our faces perfectly happily when we marched in triumphantly a few months ago,' Alleen snapped. 'Threw flowers at us, made us very welcome in every possible way, then. They were perfectly happy and alive and most of them seemed to be enjoying themselves.'

A great big feast. The city's fountains running with wine instead of water. King Marith and Queen Thalia distributing largesse in the streets. Girls wearing crowns of roses. Singing and dancing all day and all night. Yes, the people of Arunmen had seemed happy and alive and enjoying themselves. Alleen and Osen and the other generals had been virtually fighting admirers off.

'So why? Why?'

The prisoner stared at him in silence. Shit pooling on the marble. Phlegm dripping down the gold-painted steps. Stared. Lowered his eyes, stared at the floor.

Spat again.

'Filth. Pestilence. Rot.'

Osen rolled his eyes at Marith. Mouthed something that might have been 'hurry up'.

Always the same. Every few months, somewhere in his empire. Someone standing up, sword in hand, promising they could over-throw the tyrant, save the world from something it was never quite clear what. Being ruled by one man rather than another, perhaps. Overthrow the rule of evil! Freedom beckons! Kill the tyrant, throw off our chains, make me king! And all the young men and women jumping up shouting agreement, muttering proph-ecies, singing uplifting bloodthirsty war songs. And he'd have to break off whatever he was doing, march over with an army, deal with them. And they were all freed from the tyrant indeed, and never again had to suffer beneath his yoke.

The smell and the sight of the filth dripping on the dais was making him feel nauseous. Really seriously worried he was about to be sick again in front of them all. Curse Alleen Durith and his choice of drinks.

Hang on, hang on, it suddenly occurred to him. I'd already drawn up my battle plan giving Osen command of the assault on the Salen Gateway. There's no way I would have changed it if they'd asked me to. They tossed for it? What?

'Shall I kill him?' said Osen. Osen's hand was hovering on the hilt of his sword.

28

Marith nodded wearily. The prisoner's shoulders sagged. Osen drew the sword.

The prisoner raised his head, shouted out: 'You think yourself so powerful! But one of your own generals plots to betray you! Conspires against you! Thinks you nothing but filth and death! Think on that, King Ruin! Even those who serve you wish you dead! Betray you! I know!'

The prisoner's face leering at him.

The hate in those eyes. Why? Marith thought again. Why? I left your city untouched. I. Left. Your. City. Un. Touched.

'I won't tell,' the prisoner whispered. Smiled at Marith through bloody lips. 'I won't tell you. Even those closest to you loathe you. Plot to destroy you. See you for what you are. Encouraged me. Gave me money. Betrayed you. I know. But I won't tell. I won't tell you the name.'

'You're lying!' Hot desperate flush in Marith's face. 'I left Arunmen untouched!'

'Filth. Rot. Corruption. They all loathe you, King Ruin. Want to see you dead.'

'Marith—' Alleen Durith gestured to the guards. 'Take him away. Get him out of here. Now.'

'Betraying you!'

'Get him out of here now!'

Osen ripped down with his sword. The Calien Mal. The Eagle Blade. Sword that had killed mages and lords and kings.

No sound. The prisoner dead on the floor.

Alleen rubbed his eyes. 'Marith . . .'

'He was lying,' said Marith.

Alleen said, 'Gods, Osen, we needed to question him.'

'He was lying. There was nothing to find out.'

Alis Nymen made a croaking sound. Dansa Arual was staring at Osen with her mouth open.

'He was lying, he was a traitor,' said Osen. 'Who wanted to listen to any more of that poison?' He shrugged at Marith. 'Let's go and get a drink.'

Four glorious years. Half the world broken at his feet. Broken towers, burned fields, silver crowns, gold crowns, thrones of gold, thrones of iron, thrones of wood, thrones of stone. We march on and on to the horizon, places I barely knew existed places that I cannot imagine. Impossible to think, really, that these places drawn in ink on a map are real places where real people live. Look to the far south, stare at the clouds where the land and the sky meet – there are people living there, houses, tilled fields, people dying and being born, people thinking feeling dreaming as I dream. Children, he thought, live there. And it is absurd that they are real and exist there. I cannot imagine these places these people. I march my army on. We kill them. All across Irlast my dead lie scattered, mounds of them, my soldiers, dead! Their bones lie on the dark earth for the crows and the dogs, all out of love for me. They march beneath my banners to die for me in places they do not believe are real places, killed by men they cannot imagine are real and live. Ask them why and they will give a thousand excuses. And yet they are ordinary men.

'I need to earn coin, I need to feed my family, my children will starve unless I earn a wage somehow.'

'I've got responsibilities to the rest of them in the squad. We're a team. I can't let them down.'

'I swore an oath to fight for my king. I am a man of honour. I cannot break my oath.'

'I didn't want to do it. But I was ordered to. If we all stopped doing anything we didn't completely agree with . . .'

None of us know, in our hearts, why we do these things. Because we can. Because we do. They really think I don't know they're all waiting to betray me?

Two more days of victory feasting. Outside in the city, the Army of Amrath swarmed over the ruins, killing everything they found. Marith took Osen and Alleen Durith with him to visit the temple of the god spirit of Arunmen. See the house of the enemy that had defied him. He had visited the temple after he had been crowned here, and the presence of the god spirit had been welcoming to him as a king and an equal. So now he must come again as victor and conqueror. Killer of the god. Have a smug but entirely justified gloat. Twice, you beat me off, but in the end I was the stronger. You promised to defend your city, and you failed, like all the weak things of life. The black stone that was the god's physical form had shattered, they said, at the moment his blow had struck.

Also, the temple was the architectural highlight of the city, and thus of all Calchas. A very beautiful building. Huge and elegant. Loaded with beauty in gold and gemstones. Famed for its treasurers in jewels and silk. As one might expect. He was looking forward to seeing it again.

Soldiers were pouring over snow-covered rubble. Digging up lumps of melted smoke-blackened gold. A group of them were having a fight.

'What . . . what happened?'

Alleen said, 'The dragons . . .'

'. . . sat on it?'

'They took against it, certainly.'

Osen said, 'I think we might have managed to get some of the best things out of the remains. I can have the rest tracked down, if you like. The temple vessels and things.'

'No. It's fine. The soldiers can keep it. But the paintings on the walls . . . it's a shame, I liked them.' There had been a picture of a woman done in jewels above the west window, her face was quite wrong but her golden hair, the way she held her arms – reminded him—

'The dragons destroyed it. Good.'

Osen scuffed at the snow. A lump of plaster. A suggestion of yellow paint. Not his mother. She hadn't been his mother. The woman who killed his mother. She did. Remember. She did. Killed his mother and replaced his mother as queen and tried to put her own son in his place as king. And so he'd killed her and hung her body from the walls of Malth Elelane. Her and her son beside her.

'Please, Marith,' she'd begged him.

31

He went next to the place where they kept the wounded. Osen and Alleen did not come. A long walk. As was only correct and proper by every rule of warfare, the wounded were housed far off from anything, in tents far from the army's camp. A presence to it that Marith could feel pressing down on him. When he reached the place he was clammy with cold sweat.

Not so many wounded. Two days after the battle, most of them lay sleeping in the black earth with the dust between their teeth. They had marched through the Wastes and the Empty Peaks, crossed the Sea of Grief, tramped up and down Irlast from shore to shore. Desperate to share in his glory, reaching out for a tiny crust of what the *Ansikanderakesis Amrakane* had to offer. Four long years they had marched with him, they were the Army of Amrath and they would march and follow and pace out their lives following him. I don't even know where I'm going. I could close my eyes, stab my knife at random into the map. And they would follow. And they lie in the black earth dead and forgotten. And they lie here in the sickhouse, rotting.

Wounds like eyes. Wounds like open mouths. He could not look and he could not look.

The flesh grew over them, wounds healing puckered and distorted. Excrescences of blood and skin. Black traces embroidering their bodies. Arms and legs pus-swollen. Their mouths moved with scabs growing over them. Mould covering their faces, in their bones, their teeth, they spat and choked and swallowed it. Mould, eating them. Hard cold as marble. Soft and damp as leaves. Rippling dry as driftwood. He heard them breathing. Saw them breathing. No face, no hands, no eyes, no mouth, no ears. See hear feel taste touch red. Where they moved, they left black trails of their flesh behind them. Shapes and words. Their living bodies seeping away into liquid. They moved and jerked, some of them. Spoke. Knew. Wounds that had once been human faces turned groping towards him. Bodies swollen up vast with fluids, bodies shrivelled down, lumps of flesh men without arms or legs. Burned men. And at those he almost could not look. Yearning reaching towards him.

32

The worst, he thought afterwards, were those who did not seem so badly wounded. Like fruit rotted inside with maggots. They looked even strong, some of them.

'The king, the king,' the wounded whispered. Their voices thick and dry with pain. An old woman with no teeth in her mouth limped between them, giving them water, pressing a wet cloth to their cold, sweating faces, smoothing her fingers through their matted hair, running her hands over the pus of their wounds.

'Hush now, deary, my boy, my boy, hush, hush, you sleep, you rest, you'll be fine, you'll be fine, deary, my boy.'

'Water . . . water . . .' A man clutched at Marith's arm, not knowing him. 'Water . . .' His stomach was a mass of bandages, fat with bandages, spreading blood like cracks on ice. A deep wound to the gut will kill you, sooner or later, no matter what you do. Every soldier knows that. Yes. 'Water . . . Mother! Mother!' Verdigrised hand digging into him.

'Hush, hush, deary, my boy.' The nurse limped over wetted its black lips, pressed her wet cloth onto its white face. 'Hush, deary, it's well, you'll soon be well.'

At the far end of the tent the dead were piled. They should be taken away for burial each day. They had not been taken away. Some of the bodies must have been there since the first day of the siege. Beetles had got in there, and flies. A seething column of ants ripped the dead wounds open. Mould grew over black meat.

'Be well,' Marith whispered to his men. 'Be well. You who died for me.' He should know their names. He used to know all his soldiers' names. After his victory over King Selerie he had visited all the wounded, thanked each of them by name.

He thought: but I had a smaller army then. That's unfair.

He thought: half of them died within hours. Whether I knew their names or not. I stopped bothering.

Thalia arrived the next evening. Sieges bored her now; she had decided to stay in Tereen in comfort until it was done. Her party swept into the palace courtyard, red banners crusted with snow.

She rode a white horse, saddled and plumed in scarlet; she was wrapped in thick white furs showing only her eyes and her gloved hands. She slid down from the saddle into Marith's arms.

'Thalia!'

There were snowflakes caught in her eyelashes. Marith kissed them away. Her eyes shone. The torchlight showed his reflection in her eyes smiling back at him. Dancing in the flickering light. She pushed back her hood, and the snow began to gather on her hair.

'Thalia! I didn't think you'd make it today, through the snow.' He frowned. 'It was foolish, to come in the snow.'

'I made them press on.' She took his hand. 'I was worried about you.'

'Worried? Why should you worry?'

Off behind her he noticed Osen and Alleen again exchanging glances. Well, yes, okay, so he'd only managed to get out of bed and stop throwing up about two hours ago, there'd been a nasty while when it looked like Osen might have to receive her in the king's place. But it had been a hard few days. Tiring. And it was Osen's fault, really, he'd chosen the drinks last night.

Thalia bent her head closer. 'And I . . . I have news.'

'News?' Oh? Oh! A hope ran through him. And a shudder. Tried to brush it away. The things he had seen in her face, shining there, when he first saw her, and knew, and was so very afraid of her. *Why have you come to me?* But she had only smiled, and looked puzzled, and shaken her head. He took her hands protectively now. 'You shouldn't have risked it, in the snow. You're getting snow all over you. Let's get inside out of the cold. I've had men out scouring all the jewellers' for you. Such beautiful things!'

There was a stirring on the other side of courtyard, people moving forward around another horse, helping Kiana Sabryya down. The joy faded. Watched a servant thrust walking sticks into Kiana's hands, take her weight, help her steady herself on her feet. Kiana saw Marith watching and her eyes flashed in irritation. Osen hurried up to greet her. Marith heard her sigh.

'Marith . . .' Thalia squeezed his hand. 'Leave her.'

Osen and Kiana seemed to be arguing about whether Kiana needed Osen's arm to lean on. Marith turned away.

'It wasn't your fault,' Thalia said gently.

War kills people. War hurts people. That's not exactly a big surprise, hey? She fought a demon, it injured her. What did she think it would do?

He shook himself. 'Obviously it wasn't my fault.'

They went slowly into the throne room. Servants, lords of empire, all falling to their knees as they passed. Thalia's wet furs were swept away: beneath, she wore a dress of pale grey velvet the colour of the winter sky, embroidered with a thousand tiny diamonds. She was blazing fire. Too brilliant to look at. Light rippled off her perfect face. Marith escorted her up the dais, seated her on the throne.

'The Queen of All Irlast!'

She laughed sadly. Bored laugh. I was already the Queen of All Irlast, Marith, her face said. 'The Queen of All Irlast.'

Everyone present prostrated themselves on the floor.

Marith gestured to Alleen. Servants hurried in carrying boxes. Poured out a river of gemstones at Thalia's feet. Her smile was sadder even than her laugh.

She is carrying my child. My child! It will all be better now, he thought. There was a memory, he was sure of it, his mother holding Ti in her arms, newborn, wrapped in white lace. 'Come here, Marith, look, you have a little brother, thank the gods, Marith, thank Amrath and Eltheia, you have a brother.' A tiny pink fist waved at him, and he had bent, kissed his brother's pink face. Such love . . . Such a precious little thing. They were so close in age, he was a baby himself when Ti was born, a false memory, his nurse had said, he was too young to remember, and besides an Altrersyr prince would have been wrapped in red silk, of course, not white lace. But he remembered it. A child! Oh, please. This time, please.

He reached down, picked up a necklace of rubies from the

glittering pile at Thalia's feet. Held it up and placed it around her neck. His hands shook so badly he couldn't fasten it. It fell limply on the dais. In the light from her face the rubies winked up at him like scabs.

Chapter Five

The next morning they went out riding.

'Are you sure it's wise?' Marith asked Thalia.

'I rode here, didn't I? I . . .' She frowned. 'I don't want – I mean – it seems better, this time – but it could still – like before – and I – I don't want . . .'

'No. Yes. Of course.' Had absolutely no idea what she was trying to say to him. Except that it hurt her. Saying it.

She had lost three pregnancies. Miscarried three times in the first few months. She was four months gone this time already, she said, you could see the swell of her belly through her dress if you knew to look. Waited to tell him, this time. Spare him false hope and grief. After three months, four months, the pregnancy becomes more certain, the wise women and the doctors all agreed on it.

'The doctors say that I should keep myself strong.' Her hand moving to her stomach, up to her throat, to the knife scars on her arm. 'Last time, I . . . I didn't go out at all. Didn't ride. Barely walked, even. Rested in bed. You know. And—'

He grasped her hands. Kissed them. Deep luminous bronze skin. His own skin white as moonlight. Our children must have your skin, he had told her once, and your eyes, and my hair. 'I know you did,' he said. Don't say it. This time it will be good and well, it will, it will, it must be. I am a king. A god. A peasant in a hovel

37

can father a living child, if my father could father living children
. . . I raise my sword and a thousand men lie dying. I close my
eyes and stab my knife into a map and an army marches and a
city falls. I can father a living child, if I can do that.

Tiny pink flailing fists . . . Such love.

He said, 'Well . . . Come on, then. If you're sure.'

But the riding was good, for both of them. The snow cold
washing them both clean. Forget. They avoided the city, skirting
out to the east towards the Ane Headland. The wind was blowing
against them. Blowing the smell of smoke away. The ground rose
smooth and open; thick grassland, good horse country. Thalia
spurred her horse to a gallop. The wind blew back her hood, her
hair whipping up. Like black bare branches. Like birds' wings.
The snow flew out from under the horse's hooves; the sunlight
caught it, made it sparkle, it looked like the waves of a churning
sunlit sea. Marith raced his horse to catch her, shouting 'Ha! Ha!'
as he went. His breath puffed out like a dragon. 'Ha! Ha!'

Thalia pulled her horse to a standstill at the top of a high
ridgeway. Marith stopped further down the slope, looking up at
her outlined against the sky. The light was changing, clouds gathering, the light becoming flat and white and heavy, waiting for the
snow. He trotted up to join her, looked down in delight at the
plain spreading out before them like looking down into a pool.
Thick with snow, untouched. And there, on the horizon, the dark
line of the Sea of Tears, and what he could pretend in the blur of
far distance were the fire mountains of Tarboran beyond. A farm-
stead with a copse of firs behind it, hawthorn hedgerows flushed
red. Tiny black shapes that must be cattle. A beech tree in brilliant
copper leaves. Thalia pointed and he saw a hawk holding absolutely still in the white air. The hawk dived. Fast as thinking. A
dog barked somewhere below them, loud, another barked in reply.
The cattle moved in their field. He thought he could see the hawk
flying up again. Perhaps it will all be well, he thought. Different,
this time, or the next time. Look at it there! A beautiful world.
Waiting for me.

Thalia slid down from her horse.

Threw a snowball at him.

Marith laughed, threw one back, missed. Thalia retrieved it, threw it, it smacked into his shoulder and the snow stuck to his cloak. He gathered a handful of snow, tossed it up into the sky, aiming over the edge of the ridge into the world spread beneath. Tossed another handful over Thalia, showering down around her as he had showered her with gems the previous night. Snow on her face. She wrinkled her snow-covered nose. Pushed him over in the snow. Dropped snow right on his head.

'Stop! Argh!'

'Stop?'

'Stop, oh my queen!'

She pulled him to his feet again. Furry with snow: he felt like a furry white bear.

'I am absolutely bloody freezing now.' So Thalia wrapped her arms around him. Her skin was warm as the summer sun. They looked together at the view before them, the white frozen world waiting. Our world, he thought. Beautiful for us together. And there is hope, still.

Marith said, 'Don't for gods' sake tell anyone, but I much prefer it out here to Illyr. You can see why Amrath started out to conquer the world, when you look at Illyr.'

'Oh, but Illyr's beautiful. Everywhere in the world is beautiful.' Strained voice. Joyful voice. Her nose wrinkled: 'Apart from the Wastes.'

The sun broke through a gap in the clouds, a crack of light in the sky too bright to look at, so bright it was almost black. Like the cloud was the edge of the world, the light beyond a void pouring some other life in. She pointed. 'Look! There's the hawk again.'

Black against the white. Closer, now: they could see the frantic beating of its wings. On the top of the ridgeway they were almost at its eye level. Marith thought: I wonder if it can see us watching it? Could I call it to me, like I can call a dragon?

The hawk dived. He couldn't see it land.

Thalia said, 'Do you remember the hawk in the desert? I'd never seen a hawk before. And the eagles, dancing around the peak of Calen Mon. I'd never seen an eagle before, either. Or a mountain. Or the snow.' She smiled. Kissed him. Wrapped herself around him. Warm as the summer sun. 'All those things, we have.'

'All the world,' Marith said. 'All the world, I promised I'd show you. All the wonders. And our children. The world will be for them. Heaped up for them.'

On and on. Over and over. Pressing forwards to the end.

'We will announce soon that you are pregnant.' He was King of All Irlast. Of course he could father a child that would live.

Thalia laughed. 'I should think everyone in our army knows already. I see the faces of my servant women every time they come to change my sheets. The way they stare at my stomach when I dress. It's the only thing that seems to interest them.'

Had to think about this. 'Yes . . . Well . . . Anyway . . . But . . . Yes. Yes. We'll announce it soon. The army: gods, they'll rejoice! And when it's born! It's lucky for a baby to be born at Sunreturn. Well-omened.'

'Is it?' She said, 'The doctors said after Sunreturn, Marith.'

'Oh. Yes. Well . . . Yanis Stansel's youngest son was born at Sunreturn, always complained everyone forgot his birthday. I'm sure it's just as lucky for a baby to be born in the spring.'

She said, 'We're marching south, Marith. By the time the baby is born we'll be in the south. Where there won't be a winter or a spring.'

'So . . . maybe we'll march north again.' It should be born in Ethalden, perhaps, he thought. Or Malth Elelane. A king's palace for a king's heir. It would be nice, he thought, to go home for a while. Show his child the places of his own childhood. Sit in the hall of his ancestors, watching his children play on the floor with the dogs in the warmth of the hearthfire.

I will take her back to Malth Elelane, he thought. Go home. One day. I didn't want to go back home at all once and now here

I am, king. It cannot be so very hard to go back there now. All I need to do is give an order to march north. All I need to do, he thought, is turn my horse now to ride north. Come with me now, Thalia. We'll ride away home to live in peace. You want that, too, I think. Do you? Raise our child in peace.

It was beginning to snow again. He began to worry suddenly that the cold . . . She has lost three pregnancies already. His mother had died in childbed. Take care of her and the child.

'She must not die!' he had screamed to the doctors, the first time she miscarried. 'If she dies, I will kill you.'

'It is not uncommon, My Lord King, for a woman to miscarry in the first few months. There is little danger to the mother, this early. A tragedy, but not a dangerous thing, in these early months.' Just a lump of blood. Like a woman stabbed with a sword thrust. So three times now he had wept tears of relief. But it was snowing, and she must be looked after, though she was smiling with pleasure at the snow. Put her head back, stuck out her tongue to catch the snowflakes.

'We should go back, Thalia.'

She looked out over the frozen landscape. 'I suppose we should. I could stand here forever.' She sighed, laughed, put her hands on his wet snow-crusted cloak. 'You're getting cold?'

'The horses,' he said with dignity, 'are getting cold.'

They rode back through the ruins of Arunmen. Thalia wanted to see. Always, she wanted to see.

'I need to remember,' she said. 'I am not ashamed of it: they fought us, they lost. Such is the way of things. Some draw the red lot, some draw the black or the white. But . . . I should remember. See it for myself.'

The city was a desolation, black rubble, the great obsidian walls tumbled down. Pools of blood, frozen, black and hard like the stone, the whole city glazed in blood. Fires still burning, dragon fire so hot the very stones were cracked open, holes in the earth where the fury of the fighting had devoured itself. Bodies in the rubble, under ice and ash and snowfall, dead faces masked in snow, rimed in blood. Burned. Dismembered. Hacked up and swallowed and spat out. Marith steered the horses carefully away from the ruined temple. Fragments of yellow paint. Around the palace, a new city of the Army of Amrath was forming: soldiers' tents, cookfires, canteens, workshops. A smithy was working: Marith heard again the ring of the hammer, breathed in the hot metal scent. A hiss that was molten bronze being poured. A boy in a scarlet jacket embroidered with seed pearls, gold at his neck and waist and ankles, his face running with hatha sores, touting offering himself for one iron piece. A pedlar shouting his wares: 'Tea and soap! Salt and honey! Spices! Herbs! Lucky charms!' Two women washing clothes in a silver bowl that must once have graced a lord's table. Plump glossy children in fur and satin, playing snowballs in the ruins of a nobleman's great house. One of them hit another straight on, got snow all over her coat, and Marith laughed.

Some enterprising person had got a tavern back open. The front wall and the roof had been completely demolished; they'd made the best of it by setting up a fire for mulled wine and laying out some brightly coloured rugs; rigged up the remains of a soldier's campaign tent to keep off the snow. It all looked very charming. Marith nodded at Thalia, they dismounted and tethered the horses, wandered up.

Everyone recognized them, of course, so they walked through a sea of prostrate bodies, more and more people running to kneel, to be in his presence, to see him through half-closed eyes. Voices ran like seawater: 'The king! The king! Amrath Reborn! *Ansikanderakesis Amrakane!* The king! The king!' Someone starting a song of praise for him.

Bliss.

Blush rising in his face from sheer delight at it. He laughed with joy.

They sat down on the bright pretty rugs, the woman running the place rushed over with cups of hot spiced wine, a dish of keleth seeds, a dish of cakes. The cups were enamelled silver, yellow garlands around a scene of fighting birds. Very finely done, actually: he'd guess not from the tavern but looted from somewhere in the east and lugged halfway across Irlast. The wine was delicious, thick and golden. Also looted. The cakes were stale and dry as sand.

The tavern woman prostrated herself flat on her face in the snow. 'I am honoured beyond all honour. My Lord King, My Lady Queen, I kneel at your feet, I am your slave. Take the cups, the plates, everything here in this tavern, our gifts, our token of our love for you.'

Beyond bliss. Ah, such a good thing, to be loved like this. He smiled down at the tavern woman, told her to get up, kissed her hand. Drained his cup, waved over a passing soldier: 'Take this cup back to the palace. Have Lord Durith summoned, tell him to send a dozen gold cups to this woman in place of this one she has kindly given me.' The woman went pink with astonishment. Tears in her eyes. Thalia laughed with delight.

'My Lord King. My Lord King. Thank you. Thank you.'

'I'll take a bottle of this wine, too, then, if I may?' Marith said, smiling at the tavern woman. 'It's better than the wine they served my court last night.'

More laughter. The woman said, a look of great daring in her face, 'I need the wine, My Lord King, for my customers, who must have higher standards in drink than your court.'

Ha! 'They do. They do. Anyone in Irlast has higher standards than my court.'

He settled himself further back on the rugs, stretching himself leaning against Thalia. Ate another stale cake. The tavern woman poured him another drink in a new cup. She was wearing a ring on every finger; they clinked musically against the glass of the bottle. She had silver earrings that jingled, her dress was green velvet. She was positively fat.

Raised a toast to her. 'I'll buy a bottle for a hundred thalers. Make you a lady of my court.'

'But I'll make far more than a hundred thalers, My Lord King, telling my customers they're drinking wine I refused to sell to the *Ansikanderakesis Amrakane* the joy of the world the King of All Irlast.'

Gods, she was good. He got up and bowed to her. 'Like the wine, you're too fine for my court. I'll give you a hundred thalers anyway.'

'And I'll give you another bottle of this wine for free, My Lord King.' Her earrings rattled, she looked at Thalia sitting in her thick fur cloak. 'And, if I may, if I may be so bold, My Lady Queen . . .'

Oh ho. Marith tensed, Thalia tensed, relaxed both together, smiling at each other, squeezed hands. The whole army knows. The tavern woman went into the back of her shop, Marith ate a third stale cake in the time she was gone.

Thalia whispered, 'A horrible itchy baby's dress? A blanket? A pair of absurdly tiny booties?'

'A blanket. Hand-knitted. Shush. You're being cruel.'

'And you're getting cake crumbs on my cloak. How can you eat them, anyway? They must have been baked last week.'

'Amrath lived rough with his army . . .' Wiped crumbs from the white fur, leaving a yellowy smudge. Whoops. Maybe she wouldn't notice. He tried surreptitiously to pick at the mess. 'Anyway, shush, she's coming back.'

'A blanket,' Thalia whispered. 'Dark red. With a sword pattern on it.'

He almost choked crumbs over her. 'Shush!'

The woman returned smiling. Didn't look like she was carrying a blanket . . . She held out a branch of white flowers to Thalia. 'The tree behind the tavern here flowered this morning, My Lady Queen. All out of season – the dragon fire, we thought maybe, My Lady Queen, the heat. But here. Perhaps it flowered for you.'

'Thank you.' Thalia bent to sniff the flowers' sweet perfume. 'Thank you very much.' They finished the wine, Thalia made a face of mock terror at Marith that they'd be offered another plate of cakes. When they had ridden away out of earshot they both burst out laughing. The sun rises, the sun sets, and not everyone in the world thinks only of tiny booties and baby blankets.

'But the flowers are very beautiful,' said Thalia. 'How strange, that the tree flowered in the snow. Do you think it was really the dragon fire?'

'It's wintersweet blossom. It's meant to be in flower now.' He was beginning to feel rather sleepy after all the wine and cakes. 'That's what it does. Hence the name.'

Thalia looked down at the branch, which she had woven into her horse's reins. 'It's still beautiful. We should plant it in the gardens at Ethalden.' Looking down at the flowers, she noticed where he'd got crumbs rubbed into her cloak. 'What's this? My new cloak . . . Oh, Marith. Cake crumbs.'

He looked at her belly. 'Get used to it. I had to have cake crumbs cut out of my hair once.'

Chapter Six

'I had to have cake crumbs cut out of my hair, once.'

Ti's hair. His mother – his stepmother, the bitch who killed his mother, remember, remember that – his stepmother had had to cut cake crumbs out of Ti's hair, once. He had killed Ti and he had killed his mother. Hung their bodies from the walls of Malth Elelane. He remembered the way his mother's hair had blown in the wind.

Three miscarriages. But after three months, four months, the pregnancy is more established, the baby is more likely to be born and live.

He felt sick. The stupid stale cakes.

The next day Marith rode out alone. The land was very empty, the burned fields blanketed in snow. A few surviving villages clinging on in the ruins, ragged-faced farmers tending their cattle. His soldiers were out, rounding up the cattle, pillaging the villages for food and men for the army to consume. A ravening beast, an army. Never ceased its hunger. Indeed, its hunger grew and grew.

Rode past a line of men and women in tattered clothing too thin for the weather, sick faces staring. Rounded up to march in his army. Men and women and children and old men and cripples and the maimed and the half-dead. It didn't matter who they were.

Whether they were strong or weak. If they had no other use, they would deflect an arrow or a sword. If they had no other use, they would die. The soldiers with them prostrated themselves in the snow when they saw him. The new conscripts stared, then did the same. Whispers. His name cried in blessing. The joy in their eyes, radiating off them, the fulfilment of their lives, to see him.

King Marith! King Marith! *Ansikanderakesis Amrakane!* I can die now, for my heart and my eyes have beheld him.

Marith pulled up his horse before them. 'We will fight,' he called to them. 'You will march in my army, and you will fight, and you will be victorious, and you will conquer the world! This gift, I give you. All of you, you will do this. Conquer the world!'

'Death!' the soldiers cried back to him. Shining in ecstasy. 'Death! Death! Death!'

He stopped around midday in a bare high place without any signs of human life. No – there, to the west where the land dropped down into a valley, a single plume of hearth smoke rose. A little village sheltering there, perhaps.

No matter. He dismounted, stood against the white sky. Raised his arms. Called out.

'*Athelamyn Tiamenekyr. Ansikanderakesis teimre temeset kekilienet.*'

Come, dragons. Your king summons you.

A long silence. And then the slow beating of vast wings.

Weak things, dragons. Far weaker than he had first thought. Ynthe the magelord saw them as gods and wonders. Osen and Alleen thought of them as toys: 'Ride it, Marith', 'Just use it to kill them all, Marith', 'Make it sit up and beg and roll over at your feet'. He himself had thought that the dragons were like him, once. The only things in all the world that might understand him. Things of love and desire and hunger and grief and need. He had been a fool, to think that.

He thought: do dragons rear their children? Care for them? Feel love?

He thought: no.

The dragons came down in the snow before him. One black and red. One green and silver. Huge as dreams. He had summoned them out of the desert along the coast of the Sea of Grief, called into the dark and they had come together side by side, their wings almost touching. They could be mother and child, lovers, siblings; what they thought towards each other he did not know and could not know. What they did, when he did not need them, he did not know. Dark eyes looked at him. Like looking down into the depths of the sea. Never look into a dragon's eyes. Look into a dragon's eyes and you are lost. Eyes black with sorrow. Such hatred there, staring vast ancient unblinking down at him.

He thought: I call them and they come to me.

The dragons turned their heads away from him. Lowered their eyes. The red dragon spoke in a hiss of fire. Dry rasp of pain. Its breath stank of hot metal. Dead flesh rotting in its yellowed teeth.

'*Kel temen ysare genherhr kel Ansikanderakil?*'

What is it that you want, my king?

I don't know, he thought. What is it that I want? I want to die, he almost said. The red dragon almost spoke it. The words there in the stink of its breath. I want to die: kill me, he almost said.

Or kill the soldiers. My soldiers. Come down in fire, burn my army to dust. We spread out across the world in blood and fire, we have destroyed half the world but the world is endless, the road goes on and always there is another conquest waiting on the horizon. All I need to do now is speak one word to make it stop.

Dragons are not gods, he thought then. Not wonders. There was nothing in the world that they could give him. Huge things, huge as dreams; he stood between them tiny and vulnerable. He could crush them.

'*Kel temen ysare genherhr kel Ansikanderakil?*' the red dragon asked again.

'*Ekliket ysarken temeset emnek tythet. Ekliket ysarken temeset amrakyr tythet. Ekliket ysarken temeset kykgethet,*' Marith said in reply.

What is it that you want, my king?

I want you to bring death. I want you to bring fire. I want you to kill.

Always the same words. The same commands given. Kill! Kill! Kill! On and on forever. On and on until the world ends. So close to asking. But I don't ask. Why do we waste our breath saying it?

If my army was destroyed, he thought, I would cease to be king. What would I be, if I were not a king?

'You are tools,' Marith shouted at the dragons. 'Nothing more. Things I send out to kill.'

The dragons nodded their heads in obedience. The green dragon might smile, even. Scars on it deep in its body, wounded, its body moved with the awkwardness of something in pain. The red dragon thrashed its tail. Hating him. Tired. Old. Just wanting to sleep.

The green dragon said, as it always did, '*Amrakane neke yenkanen ka sekeken.*' Amrath also did not know why. '*Serelamyrnen teime immikyr. Ayn kel genher kel serelanei temen?*' We are your tools. And what are you?

They leapt into the air together. Red and black, green and silver, so huge he was left blinded. The snow where they had crouched was melted. He watched them spiralling up and outwards. Off to the south, towards the Forest of Calchas, the Sea of Tears, the Forest of Khotan. Tiny jets of flame on the horizon. Or perhaps he was imagining them. But when he closed his eyes he saw it burning. The trees burning. The sea rising up in steam.

Go back four years. Marith sits in his new-built fortress of Ethalden, new-crowned King of the White Isles and Ith and the Wastes and Illyr. He has taken his father's kingdom. Yes, well, any number of sons have done that. He has taken the neighbouring kingdom. That's not exactly novel behaviour from a new ambitious young king with his people to impress. He has taken the kingdom of his holy ancestors, he is a king returned in glory, he has restored a blighted land to greatness, he has been revenged on the evil-doers who ill-treated him. That's absolutely right and proper. Expected by everyone. And then . . .

'Gods, this is glorious,' Osen Fiolt says one night in the new-built fortress of Ethalden, as they sit together in a feasting hall with walls and floor and ceiling of solid gold. 'Goodbye sleeping in a stinking tent in the pissing rain. Hello sitting by the fire with our feet up. We're richer than gods and worshipped like gods and we've still got our whole lives ahead of us to do absolutely nothing but enjoy ourselves in.

'Look at my hands,' Osen says, stretching out his right hand. 'Look, the calluses are finally going down. I might grow a beard, you know? Befitting my noble status as First Lord of Illyr. Or get my wife pregnant. You're going to have a child, Marith, you should maybe grow a beard as well. Dress like a respectable family man, stop wearing all black. Kings wear long robes, have well-combed beards, feast and wench rather than drink and mope. Those pretentious boys quoting godsawful poetry and weeping over life's burden . . . and now we've got wives and children and kingdoms to rule. Gods, who'd have thought?

'I will do nothing,' Osen says, 'but sit by the fire and drink the finest wines and eat the choicest meats and fuck my wife and my servants. Raise a horde of spoilt brat children. Never pick up a sword again.'

'It feels strange walking,' Marith says, 'without a sword at my hip. Unbalanced.'

'Lighter,' Osen says. 'Much lighter. The joys of not wearing armour! A real spring in my step.'

'That too.'

They both go to bed early, dozy with warmth. It's very restful, doing nothing. It's amazing how tiring paperwork and bureaucracy and helping your wife choose baby things can be. He goes to bed early, wakes late in a warm room in a bed of gold and ivory and red velvet, soft as thistledown after campaign beds. His bedchamber looks very much like the one he slept in at Malth Salene. He is not sure whether Thalia realizes this. Unlike at Malth Salene, the morning sun shines in on his face. He tries to put this thing he feels into words; even to himself he cannot say what it is.

Two days later he is reviewing the Army of Amrath. Dismissing most of it. Illyr is taken. The Wastes are taken. Ith is taken. The White Isles were and are his own. He is king. War is done. All is at peace.

'You have to disband some of them,' Lord Nymen the Fishmonger says to him. 'They are driving the people of Ethalden mad with their brawling, the women fear to walk the streets after dark because of them, innkeeps and merchants shut up shop at a soldier's approach. As they say: a friendly army without a purpose is more dangerous than an enemy army at the gates. Also, more seriously, My Lord King – do you know how much this army costs?'

'I have the wealth of three kingdoms at my feet.'

There is a short pause. 'You had the wealth of three kingdoms at your feet, My Lord King,' Aris Nymen says.

A thousand times a thousand soldiers. And horses. And armour. And equipment. And engineers and doctors and weaponsmiths and farriers and grooms and camp servants and carters and . . .

'Yes, yes, I suppose. I see. Yes.'

'The cost of Queen Thalia's temple, My Lord King . . . It being made of solid gold . . . Amrath's tomb . . . The work on the harbour is proving more expensive than we thought . . .'

'Hang the man who thought up the original cost then. No. No. I'm joking. You're right.' I am King of Illyr and Ith and the Wastes and the White Isles. I am invincible, invulnerable, soon I will have a strong son to follow me. What am I afraid of, that I need an army of a thousand times a thousand men? He rubs his eyes. For the first time since he took Illyr, he does not sleep well. He stands in the great courtyard in Ethalden, raised up before his army on a dais of sweetwood hung with silver cloth. They cheer him. They hold out their hands to him. Their faces shine with love.

'Amrath! Amrath! Amrath! King Marith!'

He smiles, basking in it. They shine so brightly, his soldiers, so strong, so proud. He begins to speak.

Stirring. Faces grow pale. Eyes stare up at him in astonishment.

The war is over. They have won eternal glory, until the drowning of the world the poets will sing of them. They can go home now in triumph to their friends and families, tell them of their prowess, show them the riches they have won. If they do not want to go home they can have land in Illyr, slaves to work it, a life of leisure, farming: the soil in Illyr now is rich and good. That is what all men want, isn't it? A house, a garden in which children are playing, fruit trees, clear sweet water, fresh meat, fresh bread. Long days of peace stretch before them. They are heroes from the poems, every one of them. They will look back on what they have done with pride all their lives.

Muttering. Whispering. He can see tears on some of their faces, at the thought of this time ending. Feels tears himself, to dismiss them. They who have made him all he is. He hears his voice unwinding out of his mouth.

Their voices come back mournful as seabirds: 'But . . . But . . . My Lord King . . .' 'You can't . . . you cannot abandon us, Lord King . . .' 'We fought for you. We shed our own blood for you. You can't abandon us. Please, Lord King, do not abandon us to live away from you.' 'We are the Army of Amrath! You are our king! Without this, we are . . . we are nothing.' 'Please! Please, Lord King!'

It feels . . . shameful, and sad, and delicious.

'A farm?' a voice shouts, bitter, croaking, it sounds like a raven cawing, like one of the old women who sell meat in the army's camp. 'A farm? What do we want with farming?'

'What about our pay?' a voice shouts. 'Never mind bloody poetry. We're two months' pay in arrears, Lord King!'

There is something in that voice he has not heard for a long time. '*Prince Ruin. Gods, you stink.*' '*You're disgusting, Marith, look at the state of you, how can you do this to me? To your father? Look what you're doing to him.*'

'What about our pay? Yes!'

A great roar, like the waves when the tide is high and the storm wind is blowing, wave crashing against wave: 'What about our pay, you cheap bastard? Pay us!' 'You can't abandon us! You are our king! Don't abandon us!' 'Pay us, you cheap bastard shit!' A voice shouts, 'Pension us off, will you? Who made you all this, eh? Who made you king?' 'You've got a fucking palace!' a voice shouts. 'What have we got?' 'You can't abandon us,' a voice shouts. 'You owe us. We made you king.'

He looks down on his army who have conquered three kingdoms for him, and a great fear takes him.

'You will have all that you are owed. Those who wish to remain here in Illyr will have land to farm. Those who wish to go home to their families I will provide with passage.' His voice is shaking. His hand goes to the hilt of his sword. 'You are dismissed.' A few of them still jeer. Dogs' faces, snarling at him. Many of them stand openly weeping. Frozen. The tears on their faces look like snowflakes. 'You are dismissed,' he shouts at them. He walks down from the dais away from them into his palace. His back is turned to them inviting a sword blade between his shoulders. He can almost, almost feel one of them stabbing a sword blade into him. No one dares to go near him: they see his eyes, they see the shadows around him, they hear the shadows scream in triumph. If he had dismissed them after he took Malth Tyrenae. After he took Malth Elelane. If they had never crowned him king . . . They howl and moan behind him, prayers, entreaties, curses, 'Amrath,' they beg him, 'Amrath. You cannot do this to us.' 'They are dismissed,' he shouts to Osen Fiolt and Alis Nymen. 'Dismissed.'

Thalia looks at him with sorrow. 'They don't mean it, Marith. They have shed their blood for you. Of course they are upset.' She says, 'They will be glad enough soon, when they have got back home safe to their families.' She is pregnant, soon he will have a family. 'We marched all across the Wastes with them,' she says, putting her arms around him as she will soon put her arms around their son. 'They suffered for us. They shared in our glory, crowned us, celebrated victory with us. I feel sad myself,' she says, 'to see this ending, to be dismissing them after everything they have done for us. But we will be glad of it,' she says, 'and they will be. When we have our son and they have their homes and their families around them.'

Yes: he thinks of his own father King Illyn, running with him in the gardens of Malth Elelane, his father's stern face creased up with laughing. '*Catch me, Daddy*!' '*Caught you, Marith*! *Caught you*!' He walks up and down in his chambers, trying to block out the sound of their voices, cursing them.

'Leave them,' Thalia says, 'Marith. Look,' her face changes, 'look, Marith,' she says suddenly, 'they are beginning to disperse.'

'They are?' He comes to the window to join her. It is coming on to evening, growing colder, the smell of their evening meal cooking hangs warm in the air. It is true, they are beginning to drift away, more and more of them. Their shouts are fading. The courtyard cannot be more than half full.

'I told you they would,' Thalia says. Her voice too is almost regretful. 'They suffered so much for us,' she says. 'Pay them double, Marith, when you send them off.'

'I can't afford to pay them double. I can't afford to pay them anything. You wouldn't happen to have two months' pay arrears in your jewellery box?' Already, he thinks. Already. I thought they might stay there calling on me a little longer. As Thalia says, they suffered for me, they were victorious with me, they shed their blood for me. And yet this is so very easy. I have my kingdom, my palace, my queen, soon I will have a son. Sweet golden dreams of peace. In the courtyard only a very few of the soldiers are left now. Outraged shouts turn to muttered grumbles. Grumbles to knowing complaints. 'Oh well,' they say to one another, 'oh well, we knew it would be coming. If he packs us off soon at least we'll be home for the spring.' 'Got my wife a diamond necklace when we sacked Tyrenae. Was looking forward to giving it to her. Lost it to a whore one night when I was hammered. If the bastard pays us off, maybe I'll buy her another one.' 'A farm, yeah? Never been outside Morr Town's walls before we started marching. A farm might be nice.' 'Bastard. Throwing us over. But that's kings, yeah? What else did we expect?'

That night the city of Ethalden is filled with whispers. Some of the soldiers drink to celebrate their return to homes and families. Some sit in lonely silence, weeping. Some shout their anger to the night sky and the sea. Marith walks the walls of his fortress, paces the corridors and halls. Seabirds scream in the darkness. Something that might be a hawk screams. It cannot be this easy. In the grey light of dawn he comes back into his chambers. In the bedchamber Thalia lies asleep, her face crumpled and strained.

'The day when we were crowned King and Queen of Illyr, Thalia. Do you remember that?' Little more than a month ago. He cannot remember it properly now. Too bright. Too unreal. Too wonderful. They stood in the great golden feasting hall, silver trumpets rang out like birdsong, every living soul in Illyr acclaimed them, the air itself seemed to blaze with gold. 'The most perfect moment in any human lifetime.' Grief overwhelms him. Self-pity and shame.

There are reports the next morning that there has been fighting in the city, groups of soldiers fighting each other, a mob of soldiers has been looting houses and shops. A small group of soldiers returns to the great courtyard to entreat him. Alis Nyman and Yanis Stansel go out to them, pay them off with silver pennies. They are grateful. Cheer their king. File away. Marith and Thalia, Osen and his wife Matrina, Kiana Sabryya and Ålleen Durith go out for a day's hunting. Blackthorn is budding in all the hedgerows. There are snowdrops in bloom by the roadside and faint traceries of frost on the north slopes. In the distance the great central spire of his fortress flashes out silver and pearl, hung with red banners that dance in the morning wind.

'Are you growing a beard, Osen?' Thalia asks.

Osen strokes the stubble on his chin, grins at Marith. 'Possibly.' He seems to be wearing a very ugly new brown coat as well, loose and badly fitting.

Thalia looks very hard at Marith's chin.

They ride past a stream where the willow trees are furzed yellow with catkins. In the fields, they are ploughing the soil for the summer wheat. Thalia says, 'I might well have two months' pay arrears in my jewel box.' The air smells so nearly of spring. When they get back to Ethalden there are petitioners waiting to ask the king's judgement. A dispute needs to be settled concerning an Ithish lord's inheritance rights. A messenger has come from Malth Tyrenae to report on the work rebuilding the city. The tax official on Third Isle has been dismissed for embezzlement, the king must approve his replacement. There is a letter from Malth Elelane reporting the financial situation on the White Isles, so that the king can be advised and take action. There is a letter from Malth Elelane reporting that a lord's son on Seneth Isle has run off with another lord's wife, the lord's son's mother is asking the king to do something.

That evening a group of soldiers gathers before the closed gates of the fortress, shout demands to see the king. But in many taverns the soldiers are drinking happily, raising a cup to their king who will soon send them home.

He goes to bed early. Thalia is tired out after hunting. He lies in bed listening to her breathing, and he cannot sleep. He goes up to the window, throws open the shutters, Thalia makes a moaning sound in her sleep. The night is clear and cold. He thinks of riding down to the sea, standing in the dark to listen to the waves beating on the shoreline. Tastes the salt damp on his skin. A gull screams high in the rooftops of his fortress. He thinks of dead bodies cast up on a beach.

At noon the next day he again summons the Army of Amrath before him. Stands again to address them on a dais hung with silver silk. The men stare up at him. They are wary. Frightened of themselves. Frightened of him They move and murmur like waves. A voice shouts, 'Pay us!' and is hushed. A voice shouts, 'Don't abandon us! Lord King! Please!'

How could he have thought it could simply end?

He cannot speak, at first. His mouth feels dry as desert sand. He stares down at them. They stare back at him.

His hand rests on the hilt of his sword. I don't have to do this, he thinks. All I have to do is walk away.

He rubs hard at his eyes. His voice and his hands tremble as he speaks. 'The army will not be disbanded. Not a single man of you. My companions, my most loyal ones, my friends. The Army of Amrath will be doubled in number! Every one of you shall be re-equipped in new armour with a new sword sharp enough to draw blood from the wind. There will be places in my army for your children, your lovers, your friends. All your arrears of pay will be compensated twice over. And in three weeks' time the Army of Amrath will march out! You will be glutted with gold and with killing! My companions! My friends!' He draws the sword Joy, holds it shining aloft, white light dancing along its blade. 'We will see victory and triumph!' His soldiers cheer with tears of happiness running down their faces. Alis Nymen cheers. Osen Fiolt cheers louder than any of them.

He thinks of Thalia cupping her hands over her belly. She just about shows now, when she wears a tight dress. The women of the court croon over her, fussing, 'Oh, My Lady, how wonderful, how wonderful, oh, the greatest blessing a woman can have, My Lady, oh, joy to you, joy to you, My Lady Queen, My Lord King.' Many of them had mothers or sisters or friends who died in child-birth. His own mother died in childbirth, a dead child rotting in her womb, it had to be cut up inside her, they say, extracted piece by rotting piece. The sounds a woman makes, in childbirth . . .' The greatest joy of your life,' the women say to Thalia, fussing. He knows it is.

He has some claim to the throne of Immier. His great-great-great-great-grandfather's second wife was a princess of Immier; her father died without a male heir and the crown passed to someone else. Disgraceful. The throne should have gone to . . . whatever the girl's name was. And the first Amrath conquered Immier a thousand years ago. Well, then. Immier is not a rich land. But there are many people there for his army to kill.

'Death!' the men chant, loud as trumpets. How much they love him! 'Glory! Glory! King Marith!'

His uncle's voice, mocking him: '*You were such a happy child,*

Marith. But one might have guessed, even then, that this would be where you'd come to in the end.' Where any man would come to, once they started on this.

He thinks: Immier, Cen Andae, Cen Elora, the Forest of Maun in the furthest south of Irlast . . . it doesn't matter where we go. We will march, we will fight, we will kill, we will march on. We dream of glory, and we must have more glory, and more, and more. Men grow restless, look wistfully on swords growing blunted, dream of times past when they were as gods. Looted coin is soon spent.

Thalia miscarries that same evening. The first of them: she has lost two more children since, on the march; they are marching still and now she is pregnant again. He still owes his men two months' arrears of pay. But, now, behold, half the world is conquered.

The dragons were black dots in the white snow sky. Marith rode back to Arunmen through the snow falling heavier. Thick soft white flakes like feathers. Falling until he could barely see his hand in front of his face. He rode along unconcerned. A king in his kingdom. Silent in the snow. A wolf slunk past almost in front of his horse's hooves. Looked at him. Sadder eyes than the dragons. What might have been a scrap of human flesh in its mouth. The horse snorted, rolled its eyes. The wolf was injured, like the green and silver dragon, a long wound running down its flank. Maggots crawled there, even in the winter snowfall. It was heavy and fat from glutting itself on his dead.

'*Denakt,*' he shouted at it, as though it was another dragon. *Go. Leave.* It stared at him. Padded off, disappeared into the snow. He rode on, in a while came across the body it had been feeding on, a man, torn apart lying there. Someone who didn't want to be a soldier, he'd guess. Tried to escape his men. The face was untouched. Mouth open. Eyes open. The snow slowly covering it.

Chapter Seven

Envoys came to Arunmen from Chathe and Immish and every city of his empire, brought him gifts from every corner of the world. Treasures and jewels, objects of great beauty and wealth. White horses. Silver cloth as light as sea foam. A thousand ingots each of iron and copper and lead and tin. The emissaries from Chathe came to kneel before him, swear their loyalty. He smiled at them, raised them up, promised them his faith back in return as long as they remained loyal to him. Ryn Mathen nodded, eyes bright with happiness. On a whim, Marith ordered the emissaries to be given a hundred chests of gold and silver, to bring back to King Heldan as an honour gift. The lords of Marith's empire knelt and crowned him with wreaths of flowers. He held races and dances and feasts. The soldiers paraded for him, dressed in their finery, polished bronze, red plumes nodding on their helmets, red cloaks, gleaming, marching and wheeling in the snow. The music of the bronze: they danced the sword dance, clashed their spears, shouted for joy. So many of them, uncountable, like the trees in a forest. They roared out his name with triumph, he who had given them mastery of the world, made them lords of life and death. Their love burned off them, warm and joyous; Marith gasped as he watched them, his face radiant, breathless, still, after everything, half unbelieving, all this, all this, for him. The emissaries departed, leaving more allied troops in his army's ranks. The Army of Amrath prepared to march out. The forges rang with the clash of hammers, the glowing fire of liquid metal, burning day and night. More swords! More spears! More helms! More armour! Grain carts rumbled in beneath the ruins of the gateways. Provisions for a long hard march. A new levy of troops marched in from Illyr, young men who had not yet seen the glory of his conquests, staring wide-eyed and hungry at the ruins of the city, the tents piled with plunder, the campfires of his army numberless as the stars. They marched in between towers of white newly slain bones, white skulls grinning, the shriek of carrion birds. He saw in their eyes the wonder, the longing to be part of this. They saw him, and he felt their love rise like mountains. A marvel, a gift unparalleled, that they could look upon him, fight for him, swear to him their swords and their spears and the strength in their body and all the length of their lives, to kill and to die at his will.

Onwards. Ever onwards. New lands to conquer. The road goes on and on. Issykol. Khotan, with its sunless forests. The lawless peoples of the Mountains of Pain. Turain, with its wheat fields and its silver river. Mar. Maun. Allene.

The Sekemleth Empire of the Golden City of Sorlost.

Gods, he sees it, so clear in his mind. Yellow dust, yellow sand, yellow light. Magnolia trees and lilac trees and jasmine, all in flower; women in silk dresses, bells tinkling at their wrists and ankles; in the warm dusk the poets sing of fading beauty and the women dance with grief on their crimson lips. The golden dome of the Summer Palace. A boy falling backwards through a window, lit by a thousand glittering shards of mage glass. In Sorlost I saw her face for the first time, radiant, and when I saw her I knew. My hands wallowing for the first time in innocent blood there. In Sorlost I killed a baby, I looked down and I ran my sword through it because I could. Sickness filled him. Fear. He thought: don't think of it. There are so many places to conquer before I have to go back there.

At night he lay with Thalia in the bedroom with the green glass windows, beneath the mage-glass stars. Thalia naked and glowing, bathed in light. He rested his head on her stomach, imagined he could hear the child's heart beating. In the dark inside her body it swam and dreamed. Absurd and impossible.

'I can feel it move,' she said. 'Fluttering inside me. Like a bird. Like a butterfly landing on my hand.' My child! he thought. My child!

He said, 'This time it will live.'

The shadow flickered across his mind. He who had killed his own family. The fear, that it would live.

Alleen Durith held a celebration dinner the last evening before they marched. A private thing, Marith, Thalia, Osen, Kiana Sabryya, Dansa Arual, Ryn Mathen. Alleen's chambers were decked with silk flowers. Marith was noisy, happy, laughing, the lights were very bright, the air smelled fresh and good. Thalia glittered in his vision, silver and bronze, silk and water, summer rain.

'Do you remember the morning it rained,' he said to her, 'in the desert, and the flowers came out pink, and the stream came rushing down?'

Thalia said in surprise, 'No. I . . . I don't remember.'

'I remember it so clearly. The way the desert came alive. How can you not—?' Or . . . ? 'No, that was before, wasn't it? You didn't see that. We saw the stream with the willows, and that first stream, where we threw pebbles, and I told you who I was. It didn't rain in the desert when you were there with me. But you'd never seen running water, until I showed you the stream, and you bathed your hands and feet in it . . .'

'No,' Thalia said, confused. 'No. I hadn't. I—' She smiled then: 'It was beautiful, Marith, when we saw the stream. I remember that. I'll never forget that. Like seeing the hawk – was that on the same day?'

The hawk? What about the hawk? 'We'll go back there soon,' he almost said.

'Drink up, everyone,' Osen shouted. Bustling around, refilling cups. 'Tastes like goat's piss, but we can all manage another cup.' A good and clever man, Osen Fiolt. A good friend.

'Goat's piss? Goat's piss?' Alleen raised his cup. 'I looted this stuff personally, Osen, you barbarian. Horse's piss, at least.'

Kiana threw a flower at Osen. 'War horse's piss. I helped him choose it.'

'Did that woman ever send a bottle of her good wine?' asked Thalia.

'I don't know.' Looked at Osen and Alleen. 'Did she?'

'I have no idea what you're talking about, Marith.' Osen chucked Kiana's flower at him and shoved over a plate of sweets.

'I found a girl in Arunmen who can sing like a skylark,' said Alleen, 'if anyone's interested in hearing her sing?'

'"Sing like a skylark"?' said Kiana. 'Cousin, really.'

Thalia yawned. 'I will go to bed, I think, Marith. I'm tired.' She was very tired, suddenly, the last few days, slept and ate a lot. But she looked well, her face was shining, it would be well, this time, surely, the doctors said that it was good that she was tired, because it showed that the baby was strong. It will live, it must live . . . he felt sickened, thinking of it, gulped down his drink, found himself looking away from her. My child. My child. I who killed my mother and my father and all of them, what will my child be if it lives?

'Stay a bit longer, Marith,' said Osen. 'This girl of Alleen's can sing *The Deed of the New King* and *The Revenge of the King Against Illyr* like a skylark. The proper songs and the dirty versions.'

'Her dirty version of *The Revenge* is . . . dirty,' said Alleen. 'You have no idea.'

Osen began to sing, '*His big big sword thrusts hard and wide.*'

'I will certainly go to bed,' said Thalia.

'I fear you may be wise, Thalia my queen,' said Osen. '*Whole cities call him to thrust inside.*'

'Come to bed soon, Marith,' Thalia said as she left them. Her hand brushed his arm as she walked away. 'Won't you?' Pregnancy seemed to leave her insatiable. It made her flatulent, also. Slept and ate and farted and wanted to fuck. All the good things.

'And she sings it completely straight-faced, too,' said Alleen. 'A marvel.'

Umm . . . ? Oh. Yes. 'Do I really want to hear a woman singing obscene songs about my triumphs?'

'Of course you do,' said Alleen.

'Do I really want to find myself humming it the next time I . . .?'

'Of course you do,' said Alleen. 'And it makes me happy just thinking of it. Why else are we conquering all the world, wading through the blood of innocents, if not for people to make you the subject of obscene songs?'

A loud click of metal as Kiana put her cup down. Alleen went white.

'It's no worse reason than some.' Try to laugh. Try to smile. Try to laugh. His face felt so hot. That feeling, that he had had when they were cheering him, singing his name outside the ruined wine shop, joy, bliss, wonder, but I felt shame, he thought, then, hearing them, and I feel shame thinking about it now, and thinking about a girl singing songs about me . . . *My eternal fame, my glory, the songs of my triumphs* . . . His face felt hot and red. Like it's humiliating, that they praise me. Like they and I are both wrong, should be ashamed.

My head hurts, he thought. I need to go to bed as well. I should have gone with Thalia just now.

'I won't have the girl summoned,' said Alleen. 'I'm sorry, I don't know where that came from. Stay and have another drink, don't leave looking like that. Please.'

'One drink.' It is no worse reason. He's my friend, I . . .

Osen and Alleen were singing something. Kiana was crying with laughter at it. He was singing it too. He was stumbling back to his chambers. It suddenly seemed to have got very late. The girl had sung like a skylark. Even Kiana had admitted as much. Kiana had smiled at Osen: it would be so good if she was to return

Osen's feelings. Make him happy to see it. Poor old Matrina, Osen's wife. He had always rather liked Matrina. But Osen liked Kiana. Kiana didn't seem to like Osen. I wonder if Matrina would like Kiana? he thought.

'My Lord King!' his guardsman Tal shouted.

He was blind. Felt like he was being buried in sand. Thrashed about, gods, it was sticky, coating him. Hands flailing. Filth, coming all over him. His skin burning. Itching. Filth coming up through his skin. He had seen a dog once all covered crawling with ticks and sores and lice, its skin its fur moving. His skin was crawling. Erupting. Rotting. He retched. Vomit filling his mouth, vomit and sand, and he tried to swallow it, he couldn't swallow it, it burned at his lungs, felt it in his nostrils, his eyes bulging, his head going to burst, choking, trying to claw at his nose and mouth. I'm drowning. Gasping to breathe and there was nothing. His arms and legs trembled. Cold sweat pouring off him. Tore at himself he itched he was crawling his skin was crawling his skin erupting his throat erupting choked blocked crumbling he was choking, drowning, his skin, his throat blocked with filth.

The sound of metal. Voices cheered. A trumpet rang.

Swords, he thought. Fighting. A vast battle, men fighting in their thousands in the hallway around him. A hundred thousand shining sword blades.

Gasped, vomited up sand. On his knees, sand pouring out of his mouth. Great gouts of it, like the dragons pouring out fire. Breathing again. Gasping down air. His throat and lungs raw. Sand and vomit dripping from his nose and mouth.

A shadow stood over him. A thing like a man. Dark, like a shadow, featureless, an outline of a man, like a man's shadow in the half-light, and then it moved, poured itself back towards him, a thing like a man but all formed of black sand, crumbling away as it choked itself over him.

He had seen such things in the ruins of his victories. The destruction of the body in a wave of dragon fire. Flesh and bone turned into black ash.

Its hands reached again for him. Pouring towards his throat.

Buried his hands in it. It came apart around him. Flowed over him. The faceless head pressed towards him. Its arms embraced him. Pouring itself into him.

Threw his hands up over his face. Covered his mouth with his hands, bent down pressing his face into the stone floor. Hugging him to itself, kissing and devouring him. In his eyes. His ears. His mouth.

Vengeance. Hiss of sand in the wind. Tried to squeeze his eyes closed, tried not to breathe. It clambered itself swarmed itself over him into him. *Vengeance.*

A hand on his shoulder. He sat up.

'Easy there, My Lord King. Careful.' Tal helped him up carefully. Propped him against the wall. Marith bent forward and coughed up a last trickle of vomit.

'Heavy night, was it, My Lord King?'

Blinked, stared down the corridor. 'There was . . . was . . .'

Tal helped him up the stairs towards his own chambers; he had hardly gone a few steps when Thalia was rushing down to him, her guard Brychan there beside her with his sword out. Pain in her face when she saw him.

'Marith!'

'It's nothing. Nothing.'

Her foot slipped on a step, he cried out but Brychan caught her arm, then she was beside him.

'It was nothing,' said Tal.

Black sand gushed off him. When he looked there was no sand on the floor. Sand crunched in his mouth. He spat. Thalia looked shocked at his spit on the floor. Gleaming. Someone else spat, he thought, I saw a man spit green phlegm at my feet.

'Have some water, Marith.' A cup in his hands, heavy goldwork that heaved beneath his fingers. Itching, crawling, moving. He drank and gulped it down. Tasted so sweet. A grating feeling in his throat as he swallowed. Hair and gristle. Dirt stuck in his throat. His mouth was running with lice. He gagged, his hand over his mouth, don't be sick here in front of her, my wife, do I want my wife to see that? The shame . . . once I didn't want her to see my face, because she'd see it there, vomit and death, I'm human fucking vomit, filth like I'm choking down.

Thalia brought all the lamps in the room to burning. They were in their bedchamber. He couldn't remember walking there. The green glass windows were black and hollow, black voids; the lamplight made the mage-glass stars in the ceiling faint and dull. The silver hangings on the bed moved, trembled: the warm air from the lamps, someone had told him, one of the maidservants. Her sweat in the lamplight, running down inside the neck of her dress . . . The leaves and flowers on the walls looked too real, like wax flowers. Obscenities like a swollen body. Draw his sword, hack them down to bits. The scabs on his left hand were diseased. The scar tissue alive with parasites. The scars on Thalia's left arm were alive with parasites. The scars on her arm were crusted cracking infested with maggots. His throat was dry with dust.

'You almost slipped,' he said. 'On the stairs.'

'Brychan caught me.' She put her hands over her belly. Her nightgown was very sheer, very fine silk, he could see the swell of the child growing there. No other child had grown this big in her womb. Blood smear things on her thighs. Clots of stinking blood. Pregnancy had made her breasts huge. Sweat on her, between her breasts, staining the sheer cloth. He felt sick. For a moment it seemed to him that her belly was swollen not with a child but with ash.

'He's safe,' she said. 'I was worried about you.'

'He?'

She blinked. 'Our son.'

'You know? How can you know?' I don't want it to be a boy, he found he was thinking, not a boy, not another murderer, parricide, dead thing, rot thing like I am. Will it kill her, tearing itself out of her? Cut her up into shreds, laugh in her face, curse her, take her heart to pieces slowly over years and years? I don't want a child. I don't want a boy. I want it to die like the rest, before it can harm her or I can harm it. It struck him suddenly: it is not dangerous for the mother to lose a child in the first early months.

She said, 'I . . . Of course I don't know.'

Did I kill them? he thought. The other children? Kill them in her, will them dead, give her poison in her sleep? *I cannot father a living child. One of your generals himself plots to destroy you! Conspires against you!* What if one of them is poisoning her, killing our children?

'Why do you call it "he", then? As though you think it will live, as though you pretend it will live?' A wound, a rotting wound inside her already infected and dead.

'He will live.' Her hands clutched over her belly, tight, so tight like she might crush it, smother it in the womb. She was lying, they both knew it, it would die soon, any day, any moment, like the rest, just let it live let it live.

'Don't call it "he".'

'I – I want—' And it came to him sick and horrified that she did not want it to be a girl. Look at her, the former High Priestess of the Great Temple, sacred holy beloved chosen of god who was born and raised to kill children, men dreaming in hot sweat about her hands stabbing them. She doesn't want to have a daughter any more than I want to have a son. A perfect clarity, as he coughed the black sand of human bodies from his lungs: we both want this child more than all we have in the world, the last hopeful thing left to us, the only reason for anything. A child, to build an empire for. A child, to show our happiness and love. And we both want it to die unborn.

He remembered, so clearly, kissing Ti's pink screwed-up face, kissing Ti's pink flailing fist.

'He will live,' Thalia said again. 'We should not be talking about this, Marith. Not now. You're frightened, angry,' she said. 'You need to calm, to sleep.'

'I saw . . .' I can't tell you, he thought, not you, I can't speak it, I can't have the child, my son, he can't hear. Black sand crunched between his teeth.

Chapter Eight

It was a nightmare brought on by drink and stupid songs, he thought the next morning. There had been grains of black sand in the bed, he had woken to feel them itching him. A scalding hot bath; he drank and spat water, drank and spat, drank and spat. He still could not speak of what he had seen.

He drank a cup of wine and his mouth felt cleaner. He was dressing when a message was brought that Alleen wanted to see him urgently. Thalia looked at him in fear and surprise.

'What is it?'

'How should I know?'

'Show him in, then.'

Perhaps, he thought for a moment, he should see Alleen alone, without Thalia there.

'Marith . . .' Alleen was nervous. Excited, afraid. 'Marith, I've someone here you need to see. Now.'

'I . . . Bring him in, then.' Should I tell Thalia to leave? he almost thought. He could hardly tell her to leave in front of Alleen and the guards prowling around.

What will I do, he thought, if it is coming now that she is the one betraying me? Or Osen? But I love her, and Osen is my best friend.

There was a young man waiting in the bedroom doorway. A

servant, from the look of him . . . no, Marith looked closer, a soldier, unarmed and as frightened as Alleen was, but a soldier. Blood smell on him. Bronze and blood ground down onto him, marking him. The man was looking down at his feet, too afraid to look up.

'Well?'

Gods, he needed a drink.

'Speak,' Alleen said.

We've been here before, and he'll say . . . Not Thalia. Not Osen. Please. He'll say it.

'Lord Erith,' the man said.

'Valim Erith offered him gold,' Alleen said, 'to kill you. Gold and—'

'Lord Erith gave me this.' The man held up a dagger. Carefully, cautiously, between finger and thumb, hanging down like a live thing. Blue fire on the blade. A blue jewel in the hilt. Marith reached for it.

'Careful!' Alleen pulled his hand back away. 'The blade is poisoned, he says.'

'Poisoned.' Marith took it, held it up to see the light move in the jewel. Pressed the very tip against his finger, drawing out a single bead of red blood. Heard voices gasp and wince.

'Valim Erith gave it to you? To kill me? You swear this?'

'Valim Erith gave it to me, My Lord King, I swear it.'

'On your own life?'

'On my own life, My Lord King.'

'Why you?' Thalia asked. 'Who are you?'

A long, stuttering, gasping noise. The poor man. Wretched man, brought to this. He's nobody, Thalia, Marith thought. Some poor man doing as Valim Erith ordered him.

'Speak,' Alleen said harshly.

'My name is Kalth, My Lord King, I am an Islands man, My Lord King, I've been a soldier under Lord Erith since you were crowned king at Malth Elelane, I've fought in every one of your battles since you sailed to Ith, I've fought and survived them all.'

There was so much pride in his voice as he said that; his pride filled the room with warmth. 'My brother died at Balkash. My lover died here in Arunmen, on the first day of the siege. Perhaps I . . . I said some things I didn't mean, after he died, mourning him. He . . . It took him five days to die. So I was angry, and perhaps I said things . . . I'm sorry. But Lord Erith – I served him, my family have served the Eriths as soldiers and servants for a hundred years, he himself was a guest at my sister's wedding, but I would not do it, My Lord King, not what he asked me to do.'

'He came to me this morning,' said Alleen. 'He was supposed to do it last night. He hid, came to me instead.' Alleen rubbed his eyes. 'A hangover and four hours' sleep. Curse Valim.'

Thalia said, 'Can we trust him? This man?'

Alleen said, 'Look at him. He has no reason to lie, I think.'

Thalia looked thoughtful. Marith rubbed at his own eyes, 'Have Valim brought in, then. And fetch Osen here.' Valim: yes, it made sense to him, he could see it; Valim whom he had known since he was a child, bright in his bright armour, his hard face, a proud young man in King Illyn's hall. Not a friend. A friend of his father's.

Valim Erith was brought in shaking his head, chained, guards all around him. His eyes bulged when he saw Kalth. But he did not speak.

'You conspired to kill me.' It was not a question. Managed to keep the question out of his voice. He remembered Valim Erith from when he was a child. A stern, cold man. He had always known that beneath the cold Valim Erith was weak.

'Why?' What do I expect, Marith thought, that he'll say anything more than anyone else ever does? The same old same old things, the same words, *the Altrersyr are vile and poison and hateful and should be wiped off the face of the world and I, I alone will manage it . . .*

'Where did you get the knife?' Osen asked Valim.

Valim said in a whisper, 'It's not mine. I have never seen it before.'

70

'Your man has told us everything, Valim,' Thalia said, 'stop lying.'

Marith held the knife up close to Valim's face. 'Was it you the prisoner was talking about? One of my generals, betraying me. You.' Brought the knife so close to Valim's face.

In the eyes. His own eyes itched and burned.

In the eyes. The blue jewel in the knife handle, blue as Thalia's eyes. Is that some joke?

'Are you killing my children?' he shouted at Valim. 'Are you making my children die in the womb? What are you giving her, to make it happen?'

In the eyes. So close to the eyes. His own face, reflected there. The knife, reflected there.

Thalia moaned in pain at that.

'Are you conspiring against me? Are you?'

Kill him. Kill all of them.

I don't want the child to live. Thalia doesn't want the child to live. Thank him.

Valim said, 'No. Marith. No. No. No. No. No. No. No.' A flood of filth coming out of his mouth. Puking out his lies.

'Stop it,' Marith almost screamed at him. All the voices, so many, his own: no don't do this please please no please. 'No no no no no. Marith, no,' Valim screamed.

Alleen said, 'You cannot possibly have thought Arunmen would be able to defeat us.'

'You were the one who brought the Arunmenese ringleader in to judgement,' said Osen. 'Gods, you snake.'

'No,' Valim whispered. 'No.' He stared at Marith, pleading. Stared at the knife. His body slumped. 'I followed you, I loved you, I . . . You are my king, Marith . . . My son died for you . . . Marith!' His voice rose again screaming. 'It wasn't me! You cannot believe this! You are my king! Always! Always!' Scrabbled towards Marith, chains rattling stupidly. Dead body on a gibbet. 'Always!'

Marith took up the knife again. Blue fire blue jewel. Fine bronze blade. A good weapon, well-balanced. It felt good in his hand.

Could imagine it, very easily, sinking in. Now he knew it was poisoned, he could see a slight sheen to the killing edge. A slight scent, even, sweetish, dirty, reminding him of childhood sickness, over the cold smell of the bronze. His finger ached, where he had pricked himself with the knife. Wondered if this really could have harmed him.

'Curse you! Curse you!' A pause, a sudden look on Valim's face like a cruel sly child: 'I wish now that I had done these things.' Then Valim said nothing more. Silent, hate in his eyes, as Marith killed him. The man Kalth screamed and shrieked, tried to break away, ended up on his belly wriggling, pleading, mass of snot and tears, clawing at the ground. Tal and Brychan killed him.

The wounds on Valim's corpse blackened. Smoked and crumbled away. Black slugs, crawling over the knife wounds.

'Bury it. Bury the knife, too.' The first man to touch the corpse leapt back screaming. His fingers turned black. They had to wrap the body in raw hides, bloody and dripping, before they could carry it off. They threw Kalth's body on top, shovelled the earth fast over it. Marked it with a pile of white stones: this place is cursed, keep away.

There was a sense of relief, afterwards. Marith felt a kind of lightness in him. Purged. Younger, brighter men than Valim around him. It must have been Valim. It must. Don't speak more of it. Ignore it. His skin crawled running crawling with lice sand in his throat. Never speak it.

'He was never part of it, not like we are,' Osen said, 'he was thick with your father, gods know how long he has been plotting it.'

'Filth,' said Alleen. 'You heard him at the end, confess it. *"I had done these things"*. I've been through the men who fought under him,' Alleen said. 'Had a good think and killed a couple of them.'

Thalia frowned, looked troubled, agreed it was for the best. 'Are you sure, Marith? That it was Valim Erith?'

'Yes.'

'It just seems . . . I don't know . . .'

Too neat, is I think what you may be saying, Thalia my wife. But blink it and drink it away. If it was more complicated than that, well. It's done You did it, I think, or Osen, or someone all of you my dead children my unborn son. Valim Erith probably deserved it for something. Sand crunched in his mouth. So don't think of it, don't talk of it. Close your eyes, point at the map, give an order, march on.

The Army of Amrath left Arunmen behind it. Marched south through the wheat fields of Tarn Brathal, following the course of the sacred river Alph. The river ran cold through frosted landscapes. The earth was fresh and hard, the horses pushed on eagerly, the men marched singing, their voices crisp in the cold, puffing out their breath as they went. 'Marith! Marith Altrersyr, *Ansikanderakesis Amrakane*! Death! Death! Death!' Tereen, he besieged and destroyed, despite it having sworn allegiance to him as king. They had been lying. They would have betrayed him eventually, as Arunmen had. Risen up, cast off his rule, cursed him. Thus better to get it over with. The city fell and he went through the streets killing anything in his path, and he felt triumph and shame and relief. *Filth. Rot. Corruption. They all loathe you, King Ruin. Want to see you dead.* They deserve this, he thought. They would have come to this in the end.

Samarnath, he loosed his dragons on. A champion came out, dressed in black armour, a mage blade running with blue fire in his hand. 'Fight me, Marith Altrersyr! Amrath! Fight me, I will destroy you! I have sworn it! Fight!' They fought together, Marith and the challenger, wrestled and hacked at each other while all the living men and the dead looked on. He is invulnerable. He is death and ruin. He ached and stumbled and sweated and his mouth tasted of dust and blood and vomit, and he killed the fool in his black armour and sent him crashing down to the earth where his teeth stirred up the dust.

On again, still southwards, leaving the river Alph behind them. At its mouth was a great delta, a thousand miles of marshland, reeds and waterfowl, the people there lived on islands made of reeds, in huts raised up on poles above the water, in houseboats that rocked on the tide. They lived by hunting and fishing, prowled the wetlands on stilts looking like the wading birds they sought. Some of the marsh dwellers, it was said, had never set foot on firm hard ground. Stone to them was a marvel, more precious than bronze or iron: and what use was iron, indeed, when it rusted away in the constant damp? They worshipped the mud and the waterbirds, believed that the world was hatched from the egg of a giant black-winged crane. It might have been pleasant, Marith thought, to visit there, go hunting in the marshes, it was the season when the cranes would be gathering there to breed, from Theme, Cen Elora and Mar and all of Irlast. The sky would be dark with them; their wingbeats were said to make a sound like heavy rain. It was almost Sunreturn: back home on the White Isles it would be icy cold, dark even at midday, but here they were moving south, the air was warmer, the air had a different feel on the face, a new taste in the mouth.

The marshes were dying. Scouts brought the news in, proud and delighted to be the first to tell him. The waters of the Alph brought down rotting bodies, blood, disease, banefire, ash. The marshes choked on the poisoned waters, the reeds withered, the birds and the fish floated on the surface of the water bloated and green. Children sickened, their lives dribbling out of their mouths. Babies were stillborn. The old and the weak died of hunger. The strong died of grief.

So not much point going there, then, to hunt and boat. The cranes, the scouts said, were dying in such numbers that the channels of the river were choked with their bodies and their unhatched eggs.

The river is cursed. From being sacred, it is a river of death. It is punishing you, King Marith, by destroying itself. It worships you, you see? They marched instead for the Forest of Calchas, fragrant cedar wood, wild pears, walnut trees. Burned it. The dragons swept over it, belched fire, and the smell of the burning was sweet, as it always was. The flames, like the water, worshipping Marith the king.

Another feast, by the light of the forest burning. Osen had found a troop of acrobats who could jump and tumble higher than should be possible, they wore bells sewn over their costumes, mirrors on their costumes and on masks covering their faces and their hair. The air was warm, they could sit beneath the open sky. A great wall of flame and smoke to the west. The flames must be visible in Issykol, even on the shores of the Small Sea.

A cheer rose up in the distance. The whole camp was celebrating, the army enjoying itself. Singing and music. It would be lovely, Marith thought, to wander down there, join them, dance and drink with them as a man among them.

'The Battle of Geremela!' the lead acrobat shouted. The troop formed itself into two sides, took up long poles painted bronze. They vaulted, climbed the poles, flipped and darted over and under each other; clashed the poles together in the air; fell and leapt back up. It did look like a battle, a little, if one had never seen a battle. Osen and Alleen Durith cheered and clapped, their eyes very bright. 'Do you remember?' 'Do you remember?' 'Do you remember?' Gods. He could remember everything, every sword stroke, only had to close his eyes and he was back there. That moment, kicking his horse to charge down on the Ithish ranks, his men and his shadows following him. He had been the point of an arrow, the tip of a sarriss. That moment as he struck the Ithish ranks. So long ago now it seemed. The acrobats unfurled red scarves, whipped them behind them as they leapt, red banners snapped out from the tops of their poles. Bodies falling, leaping over each other. A final clash of all the poles together, the red silk burst over them, a girl threw a clay pot into the air, struck it with her pole to break it: white silk flowers showered down. 'Hail King Marith! Hail King Marith!' the troop shouted in unison.

Oh, that was lovely. Nothing like Geremela, but lovely. The acrobats bowed, a servant passed him a pouch of gold to throw to them.

'Very clever. Very fine. Where did you find them?'

Osen was beaming, 'Samarnath. Good, aren't they? And the girl there, the one who threw the pot at the end . . . the things she can do . . .'

Kiana tossed her head at that, like she didn't care. Which she didn't. But who wants to be scorned even if they don't return their suitor's ardent love? Now you have a wife and a child and a true love and an acrobat mistress, Osen, Marith thought. A positive crowd of women. It was pleasing. The second most powerful man in Irlast shouldn't just be moping about after Kiana Sabryya. And Alleen has his foul-mouthed singer; isn't it a joy to see my friends so happy in love? Why else are we conquering all the world, wading through the blood of innocents, if not to meet beautiful young women with unusual talents?

A few days later he led an assault on a village fortress on the coast south of Calchas, a bandits' nest, nothing of importance save that it sat on their march bristling with spears, could sit thus on their rear as a threat. Three days alone in command of fifty men, sleeping without tents or blankets under clear skies brilliant with stars, then a short sharp fight hand-to-hand at the end. The fortress was built over a spring of ice-cold water, tasting strongly of iron, Marith bathed in it, drank great gulps of it, it washed away any last memory of sand crunching in his mouth. When he got back to the army Thalia said his hair was curlier, too, from washing in it. In the bandits' treasure store there was a necklace of rose-pink rubies, made for her, surely, and a string of green pearls that she gave away to Alleen's foul-mouthed skylark-tongued girl. 'Osen is happier, also,' Thalia said, 'than he has been. His acrobat is good for him.' She laughed in bafflement at these men.

'Why was Valim Erith such a fool?' Marith asked. 'Why? When he could have been part of this?'

Thalia opened her mouth to speak. Shook her head. 'Because he was a fool,' she said. 'I don't know.'

Thalia dreamed still of sweet water, wild places, birds: the feel of water, the smell of water, would be good for the child, she said. They made a fast ride to the shores of the Small Sea, Marith and Thalia, Osen and Alleen and Kiana and Ryn Mathen, camped there, watched the sun rise over the water. There was a great mystery in its waters, which in places were saltier than the Bitter Sea, in places sweet and fresh, safe to drink. One could swim, even, between areas of the two. It was the season in which the birds of the Small Sea raised their young, and the sky was filled with them, white feathers floated on the water's edge.

'We will take our daughter here.' He stretched out full-length on the grass. He could no longer rest his head in Thalia's lap but she ran her fingers through his hair. 'We can teach her to swim in the water – much nicer than the freezing ponds I learnt in. The White Isles in winter, for snow and sledging and skating. Illyr in the summer, when the meadows are full of wild flowers for her to run through, as high as the top of her head. The shores of the Small Sea in the spring and the autumn, when it does nothing on the White Isles but rain and Ti and I would go mad stuck indoors for weeks.'

A great flock of white egrets came down on the water together, churning the water up, sending waves lapping against the sand on which they sat. So thickly packed that where they floated together they looked like an island. There were said to be dolphin in the water, and silver-coloured fish with long yellow curling hair like women. On the further shore the river Ekat ran down from the Mountains of the Heart, tasting of honey, the mountains were so high and so shrouded in ice that no one knew where in the mountains it rose. Some said the river Ekat was the tears of a dragon chained to a mountain. Some said it welled up from a great cavern glittering with diamonds, that led down to another world beneath. Some said there was a valley in the Mountains of the Heart where the people had wings like birds. Some said there was a city in the Mountains of the Heart where dragon princes lived.

Osen said, 'When we get to Mar, the far south coast . . . we'll have marched from the furthest north to the furthest south, when we get to Pen Amrean. The far end of the world. The Sea of Tears, and they say it goes on forever until you are no longer sailing on water but on . . . light, perhaps, or mist.' He shrugged. 'Until nothing. No one has ever sailed out, to come back. Unless they have tales of it in Mar or in Pen Amrean.'

'I should like to see it,' Thalia said. They had stood on the cliffs of the far north coast of Illyr, looking into the northern sea that has no end: 'I should like to see it here at the south,' Thalia said.

'We can set up a marker there,' said Osen. 'They say the sea is warm there, the sea winds smell of spices there and the cliffs are silver-shining. An empire stretching from sea to sea. A tower, a monument, a mirror-image of the tower of Ethalden, silver and pearl. A tower greater and more beautiful than Ethalden, a palace, a house of glory for the king who had conquered from the furthest north to the furthest south, a monument to all his victories.'

Yes. On and on. On and on. Alleen shouted in agreement. Marith said, very quietly, 'And then what we will do?'

'Then what will we do?'

The sound of men's feet, marching. The flash of their bronze spears held high. *'Don't abandon us, My Lord King!'* *'Pension us off, will you?'* *'Pay us, you bastard shit!'* Marith and Thalia, Marith and Osen, sitting by the fireside, children rolling happily at their feet, Marith and Osen have well-combed long beards, Thalia is stout and grey. Marith said, 'When we have conquered the world. When there is nothing left to conquer. What will we do?'

Thalia sat up, looked at him. Osen said, laughing, 'What do you want to do?'

'Eralad, Issykol, Khotan, Mar, Allene, Maun, Medana, Sorlost . . .' The awkwardness in his voice again, Osen was frowning, still trying to think it was fooling, Thalia made a little laugh noise in her throat to show she understood, and he brushed it away. 'Chathe is our ally, Immish is our ally.' Counting the places off on his fingers as he named them. 'And then . . . we've conquered the world. There's nothing left. So what will we do?'

'That's still a lot of places still to conquer, Marith,' Ryn Mathen the King of Chathe's cousin said.

'Fewer places than we've conquered already, Ryn.'

Kiana said, 'Pol Island. The Forest of Maun where there are a thousand miles of wilderness where a man has never been.'

'Ae-Beyond-the-Waters!' said Alleen Durith. 'If Ae-Beyond-the-Waters is even a real place!'

'That bit of rock off the coast of Allene!' Osen shouted. 'Those bits off rock off Maun's coast! Places we've made up!'

Thalia grasped his hand. 'Marith—'

'Yes! We'll load the Army of Amrath aboard a flotilla of war ships, sail away into the west. Ae-Beyond-the-Waters. Places that do not and cannot exist. All of them! How glorious, we'll conquer the sea, the waves beneath the ships' keels, all the creatures of the land and the water, all the birds of the air, we'll conquer the sky and the rain and the wind and the snow and the summer heat. Tear the sun and the moon from the sky and trample them. Rip out the stars of heaven and give them to my men. *To the eternal glory of the god Amrath! From the sea-eaten shore to the grey of the mountains, from the north to the south, from the sunrise to the sunset, to the end of the world, we will hail Him king!* Do you think they will be satisfied if I give them the stars to rape and pillage? Do you?'

'Marith,' Thalia said to him quietly. He thought he saw her belly move, where the child kicked.

'And by then the cities of Irlast will have been rebuilt, their towers and their walls will shine bright again, their armies, their treasuries, swords, spears, helms of bronze, and we can go around and do it all again. And again. And again.'

'Don't abandon us, My Lord King!' 'Pay us, you cheap bastard shit!' Thalia's hand dug into his wrist.

'We'll go round and round Irlast killing and burning, round and round and round and round. Pay them to rebuild, so we can sack them again! Rebuild them ourselves then tear them down! I've got all the money in the world now, after all. What else is there to bloody do?'

'Stop,' said Thalia. 'Marith.'

He laughed and sat down and thought he would break down sobbing. 'What else is there to bloody do?'

Silence.

'Let's go for a swim, Osen,' said Alleen at last. 'They've caught us a feast of fish for dinner, come and swim while they cook it.'

They slept that night on great rafts floating on the water, like waterlilies, a thing that the people who had once lived there were said to have done. It was pleasant enough.

They marched on south down the coast. Issykol he drowned in a storm. Ranene the weather hand's masterwork: black sky, black sea with white waves, rain so heavy it bruised the skin. The earth turned to liquid. The earth and the sky and the sea and the wind and the rain blurred into one howling, screaming maelstrom. This was what the world was like before sea and sky became separate, at the dawning of all things before sea and sky and land were formed. The soldiers huddled in dug-out shelters. The storm downed them. The storm buried them. The storm ripped them away screaming into the air. Marith stood out in it, face thrown back, arms raised to the wind.

'Like rainfall, like storms in the desert, drowning, engendering,
Soaking the parched earth and washing away all that survives there.'

The Song of the Red Year. The storm drowns all to recreate it. Only through death can the world be remade. Beautiful. Like all illusions. The wind tore at his hair, the rain poured over him, the force of it almost overpowering him. The waves shattered cliff tops. The wind tore down buildings, uprooted trees. Like a child bored while his mother tends her garden, and he plucks leaves, breaks off flowers, snaps fresh green stems. The world was mud and ruin. Dead bodies floated on the mud. Broken stonework. The remains of houses. The remains of ships. The city drowned and gone.

The storm died. Clear pale sky.

The joy of it faded in Marith. Ranene crouched at his feet, exhausted.

'It . . . is done,' said Ranene, wheezing out tired breath.

'Good. Well done. We'll have a feast tonight and you'll have the place of honour.'

Turned away from the ruin before him, his eyes already fixed south on the ashes of the forests, the high mountain peaks.

'Then tomorrow we'll march on. Khotan. The Mountains of Pain.' Thinking, thinking, how to destroy them. 'Turain. Pen Amrean. Allene.'

Sorlost.

The dragons circled overhead. Like gulls. Circling in the clear washed liquid sky. They are laughing, he thought. They were wise beyond all imagining, all the wisdom in the world was there in their eyes. Thus they knew. Valim's voice, cursing him: *You are my king. Always. I wish now that I had done these things.*

Thalia stared at the mud with big sad mother's eyes. He'd played in the puddles with Ti and once he'd pushed Ti over and Ti had pulled him down after him, they'd got soaked through, ruined their clothes, their nursemaid had been whipped, their mother had scolded them.

On. On.

Chapter Nine

The storm passes, the sun comes out, and the earth is shining. I had forgotten what it feels like in the warmth of the south. Damp heat, lush with growing, not the dry deserts of my other life. We go riding together, away from the columns marching. Up into the mountains, feel the spray from the river where it comes down in a waterfall over a gorge, sends up rainbows, there is snow up there on the highest peaks, the ground is mossy, soft as silk pillows, the high meadows are so rich in flowers the gold of their petals shines on the skin. We find a lake up there, clear as mirrors, the birds of the mountain are reflected in it, Marith smiles and says it is almost as blue as my eyes. 'Our child must have your eyes,' he tells me. 'Your eyes, and your skin, and my hair.' The Mountains of Pain, the mountains are called. They are sharp as blades. But I cannot see pain in them. They are beautiful. Not a place for men, no, very few live here, if one goes too high into the mountains one's breath is said to come heavy, the head feels dizzy, in the snow at the heights a man can sicken and die. But they are not things of pain. The name is from a story, I am told, a woman, a princess of Turain with black skin and silver hair, very beautiful, and her heart was broken, and she raised up the mountains so that she might live alone there, in solitude. Her pain, alone.

Yellow cranes fly up from the south to build their nests in the mountain heights. Wild goats with horns as sharp as sarriss points; mountain eagles; grey wildcats that have no shadow as they hunt in the dusk. Walnut trees. Peach trees. Rose trees. Trout and perch in the rivers. Gellas fowl. Wild peacocks. Meadows like a carpet unfurled, cloth laid out in a market place. In the valleys the earth is good, golden woodlands, fields basking in the sun and watered by streams from the mountain heights, the crops grow up so fast here that the mountain people can gather three harvests a year; in the gardens the trees are so heavy with fruit that it does not need to be bought and sold, one can simply reach out to take. Here, in the warmth, we rest the soldiers, load ourselves with supplies, let the horses rest and fatten. The dragons are gone into the mountains. Weary, after the great labours they have done for us. We settle ourselves in the foothills, build a city of soldiers' tents. The men of the mountains come to do us honour, kneel before us, crown us with silver, offer up gifts of animal skins and sweetwood and wine and fruit. 'Dragon King', they call Marith. He smiles radiant at that. They call me 'Queen of Flowers'. We hold feast days and games, the Army of Amrath parades, dances, sings songs, stages races and mock fights. The winners are crowned as we are with flowers and gold. There are weddings, celebrations of births and birthdays, commemorations of our dead. Osen talks of writing a book, a history of our conquests, until Alleen Durith laughs him out of it.

'What will we do, when we have conquered the world?' I say to Marith. 'We will do this. Celebrate and enjoy ourselves, fill the world with music and dancing and poems. Pass all this beauty on to our children and their children after them.'

Marith tries to smile. 'We have sacked all the great cities of the world, Thalia. Killed all the poets and the musicians who live in them.'

'As you said, we will rebuild them. More beautiful than before. Never mind offering your soldiers a farm each: every soldier in the Army of Amrath can hold court in a palace in a great city, with retainers and painters and poets.'

He rubs his eyes. But I lived for twenty years in one building,

I fasted, I killed, I knelt in the darkness with a knife in my hand, I knelt in the blinding light for days without sleep. If there is nothing else for our armies to do . . . yes, we can sack them again and again. If there is nothing else for us to do.

The child is growing so strong inside me, I feel her swimming within me, moving like a fish. Soon she will be born. Sometimes now she kicks so strongly Marith can feel it, if he puts his hand on my belly. 'Quickly, quickly!' I call to him, and he puts his hand where I show him. 'I feel it!' he cries. The wonder of it, each time, he laughs and shouts like a child himself, for pure longing joy. 'My daughter,' he says to it, he kisses my belly where it lies. The baby kicks and wriggles within me, as if she too is delighted by it.

I say to him, 'We won't have time to conquer any more of the world, when we have our children to bring up.'

I want my child to grow up happy and contented. Never to know hunger or helplessness. I want to give her a rich good life, far better than my own. I want her to have everything, wealth, status, for her life to be free from want, from sorrow, from grief. I want her life to be perfect. I would put my child's life above others' lives, I would do anything for this child inside me. Is this also a bad thing?

No one, I am certain, has thought or done such a thing before. You, I am sure, have never thought these things.

In the blazing light and heat of the south we celebrate Sunreturn. 'Year's Renewal,' I say; Marith says with a laugh, 'You heathen, it's called Sunreturn.' 'There is no need for it to return,' I say back to him, 'you barbarian, look – the days are no shorter, the sun has not gone.' He shakes his head, 'True, true. But in my empire, Sunreturn is its right name.' Indeed: such an absurd joke to us in the city of Sorlost the city of the dawn, that the people of the north should fear the death of the sun, this fool's idea that the sun is so fragile. Sunreturn and Sun's Height, what a strange joke! Yet I find that I miss the long days of the north. In Illyr, the summer days were so long I would go to bed sometimes when the sun was still golden, the light in the air as I lay waiting for sleep would be comforting. Like sleeping wrapped in light. I would fall asleep to the sound of birdsong; wake in the morning to a world already brilliant with light.

On the feast day the fires of the camp from the mountain are like stars; the air rings with song; the servants are garlanded with hyacinths, they have spread the floor of our tent with rose petals, Osen Fiolt brings us crowns of white blossom, caught and frozen, alive, cold with frost. A new gown is waiting for me, rosy silk so fine it looks as though I am wearing the dawn sky. A necklace of spun gold flowers, delicate as breath. There is music and singing. Silver bells ringing in the air above our heads. We drink perfumed yellow wine out of diamond cups. Poets tell of his triumphs, the beauty of his battles: *The Deeds of the New King; The Ruin of Tyrenae; The Fall of Tereen.* Osen Fiolt raises his cup in a toast to us. As the others join him, gold and silver stars begin to fall from the ceiling of the tent. Outside, in the warm summer darkness, the soldiers dance in their costumes of branches and bones and ribbons, run and leap with burning torches to light up the night. 'Luck! Luck!' their voices shout. Inside me, I feel the child kick. Alleen's servant girl begins to sing, her voice sweet and soft as honey, warm, rich. A man beside her accompanies her on an ivory flute. She claps her hands, stamps her feet as she sings, a fast rhythm, joyful. She has the heavy accent of Illyr; I think, from the words I can understand, that she is singing of Amrath and Eltheia, how much He loved her and she loved Him. Dansa Arual gets to her feet, begins to dance. Alleen Durith joins her, and Osen Fiolt, soon almost everyone is dancing. Marith sits and watches beside me, until Dansa Arual grabs his hands and I tell him to join them. The tent smells of crushed flowers, rose petals kicked up by dancing feet.

In the grey light of the next morning, a pain grips my belly. I see the sun rise, I lie awake in the first light with the sounds of revelry around me. I begin to bleed.

* * *

When the sun sets in the evening, my child is dead.

Marith sits at my bedside, and we both knew that this would happen, and we both scream with grief. The greatest pain a human heart can endure, I am told, to lose a child, and I believe it. Marith's voice, calling the shadows, his eyes are dragon eyes: 'No. No. Please. Please. Just let her live.' I hold her, for a little while. She moved, once, after she was born, her mouth opened, her eyes opened, she opened and closed the fingers of her hands, balled them into fists. Marith says that she did. Swears that she did. She is very cold in my arms, but very soft. She has tiny fingers all wrinkled up. She has tiny fingernails. Her ears are like tiny shells, she has fine black hair almost like feathers all over her head. Her skin is red-brown. Like apples. Her eyes are closed and I cannot bear to know what colour her eyes are. Her eyelashes are long and black. She has a smell on her like blood and like the sweat of a clean body after running, and like something else that I cannot describe and will never forget and already forget.

They say that an unborn child's heartbeat sounds like horses' hooves galloping. A healer woman came to our tent once, pressed her head to my belly, listened, drummed her fingers on a stone to beat out the sound of my child's heart. 'It is strong, your child,' she told us. 'Listen. It sounds like your army racing into battle, My Lady Queen, My Lord King.' But that child died inside me, unformed, a little smear of dark blood. It was not strong. We were camped in Cen Elora, then, when my last child died. The great pine forests that grow on the shore of the Closed Sea. The floor of our tent was soft, from being pitched on pine mast, the air smelled of resin and wood smoke, the flames of our campfires would flicker up suddenly green and blue. The woods were very silent, empty of birds or animals. The streams in the woodlands were very clear, dark and empty also. There is something in the pine needles, in the resin from the trees, Marith said, that makes the water unpleasant for creatures to live in. The stream beds were fine gravel; one night our tent was pitched beside a deep pool, delicious for bathing. Purple iris grew up beside it, ringing it like a garland. We ate venison roasted over pinewood, fragrant with pinesmoke. My last child died the next day. We marched on three days later, I was still bleeding, horses' hooves drummed on the earth. One of my guardsmen brought me the skin of a marten, made into a scarf. That evening they paraded before my wagon, red banners and trumpets, drum beats, hoof beats. 'Hail to the queen! Hail to the queen!' They did not know how to comfort me and they were trying to comfort me. Again, now, they will try to comfort me.

They take her away. My dead child. Someone takes her, wraps her in red cloth. I cannot bear the feel of my arms where I was holding her. She weighed nothing at all and they take her and it feels as though I was holding a great weight that is gone. Like I am looking around having been holding something that I have forgotten, panicked, what was it that I have dropped? Her face was perfect. Like a painting of a child's face. Already I cannot remember it, what she looked like, what she smelled like. My hands smell of her but I cannot remember it, name it, her scent.

I weep. Marith weeps and howls. We cannot make any human sound.

But admit it: somewhere, deep down, you think that we deserve this. You believe we deserve this.

PART TWO

THE GOLDEN CITY

Chapter Ten

Tobias the bastard-hard sellsword failed fucking assassin waste of bloody space

The camp of the Army of Amrath, the scourge of the world, the conquerors, the bloodletters, the plague-bringers, the despoilers of all that lives, somehow in some complicated way kind of his friends

'More porridge? It's calling your names, lads . . .'

'It's calling out for something, certainly.'

'So put it out of its misery and finish it, won't you?'

'Its misery? What about my misery having to eat it?'

'Mercy, mercy, I'll do anything, mercy! Just don't offer me any more of that porridge, please!'

'I'll have another bowl, if it's going.'

'Ah, gods, hear that? Clews wants another bowl. Make sure you're marching well upwind, yeah?'

'Better out than in, man. Better out than in.'

'That goes for the porridge, too.'

'Piss off, man. You want to be the cook, you can be the bloody cook.'

'That was my damned bag you just dripped porridge on!'

A troop of fresh new soldier boys finishing up their breakfast, their armour so new and shiny, their faces so young and ardent; it was positively freakish, to see them beside the old hands.

Tobias sat and watched them for a bit. Kind of pleasure/pain in it. Like probing a wound with a fingernail. Seemed to be becoming more and more of a masochist in his old age.

Regrets? I've had a few. But if I could fix one moment in all my life . . . Warp and weft of it, backwards and forwards, some company of an evening, two hot meals a day, the odd barrel of strong drink. Him and Geth and Skie, the lads with their innocent killer's faces, playing dice and arguing and ignoring him and Geth and Skie when they ordered them to stop arsing around and polish their kit and then get some sleep. The Free Company of the Sword, a troop of bastard-hard sellswords and lonely blokes with no other job prospects. An old name, if not a famous one. Well-known in certain select political circles. Specialized in stabbing people in the back. Skie the commander-in-chief, thinker, broker, scariest hardest hardman Tobias had ever met. Tobias and Geth the squad commanders, hard-bitten, respected, maybe even kind of father figures to the squad boys, certainly both agreed they felt guilty when they stabbed the squad boys in the back. To be fair to Tobias, the clients did pay a lot more if the job included stabbing the squad boys in the back. 'It's good here,' one of the squad boys had said to him, 'don't you think?'

Recruited some new boys. And one of them was Marith pissing Altrersyr may his godsdamned kingly dick rot off with pox. Decided it would be a great idea to stab Skie and Geth in the back and strike out on his own, Commander-in-Chief Tobias, build up a new troop around him, be his own man, do his own thing. Or just retire, drink beer, find himself a woman, keep her well enough she'd grit her teeth and ignore him getting fat and sweaty and farting all night.

Yes. Well. The best laid plans and all that, if ifs and buts were pots and pans, etc etc to the bitter clichéd end. Think it would be fair to say things didn't entirely go quite to plan there, yup.

Four years, Tobias the bastard-hard sellsword had been floating around following in the Army of Amrath's wake. His leg hurt where he'd once jumped out of a bloody window. His arm hurt, where Marith shitting Altrersyr had once stabbed him. His ribs hurt, his knees hurt, his frigging arse somehow hurt, hair was grey and thinning, his gut hung over his belt-buckle and he did indeed fart all night. 'We can kill him, we can stop him, we can . . . we can do something. Right?' And lonely. One man, stumbling along.

There had been others, once: Raeta, Landra. *Friends*. Raeta was . . . not human. Antlers. Claws. Wings. Green leaves, wet earth. Life god wild god thing. '*I am his death, Tobias,*' Raeta had whispered. '*I am his death, I will follow him and follow him, I will destroy him.*' Raeta the life god was four years dead. Landra Relast had finally fucked off two years back. 'We have to destroy him, we have to kill him, I will find a way to destroy him, I will, I swear it.' She had sounded the voice of reason. But there had been something in her face that made him glad, still, that she had gone off alone. Her eyes were like a wild dog's eyes. Running her hands over a knife blade, whispering her father's name and her brother's name, promising them vengeance. Sometimes thought of her and shivered, right down inside his manhood. Raeta . . . Landra . . . Gods and monsters . . . '*It's worse than he is,*' Landra had cried out once, before Raeta died. And he might almost understand that, thinking of Raeta's eyes, dying. Thinking of Landra's eyes in the last days before she left him. 'Kill him. Kill him.' Grinding her teeth whispering it in her sleep. Wild dog's eyes, wild dog's moaning howling, 'We have to kill him.' So bloody empty, she'd looked. 'I will be his death, Tobias. I will end this. I will stop him.' Thank the gods he himself was old and sore and ached.

Gods. Shivered now. Anyway. They're gone, like rainfall. Don't think of them. Four years, Tobias the bastard-hard sellsword been floating around old and sore and farting, marching up and down behind the army. 'I'll think of something, right? Okay?' I'm not complicit in this shit that's happening here. I'm a hero, me. I'm following him around because one day, one day, when he's old and sick and abandoned and ruined and his army's left him and he's nothing, I'll still fuck up and fail to kill him. If Landra's a wild dog, I'm just a fucking dog too. I'm walking here in the darkness in his footsteps forever. Following him because there's nothing else. This is all there is of the world. The fire burning hot and light and there is no heat and there is no light. I can't kill him. Terrified to even think of killing him. But I'm alive. Just about.

'Gods and demons, look at that, Clews has finished the whole of his second bowl.'

'Clews, man, your insides must be made of bronze.'

'Iron, Turney, mate. My insides are made of iron.'

'So . . . your insides are rusting away, then? That would explain a lot.'

'Petros, mate, you see this empty bowl . . . ?'

'I see it, Clews. I'm thinking of giving you a special medal, in fact, for emptying it.'

'Oh yeah? Oh yeah?' The whole company turned to Clews, who in turn turned to Turney. Ooooh. There going to be a fight?

They were getting bored. Arrived ready and eager, 'March like all hells, lads, no slacking now, got a war to fight,' halfway across the whole of Irlast, 'you'll be men, soon, laddies, real men, you just need to bloody get there,' and now they were waiting around in a mountain valley in the middle of nowhere, five days now just sitting here, no slaughter no looting no torture no rape. Okay, so Sunreturn had been fun and games, if a bit weird here in the south, they could use a day afterwards to rest, yes, but now it was over lads like these needed to get on. The latrine trenches were filled to overflowing, apart from anything else.

Rumour going round that the queen was ill. That was why they were hanging around. Obvious what 'ill' means, in a pregnant woman. Nobody dared say it. But.

Don't. Just don't.

The lads' squad commander turned up, bawled at them to get themselves sorted out, they were marching in an hour or so, look at the bloody state of them, thought he'd told them twice already to polish their bloody kit. The lads shuffled up grumbling, faffing around in time-honoured fashion with random bits of stuff.

'And get that bloody cookpot cleaned up. It stinks. Looks less like food, more like someone sneezed in it. Cleaned. Now. You, Petros.'

'Me?'

'Chuck it away, mate,' Clews said. 'We'll be in Turain, soon. Famous for their metalwork, they are, the people of Turain.' They'd never even heard of Turain before yesterday, Tobias thought. No idea where it is. Don't think they're even pronouncing it right. Good King Marith could just be making these places up.

The lads got themselves sorted, Petros humming *Why We March* like it was a love song, Turney having lost half his equipment, Clews regretting out loud having to march on two full bowls of the porridge.

'Turain, here we come!'

'Woop woop!'

Tobias wandered off. Gods. Fucking gods. Tears in his eyes.

We were all that bloody innocent, once.

His own belongings were the basic definition of basic. A blanket. A cookpot. A couple of spare shirts and leggings. A spare pair of boots. The blanket was silk velvet, a stunning deep emerald green with a pattern of silver flowers, seed pearls crusted around the edge. The cookpot was copper and had an enamelled handle in the shape of a peacock, its tail fan spreading across the side of the pot. The shirts, leggings and boots must have been made for a prince. Several princes, as none of them matched. The Army of Amrath and the second army of camp followers following it marched around looking like peacocks themselves, resplendent, dazzling, a riot of colour, nothing fitting with anything else, nothing quite fitting the body it was draped on. There'd been excited chatter in the camp about Turain's fashions and craft traditions for days now, everyone working out what they might want to get their hands on, putting in early orders with the soldiers, haggling over prices. Vultures. Though Tobias wouldn't mind a new coat, if one happened to turn up.

Anyway. He bagged everything up, shouldered it. The whole camp was stirring, busying itself for the march.

'Finally getting off, then,' Naillil said cheerfully. A woman he knew, made her money doing the soldiers' washing and sewing. She'd been with the army since Ith, way back. Longer than Tobias, in fact, technically. When Naillil started following the army, Tobias was still labouring under the impression he could do something else with his life.

Tobias nodded. 'Finally.' Had to say something more, really, somehow. Speak, Tobias! Don't mumble at her and walk off.

Rovi said in his horrible dead voice, 'Maybe King Marith's hangover was really crippling him?'

Tobias shuddered. All this time and you'd think he'd have got used to Rovi's voice and he never did and never would if he lived a thousand years and heard it every day.

Naillil said, 'Rovi!' Pretending shock.

'Four days, we were all sitting around, after Lord Fiolt's birthday. Ander almost had to sack itself.' Dust puffing out of Rovi's rotting toothless scar-tissue mouth. Smell like when you dredged the bottom of a pond after a sheep fell in. Rovi had been a goatherd. Thirty years man and boy tending his flocks in the highlands of Illyr, until the Army of Amrath turned up. Rovi had got stabbed in the chest and the gut and the neck during the battle of Ethalden. Rovi had ended up face down in the river Jaxertane, sunk in the mud and the filth for three days. Only somehow Rovi . . . hadn't died. Kind of. Naillil had found him when she went to wash some shirts out. 'Helpful for carrying my wash bags,' she'd said once, and Tobias really wasn't sure whether she meant something dirty by that or not. Really, really, really hoped not.

'Here we go,' said Rovi.

'Here we go.'

Trumpets rang. Strange gathering sound of an army beginning

to march. Tramp of feet and clatter of horses' hooves. A rhythm to it, a music.

All day marching, through the mountains, beside the river that rushed down fast and wild and cold. The mountain slopes were covered with fruit trees, rich in birds and deer and wild goats. The sunlight came down through the leaves thick and golden, dappled the light, bathed their skin green. The men laughed and sang as they marched. A green tunnel, they were marching through, like being a child forcing your way through hedgerows, unable to see the sky, parting the leaves like parting the water of the sea. Then the path would rise, the trees would thin out, the sky would explode huge above them, deep joyous blue. The mountain peaks would appear then, and even in the warm damp growing heat, on the highest peaks of the mountains, there was snow. Marching on soft green grass, green bushes crusted with purple flowers, sweating in the sunlight, dazzled by the light and the blue of the sky. Then the path would dip again, the trees would close in around them, green soft damp cool heat. Felt different. Sounded different. The air tasted different in the mouth.

The fruit on the trees was poisonous, the camp followers had been warned. If you ate it, you'd swell up and sweat and die. When they stopped that night the trees had great knotted roots and twisting branches reaching almost to the ground. Hiding the world around them. Huge waxy pink and red flowers that attracted more insects than you'd believe possible. There were birds in the trees eating the insects, they had brilliant red feathers with black undersides to their wings. Tamas birds. They shrieked and called, sounded like they were speaking.

A whole village of camp followers setting down for the night. Endless babble of women warning their children against eating the poison fruit, smell of food cooking, smell of sweaty bodies, smell of human excrement. The sun was just setting. Warm and red like a healing wound.

Naillil was cooking stew. Asked Tobias if he'd like to join her and Rovi in having some.

'Uh . . . Yeah.' Paused. He could sit downwind of Rovi. And the stew smelled good. 'Thank you.'

'Want to help me wring out some shirts, afterwards?'

'Uh . . . No.' Paused. 'Okay, then. Just this once.'

Tobias the bastard-hard sellsword! Hell yeah! Eased off his boots. Gods, his leg was bloody killing him this evening. Bad enough to make him forget about the pain in his arm and his ribs. When they'd eaten, Naillil called him over; he bent down over a pot of warm water, sank his hands in. Lifted the wet cloth up, water running back down into the wash-pot, the heavy feel of the wet cloth, solid and satisfying, the smell of the warm water in the warm air, the smell of the wet cloth. Twisted the shirt up to wring out the water, flicked it out with a good loud noise to get the creasing out. Water sprayed on his own clothes.

'You're good at this,' Naillil said. She sounded surprised. Made a noncommittal secretly pleased nothing sound in his throat in answer, wrung out another shirt and enjoyed the feel of twisting the wet cloth. Naillil said, 'Want to help me soap the next load, as well?'

Raeta the *gestmet*'s voice, weary: *Not much else you can do with your life, I'm guessing, except kill?* Tobias flicked the shirt out with a snap. Showered water over Naillil, who swore at him and laughed. Rovi sort of laughed.

From somewhere far off in the trees, a voice screamed.

Naillil looked up. Tobias looked up.

A howl in the air. A great gust of hot wind. More voices shouting. Screaming.

'The dragon! The dragon!' The sky lit up crimson. Fire blazing across the sky. 'The dragon!' a voice screamed. 'The dragon!'

It came rushing over them, green and silver, huge as thinking, writhing and twisting and tearing at itself, swimming in the flames. Spewing out fire. Again. Again. Again. Again.

Soldiers came tramping towards them. Armed. Began killing

them. Killing women. Killing children. The trail of lives that followed where the army led. Their women. Their children. Killing them.

Run.

Just run.

Tobias was gasping, wheezing, limping. His leg shrieking in pain and his arm shrieking and his heart and his ribs. Rovi next to him staggering, gasping, rot stink coming off him. Almost fell. Teeth gritted with pain. Up the slope of the mountain, towards . . . something. Nothing. Just run. Good rich black earth clinging sucking to his boots. Streams of people. Soldiers. Panic. Naillil shouted, 'Look.' A dark little cleft in the rocks, a cave, could hardly see it in the night and it looked like a wound in the hillside and it stank of blood like everything everywhere they had been. They scrambled up to it, crouched into it, sat in the dark, like sitting inside a wound. Stone walls close around them. Tobias gasping and sobbing in pain. Trying to gasp loud enough to drown out Rovi wheezing his horrible broken dead bad-water breath.

'It will be over soon,' said Naillil. 'Few hours, at most.'

'Yeah. Few hours. Like last time.'

'She'll stop it. Or Lord Fiolt will.'

Noises in the night. Wing beats. Voices shouting. Then horsemen passing very near them, riding hard. Trumpet calls. Then silence.

They emerged from the cave in the first light of morning. Voices crying. Footsteps on loose pebbles, jangle of bronze. A soldier's voice shouting commands.

'Line up there! We're marching now.'

The slope of the mountain fell away very steeply beneath them, they must have scrambled up it climbing, Tobias could barely remember except that it had hurt. In the valley beneath them, a column of soldiers was marching off south. Staring straight ahead, everything neat and tidy, armour polished, red crests to their helmets very bright. They marched past in silence. Another column, spearmen with long sarriss, a raw red banner at the head of their files. It hung limp in the still air. Further up the slope, very near them, a party of horsemen. The smell of the horses was strong and pleasant.

There were great burn marks across the mountain. The fruit trees were burned away, rocks smashed up. The earth bare and black and dead. Figures picked their way across a wasteland of black ash.

A woman was standing a short distance from them. A dead baby in her arms. Her face and body were streaked with blood. Further down the slope a dead child lay sprawled, flies buzzing over it. A dead woman lay near it, her arms thrown out towards it. There were flies everywhere.

Oh Thalia, Tobias thought. Oh Thalia, girl.

'She's lost four pregnancies now,' said Naillil. 'Four pregnancies in four years.' Naillil's hands folded over her stomach. 'You could almost pity her.'

She must have heard the sound Tobias was trying not to make. 'I said almost,' she said.

They began to walk slowly down the burned slope. Following the way the horsemen had gone. Tobias groaned in pain, rubbed at his arm. 'Any chance any of our stuff survived, you reckon?' One of the pointless things they said. Survivors coming together, the old hands who knew what to do to avoid the soldiers on the bad nights. Pedlars began to shout that they had cloths and blankets and cookpots for sale, cheap and best quality, lined up waiting for those who had lost everything overnight. The woman holding the dead baby began walking behind them. After perhaps an hour she grew calmer. Dropped the baby's body. Walked on and walked on.

They stopped that night to make camp on the banks of a stream. Tobias made up the fire. Naillil began to prepare a pot of stew. Rovi sat and stank.

'Why . . . why did he . . . do it?' the woman whose baby had died asked them. Her name was Lenae. Couldn't bring himself to

ask about the baby's name. Her hands moved and for a moment
Tobias almost saw a baby cradled in them.

Why? Oh gods. Don't ask that.

'You haven't been with the army long, then?' said Naillil at last.

Lenae flushed red as the fire. Pulled her cloak around her tight.
'I . . . My husband was a merchant in Samarnath. When the
Ansikanderakesis Amrakane's army came . . . One of the soldiers
was kinder to me. Stopped another from killing me. He – so I –
everyone there was dead, and he – I – then he must have been
killed, at Arunmen.' She looked away. 'Why did he do it? Kill the
children? Burn the camp?'

A branch moved in the cookfire, sending up sparks. The fire
died down to embers. 'Damn,' said Naillil. Tobias got up and
poked at the fire and moved bits of wood around and eventually
it flared up bright and hot.

'The queen lost her baby,' said Naillil. 'She was pregnant, and
she lost the child . . . And last night the king . . . He . . .'

'He was angry,' said Tobias. Say it. That fucking poison bastard
Marith. That sick, vile, diseased, degenerate fucking bastard. My
fault my fault my fault my fault. 'He ordered the . . . the dragon
. . . ordered his soldiers to kill the children. All the children in
the camp. He's done it before. Twice.'

'He'll feel remorse, soon enough,' said Naillil. 'He probably
does already. Gets drunk, orders it, cries when he's told what he
did. He'll probably give a bag of gold to anyone whose child died
in it. To make amends.'

'Like he did before,' said Rovi. 'Twice.'

'So you're quids in, then, woman,' said Tobias. He stared into
the fire. 'You can go home to the smoking ruins of Samarnath and
live rich as an empress in the ashes there.'

Thought then: I let Marith kill a baby, once.

Once?

A few years ago.

Let Marith do it?

Encouraged him. Swapped a baby's life for a sleep in a bed.

You look like what you are, boy, he'd told Marith before the boy did it.

Three days later, Lenae had five thalers in a bag around her neck she didn't know what to do with. Buy a house somewhere and live long and peaceful. Bury them in a hole and piss on them and curse Marith Altrersyr. Drink herself senseless and pay someone to slit her throat.

The first, almost certainly. That's what most of the women had done. Twice before.

That's not fair, Tobias thought. Not fair. She's got every right to make the best of her crapped-on ruined wound of a life.

Chapter Eleven

Turain! The land fell away sharply, the plain of the Isther river opening up, black earth and rich fields before the desert and the mountains rose again. Groves of white oleander. Peach trees. Dates. Golden plump wheat. Ah, gods, the smell was mouthwatering. The wind blew up from the south scented with ripe fruit, everyone drooled as they breathed it in. The river lay a wide silver ribbon, fat, smooth and sleepy, worn out from rushing through the mountain slopes. It is good here, Tobias thought. Really bloody nice. Turain smiled at them on the horizon. Not a very big city. Maybe even just a large town. Not much to look at, either, said someone who knew someone who knew some bloke. Grey and square and low, houses with narrow windows, gloomy inside and out. It had been sacked and pillaged and burned and smashed up and basically completely annihilated a surprisingly large number of times. So it had very, very, very, very strong walls. Not like they weren't short on old stone.

'Is it really worth the amount of pain it's going to take to take it?' Snigger. 'Stupid question, yeah.'

The whole army sat and looked down on it. It sat and looked up at them back. The land around was completely empty. Abandoned villages, no people, not even a stray goat. Everyone and everything had fled inside the city. You got very, very, very,

very strong walls, you're hardly likely to do much else, are you?

'They'd have been better off staying outside it, I'd have thought, myself,' Tobias said conversationally to Lenae. 'Those walls are like an insult to him.'

'Never seen a city the Army of Amrath can't break to tiny bits!' a passing soldier shouted, riding past them leading a squad all in silver helmets, all mounted on beautiful white horses with gold saddle cloths. 'Gravel, we'll make of those walls. Use them as a grindstone for their defenders' bones.'

'Cowards, cowering there behind their walls! We'll teach them the cost of cowardliness!'

Oh my eye, didn't Lenae look impressed.

Tobias made a face after them. 'Yup. As I was just saying. Only in a less naff way.'

The siege train got itself ready for action. The army went down into the plains and brought back a feast of ripe, slightly ash-stained fruit. Wonder the people of Turain hadn't burned the fields themselves, in all honesty. But maybe they had too much pride for it. Or too much misplaced hope. Marith ordered the dragons out to soften up the city a bit. Everyone sat on the mountain slopes munching peaches and drinking date wine, to watch. Dazzling. Impressive. The red dragon had a great turn of speed on it, turned in the air on a penny, had this neat trick of rushing over, spinning around, rushing back so quick its fires almost seemed to meet. The green dragon was slower: it came down low, tore at the buildings with its claws as well as burning them with its breath. The people of Turain did pretty well against them, considering, loosed off various big missiles that did nothing, surprise surprise, but looked impressive and must have made everyone involved feel slightly better about things. Some mage bloke blasted light around: the spectators applauded politely when the green dragon shot up into the sky with one wing on fire, howling. Like watching a wrestling bout, you kind of wanted it to be a bit more of a matched fight. Support the underdog, like, for a while at the beginning. Not so interesting if the other side just caved from the off.

'Date?' Tobias asked Lenae. She shook her head, her mouth stuffed with peach. Juice running all sticky down her chin. Yeah. Nice to look at.

The mage bloke got the green dragon again, hurt it. Big groan rang over the mountainside. Gods, thought Tobias, gods, don't tell me something's actually going to go one up on him?

The green dragon and the red dragon met in the air. Quick conflab. Flew down over the city together. 'Come on! Come on!' the spectators all shouting. Underdog forgotten. Cheer of 'Yesssss!' as the mage sent up a blast of light that was abruptly snuffed out. Widespread applause. A curtain of fire came down over half the town.

The dragons seemed to decide that was game over. The place was indeed looking pretty well scorched and bashed up. They flew off overhead into the mountains, to oohs and aahs as they came low over. Nasty smell from the green one's injured wing.

'I'll have a date, now, thanks,' said Lenae. She got up. 'That was amazing. When do you think we'll go in?'

Weird, really, looking at the city, thinking this time tomorrow it was going to be rubble and human mince. The whole army lining up there, waving their sarriss around, marching back and forward pointlessly so King Marith can feel good about himself, knowing this time tomorrow they could be dead and there's absolutely nothing any of them can do to make it any different.

Tobias sauntered off to use the nearest latrine trench. Most of the camp followers didn't, filthy ignorant bastards, but. Pleasing, as always, that all the practical advice he'd given Marith about latrines had paid off. A lot of soldiers were squatting there with him, fresh from helping to chuck big rocks around and gasping with relief. All the fruit they'd been eating was, uh, having something of an effect.

'Lovely display,' said Tobias. Seemed apposite to say something, when you're shoulder to shoulder with a bloke hearing the sound of his shit come out.

'You what?'

Wait, no, not the— Oops, gods. Disgusting mind, you have, mate.

'He means the siege, obviously,' bloke on the other side of him said. And: thank you. Someone with a clean train of thought. Face burning, Tobias shuffled himself to sort of facing him.

'Clews, man!'

Pause. 'Uh, do I know you?'

Porridge boy. Yeah?

Oh, wait, no, he doesn't know me. Can't really say, 'No, you don't, but I wept over you, just recently, cause you reminded me of the life I fucked up.'

'He's a camp follower,' the man who'd thought he was talking about the men lined up shitting said. 'They know all our names, the camp followers do. Idolize us.' Big, strong, solid-looking man, flashy hair, expensive cavalryman's boots . . . some of the camp followers probably did know his name, yeah. He probably paid them extra if they screamed it.

'Pathetic, they are, camp followers,' Clews said. Sneer in his voice. Trying to make his voice sound loud and strong. 'Men camp followers! Cowardly. Should be soldiering.'

Don't rise to it, ignore it, you know what he's doing, he's a boy, it's only bugging you because . . . 'I was a soldier,' Tobias said. 'I spent years soldiering, I'll have you know.' Killed more men than you've had hot meals – for the love of all the gods, don't say that, don't. The cavalryman was grinning at them both, still crouching over the latrine trench. He's got you right riled up, Tobias, this kid, and you know why, and just finish your crap and walk away.

'Got scared, did you?' Clews said.

Tobias stood up, knees creaking. 'Got old and aching.' Started to walk off.

'That's no excuse. My squad commander's probably older than you.'

Stopped. Oh, gods, this boy. 'Your squad commander got a knackered leg and a knackered arm and a broken rib that never properly healed?' Your squad commander fought a demon and a mage and a bloody fucking death god?

Clews snorted. 'Got men in my squad injured worse than that, still fighting on. A man in my squad with one arm. A man in my squad with half his face burned off. A—'

'Yes, all right, okay, great, well done them.' Gods, if I had a sword right now, a knife, a bit of sharpened stick . . .

'When Turain falls, tomorrow,' Clews said, 'I'll bring enough loot home to my family that they can get my sister married. If we get through the gates early, get the pick of the houses, I can bring home enough so my dad can stop having to work. And they paid a silver penny a head, they say, at Tereen. Couple of good strikes, that'd be enough we could buy the next field, hire a man to work it . . . And look at you, pleading your knackered leg.'

The cavalryman with the hair was sniggering now. He and Tobias exchanged looks. Rolled their eyes at each other. Well, yes . . . There's that, yes, true enough. Gods, poor dumb kid.

'It's fucking awful, the actual fighting,' Clews said. 'But worth it.' Sneer came back, faking it so hard it hurt you to watch. 'If you're brave enough. A silver penny a head, they said.' He gestured vaguely towards the camp. 'As we're talking . . . you want to go for a drink?'

Suppose the kid could just be desperate to fuck someone on possibly his last night of living. Let's try to be charitable here. Part of him wanted to take the kid off and listen, even, lend him a handkerchief, tell him it would be all right in the end.

Tobias said, 'I've got things to do. Cowardly old-man camp-follower things.'

Decided to turn in early. Curled up in the tent. Went to sleep thinking of dragons dancing, peach juice dripping down Lenae's chin.

You miss it, Tobias, man, he thought as he drifted up off to sleep. Bronze and blood and fire and killing. You lie to yourself, but you always will. You, washing clothes? Yeah, right.

Warm water smell, heavy feel of wet cloth, washing the fucking blood out.

Symbolic, yeah, don't you think?

Chapter Twelve

Landra Relast, Marith's enemy, sworn to defeat him and destroy him
Ethalden the Tower of Life and Death, the first Amrath's capital, the City of the *Ansikanderakesis Amrakane*, the King of Ruin, the King of Death

When Landra had last been here, Ethalden had been a city of workmen, of raw stone slabs and stacked timbers, building rubble, scaffolding, workers' huts, soldiers' tents. The air had smelled of sawdust and stonedust, great clouds of it stirred up; the air had resounded with the shouts and songs of labourers and craftsmen. Marith's fortress had risen up in the midst of this chaos, a glory of gold and mage glass and marble, heavy silk and shining fur and bright gems. Throne rooms, banqueting halls, pleasure gardens, crystal fountains pouring out perfumed water coloured red or blue or deep lush forest green. A central tower like a beam of sunlight was set at its very centre, so high it seemed to come down from the heavens to the earth. It was made of silver and pearl, hung with red banners; on balconies at its heights bells and silver trumpets rang out. Beside it stood two temples, one of gold dedicated to Queen Thalia, one of iron dedicated to Marith himself. In its shadow stood a tomb of onyx, holding the bones of the first Amrath.

Every master builder in Irlast had been summoned to Ethalden. Men who could work stone to create marvels, for whom stone could flow like water, who could pour out beauty onto the bare earth. Men with hands running with magic, with power over stone and metal to raise them up into dreams. Thirty days, Marith Altrersyr *Ansikanderakesis Amrakane* had given them to build him a fortress. If it was not completed as the sun rose on the thirty-first day, he would kill them. On the morning of the thirty-first day, the feast of Sunreturn, Landra had watched Marith ride into his fortress to be crowned King of Illyr and of all Irlast.

And now around the fortress a city was forming. Palaces for Marith's lords. Storehouses for the wealth of his empire. Barracks for his armies. Docks from which ships sailed across the world. He had emptied the towns and villages of Illyr, resettled the people here. The streets were wide and well-made, the houses tall.

Landra had once been betrothed to Marith Altrersyr. Her father had been Lord of Third Isle, one of the greatest lords of the White Isles, a companion of King Illyn Marith's father. Her brother Carin had been Marith's lover, until Marith killed him. It was in her father's house of Malth Salene, the Tower of the Shining Sea, that Marith was first crowned king. Marith had killed his own father before Malth Salene's walls. After he had killed Landra's father and her mother and her sister, and thought that he had killed Landra herself.

In the ruins of Ethalden, as the great battle for the ruins of Amrath's city had still raged, Landra had uncovered the bones of the first Amrath, used a power they held clenched within them to try to destroy Marith. Failed. In the new city rising on the rubble of the battlefield she had seen Marith crowned in his new palace he had built himself on the site of her failure. Her brother would have wept for him, she had thought. She had tried herself to weep for him.

Don't go looking for vengeance: but, oh, it is too late for that. No other arguments left. Anything else is weak. She thought now:

I did not want to come back here. I do not want to do this. But I must. I must. It hurt to her soul, guilt and anger mixed together. Shame, dry and crouched, flaked with dried blood. And the joy, on top of it. Perfume to her soul. Landra Relast, who had nothing left. Do it! Do it! You must! She had crossed half the world, to return here, to do this. She was not certain whom she thought of, when she thought of vengeance. Against Marith, or against herself. When she had found him he was dead, nothing, forgotten, a sellsword in a rough company of failed killers. He was content enough with his life, he had claimed. All he had ever wanted: to be nothing. She had brought him back to his kingdom to punish him. Ah, gods, Amrath and Eltheia, she had punished him. The great tragedy of all our lives, she thought: that I walked the wrong way down a street in a distant city, and thought I saw his face, and followed him. If I had been looking the other way, when he passed me . . . If I had walked left rather than right out of a shop . . . Through such absurdities the world is brought to this.

A soldier spares a child in the sack of a city: the child grows up to be a man who beats his wife. A cruel master dies, his heir frees his servants: they starve and freeze on the road, homeless, lost. A woman chooses one dress over another: a dressmaker's child eats or does not eat that night. Deep inside her, a voice laughed and stirred. Rustle of green leaves. Giggle of running water. Scream of grief. It is not vengeance, she thought. It is just and good. He is Ruin. The world will be a better place without him.

What would I have done, Lan thought, if he had asked me to forgive what he did to me?

She spat in the dust, mounted up on her horse, rode slowly down the hill towards the city that shone before her.

Reached the city's gates in the late afternoon. All of white marble, and the city walls themselves were solid gold. As though he had thought of the bronze walls of Sorlost and promised himself that he would outdo them. Measuring himself by this. And the green and gold walls of Malth Salene, she thought. Somewhere here was a boy clasping Carin's hand with a smile.

Guards at the gate in bronze armour and red badges, the Altrersyr colour, red banners above the gates snapping in the cold wind. Bored-looking, guarding a city at the end of the world: they must dream of being in his wars. She could feel the spear points whispering to them. A wagon came out through the gates with its cargo safely muffled against the weather. It was so cold that the oxen drawing it steamed out breath like dragons; Landra could smell the sweet hay scent of them, a good smell.

'What is your business?' the guard on the gate asked her, when it was her turn to enter.

'I am seeking work,' she lied in a flat voice. He looked at her, and she saw what he must see, her head swathed in cloth covering what should be her hair, her scars, the dry cold of her eyes, the stiffness in her body of knotted wounds. Still a young woman, somewhere beneath it all, but her face was the face of a thing carved from rock. 'It's not as bad as you think,' she used to hope for Tobias to tell her, when he caught her looking at her reflection, 'people always look worse to themselves, yeah?' It can't be as bad as you think.

The guard shrugged. 'Come in, then. Ethalden the City of the King welcomes you.' A rich man with a guard around him rode in after her and was not questioned. She still noticed that she noticed that. She found an inn, argued with the innkeep over the cost of stabling, argued with the innkeep again until he moved her to a room with a door she could lock. The whole inn smelled of sawdust. Joists still creaking and settling, plaster in places still damp. The stairs to her room were badly made, the steps uneven; the bedroom door struck in the frame. But she had never been in a place so new and clean. They could only have finished building it in the last week.

She ached. Her whole body, aching. Deep pain, down to the bones, in her back, her stomach, in her chest when she drew a breath. In her hands, up her arms, pulling and twisting up her right arm, the fingers on her right hand puffed up red and numb. She spat on her fingers, rubbed the spit into them, took a water bottle from her belt and poured water over them to try to ease the pain.

Chilblains, she told people. Winter is a cruel goddess, gnawing at the flesh. The skin looked heavy, mottled like old meat. She had seen people wince, rub their own hands, when they saw it. She opened and closed her fingers. Shook her hand out. The pain faded a little. It would not heal while Marith lived.

She went over to the window, which faced north over the city out towards the Bitter Sea. The end of everything. An hour's walk, and then sheer cliffs, and then the sea going on into eternity. No ship would sail on those waters. Wave upon wave upon wave of dark water, on until the world's end. It was pleasant looking out in that direction, thinking of the sea beyond the walls. Far beyond human hopes or cares. Ignorant of all human things. No hope no pain. Calming. The desire to be herself beyond human things.

The wind was getting up, shaking the branches of a tree opposite the window A birch tree, its bark white as bone. Its branches rattled like bone. '*His city is built on bones and blood and tears, His city is built on the flesh of living men,*' the songs of praise to King Marith said. '*Is it true?*' one of soldiers had once asked her, a new recruit, young and ardent and eager, all his love for Marith glittering out of him, '*is it true, that he ordered his fortress to be built on living bodies, that he mixed the mortar with human blood?*' The Army of Amrath had just taken Raen, had built their towers of skulls where the walls had stood. And the soldier's eyes had gleamed, looking past the skulls, seeing greater, more terrible things. '*Is it true? Really? They say you were there, Lan, they say you've been with the army since Illyr. Tell me it's true, won't you?*'

She had tried to speak, but no words had come from her mouth.

'*It is,*' Tobias had said. '*I saw it. I saw.*' And then he'd rolled his eyes. '*And other places aren't, of course. Alborn, Morr Town, Sorlost the Golden, Malth Salene . . . no one suffered and strained and got hurt building them. Light as air, the stones that built Malth Salene, and the labourers were paid in gold.'*

'*That's not the same, Tobias,*' Lan had said.

'*No. It's not. Obviously it's not. But . . .'* Tobias had shaken his head. '*Never mind, then. I'm being cruel.'*

Raen had been chaos, the usual maelstrom after a sack. Landra had taken her knife in her injured right hand, buried the blade up to the hilt in the soldier's heart.

Filth. Her heart had sung out for joy. One less of them. A tiny bright difference: somewhere in the heart of a loving world a joyous song is rising. Her shame had been a void beneath her feet.

'*You know what I mean,*' Tobias had said. '*Don't you?*'

'*Perhaps.*'

'*Better get your knife clean, Lady Landra,*' Tobias had said. '*And get away from that corpse.*'

She had left Tobias the next morning, fled away north towards the cities of Ander and Balkash. Warn them. Beg them. I can no longer bear it, she had told herself, I must act, make it stop. Something can be done and must be done. She had once loosed a *gabeleth*, a vengeance-demon; she had once fought beside a *gestmet*, a god of life. Thus she could do things. A bright light in the world, was Lady Landra Relast. A joyous song, a good sweet song to make the world a better place. Thus every night she cursed him. I will not rest, she swore to herself, until he is defeated and all who follow him are dead.

Knife in her heart. Shame and pity. Her hands ached sore heavy wound red. The wind blew in the branches of the tree opposite, and the branches scratched together like bones, and the bark was white like bones in the fading light.

But in the dawn, ah, Ethalden was beautiful. Grey mist around the towers, fading, they were unreal, they were not buildings but statues, stone dancers, robed in clouds, they were giants dancing, they wore the dawn as jewels on their skin. Landra slept well and peacefully. Her ancestor Amrath's city: so perhaps He blessed her, eased her pain, let her sleep. Perhaps her hair and her skin were healed a little. Her wounds less harsh. There were a thousand birds in the city of Ethalden, and every one of them seemed to gather beneath her window that morning to sing. She rested her hands on the windowsill and gazed out at the city, over towards the gold walls and away into the horizon where the sea would be. Peace. Peace. The streets already busy with people, animals, voices chattering, the sound of building work. Women in fine dresses, workmen already covered with stone dust clinging damp to their clothes, slave labourers from half the world chained in filth. Trades being made, goods bought and sold, gold and treasure and living men. The patterns and circles of every city: those who dance begin to dance, and those who weep begin. Beggars, naturally, as in every city – but fewer than in other cities, she thought, where the wealth of the world did not now come. Even as she watched, a woman gave a beggar a coin, smiled at him. Children playing – she watched a pair of them, a boy and a girl, from their matching curls they must be brother and sister. The girl ran and the boy chased her, the boy caught her and pulled at the girl's dress; they began to quarrel, the girl pulling her brother's hair; a woman ran up to scold them, kiss the boy's curls, take their hands firmly and walk on. Pilgrims were making for the tomb of Amrath. Strong young men and women were looking to join the Army of Amrath. Some kind of absurdity here that she, Landra, was a descendant of Amrath.

'*Your great-great-great etc grandma got knocked up by your great-great-great etc grandpa. Get you! Astonishing achievement, having ancestors, isn't it? Very rare thing.*'

'*That's not fair, Tobias.*'

'*Oh, no, I'm sorry, his great-great-great-grandpa having knocked up his great-great-great-grandma certainly means he's entitled to all this.*' That had been on the day of Marith's coronation. Tobias had spread his arms wide, taken in all the towers of the fortress, the cheering crowds, the banners and petals and jewels, taken all of it into his outstretched embrace. '*His birthright. His destiny.*

For being able to reel off a list of his ancestors' names.' As Tobias said it, the sun had put out golden beams that had struck Marith's face perfectly, lit up his face and his eyes and his crown, made him shine.

'Honey cakes! Saffron! Curd cakes! Dried plums!' Landra shook her head. A foodseller positioned himself opposite her window with a tray of cakes, his own face thin and hungry. The children came running back with their mother to buy some. Workers were swarming up a great tower of ivory beside the north gates shouting to each other in a babble of languages, up ropes and ladders, calling, whistling.

'Get on! Get on! Get it built!'

A great spike of carved sweetwood was rising there: Landra watched the workers struggle with it, drag it awkwardly up the building. Ropes flailing. Many curses. It almost slipped, three men almost fell. It was carved to look like a garland of flowers, gilded in silver leaf, skeletal faces staring empty-eyed between the blooms. They got it upright, finally, struggled and fought with it. Almost done it . . . then a scream, as a man did fall. His arms flailing as he came down. Horrified cries from his fellows. Landra could not see him hit the earth but turned her face away anyway. Such a long sickened pause. All the men looking downwards, each must be thanking all gods and demons that it had not been him. The foreman shouted at them to get back to it. The carved wood shuddered; they got it steady again, slotted it finally into place. The thud of a mallet on wood. Landra breathed a great sigh of relief. The tower looked beautiful, with the wooden spike at its height. The morning light caught the gilding; from her window, Landra could see the flowers and the faces clearly, like one of Marith's skull towers, blossom growing up over dead faces all those dead eyes. At the base of the spire, workers scrambled with blocks of marble to build a parapet. I wonder whose palace that will be? she thought. And if they will live to see it? Osen Fiolt? Valim Erith? Alis Nymen, who had once sold fish to the kitchens of Malth Salene? The new lords, his new friends, from all over

Irlast. He betrayed Carin's memory, surely, by making these fine new friends from every corner of Irlast.

A block of stone was being hauled up now, carved with a pattern of hunting beasts. There seemed to be an argument going on over it, the foreman waved his arms, seemed angry, the workers lifting it shrugged and gestured back. The block was lowered down again. The foreman climbed down a ladder, began to argue with someone else, pointed at the block. The two of them disappeared from Landra's sight, still arguing. The thin-faced cake seller, she noticed, was now eating one of his own cakes. He looked delighted by it. Two men came hurrying up with a bier, to cart off the remains of the workman.

Anyway. Things to be done. She adjusted the headscarf covering her burns. Went down out into the city.

She went first to the tomb of Amrath. Already crowds were gathered there to leave offerings. Just to see it. Amrath's bones. The tarnished shards of Amrath's sword and helmet and armour, twisted and boiled with dragon fire, eaten into lace by dragon blood. Marith had killed his brother Tiothlyn; the first Amrath had killed His brother that was a dragon, been killed by it as He died. Ever were the Altrersyr fratricides and parricides and cursed men.

The bones of an arm. The bones of a hand. A shattered ribcage. A shattered skull case. Blind eye holes, a hole where the nose had been, white pearly teeth but missing its lower jaw. Yellow old dry bare cold bone. A man who died and lay dead and unburied. A man who had no one left at the end to mourn for him. Marith had gathered up the bones in his own arms, laid them with reverence on a bier of white samite in a coffin of cedar wood in a coffin of iron in a coffin of gold. Over them a temple of black onyx had been raised, sat glaring in the shadow of Marith's fortress. The doorway was high and narrow, like the doorway of the Great Temple in Sorlost. The whole tomb building, Landra thought with pity, was modelled on the Great Temple in Sorlost. Inside, the floor was black iron, the walls smooth stone. The gold coffin stood on a plinth of white marble. It was huge, to look as though the bones inside it had been huge as a giant. Braziers burned all around it, sending out smoke that was rancid with incense. The smoke made the air dry.

A woman leaned forward to kiss the coffin. A man placed a knife in offering at the base of the plinth. 'Amrath,' voices murmured. 'Amrath. Amrath.'

Landra's hands itched. The skin red and dry, her fingers puffed up, swollen, the skin cracked. She followed the woman worshipper, reached out and placed her hands on the gold. They ached. The metal felt very cold. She could feel herself shaking. Hear her fast shallow breath.

What do I expect to happen? she thought.

The air in the room whispered. Something will happen. Waiting. Her face reflected in the gold. Wait a little longer, and you'll see, something will come, the face there will change, the dead will rise. Stare and her reflection is changing, no longer can she recognize that face.

Pity. My ancestor, Amrath, cruel hateful man of anger: unmourned, unburied, raw bones. You, also, would not have chosen this. Did not want this. The face there, so close, thinking it, feeling it: you trampled the world beneath you, who would ever wish this for their life? Everyone in the world, and no one. Amrath, my ancestor, you had what all hearts desire, all it ever can be is grief. To be touched by the gods is cruelty and suffering. To be as a god is to be nothing but death.

My ancestor, Amrath, help me. Grant me strength.

The face in the gold, a different face not her face. Eyes open, mouth open wide, it will speak, it will speak, tell me, help me . . . Pressed her hands onto the gold. Closer. Closer. Amrath, my ancestor, Your bones lie here, show me what to do, help me. A ringing in her body, a pulse there tolling. The heaviness of it. Trying to reach the surface, swimming, and the surface of the water hanging out of reach. The cool of swimming with open eyes, seeing another world.

There, a face, a mouth opening in the gold, sinking up through the gold towards her. Help me.

A man beside her jostled her, bending awkwardly forward to press his own forehead to the coffin.

Broken. Landra backed away. Dead old bones.

The man who had jostled her was garlanded in flowers, he took them off and threw them in offering. 'A son, Amrath, World Conqueror, Lord of Irlast, grant me a son.' His voice was sad and cracked.

Voices, echoing around the black walls, babbling.

'My wife is sick,' another man said, 'let her be healed.'

'Let him marry me. Let him love me again.'

'Heal the pain in my leg, the wound there, Amrath, World Conqueror, I was wounded fighting for our king, heal me.' Smell of flesh rotting. Swirl of incense smoke.

A woman stood silent, staring at the coffin, her face rigid. A man beside her stared not at the coffin but at the people praying there. A man beside him wept.

Mourning?

Rejoicing?

The woman cut off a lock of her hair, laid it before the tomb. 'Amrath, Amrath, World Conqueror, keep the king safe. That is all I pray. All that any of us pray.'

A note of sorrow then, Landra thought, in the air, in the gold of the tomb.

The red pain in her hand felt no different, if she had hoped that coming here would help it. Touching the bones had caused it, could not now cure it. Dead old yellow bones without power for anything. 'Tear it down,' she whispered. And a pain stirring inside her. Itching like lice across her heart. Grief. Pain. Rage. Hope.

Such ordinary things, they wanted, these people, that they must be punished for.

Outside the tomb the city was churning with people. Thalia's temple was empty, almost ignored; the doorway of Marith's temple was crowded with soldiers making dedications and prayers.

'A strong right arm, my Lord Marith *Ansikanderakesis Amrakane.*'

'A strong right arm and my sword coated in blood.'

In the temple forecourt, a horse's head had been raised up on a pole of bleached white wood. It grinned through skeletal jaws. Sinews drying curling back its lips. Its eyes were almost still alive. Its mane moved in the wind. Landra found herself staring at this, also. Disgusting thing. A sacrifice. To Amrath. To Marith. Imagine it, making a sacrifice to yourself.

'The luck horse,' a woman said, seeing her staring.

Landra nodded. 'Yes. I know.'

'The king killed it,' the woman said, 'on the day he rode out to rebuild Amrath's empire. Jet black, it was, with a blaze of white on its forehead like a star. The most beautiful horse I've ever seen.'

The woman was dressed in tatters, her hair matted and filthy. She had a strip of rotting horsehide wrapped around her right arm. A bone that might have been a part of a horse's backbone hanging on a chain around her neck.

'You saw it?' Landra asked her.

'I held the horse's bridle,' the woman said, 'while he killed it.'

Landra thought: she's mad.

'It was a wild horse,' the woman said. 'Running loose on the shore out to the north, where the land is dead. Left over from the army that fought him here, the traitors, the blind ones who did not follow him. His enemy's horse, that fled when the battle was lost, its rider dead. On the day the army was to march my husband found it, out on the shore there where the traitors' bones lie. He brought it to the king and the king sacrificed it for luck. To bless his army as they marched. Four years ago. Now I sit here beside his temple. To guard it.'

A horror of something gripped Landra. She said, 'And your husband?' But before she had finished speaking, she guessed.

'The horse killed him,' the woman said. 'When the king drew his sword it reared up, its hooves shattered my husband's skull. He lay there dying while the sacrifice was made: his blood and his life, as well as the horse's, they marched through, to bless the army and the king. Now I sit here. Guarding it.' She looked at Landra keenly. 'They say that if you give me a coin, any prayer you made in the king's temple will be more likely to come true.'

'I haven't been into the king's temple,' Landra said. She reached into her pocket to hand over a coin. The horse woman raised her hand to thank her. Stepped back. Grimy eyes blinked at Landra.

'Any prayer,' the horse woman said. 'Any prayer, and it will be granted. Think on that.'

'What happened to the horse's body?' Landra asked. Why she asked that she had no idea.

'They sold it for meat,' the horse woman said.

Landra went back to the inn, ate a meal, paid the innkeep's boy a handful of copper to saddle her horse. Rode out of the north gate of the city, along the banks of the Haliakmon river, towards the shore of the Bitter Sea. Silt-blackened water, rushing down fast from the hills, singing as it ran. Fields on the riverbanks, stubbled with winter wheat. Apple trees, plum trees, ghost leaves and ghost fruit still clinging to their branches. Yellow broom flowers, wild clematis down like wool in the hedges. Beside the river the land became marshy, irises on the riverbanks, bulrushes, willows, alder, the banks of the river smelled of rotting leaves and of mint. Water fowl in great numbers. Herons, still and grey as godstones, long long legs, their wings raised over their heads. Kingfishers, perfect blue. An arrow flight of white geese. Red cattle in the meadows, shaggy and long-horned, raising their heads from the grass watching with dark liquid eyes; sheep on the hills beyond with thick wool for war cloaks. A herd of deer come down to a sheltered pool in the marsh to drink.

The plain of Illyr where no grass grows. He did this, Landra thought, dazzled. He brought this land back to life.

Where the land rose in a hillock a village had been founded, the house timbers still raw, everything clean and new. Good, big houses; bigger, Landra thought, than the houses of most of the peasant folk back home on Third Isle. The air smelled of roasting meat and new-baked bread. A child came out to stare, ran along the road behind her horse. Landra waved to her.

The first few months when Marith had been with Carin, the first summer, when he had come to Malth Salene . . . He had seemed to her like a man sick and dying but standing warm in the beauty of the sunlight. Like a woman dying in childbirth but she holds her baby safe in her arms, kisses it, names it, rejoices in it.

He will never come back here to see this, Landra thought. What a waste it all is.

After perhaps an hour's ride the sea appeared, a thin line of grey on the grey horizon. The fields and the trees ended. Here, still, no grass grew. The earth was grey and sallow. Flabby-looking. Diseased skin. There were cracks and folds in the ground, eruptions of soil, broken lumps of rock. Seashells and sand. More tarnished broken weapons. More human bones. The Illyian army had camped here at the end of the world before Marith destroyed them.

The horse would go no further. It snorted, stamped, restless. Landra patted its neck.

'It's fine, horse. This is bad place, I know it is.' She took it back a few paces. Hobbled it. She took an apple out of her pocket and fed it to the horse. The horse pissed loudly while it ate.

She walked carefully on through the rubble of a world's dying. To the very edge of the Bitter Sea. Looked out over the waters. Low cliffs sinking down into the waters, rotten seaweed heaped on the black rocks. More bones. A single gull floated in the grey sea and as she watched it lifted into the sky and circled, shrieking; a seal broke the surface, seemed to stare at her. Dark eyes like a baby's eyes. It was gone again in an instant. The gull settled back on the water, further out into the endless sea.

The end of the world. There was a seacave in the cliffs somewhere, she could hear the waves as they sucked at the cave mouth.

The end of the world. Where the luck horse had come from.

She had crossed and recrossed Irlast with Marith's army. She had screamed and raged at the people of Irlast to resist him, to fight him, to hope. They resisted and they were destroyed. They fought him and they died. They hoped and they saw him, shining, glorious. They believed in him, those that lived, in all their hearts and their souls. Or they did not care, those that lived. Or they did not know. A thousand thousand miles away from them. Rich black earth, flat flocks, fat herds, their children healthy with strong clean limbs.

She turned her face up to the sky. The waves broke and broke on the rocks like whispering.

Voices. Always voices.

She whispered back to them, 'Vengeance.'

The water and the air began to stir. The earth began to stir. Rattle of bones.

Chapter Thirteen

A man and a young woman, alone in a tall narrow room in a fortress.

'Of course I won't agree to him! Osen Fiolt! But Mother wants me to accept him,' Landra says with bitterness.

'His is rich,' her father says. 'Already a lord in his own right. You would be Lady of Malth Calien.'

'I would be nothing,' she says. 'I would rank lower than my own little brother.' One day Carin Relast will be Lord of Third Isle. And Landra Relast will be wife to someone. 'I will not marry some minor lord,' she says. 'You tell her I won't.'

Her father says, 'I have told her I forbid it. I will tell her again.' He looks tired. She is older now, and wiser, and she knows that she caused her parents to argue when she set her father against her mother like this. Chipped away at both of them.

'But Lan,' her father says, 'your mother's right that you need to marry soon.'

'I won't be some petty lord's wife! You tell her!' Landra shouts. Her father's favourite child. He looks at his own wife, he wants more for her than that. She can see.

'Lan.' Her father takes her hands to speak to her very seriously. 'If you marry well, you will have land and people to manage, you will share your husband's responsibilities. You will be a lord,

124

almost, you will rule all your husband's lands when your husband is away. Your mother wants you to marry Osen Fiolt because you would be near us.'

'You'd be a far better Lord of Third Isle than I will be,' Carin her brother says to her. He's useless, their father despairs of him. 'I'm the feckless younger son,' he says wretchedly.

Yelling and shouting, she's tried to help him enough times, poor little brother. 'Why do you find it so hard? It's Immish grammar, not Itheralik. You just need to learn it. Recite it over until you can get it.' She says, helplessly, to him, 'Just . . . think about it.'

He throws up his hands: 'Why does he make me do all this?'

'Because he wants you to be a good Lord of Third Isle. And because he wants the people of Third Isle to have a good lord ruling over them. Come on, look, gods, Carin, just concentrate. Copy it out a few times. Recite it.'

'I do. I try. I can't do it.'

He's still a child, really, three years younger than her. 'Come on, look, I'll help you.'

He says hopefully, 'You could do it for me? No one has to know. And Father would be pleased I'd done it well.'

Their father sees it at once, of course, it's so obvious. Is furious with them both, but laughs too. His laughter baffles them. Now, older, wiser, she wonders whether the disaster that struck them all was there, already, in these things.

'This is not helping me, Carin,' she says.

'You need to marry an old sick man,' Carin jokes.

She does love her brother with all her heart. But.

Marry well! There are six islands that make up the White Isles. Seven, if one counts Belen Isle, which is so small and poor and barren that no one does. Five of these islands are held by the great lords of the White Isles. She counts them off on her fingers: Deneth Relast of Third, her own father, Carin Relast her brother will be lord after him; Carlan Murade of Sel, the king's goodbrother, he has sons and grandsons, her father hates him; Rethnen Jurgis of

Heneth, he stands high in the king's favour, his younger son Kamleth is unmarried but what use is a younger son?; Valim Erith of Feleane, his son is a child; Lord Nasis Jaeartes of Thirane, he is young and unmarried but he is an idiot. Of these five lords, none of whom are suitable, her father is the richest and most powerful, her island the largest, her home the most beautiful, the most famous, the finest. Even if she could marry one of them, she would still be nothing but a wife and still she would be poorer and weaker than her brother Carin. And the petty lords, the liegemen like Osen Fiolt . . . if she marries one of them, she might as well be nothing. A house, land, people: a few villages, her father means.

If she does not marry, she will stay here like a child, she will rank lower than Carin's wife when he marries, or she could go out into the world alone and be less than nothing. She thinks of her mother, bending her head meekly to do her father's will.

She thinks. The sixth island, Seneth, is held by the Altrersyr king.

'The king,' she says to her brother that evening, after they have been scolded for cheating in his studies, are sitting together in his bedchamber looking down at the sea, their ears still ringing from being yelled at. 'King Illyn has two unmarried sons, Carin.'

'He does?' her brother says. 'You astonish me. What about it?'

She says, 'You remember when Prince Marith came to stay here for the summer, when Prince Tiothlyn was ill? He was, what, eight? Seven? He followed you around, wouldn't let you alone, drove you mad.'

Carin says, '"The greatest opportunity of all our lives", that I squandered away because I quarrelled with him? Of course. I—' His face goes white. 'Yes, but . . .'

Gods, Amrath and Eltheia, she thinks. Now, older, wiser, she can see in his shock, as well as in what came after, that she was the naive one.

'They say Marith is unhappy,' Landra says carefully. 'Lonely. Quarrels with the king and queen. Quarrels with Prince Tiothlyn. So Mother says. "Poor lonely motherless boy", Mother says. You've heard her say it yourself.' She takes a deep breath, pauses. 'You are going to court with Father, in the spring,' she says.

'He was seven,' Carin says. 'He's fourteen now. He'll be fifteen, by the time we go to court.' Carin glances at the books piled by the window. 'If I get to go.' Still looks so troubled, you can see why Father despairs of him. 'I don't think he'll still be following me around because he covets my toy fort, Landra,' Carin says.

Their father looks more proud of Carin than he's ever looked of anything in his whole life, when they tell him, when it's done. It's beautiful.

Chapter Fourteen

Several hours later Landra rode back towards the north gate of Ethalden. She did not look at the land around her. When she rode through the village the children stopped to look at her. She did not look back at them.

She reached the city. At the gatehouse, two guards stopped her to question her. Where was she going, where had she been? The usual questions, the same greasy smell to them, the boredom of guarding a gate on the road to the edge of the world where there was nothing. A girl herding geese had been the last thing in front of her in through the gate. But they seemed very nervous, twitching and eyeing her as she rode up as though she might be a danger to them. Landra felt a thrill of power. Not power. Hope.

'What has happened?' Landra asked them, though she already knew. They liked her White Isles accent, had brightened up at her voice. 'The temple of Amrath,' the taller of the two said. 'It has . . .' licked his lips, stared fearfully at the ground, spat for luck '. . . it has collapsed.'

'Collapsed?' A song of joy. The sun shines and all the birds sing. Had to bite her lip to keep from laughing. Ah, Tobias, Raeta, she thought, what would you say? She could see Tobias's face, his eyes creased with laughter. '*Boy can't keep his tower up, now, can he? gna ha ha,*' or such. '*I know it's not a tower, Raeta, before*

128

you say it. "Can't keep his building up" doesn't work, though, does it?'

The innkeep's son at her inn was full of it when she asked him to tend the horse. 'A great crash, no warning, a crash like thunder, and the whole building fell. It was packed full of people, they all died, they couldn't dig them out.' The boy's eyes bulged. 'They say blood was literally oozing out of it.'

'Do they?' Gave him a couple of copper pennies. 'My horse needs a good grooming and a feed.'

The boy's eyes bulged at the state of the horse too, ashy dust on its legs, fretful. Landra went to see the ruins. The innkeep's son was begging his father to let him go when she left. The whole city was gathered there, a weight hanging over them almost visible, thick crowds packed close. Muttering, whispering, cowering. Landra could not get anywhere near it, was pushed and trampled in the crowd.

'It just gave way. A roar, a crash, it fell down.'

'Best part of an hour, they've been digging. Still haven't got anyone out.'

'Watch it. Watch it.' The crowd pulled apart as soldiers and horsemen came down the street away from the temple. Landra recognized Lord Stansel of Belen Isle, Marith's regent in Illyr, his face pale and grave. He was shaking his head, talking to the man next to him; there was black dust smeared in his hair.

'. . . fault with the roof. Built too quickly,' Landra heard him say as he rode past. 'I told him.'

The woman beside her spat. And not for luck. 'The king will have him flayed,' she said to Landra.

'It can hardly be his fault, that a building fell down?'

'Can't it? And not a building: His tomb. What will we do if His coffin has been damaged? His bones, damaged?'

'Rebuild it all twice as big as before, I expect,' said Landra. 'With more gold.' She returned to her inn, where the innkeep's son begged her for news, wanted a description of everything. Served her bread and cheese and salt meat, wanted to know, over and over, what she thought it meant. She was from the White Isles, like the king – so she must, somehow, know things.

'It means something, doesn't it?' the boy said. 'Some great thing, it means, for the king.'

'Great things,' Landra said.

By sunset, the bodies of five master stonemasons were hanging in chains from the fortress gates. The rubble was being cleared, the golden coffin emerging, magically unscathed. So the drinkers said. People moving from inn to inn, talking of it, on edge, drinking one drink and moving on to another inn to talk of it again. Later that night shouting rang out in the street, 'Look! Look!' and the innkeep rushed out to look: a shooting star had been seen, very bright and clear in the north sky, half the city had witnessed it. 'But I was too late,' he said ruefully. Later that night a great storm came in from the sea bringing thunder and hailstones. 'As big as pebbles,' the innkeep's boy said as he served Landra bread and beer the next morning. 'They broke the branches of the tree opposite, took half the leaves off, I looked out of my window last night and they were covering the ground like brown snow. Didn't you hear it?' the boy asked Landra. 'Or the thunder? Noisy enough to wake the bloody dead.' His face went pale, he made a warding gesture. 'Or maybe not that loud. Didn't mean it like that.'

'I'm sure you didn't,' said Landra. The innkeep came shouting that the hail had damaged the stable roof; the boy leapt up and out to see to it. 'Your horse will be fine,' he said to Landra as he went out, 'I'm sure.'

'I hope so. I may need him saddled, later.' The wooden spire that Landra had watched rise up the previous day was damaged, she noticed. Many trees had indeed lost branches; dried leaves had been crushed down littering the pavements. Dirt and rubbish had been washed into heaps.

The city streets were almost empty. In the ruins of Amrath's tomb people were packed thick like insects, crawling over the black stones like insects, black with dust. Landra watched them a while. Their hands clawed at the stones. They were tearing their hands raw. Bodies were beginning to be dug out. A woman, a man, a child, a woman with offering flowers still clutched to her breast. A sigh ran through the crowd as her body came up. Her face was crushed in, but her hair hung down thick and black. A voice wailed out at the sight of her. Her gown was fine pale silk, fringed with gold embroidery. They did not make such things in Illyr. From Tereen, or Arunmen. Landra turned away. Walked to the gatehouse of the fortress of Ethalden itself.

The woman might have bought the dress in all innocence. Briefly, Landra might think this, feel shame or guilt. But the man who sold it to the woman, or the man who sold it to that man . . . someone knew, could have told the buyer where the dress came from. The woman could have asked where it had come from, Landra thought. Look at the prices of these beautiful things now on sale here. It should have been obvious to everyone.

All human lives, Landra thought, are based on human suffering. Every house is built on bloodshed, our feet trample others' lives beneath them with every step. One man eats off plates of gold, another starves, a face turns away not to see. Even the kindest innocent young child . . . look behind them and there is a trail of others' blood. A child has food and clothes and loving peace because his ancestors looted and pillaged, because others still suffer somewhere far away. There is nothing that is not bought in blood.

No mercy. No one here is innocent.

The gates to Marith's fortress were white bone. Dragon bone. Only Marith Altrersyr, Landra thought, could be absurd enough to take the bones of a dragon that had died fighting for him and build it up into the gates of his hall. The gatehouse was white marble, whiter and colder beside the bone. The arch of the gates was topped with a row of gilded human skulls.

Revolting. In the cool clear air Landra smelled butchery. Human bones will never cease to smell of rot. All those smiling mouths, the empty eye sockets that still gazed out. How could he bear it, she thought, to ride in and out beneath that? His enemies, smiling down cold at him, knowing. Dripping their rot on him.

'What's your business?' the guard at the gates asked her. His helmet and his armour were burnished silver, his cloak was blood red. His helmet covered his face. Its crest was shaped like an eagle, its plume the eagle's wings. Landra thought: does he see what he looks like? He must see. How absurd he is.

She said, 'I have come to speak to Lord Stansel.' She stared at the guard's eyes through his helmet. 'Tell him that Deneth Relast's daughter is here to speak with him. Give him this.' A gold ring, too big for her finger, stamped with a bird flying. Her father's ring. She should feel anxious, handing it over. The guard could steal it, keep it, melt it down, of course, yes. She should fear that. The grass grows around the ruin of Malth Salene, the grass grows up over her brother's grave that Marith has never been back to visit since he took up his crown as king. She might fear even that Yanis Stansel will not remember her father's name.

Three things she had, in a purse in her pocket, held close. A gold ring stamped with a bird flying. An old spindle carved of horse bone. A filthy scrap of yellow cloth. Of these three things, the ring was the first and the least that she would give away.

'Wait here,' the guard said. He put out his hand to take the ring and his hand was an old man's hand, thick dried callused fingers, his nails yellow and ugly, the skin split and healed and scarred. He had a White Isles accent. He walked away stiffly, limping, putting his weight on his left leg; his left shoulder was hunched, hung wrong on him. He is an old soldier from my homeland, Landra thought, pensioned off here. He knows the name Relast.

Guards marched to and fro, glancing at her. Landra stood shuffling her feet, trying not to look back. An eternity, the man had been gone, he must have simply abandoned her, been distracted and forgotten, stolen the ring. Which was for the best. It made her ashamed, that he might have recognized the name Relast. A troop of soldiers went in through the gates, looked at her. A woman on a white horse rode out. A man on a roan horse rode out, fast, wrapped in a cloak. He had the look of a messenger, Lady Landra

Relast thought. Bringing Marith a message that the tomb of Amrath had fallen into rubble. Or bringing Marith a message that the rumour of this was a lie, hoping that he would ignore it until the tomb was rebuilt. A wagon went in stacked with sacks of grain.

A man came out of the gates to Landra. Not a guard but a middle-aged man, well-dressed, his gown velvet, fur trim on his sleeves, gold at his wrists. Red hair dressed with oil. A smooth dark face. Familiar. She had seen him. Recognized him. Where?

A companion of Yanis Stansel, she thought, a member of Yanis Stansel's household. What was his name? He was . . . was he not married to Yanis Stansel's niece?

He knew her. Through the burns and the scars. His eyes were filled with shock. The smooth voice with the accent so like her father's, as the man said, 'Come this way, please, My Lady.'

What have I done? Landra thought with horror. *My Lady*. I should not have come here. Ah, gods, Amrath and Eltheia. For them to see me, to be among them once more, all that I have been. And she remembered again Marith crying out, 'I didn't ask to come back here. I was happy, before you brought me back here.' He had said it even as they knelt before him in the Amrath Chapel of Malth Salene, placed a silver crown on his head. He had become nothing. And she had forced him to return to being a king.

She followed the man through into the fortress, down wide corridors with floors and walls set with jewels, great vaulting halls hung with silk tapestries and fur hangings, courtyards bright with the sound of fountains, audience chambers of marble and gold. They walked through chambers decked in silver, lined with pearls, crowned with flowers carved of amethyst. Real flowers, jasmine, lilies, orange blossom, things that should not grow here in the far north. Windows, mirrors, candles, jewels, gilded carvings, hangings of gold and silver, gold mosaics, gold and silver carpets. In a hall of white marble stood a tree made of ivory in which birds made of emeralds fluttered diamond wings. Beyond it, a small chamber where the walls were hung with blue satin that moved in a hidden wind like swimming beneath the sea. They walked up a staircase of green marble. Along more halls and corridors, up and down more stairs, past closed doors of silver, of bronze, of amber, of black jet. A wall all of living plants, green and soft. A wall all of mirrors and candles. A wall of living birds in gold cages, singing.

The emptiness of the place was oppressive. She thought of her own lost home, Malth Salene, of Malth Elelane the seat of the Altrersyr kings. Noise and bustle. The orderly uproar of a place filled with day-to-day life. She thought of Ru's cottage, where Ru had sat alone in silence. This place was built as a king's home, she thought, a house for Marith and Thalia and their children and their friends. This place is like a corpse at a wedding feast.

They came to a chamber opening out onto a rose garden, at the centre of which stood a statue of a woman robed and crowned. A carpet of petals on the earth bruised and faded, brought down by last night's storm. Yet every rose was in full bloom. White roses, and pink, and dark lustrous red.

Lord Yanis Stansel sat in his wheeled chair, looking out at the roses. The Lord of Belen Isle, the smallest and poorest of the White Isles. Now the right hand of the Lord of All Irlast, and he did not look happier or richer for it. He had thick black hair, despite being old enough to have four grown sons. His hair was long, falling over his shoulders, his beard was black and grey. His upper body was very strong, broad muscles in his arms and across his chest. His neck was thick as a bull's neck, beneath the beard. He sat in his wheeled chair solid, heavy, fierce. The silk gown he wore did not suit him, he should be wearing armour, his hair bound up with red leather, his eyes framed in gleaming bronze. His great hands rested in his lap. He had a new chair, Landra noticed, and then realized that the chair she remembered him in must have been uselessly old. It was pale wood, the arms carved as a pair of wolves, their bellies low to the ground, their teeth bared. The bronze rims of its wheels were snakes swallowing their own tails.

He looked a thousand years older than he had when Landra had last seen him in King Illyn's court in Malth Elelane a thousand lifetimes ago.

He was holding her father's gold ring.

He gazed at her for a long time. He had known her when she was a child. What did he see? A scarred bald old woman, honed to dry metal, flayed down to dry bone. A living scar. A human wound. A rabid dog.

Yanis said, 'It is you. I thought you were dead.' He waved his hand at the other man. 'Leave us, Tolan. Have some wine brought.'

Tolan. Yes, that was the man's name. She did remember him.

A servant brought wine in silver cups, a plate of fruit and curd cakes. Looked at her once. Did not look at her again.

'I thought all of your family were dead,' Yanis said. Landra sipped her wine and did not speak. What can one say, to that? Yanis said, 'He talked about you sometimes as if he knew that you were dead. I wondered, sometimes, whether he had killed you himself.'

'Really? He knows that I am alive. Or he did, when I failed to kill him. Thalia must know that I am alive, since she spared me.' She said, to hurt herself, 'Perhaps he is confusing me with my brother, then.'

Yanis Stansel spread his hands, pointed to the roses. 'Look at these flowers,' he said. 'Look at them. They never fade, never wither, they have been here in bloom since the day he was crowned King of Illyr. The most glorious day any man living has seen or will see. He burned the Rose Forest. Ordered the people of Chathe to burn it all. If your fool of a brother had waited a few years, Landra, your father could have been sitting here now, regent of half the world, king in all but name. Do you ever think of that?'

Every hour, every day, what do you think I think about every night, every morning, every time my wounds ache?

'You will want this back.' Yanis held out the ring to her.

Landra took it, put it back in her pocket. 'Thank you.'

'You know what happened this morning? He will curse me for it, blame me. Everyone in the city wants to know what it means, and what can I say?'

Landra thought, Yanis Stansel, afraid!

'He ordered them to build it too quickly,' said Yanis. 'The city walls, the temples, this fortress itself will crack and fall down one day soon. The workmen toiled until they fell dead from exhaustion. He shouted at them to work harder, faster, offered them more and more gold. He will blame me, of course. Have me killed. I killed the men who built it. He will blame me for that, say I should not have done it. But if I had not done it, what would he have said? All four of my sons are dead now,' Yanis Stansel said to Landra. 'Did you know that?'

It was written there in his face, as he said it. Landra said, 'No. I didn't know. I'm sorry.'

'One of them died in the first battle, in Morr Bay, before Marith was even truly crowned. One died here, taking Ethalden, after the battle had all but been won. One died of fever, outside Bakh, the water there was bad. The last fell at Balkash. A spear point took out his left eye, the wound mortified . . . I did not see him die. I could not bear to see it.'

Bees droned among the roses, a calm sound that made Landra think of sleeping in the warmth of the sun. And a butterfly, with scarlet wings. Even in the midst of the winter. There is death beneath the ground here, Landra thought, the roses grow on blood and flesh. Marith had thought perhaps of the beehives in the orchard at Malth Salene, the wild roses in the scrub on the headland, looking down over the sea. A good place to sit and think.

'Have a cake?' Yanis said to her

Landra took one, ate. Curd cheese, almonds, honey, lemon. The wine was flavoured with lemon and rosemary. Taste of home.

'The servants here think I am mad, drinking it,' said Yanis Stansel. 'I had to send for my own servants from home, to cook for me. Walk with me, Landra.'

He pushed himself along fast, Landra had to walk fast to keep up with him. The wheels of the chair creaked. Into the palace, back through the marble halls. When they came to a flight of steps in the garden Landra had to help him push the chair: a ramp had been placed there, but the slope was steep. Yanis Stansel cursed as they pushed the chair up. She had to help him again when they came to a thick carpet stretched over jade tiles, where the wheels stuck.

'Look.'

On the wall of the chamber a picture had been painted. A great battle, rank upon rank of men in armour, a tangle of sarriss points and swords and helmet plumes, rows of gurning faces, splayed muscled arms and legs. Lovingly painted wounds. In the foreground, a river ran in spate; in the background, grey mountains rose into a blue sky. In the very centre of the picture, larger than life-size, Marith was caught mid-slaughter, his sword raised. He was wearing a crown of real silver, the hilt of his sword and the brooch fastening his cloak were set with real rubies, pressed into the wall. A vast man in black armour was falling back before him, blood bursting artfully out of his cut throat. The dying man's mouth was wide open, yelling, his eyes crumpled up in terror. Marith's face was calm, a ghost of a smile on his lips.

Behind Marith, much smaller and less radiant, she could recognize Osen Fiolt, also caught in the act of cutting a man into bits of meat. Men of the White Isles she knew and remembered. Nasis Jaeartes. Valim Erith. Yanis Stansel himself, his horse rearing up as his sword came hard down.

'The battle of the Nimenest,' said Yanis Stansel. 'I enjoyed that battle. It was a close-run thing, for a while. But none of us doubted him.'

The sound of battle rang in Landra's ears, the crash of men together, screams, cries of pain, trumpets, horses, the sound of bronze striking bronze. A singer telling the tale of the battle, sweet-voiced, his companion playing a lyre, stamping his feet to mark the beat. 'I have heard the song of it told all over Irlast,' she said.

'It really did look like that,' said Yanis. 'The light in his face as he was fighting, the joy in him as he led us. That certainty he had, that he would win; the trust he had in us, that we would win for him. All our lives, we've dreamed of Illyr. You, Landra; your father; your brother . . . Your father dreamed of conquering

Illyr, sighed with regret that he was too young to have fought for Nevethlyn. The shame of failure, in every story of the White Isles. It should be ours. It belonged to our god. Curse them, the fools who cast Him out, who ceased to love Him. What did they want that He could not give them? He made them lords of the world. They tore it all apart rejecting Him. And Marith stood before us, promised us . . .' Yanis Stansel shook his head 'I have never seen anything like his face, when he spoke about Illyr. Even in the worst days, in the Wastes, on the Field of Shame, I did not doubt him. It was like being in the brilliance of the world's new making, riding into battle beside him.' Pointed at the picture. 'I have never felt such happiness as I did that day.

'Since Marith was a child I knew I would follow him to the end of the world. We were all so amazed by him, so horrified by him. He would lead and all would follow: I swore I would follow no matter what the cost. Your father knew, Landra. King Illyn his own father knew. He would bring us joy beyond imagining. And pain beyond imagining. When she was pregnant with him, Queen Marissa dreamed that fire burned in her womb. It terrified her. She tried to abort him. Or so my wife said.

'I felt the breath taken from my lungs sometimes, thinking of what he would bring. Sometimes now I wish that I had died at the Nimenest. Or . . . no: that I had died the day after I saw Marith crowned. That was the greatest moment in all our lives. Would that this whole palace had collapsed around us, when it was done.'

Yanis pointed to a table, its legs wrought-silver dragons, the table top decorated with images of dragons carved in green jade, dancing over each other, interlocking together, the space behind one dragon's wings forming another's claws or head. On it was a silver tray with wine cups and a white dish of yellow apples, speckled brown like robin's eggs. 'Do you know what that is?'

Confused. His mind is wandering. Landra said carefully, 'No?'

'The table came from the King's House in Balkash. One of the greatest treasures of the Minol kings. It came originally from one of the kings' tombs in Tarboran. No one can say how old it is. The dish is from the altar of a temple in Ander. It held offerings of salt water to the god spirit of the Sea of Grief. Marith had the King's House and the temple looted, carted all the things of value off here to furnish his palace. Dumped it all here. Your face says that I should feel ashamed.

'I thought we were building an empire to his glory.' Yanis said, 'You've come here to kill me, haven't you, Landra?'

Chapter Fifteen

They both stood and looked at the wall painting.

Confess, Landra. Tell him. Unburden yourself. Landra said, 'I was in Balkash ahead of Marith's army. I stood in the square before the King's House. I begged the people of Balkash to stand and fight. They listened to me. I went to Ander, on the edge of the Neir Forest, I stood in the shadow of their temples, I begged them. They listened to me. They were strong and confident. *Death or freedom! Never surrender! We are not afraid!* I begged them, they listened, they called their armies out.

'Balkash is destroyed. Ander is destroyed. The Neir Forest is a thousand miles of white ash.

'I went to Arunmen, ahead of his army, I saw them welcome Marith in as their king, kneel to him. There was a man there who listened to me. A young man, tall and handsome and clever. Filled with joy and hope.'

She looked at the wall painting. Marith's perfect face.

'The young man is dead now. His body hangs above the King of Arunmen's throne. Everyone I met in Arunmen is dead. Yes, Yanis. I have come to kill you. That is all that is left to me, to kill old unarmed men like you.' She heard her voice crack with self-pity as she spoke.

* * *

Tobias, on the day Marith was crowned, as they stood together looking up at the golden towers of Ethalden: 'If your brother had been alive at his side, if you and your father had lived in this stupidly OTT place . . . There's not a man or woman alive who wouldn't burn the world if it meant they could eat off plates of silver and sleep in a massive solid gold bed. And if they wouldn't . . . it's only cause they want to bask in the warmth of being a morally superior better than thou arsehole. "*Oh oh, look at me, what a good man I am, I've got a precious shining soul where you've just got power and wealth.*"'

Rattle of bones, whispers of dead voices, I am nothing, I have nothing left but my hate. He deserves this. They all do. No mercy for anyone.

She did not have to do anything. Move. Speak. The dead of Illyr, shrieking for vengeance. The gabeleth, the demon of vengeance that had never lived. Every life that a man's hand has casually destroyed. The raw wound of her own heart. Landra stood and looked at Yanis Stansel. His throat opened in a bloody gash, his heart burned up in his chest. His eyes, that had seen violence. His mouth, that had ordered violence done. His hands, that had killed. He burned and he bled. Landra bent, touched his dead body. It crumbled away into dark rot. She looked around the room and sighed, pressed her hands against the marble wall. The stone moved beneath her hands. Sighed back to her. It was made of bones and blood and tears and sweat. Marith's portrait smiled over her, his sword raised, his face flushed with triumph, looking off into a sunlight world of glory and happiness.

A hard winter rain was falling when Landra left the fortress of Ethalden. The cloth binding her head was soaked, heavy and unpleasant. Through the raindrops, as through a veil, she could see a troop of soldiers marching in through the gateway, grey and sullen in the rain. Water dripped from their helmets. A flash of red from a man's cloak, a helmet plume nodding soaked black.

How long, I wonder, she thought, before they find Yanis is dead? Those empty rooms . . . hours, days, perhaps. Time enough. She went down into the city, fetched her horse from the stable of the inn.

'He's been groomed, see, My Lady?' the innkeep's son told her. 'Cleaned his hooves, even, he had a stone in one of his frogs, he'll be happier for it, you'll see.' She thanked him and paid him, although she suspected he was lying about the stone to charge her for it. Paid the innkeep, praised the boy to him profusely, took her bag and left. The rain had stopped, just about, the sky ran with thin winter light. The streets were streams of dirty water. People tiptoed through it stained dark with wet. The smell of damp things drying: she did not like that smell now, the smell of the world after a storm has gone.

Landra rode down to Marith's bleak iron temple. The horse woman sat in a huddle beneath the luck horse, looked up at Landra tired and cold. Water dripped from the horse's skull. The door of the temple was closed against the weather. Landra dismounted, went up close to them. The iron felt hot, close up to it, as though it was newly drawn from the forge. Sick feeling inside her. Insects crawling on her skin. If I hold out my hand, Landra thought, touch it, it will be rotting. Maggot-eaten. Inside, it is not iron, it is bleeding weeping flesh. The door of the temple opened, two men came out, soldiers in armour, everything about them fresh and clean. New boots that squeaked: 'Damned things are still rubbing,' one of the soldiers muttered as they walked; arms and armour new raw-edged. 'Time for a beer?' the soldier with the rubbing boots asked his friend. When they opened the door the world should have been flooded with blood. A young woman walked past her, pushed the door open, stopped in the doorway to shake the rain from her cloak.

In the square beside the temple a merchant with a stall of cloth had not got his wares covered over before the last rainstorm, was wringing out bales of bright-dyed wool.

'Going cheap, mistress,' he called to Landra, half-rueful,

half-laughing. He held up pale hands. 'Look how good the dye is. Hardly runs.'

'My horse won't want to carry a wet bundle of cloth on his back,' she called back, trying to be friendly.

'Tell him it's for a horse blanket,' the merchant said. He squeezed out another bolt of cloth, this time brilliant scarlet, and pink water gushed over him.

'I don't want a pink-dyed horse, thank you,' Landra said, also laughing.

'A shame, a shame, he'd look fine, that horse, with more colour on him.' The merchant held up another bale. 'Or green might suit him better, perhaps?'

Trees and flowers and rushing clear river water, all laughing within her, childish, foolish. 'He'd look very fine, my horse,' she said gravely, 'dyed green, I think you're right.' He had a bolt of creamy white wool that was dry, having been sheltered beneath the red and the green; she bought enough for a blanket.

A baby was yelling from a nearby house, a gull shrieked high above her, a builder's hammer began to ring. A woman frowned up at the noise of the baby. 'I'm sorry,' she wanted to say to the woman and the cloth-merchant and the builder and the baby. She rode on to the harbour rising on the Jaxertane's bank.

She could smell the river before she could see it. Water stink, the filth of the new city. The tide was out and wading birds and mud fishers picked across the flats. The mud was littered with the new detritus of the city, wood and stone and rubbish; human bones, ancient weapons. The hull of an old boat, itself looking like a dead thing. On the far bank there were fields stained with standing water from the rain. But the river was alive with ships, rang with voices calling in every language. Warships with bronze rams and red-painted eyes; fast black galleys from the White Isles; huge round-bellied craft from the south, Medana and Mar, with two or even three rows of oars; little trader ships that relied only on sails, being too poor to purchase oarslaves; fishermen in hide and wicker coracles.

'*No one in their right minds sails to Illyr.*' Nevethlyn Altrersyr sailed to Illyr with a war fleet, his ships were driven all the way around Illyr, into the Sea of Grief, wrecked on the south coast. His army was destroyed. One of his ships made it back to the White Isles. Spared to tell. Hilanis the Young sailed to Illyr with a war fleet. Every one of his ships was destroyed. No one knows if he even reached the Illyian coast. '*Glorious they sailed, a mighty host in golden ships. I alone came back.*' Since the coming of King Marith the seas around Illyr were calm and untroubled. Ships plied their waters every day.

A ship was coming in now, edging its way through the mudflats up to the harbour place. A fishing vessel, not large, its sail dyed the Altrersyr red for luck. Its men were laughing, shouting to the people on the riverside. Piled on its deck was a huge catch of silver fish.

'Monsters, we've caught! Monsters!' a man shouted from the ship. 'Tell the people of Ethalden that we have more food here than a city can eat in a lifetime! Tell the people of Ethalden to start planning how to cook it!' A fish longer than a man hung from the mast.

'Where did you go to catch that?' a sailor on another ship shouted over.

'North,' the man shouted back. 'North out of sight of land, beyond the flight of birds, into the wild sea that goes on to the end of the world. There are mountains of ice there rising out of the water, sea mists so thick I couldn't see my hand held touching my face. But the fish and the whales came up to the bows of our ship in wonder, having never seen a man before, we could almost pick them out of the water with our hands.'

A cargo ship was waiting drawn up on a mudflat beach. A wooden causeway leading from the deck to the riverbank. The ship had a dark red sail. The sign *palle* was painted on its bows. The White Isles rune for the smooth sheen of a calm sea. Ah. Landra's head swam, looking at it. The crew rushed back and forth loading the cargo, bundles wrapped in goat hides bound up with leather thongs. Landra approached, called over to them.

'Are you bound for the White Isles?'

One of the sailors left off his work, came over to the bows of the ship. A youngish man with a dark beard plaited with red ribbons. Breathless from hurrying to ready the ship. 'Morr Town, yes.'

She fought down sickness in her throat. Her heart must beat so loud it would make the sea shake. 'Can you take a passenger?'

The man looked Landra up and down. 'Perhaps.'

'One in gold?'

'Two.'

'Two. You are sailing now?'

'A few hours still.' He shrugged at the water. 'We're getting loaded now, but the tide will need to turn. Come back here in an hour, and we'll see.'

'Thank you.' The words were a lie in her throat. The man nodded back at her.

So . . . what to do until then? She glanced back towards the silver spire of the fortress. They would have found him, she thought. They would be frightened and angry, they would be looking for her. 'Landra Relast!' Tolan would be shouting. 'Landra Relast killed him!' Soldiers, running out of the gate of skulls, looking for a woman in a green dress with burns on her white face and her hair covered over with a cloth. 'Find her. Kill her. Keep her alive and make her suffer.' They would look to the ships at once, thinking of ways she might be trying to escape them. Fast horses, their riders with drawn swords, the horses' hooves throwing up the wet earth as they came. 'Close the gates and watch the ships.'

She put it all to the back of her mind, very calmly. It will be well.

'Is there somewhere near I can get something to eat?' she asked the sailor with the black beard.

'There.' He jerked his head. 'It's expensive.'

Landra looked where he gestured and there was an inn set back from the riverside, new and brash and large, welcoming sea travellers to Ethalden with strong beer and hot meat. Landra walked her horse over. The horse was stabled, she sat by the window with a cup of spiced beer, looking out. The sea coming in slowly, silvery water sliding up over the mudflats. Too fast. Too slow. The boats loading, unloading – carts triumphantly carrying off the fishing boat's huge catch. Her own ship was being well stocked with food and water. Waste thrown overboard sending the seabirds into a frenzy. Two gulls fought in the air over something, screaming; Landra closed her eyes, tried to look away into the inn's common room.

No one had come for her. Of course they had not come. Those empty rooms. She thought then what a sad and empty death it had been for Yanis Stansel, who had been a good man, who had been a friend of her father's, who had outlived all four of his sons.

The ship was ready at last, the tide was rushing in. Landra left the horse in the stables, telling the stable boy to sell it. She left him the blanket as well. He stared at her wide-eyed then nodded, his hands stroking the fine weave of the wool. She was not perhaps the first to leave all she had here, she thought, sailing for something greater.

She could have turned the horse loose, she thought with a laugh. Let it run free on the dead shore where the men of Illyr had made their camp. The blind ones, who had not been dazzled by his light.

'Three in gold,' the sailor with the black beard said when she got aboard. Her legs swayed as she stood on the deck. 'Three in gold,' the sailor said, 'two now, one at Morr Town.'

'You said two.'

He gestured to the sky. 'Wind's getting up. We're going now. Three.'

The wind was blowing in from the south, a fresh taste to it, they went fast down to the mouth of the Jaxertane. It was a long time, Landra thought, since she had last been on a ship. Before many things. The ship felt like an animal moving beneath her. The water parted before it like skin. Voices inside her weeping at leaving Illyr. Other voices singing in joy, for being on the water free. The gabeleth reaching out to the dead who lay beneath the grey sea, calling to them. Beneath the water, bone and bronze would move in the currents. The towers of Ethalden fell away in the ship's wake, the silver and pearl spire, the gold walls. The ship rounded the headland, began to dance on the wind. The coastline of Illyr slipping past them, bare and dead. A sailor pointed up at the cliff tops: 'There, see? Where the stones stand upright like a hand, there, you see, the marks on them? That's where it was. Their camp.' Another sailor gestured at them angrily, waved them away to avert their faces from the cliff top. 'Get back to work.' Ill luck to look. Landra too averted her face, watched white foam breaking on black rocks at the cliff's base. Try to see something there, something living, but there was nothing. She moved to the other side of the ship, looked out to the north, where the sea went on forever, she thought she saw for a moment a whale breeching. A gull screamed on the wind far out to the north; a cloud of seabirds coming down to settle on the waves. She thought of killing Yanis Stansel and a part of her felt sick with horror and a part of her wept with happiness. She looked ahead into the white distance, imagined she saw the White Isles already rising before her, and thought what she must do. Grey water. Knife water. Stone water. Breaking over the bows of the ship cold and bitter, it stung the burns on her skin, her hands ached with damp cold. But the cleanness of it, also. The sting of the salt like a scourge. Movement, travelling. Racing on. Too fast. Too slow. The dead voice of the men of Illyr, who had died fighting to defend their home from Marith Altrersyr. The dead voice of the gabeleth, that had never lived. All ringing and ringing in her head. The *gestmet* Raeta hissing, 'I am his death.' Kill them. His people. All of them. They must deserve it. They live only on others' deaths. We all live on others' deaths. She looked back towards Ethalden and saw the very tip of its spire lit and shining on the horizon, a pinprick, a faint star, and then even as she watched the light flashed very bright and then died away to nothing. A dark column of smoke. The dusk came rushing up. The smoke was gone.

Chapter Sixteen

Orhan Emmereth the Lord of the Rising Sun, the Dweller in the House of the East, once the Nithque to the Ever Living Emperor and the Undying City, once the Emperor's True Counsellor and Friend, once a man who believed in himself
The City of Sorlost the Golden, the Eternal, the Undying, the decaying heart of the mummified remnant of the Sekemleth Empire of the Golden Dawn Light

The Immish guards were lined up three deep outside the Summer Palace of the Asekemlene Emperor of the Sekemleth Empire of the Eternal City of Sorlost. Thirty of them, at least. Sweat trickled down their faces beneath their helmets. A group of street children, drunk on firewine, dazed with hatha, giggled and shouted at the guards, threw handfuls of dust at them, one threw a clod of animal dung that bounced off a black-tempered shield. Flashed thin bruised child limbs, laughing calling, 'Want some? Want some? One dhol. One dhol.' The guards ignored them. Lined-up faces set blank. A child stumbled closer, spat at a guard's feet. White foam spit on bronze bootcaps. Dried quickly in the sun. No response from the guardsman. The children giggled and shouted and got bored. Drifted away.

The gate opened. The guards flicked around to attention at that.

Lord Tardein, Lord of the Dry Sea, Dweller in the House of Breaking Waves, Nithque to the Ever Living Emperor and the Undying City, the Emperor's True Counsellor and Friend. Lord Cauvanh, the Emperor's Adviser, so kindly lent the Emperor by the Great Council of Immish. An escort of twenty more Immish guards. They went hurriedly across the square, down the Street of Closed Eyes. The Immish guards went back to staring at nothing. Even the one with bits of goat shit on his shield. Lord Tardein the Emperor's Nithque and in theory the third most powerful person in the Sekemleth Empire had trodden in the goat shit, got some on his right shoe.

A street seller came into the square with a tray of preserved lemons. Her tray was decorated with sticks that knocked together as she moved, drew attention to her. She was wearing a yellow dress the same colour as the lemons. Hatha scars around her eyes and mouth. Flies buzzed over the tray; she waved her hand weakly to swat them off; her hand faltered over the tray, went back to scratching at her eyes and mouth. The guards ignored her. There was almost no one else in the square. Why would there be anyone in the square, in the dust, in the midday heat? She sat down in a corner in the shade, scratching at her eyes and mouth. The flies buzzed over the lemons. Her dress and her tray were covered with dust.

No one came to buy any lemons. Lord Lochaiel, Lord of the Moon's Light, Dweller in the House of Silver, the Emperor's True Counsellor and Friend, came down the Street of Closed Eyes, crossed the square, the gate swung open and he went through into the palace. His guards stirred up more dust that settled on the street seller's tray and on her dress.

Another man came into the square. He might have been a handsome man, once. His black hair hung down his back, streaked with grey; his skin was black tinged with grey tiredness. He stood in the square for a long time looking up at the palace. The thousand windows of the palace looked back at him. Arches and columns of white porcelain. Silver towers, gemstone balconies, silk awnings, the great golden dome. Froth of beauty like petals floating on dark water. A building like a dream. White clouds piled on a sunlit horizon. Moonlight and shadows and voices whispering, laughing, murmuring love. Candlelight catching on the jewels of a necklace. Hands moving and dancing, fingers reaching out to touch.

A reflection in a teardrop. A thousand dead, empty windows, that had once been lit with mage glass. The whole palace was blind and maimed. The Immish guards were quartered in buildings thrown up in the palace gardens. They trampled down the flowers. Pissed in one of the streams. The fruit trees that had been hung with painted apples were all cut down.

Yesterday you walked by the Temple.
You greeted friends, played yenthes –
You played badly, at that I could have matched you –
Your white hand around the stem of a wine cup.
Later we walked in your garden.
You were more beautiful than the flowers,
The moon came out, your face was more beautiful,
Your face was like the song of a nightingale.
You were beautiful, yesterday.
I counted the days, I longed for you.
Yesterday we walked in your garden.
Today, you are no longer beautiful.

A boy had once fallen through one of those windows in a shower of breaking glass.

The street seller gave up. Hauled herself to her feet, the sticks on her tray rattling. The flies buzzed up, annoyed at being disturbed. She swatted them weakly away. Scratched at her face. One of the Immish guards, finally, gave her a look. Almost a sorry look. She didn't notice. Wandered off down the Street of Closed Eyes. The flies buzzed around her.

Lord Selim Lochaiel, Lord of the Moon's Light, came out of

the gate again. Set off down the Street of Closed Eyes. Orhan set off after him. They walked across the Court of the Fountain. Down the Street of All Sorrows. Gold Street. The Street of Children. The Street of the South. Lord Lochaiel stopped to look at the goods on display in a tailor's. Walked on, went into a wine shop. Orhan loitered across the street a little while. Followed him in.

'Hello Orhan.'

'Hello Selim.'

'A drink?' Selim asked him.

'Thank you.'

Selim poured him a cup of iced wine.

'How are you? How is Bil? And your son?' Selim asked.

Well enough. No different to how they were when you last asked me. Poor. Angry.

Alive.

'How is Elolale?' Orhan asked. 'And the boys?'

Selim winced. '"The boys" have learnt how to scream at night. I can hear them from the other side of the house.'

'That will pass. If you're lucky. In several years.'

Orhan Emmereth giving advice on fatherhood!

Orhan paused. 'How is . . . How is Eloise?'

'As well as can be. Well enough. No different.' Selim paused. 'Darath is well enough, too, Orhan. If you're wondering.'

Orhan pushed his cup around the table. 'I wasn't.'

'Your inability to lie convincingly . . . is one of the reasons we're all in this mess.'

'I—'

'He—' Selim shook his head. 'Actually, you know, things are better now than they were. When was the last time anyone tried to kill you, for example? The city was on the point of collapse. Riots in the street, plague, looting, the false High Priestess murdered by a mob, and, now, look, we've got peace again. We've had peace for the last four years. Perhaps, in an odd kind of way, we should thank you.' He said with a bitter little smile, 'I know the Immish Great Council does.'

151

Orhan drank his wine. Better wine than he'd had for a long time. The cool of the ice – ah, God's knives, the cool of the ice in his mouth! Not had ice for a long time. Four years.

The perfect irony of everything. Everything he'd ever feared: Immish soldiers in the streets, camped in the gardens of the Emperor's very palace, the high families couldn't blow their noses without getting signed and sealed permission from the Immish first. Lord Cauvanh and Lord Mylt of the Great Council and a magelord. They said the Emperor himself had to bow to Lord Mylt.

Orhan had set fire to the palace and almost assassinated the Emperor and almost assassinated the High Priestess Thalia and let the demon loose in the heart of the city and killed something over a hundred people, including something over twenty people he personally knew. All to stop the Immish invading Sorlost.

Lord Emmereth, Warden of Immish! Such a cruel stupid joke. The ancient role of the Emmereth family, to laud it over the eastern upstarts, keep them under the thumb of the great Asekemlene Empire. And didn't that work out so well?

No, you are unfair to yourself, Orhan. The Immish didn't invade. You made very sure that didn't happen. No chance at all of the Immish invading. Not after Lord Tardein invited them in.

'Darath gave me this to give you,' said Selim. He put a silk purse on the table next to Orhan's cup. Orhan looked at it. 'It's not got a scorpion in it. It didn't last time, anyway.'

'He . . . I . . . Thank him for me,' said Orhan. 'Darath. Thank him. Tell him I'm grateful. As always.'

'He told me not to tell him what you said,' said Selim. 'As always.'

Well, that was pointless. As always. What do I expect, Orhan thought, that one day the palace gates will open and they'll tell me they're sorry, let me walk in? That Selim will look at me with something other than desperate embarrassment, *I'm only humouring him because I pity him, please someone get this wretched man out of my way*? He walked slowly back to the House of the East. Bil his wife was sitting with her son in the courtyard gardens. A strapping boy of four, tall for his age, glossy brown skin, red-gold curls, handsome face. His mother's face and his father's body, lucky thing. Bil laughed as the child threw a ball towards her, ran towards her shouting, hugged himself into her arms.

'My baby baby baby boy!'

No, Orhan, he thought then. The cruellest joke life ever played was to take a woman as beautiful and alive as Bilale Aviced, load her with wealth and wisdom and grace, and then give her blackscab. And then marry her to you. One day soon the boy would learn to ask questions: why has Mummy got no hands, Father? Why has Mummy got scars all over her skin? Why is our house full of whispers, Father? Why do people curse our name in the street?

Orhan picked the boy up. Kissed him. That strange rancid perfume scent of his hair. The perfect silk of his limbs. 'Hello Dion. Hello Bil. Are you having fun?'

Dion nodded. Squashed his nose into Orhan's face. 'I can throw the ball as high as the tallest tree in the garden!'

'Can you now? Clever boy.'

He'll never know he's not mine, thought Orhan. That I swear by Great Tanis, he'll never know.

Dion stuck his fingers up Orhan's nose and yanked. Hooted with laughter. Bil called out 'Dion!' helpless with laugher. The scabs moved on her face folding and crumpling; the rigid bits of scar tissue that couldn't move, that strained and ached. 'Dion, sweet one! Stop that!'

Orhan put the boy down and he ran back to his mother, still crowing. She sat down and he scrambled into her lap, put his hands on her face, smoothing it.

Orhan's sister Celyse came into the courtyard. She, too, smiled at the boy. Celyse sat down next to Bil. Ruffled her hand in Dion's hair.

'Orhan,' Celyse said. 'You've been out?'

'I went to see Selim.'

'How is he?'

'Well enough.'

'Did he say anything of any interest?'

'What do you think? No.'

'Look!' cried Dion, pointing at two pethe birds that had fluttered down into the lilac tree. Celyse turned away back to Dion. Relieved silence between her and Orhan, that they no longer had to speak.

I should have asked Selim how Symdle is doing, Orhan thought. How Holt is doing.

His sister's son. His sister's husband.

Ex-husband.

Ex-son.

Orhan took out the purse of money Darath had given Selim. Passed it over to Celyse. Dion grabbed at the gold tassels.

'You can have the bag,' Celyse said to Dion. He beamed.

'What is it?' Bil said to Orhan. She could see the weight of it in Celyse's hands.

Pause. 'Darath gave it to Selim to give to me.'

'Darath.' Bil's face went pale and thin. Her lips went pale and thin. 'I told you before, Orhan. We don't need his pity. Send it away.'

'I want the bag!' Dion shouted, reaching for it. 'Aunty Celyse said I could have the bag.'

'Buy him some new clothes,' said Orhan. 'Buy yourselves some new clothes.'

The coins disappeared into Celyse's pocket. She gave Dion the purse. He stuck his hand in it. White silk covering his hand to the wrist. Held it up, pressed the silk against Bil's face. Bil smiled.

Orhan thought: I killed his father. I sacrificed his father my sworn servant, watched him die in front of me . . . so that the Immish wouldn't invade.

Janush the doctor came into the courtyard. The last of the house's bondsmen, the only man who refused to leave when Orhan had dismissed the servants. Spare them, as he had spared the little serving girl of Bil's. 'Bound to you means I'm bound to you,'

Janush had only said. He nodded gravely as Dion showed him the tassels on the purse.

Orhan went upstairs to his study. Sat down at his desk. He could hear Dion, laughing at something, his laughter drifting up through the window. Orhan opened his desk, looked at the empty drawer, closed it again. He'd burned every sheet of paper in his house four years ago as the Immish marched through the city towards his house to arrest him. Never write down another word. Nothing anyone could ever twist up and use against him. The pile of papers, himself throwing oil on the blaze, trying to make it burn up faster, sweating and cursing. Seeing Bil's face and the boy's and Darath's in the flames as it burned. No books. No papers. Nothing anyone could ever, ever use.

My son's father is dead because I attempted a coup against my Emperor and my son's father fought for me and died.

My son's mother has no hands because she fought off assassins trying to kill him. Trying to kill him to punish me.

People curse my name because they think I betrayed the city.

No. Not think.

The truth, Orhan. People curse my name because I did betray the city.

The child's laughter turned suddenly to wailing. He must have fallen, hurt himself. 'Baby boy, it's all right, hush, hush,' Bil's voice crooned.

No books. No papers. Empty shelves. Empty drawers. Nothing, ever again, ever again. Orhan sat and stared at the wall.

The child's crying ceased as quickly as it had started. Bil comforting him. Celyse came into the room, opened the door without knocking, sniffed at the empty shelves as she always did. Tried not to look too pointedly at the patch on the wall where the plaster was crumbling, gold leaf and green paint flaking off.

'I'm going out. Spend the money before Bilale sends it back. Do you want anything yourself?'

'No.'

It must have taken her, oh, ten heartbeats to decide to use the money. Perhaps she'd fashion a wax doll and stick a few pins in it when she returned home.

Orhan said wearily, 'You can't blame Darath, Celyse.' Time and time again he told her that. Sometimes, if the birds were singing in the trees and the sun was shining and he hadn't left the house for a while to be mocked and hissed at, he might believe it himself.

Should say: 'Darath asked at the last to get involved in my plot against the Emperor. Darath had nothing to do with conceiving and planning it. Darath supported me, defended me, stood by me.'

Should say: 'Darath married his brother Elis off to my enemy March Verneth's daughter, to shore up support for me. Darath killed my enemy March Verneth when it became obvious that hadn't worked. Killed his brother's goodfather! For me!'

Should say: 'I cheated on him. I lied to him. When the Immish came, the plague was ravaging the city, Darath was sick. His brother Elis had just died. Darath had been locked in his house with his brother's corpse and his brother's dying widow, wracked with pain, terrified of death. The Immish turned up demanding entry, twenty soldiers, long spears, offers of a bargain, a doctor who claimed he had some miracle cure – who could blame him for giving in, confessing, blaming me for everything?'

'He loved you, Orhan,' Celyse said. Time and time again. 'I know he did. I envied you more than you can imagine, that Darath Vorley loved you more than anyone has ever and will ever love me. If you love someone like that . . . how can you betray them? Throw them to the wolves like that?'

I loved him. Ah, God's knives, Celyse, I loved him so much. 'He's alive and well, Celyse. Putting his life back together. I . . .'

I'm glad. Glad he's alive. Glad he's happy. I loved him. So I want him to be happy. God's knives, Celyse, would you think I was a better man if I hated him? Wished he had been brought down with me into ruin? Would you think I was a better man if I'd stuck the knife into him first, blamed him for everything, absolved myself by ruining him? I could have destroyed him to save myself. I didn't. Because I want him to live.

'I . . .'

The child cried out from the garden. A loud crow of triumph over something. Bil shouted with delight. Janush laughed.

Celyse said, 'And your son, Orhan? Your wife? Janush your bondsman? Me? Everyone in your household, who depend on you, who had nothing aside from your name and your wealth? What did you want for them?'

Bil's hands are like chewed-up leather. Dried splintered sand-scoured wood. Sword wounds running down her face. Sword wounds sewn up and knitted together over the blackscab scars that cover her face. She had almost died saving the boy's life. The boy had almost died before he had really even lived. We dismissed the servants, we threw them out to starve in the streets.

Orhan thought: love and desire like I have for Darath – sexual love is the most selfish thing in the world.

Celyse went out shopping. Bil played with Dion. Orhan sat in his study staring at his empty shelves.

The city of Sorlost had been beautiful. Rich and beautiful. Terrifying. Brilliant. It had once ruled the world – or controlled it, might perhaps be the better term, bought and sold it, traded in human lives, countries' futures, kings' thrones. The gold coins of the Sekemleth Empire that were worth more than whole cities. The word of a Sorlostian merchant that could overturn a kingdom. Its city walls were made of solid bronze. Its Emperor's palace was of white porcelain. Its streets were full of starving children. Its beggars ate rancid scraps from golden plates. Its God must have blood, that the dying find death and those waiting to live be born. And Orhan Emmereth had sacrificed his son's father, and his sister's marriage, and his friends, and his wife, and his lover, to save it. And its streets were full of starving children. And its beggars ate rancid scraps from golden plates.

Celyse came back with new clothes for Dion. Orhan was summoned to see, the boy shouting with excitement, 'Come! Come!'; Bil's face was glowing, watching Celyse dress him in a soft shirt of green and silver, scrolled flowers, 'Look,' she said, 'oh, look, how beautiful he is.' He was. He danced before them proud of his finery. Spun round and round, shouting, preening himself. A funny little strut like a bird. Celyse had a new dress for Bil also, pale yellow, like dawn sunlight against the sunset fire of her hair. Dion rejoiced at that.

'Pretty Mummy.'

Bil laughed. Her face went pink, joy- and shame-flushed. 'Say thank you to Aunt Celyse, Dion.'

The child nodded gravely. Hugged Celyse with thin boy's hands. She kissed his gleaming hair. 'Thank you, Aunty Celyse.'

'Thank Darath,' Celyse said to Orhan and to Bil.

'And I bought you this,' Celyse said to Dion. 'Now you're such a fine-dressed young man, here's a toy for you.' A spinning top, painted red, spiralled with silver. Dion took it breathlessly. He didn't know what it was, turned it in his hands admiring it, shook it. Threw it, just to see. It clattered on the stone floor. Orhan winced.

'Oh, Dion,' Bil burst out. 'Look, you might have broken it. Be careful. You need to take care with things.'

'It's all right,' Orhan said. He crouched down beside Dion. 'It's a spinning top. See, Dion?' Set the toy spinning. It was a good one, smooth and fast. The silver flashed as it spun. Dion stared. Delighted.

Dion put out his hand to touch it. It rattled over onto its side on the floor. 'Oh.' Orhan set it spinning. Dion laughed and laughed. Dion put out his hand and stopped it. Orhan laughed with him, spun it again.

'It's a bird!' shouted Dion.

'It's not a bird, my baby silly baby baby boy,' said Bil.

'Do it again!' shouted Dion. 'Again! Please!'

Celyse crouched down, tried to set the top working. She spun it badly and it rattled on its side, making a nasty sound on the stone. Dion and Orhan laughed at her.

'It is like a bird,' Orhan said to Dion. 'I see what you mean.'

'Like a fish,' said Dion, looking over towards the gardens where they had once had long golden fish in a fountain that was now dry and unpleasant with stone dust.

'I can't make it work,' said Celyse. 'Show me, Orhan.'

'There's a knack to the way you hold your wrist,' said Orhan. 'See?'

'No.' She spun it badly, made it grate on the floor.

'My turn!' shouted Dion, and threw it.

'Careful,' said Bil. 'Careful, Dion.'

'A bird and a fish and a jewel,' said Dion, running with the top in his hand held out in front.

Orhan went out that evening. A long mindless walk. Dressed in the cheap clothes of a poor man – and of course he was now a poor man, he barely had to pretend – tattered greys and creams with lurid coloured trim, cheap flashy jewels, his hair covered in a green and gold headcloth: he looked enough unlike himself that he could not be recognized. Spared the jeers. And no one really knew his face. His name hissed with revulsion, Orhan Emmereth the Betrayer, Demon-Friend, he had become a demon himself, his name haunted the city, for all the ruin that had befallen them his name was invoked in blame. But no one really knew his face. Thus the one thing he had left, walking, mindless in circles across the city, watching other men's lives. Spies watched him and knew him, reported in his doings. Item: Orhan Emmereth sat in a wine shop, drank a cup of cheap wine, left. Item: Orhan Emmereth watched a knife fight, betted one dhol on the outcome, lost, left. Item: Orhan Emmereth sat by a fountain in the Square of Children, stared at nothing, left.

The streets were darker than they had been. Buildings coming into greater decay. Empty houses, dead windows like the windows of the palace. Deeping fever had come to Sorlost in the demon's wake; whole households had died bleeding and screaming; houses sat boarded up and abandoned, falling into ruin, overgrown with weeds, birds nesting in their walls. Cursed. Rubble and ash where buildings had burned in the subsequent rioting, not been rebuilt. On one street, rebuilding had started, stopped, started, stopped again. Orhan's dream to improve the lot of the poorest in the city. A group of beggars were bedding down among the building stone. What was to have been a portico with Orhan's name on it made a convenient place to rest their bottles of drink. An argument was in progress. A bottle broke with a stench of firewine. Voices raised shouting. In Pernish, the accent of Cen Andae.

Refugees from the demon's wars, crowding into the city with stories the city did not believe. Soldiers, mostly. Strong, healthy young men. They had the strength in them to run away. They marched out of their city's walls to defend their people, and so they could run away. So they said. More and more of them, every year: they crawled around the gates of the city, begging, pleading, and the people of Sorlost, in their infinite compassion, let them in to crawl among the rubble of the city's backstreets. They set up altars and prayer stones to their gods, muttered warnings, were scorned and disbelieved.

'We are the strong ones, the soldiers, and we ran from him. He will come here. He will fight you. He will conquer the world. Fear him.'

'Cowards. Weak. They are weak. We are strong.'

On the foundation block for a column they or others like them had carved a god face, two crude eyes above a beaked mouth.

Little wars. Little kings fighting far far away across the endless desert. No concern to us. Never was, never will be. Sorlost the Unconquered, the Unconquerable, we need not concern ourselves with these petty things. Our soldiers will come tomorrow and scour the heathen carving out. We let them in, give them our pity – what more do they want?

'Why does he do it?' Bil had asked Orhan. 'Why does he do it, Marith Altrersyr? What does he want?'

'To conquer the world,' Orhan had said, astonished at her sudden idiocy.

'Yes, but,' she frowned, 'why?'

You with your maimed hands, your scars, you almost saw your child die before you . . . should you not understand? But . . . Orhan thought: but, is it the same? Just violence?

'And his men . . . They are a thousand miles from their homes, their families. So many of them will die. But they follow him.'

'They are poor,' Orhan had said at last. 'They are a people of violence.'

'Many places are poor,' Bil had said. 'And don't do this.'

'We, of all people, should know what might drive someone to these things,' Orhan had said to Celyse later. 'And yet . . . I don't know. Is it the same? Why they follow him? Why do they do this? We kill and plot and stab each other in the darkness, there is violence here, there is murder, there is cruelty and rape and theft and all of the things that the demon's army inflicts. We are cruel, bad people. No better than the men of the White Isles, I am certain. Men die every night in our streets. But we don't . . . I wouldn't . . .'

'No?' Celyse had said.

'No!' Orhan had cried out.

It was the truth. Orhan stooped, placed a single bronze dhol at the base of the refugee god's carved face, walked on.

His walking took him to the Street of Yellow Roses, the wine shop he sometimes went to there. No desire for more wine. But the sound of voices, the music of a flute, the smell of spiced food . . . Faded old men lost in their memories, living in the clouds of the past. Old tired men, who like all old men had in their lives done things they had cause to regret. There he could sit in peace.

A game of yenthes was just starting. The first player drew yellow. Sucked his teeth. Yellow and blue tiles rattled on the copper surface of the table. The player spread an arc of tiles. A semicircle, like a picture of a domed roof. The audience murmured. A few nods. His opponent drew yellow also. Another murmur from the audience at that. Looked at the pattern on the copper table. Smiled. The tiles clattered down, changing the yellow and blue dome into a circle like the sun. The first player drew red. A spiral, dancing across the table. His opponent drew white. A square, one side open like a door. A circle again, white and silver. A diamond, silver and green. Dancing tiles, and the soft rattle as they came down.

The Pearl Singer was sitting in the corner opposite Orhan, staring at the floor, a cup resting in his hands. Long thin withered fingers. Nails bitten down to the quick. Dried bloodflakes on his fingertips, from where he scratched and scratched at his eyes. Moved on from drinking firewine to drinking firewine with hatha mixed in it. He who had once been a poet such as sang in the houses of the mighty, performed before the Emperor to be rewarded with a pearl arm-ring, sang of desire so that the noble ladies of Sorlost followed him with their eyes, sent him feathers and cut gemstones, let him caress them naked beneath lilac trees. His coat was embroidered with pink flowers. A woman's coat. Tattered to pieces. Smelled of stale piss. *Today you are no longer beautiful.* Orhan dreaded some nights that the man would get up, try to sing.

In the backstreet slums the plague still lingered. Pestilence sank into the city's earth. Sweating faces bleeding begging for death.

The yenthes game ended. The first player won. The audience exchanged winnings and losings. Clicking sound, like heavy storm rainfall, bone on bone, as the box of tiles was shaken for another game. It shivered over Orhan: pleasant sound, like someone running cool fingers over his skin. Hissing of rainfall on a pool of water. The tiles falling over and over, pouring over each other like sand. Shapes and colours, patterns, pictures, falling together, every possibility of shapes and patterns and colours the tiles could form. A game of luck, as much as skill. The Pearl Singer raised his head. Blurred misted eyes. His head moved with the slow heaviness of dreams, looking for the sound.

Chapter Seventeen

Bil said, 'I am going to the Great Temple, Orhan.' She went there often now. The only place she went. Said sometimes, and Orhan was never sure if she was joking, that Great Tanis had heard her prayers, kept them alive.

'Would you . . .' Hesitation. A smile for him, weary and knowing him. 'Would you like to come?'

She was wearing a grey dress, pale grey like the robes the priestesses sometimes wore. Long, loose sleeves, a high neck. Orhan had thought she was more ashamed of her scars now. Hadn't understood, for a long time, that the way she dressed now was because she no longer cared about her scars.

'I'll come.' The God alone knew why. Something to do with himself. Something that wasn't staring at empty walls. Bil smiled. Trying to look pleased with him.

They walked out down Felling Street into a city burning already in the morning sunshine, white light beating off white stone. A child's voice shouted and Orhan almost flinched at it, waiting for it to be a voice shouting at him, calling him all the things he was. Bil smiled. All these children, every one of them, she seemed to love.

They walked through streets that were noisy with people, street girls, beggars, more children in rags and filled with laughter, merchants touting all the things in life a man could ever need. Orhan braced himself for jeers, but no one noticed them. Just two people, man and wife in simple clothing, taking a walk. A troop of Immish soldiers went by, didn't notice them. Orhan's eyes followed the soldiers. How could they not see him? How could they not know? They, too, looked weary. Preoccupied.

The ragged children ran past the soldiers. One of the street girls shouted a price, was ignored. The soldiers turned a corner and were gone in the hot dust. Some soldiers, taking a walk, looking hot and weary and preoccupied. Who cared? There is absolutely no reason in all the world to care about any of this. There never was. Some soldiers. Taking a walk. God's knives, that's hardly a catastrophe unmatched in a thousand human lifetimes. Everything I imagined came to pass, the Immish occupied our city, and that's the result. Some soldiers. Taking a walk.

In Beating Heart Lane a food seller was offering skewers of meat up cheap. Two Immish guards stopped to buy some. They were wearing bright jackets over their armour, red leather sandals on their feet. On first glance, they might have come from Sorlost. They leaned against a wall eating, licking grease off their lips.

'Buy a flower, sirs?' a street seller called to them in Immish, a young girl with a bright face. 'A paper flower, for your wife back in Alborn? A silk flower, for your mistress here in Sorlost?'

'What kind for the woman who spurns me?' one of the soldiers called back to her in passable Literan. She laughed, went up to him and kissed him on the cheek.

In the Court of the Broken Knife a woman was sitting weeping beneath the statue. Someone was always weeping in the Court of the Broken Knife. In the far corner of the square a shrine had been set up, a lump of wood bleached white, garlanded with ribbons and tiny white bones. The statue in the centre of the square stared away up into the clouds, faceless, nameless, eaten stone like leprosy, ripped away by wind and sand and dust. The broken knife blade in its right hand stabbing downwards. Futile gesture. Stabbing empty air. Scented oil glistening on the broken blade of the knife.

That looked obscene. The burden in its left hand was raised to the heavens. A shapeless nameless eaten lump. We kill for nothing. We die for nothing. We fight and fight, struggle, triumph, fail. The figure stood holding aloft its burden. Orhan was struck by a sense that it was not triumphant but in pain.

'They say you can see its face more clearly,' said Bil.

'Its face? What?'

'Its face,' said Bil. 'They say you can see its face.'

The woman shouted out, 'We carved this for Him a thousand years ago. From the beginning of the world it has stood, waiting for Him. Soon He will come to claim it. The knife will sharpen. The burden will grow greater. The knife will strike down. He is returned in glory! Worship Him!'

A refugee from Cen Andae came into the square, prostrated himself full length at the statue's feet. Shouted out, 'Death! Death! Death!'

Dead. Dead. A boy's face, falling backwards in a shower of coloured glass. Tam Rhyl's voice as he died, gasping out, '*What have you done, Orhan?*'

Balkash has fallen, they say, and its citadel is torn down. The demon met the men of Ander in the field and routed them; his magicians raised the tempest to drown their city, the Sea of Grief is choked with their dead. His dragons came down upon the Neir Forest and left it a barren wasteland. The demon spreads his shadow across the world. Vomits up human blood. We sit and hide, and it is nothing, ignore it and it will all be gone.

'Come on,' Bil said. She shuddered. It was so cold in the square for a moment, and surely the air smelled suddenly of blood.

They walked through the Street of Flowers, going more hurriedly, Bil looking askance at Orhan as they passed Darath's house. The gates were closed. Beautifully carved onyx, a garland of black stone flowers on the edge of fading, overripe petals about to curl and fall.

Dead things. I'm sorry, Darath. I loved you.

All the things . . . all the things I made you do.

Two beggars slumped against the house's walls, waiting to be beaten up and moved on.

'We should have gone the long way,' said Bil. 'I'm sorry. That was thoughtless of me.' Orhan said nothing. Nothing to say.

They stopped before the Great Temple. It crouched there sucking in the heat around it, shivering cold like it was carved of black ice. Huge as thought. Baleful. Loving. Beating and beating before the eyes like a heart.

The soldiers should stare at me, thought Orhan. The Temple should scream out to the God to strike me down.

Crowds around it, milling and talking, edgy and afraid. Immish soldiers with spears. Still faint traces of fire and blood on the square's worn stones, underneath the Immish soldiers' feet. They walked towards the steps up to the high narrow doorway. Black wood with the knots in the wood like a beast's eyes. The great clawmarks in the door, at head height.

'Dear Lord,' whispered Bil as they walked through the crushing dark of the entranceway. 'Dear Lord, Great Tanis Who Rules All Things, from the fear of life and the fear of death, release us. We live. We die. For these things, we are grateful.'

'Dear Lord, Great Tanis Who Rules All Things, from the fear of life and the fear of death, release us,' Orhan echoed. 'We live. We die. For these things, we are grateful.'

They walked through the dark of the entranceway into the Great Chamber, candles burning in massed ranks blazing against the bronze walls, so many candles, so much light, so much fire burning for the joy of living, the flames dancing, rising to the heavens, the light dancing burning the eyes, the warmth, the heat of the candles the metal walls the bodies of the worshippers calling on the power of the God with the candle flames reflected in their faces, the priestesses kneeling, grey robes like rainclouds and jewelled masks. The child High Priestess knelt before the High Altar. Bil jerked when she saw her. Thin and small, hunched up. Her fine child's curls falling over her face.

A sacrifice night tonight. Orhan had forgotten. He tried to

remember the moon from last night. Not a new moon, he thought. A waxing moon. A man. Not a child.

A more popular choice than it had been for years, giving yourself up in offering to the God.

Bil went over to an altar. Silver metal, a long low bar of silver reflecting back the candles, glowing white against the candle-lit bronze. She knelt, stretched out the ruined stumps of her hands, bowed her head in prayer. Orhan knelt and prayed beside her. A rational man. But a fearful one.

'Please. Please, oh Lord, Great Tanis Who Rules All Things. Please. Just let them live. Bil. Dion. My sister. Darath. Just let them live.'

Marith Altrersyr is a boy, a petty warlord in the far north, king of nowhere important, what idiots these people are to think of him, to fear him. He will soon be defeated, killed, slink back to his home in shame. It is all a story. It is all happening an eternity away.

Great Tanis. Please believe me.

'I will come back this evening,' said Bil as they left. 'For the sacrifice.'

'If you want to.'

'I should bring Dion again soon. He will soon be old enough.'

'For the sacrifice?'

She looked horrified. 'Not when that is happening, no. Of course not, Orhan. But to pray. To make an offering. He is old enough now to do it properly.'

'Yes. Yes, of course.'

He is not that much younger than the High Priestess, Orhan thought. The High Priestess Thalia's existence was now . . . ignored. Never mentioned. An inconvenient thing. The child Demerele who had been torn to pieces within the Temple itself was now . . . ignored. An equally inconvenient thing. The High Priestess Sissaleena is the High Priestess and was the High Priestess and does it well. Do not speak of it. Nobody speaks of it. All is well and well and thrice well.

A child of eight.

She had just turned four, when she was dedicated to her role.

She takes it better than Demerele-who-never-existed, thought Orhan. She was so young when she started in it, she had no idea what it is she does.

She drew the lot. If Great Tanis had not wanted her, she would not have drawn the red lot.

'Little thing,' said Bil, as they turned to leave.

They walked back in the blazing heat. Midday sunshine scouring away all the shadows. Bil panted, wiping sweat from her brow with the stump of her hand.

'I wish we still had the litter,' she said irritably. Then she laughed. 'But all this walking has made me strong. I'm slimmer than I ever was.' She wiped sweat out of her eyes.

They went the long way round, avoiding Darath's house. In the Court of the Broken Knife someone had put a paper crown on the head of the statue, a garland of red flowers around its neck. Three people prayed at its feet.

Bil looked at the statue. 'Is that what he looked like?'

Orhan looked at the statue. The eaten face. The knife. 'Yes,' he said. 'Yes. It does look like him.'

When they got home, there were two guards standing at the gates of the House of the East, waiting. Selim Lochaiel stood with them. And beside him, Lord Cauvanh the Immishman.

Selim said, 'You need to come with me, Orhan. Now.'

Selim said, 'I'm sorry.'

Chapter Eighteen

White porcelain gates opened before them. So fine they were almost transparent. White porcelain flowers, petals soft and full, white porcelain leaves. The air had a faint music to it. They went in under the gate of the palace into a courtyard of pools and fountains, and the fountains were made of gold. The water was coloured to look like liquid gold. Lord Cauvanh dipped his hand into the cascade of a fountain. Drew his hand out covered in drops of liquid gold.

Lord Cauvanh smiled. 'I was born in the White City. I have travelled to Chathe, to Maun, to Cen Andae. I have lived here for five years. It still amazes me.'

They turned away from the glories and the grandeur. Slunk through a little bare doorway into the warren of passages and staircases that the servants would use. Up stairs, down hallways, and everything there was dusty and unkempt. Bare wood, bare plaster. Dead flies dried out in patches of light.

Lord Cauvanh opened a door, ushered them into a room painted and furnished all in pale green. On one of the walls there was a jewelled map of Irlast.

Orhan didn't know whether to laugh or to weep.

'Sit down.' Lord Cauvanh pulled out a chair for him. It and the table it was paired with were set with milky pale jade.

'Does it have to be here?' he asked Lord Cauvanh. 'This room?' Lord Cauvanh only frowned at him.

The room's main door was gilded silver. It was closed; Lord Cauvanh was looking at it, waiting. It opened and another man entered. Tall and thin, with dark hair and skin that was the colour of fatty meat, dressed in the robes of the Immish Great Council, fur-trimmed, thick and heavy, stifling in the desert heat. Lord Mylt, one of the six members of the Immish Great Council. Thus one of the most powerful men in Irlast. Orhan stood up. Bowed his head.

Lord Mylt said, 'Cauvanh. Selim. Orhan Emmereth.' Distant, cool, dull voice. But his eyes . . . Something, as he looked at Orhan . . . Trying to look as he should look . . . Orhan thought madly: is he afraid? Of me?

'You may go now, Selim,' said Lord Mylt. 'You too, Cauvanh.'

The man frowned. 'My Lord?'

'Go.'

Selim Lochaiel rose hurriedly, bowed low, went out. Lord Cauvanh rose, bowed.

'We will speak later, Cauvanh,' Lord Mylt said in his distant voice.

'My Lord.' Cauvanh went out, and Orhan was alone with Lord Mylt.

The sound of footsteps, and a metal sound, outside the door. Guards. Sword blades.

'Will you kill me now?' Trying to keep his voice strong.

'Lord Emmereth,' Lord Mylt said. 'I . . . I do not want to kill you. I want you to . . . to help me.

'For ten years . . .' Lord Mylt smiled bleakly. 'Let me gather myself. Tell you properly. From the beginning, then . . . For ten years, your enemy March Verneth the Lord of the Moon's Light was conspiring with the Immish Great Council for an Immish invasion of Sorlost. For the last three of those years, your friend Tamleth Rhyl the Lord of the Far Waters was also, separately and quite independently, conspiring with the Immish Great Council for an Immish invasion of Sorlost. We had twenty thousand troops under arms. A magelord who swears he could have destroyed your famous walls. Food and water and fodder buried in stores across the eastern desert waiting for us. We even sent out a mage, to scout out the desert and the rumours of . . . things there, before the army was to march through.'

Orhan sat very still.

'We were three days' march from here when your conspiracy unfolded. Had things gone to plan, your friend Lord Rhyl was to have opened the gates to us and welcomed us as saviours following the outrageous attempt on the life of your Emperor by . . . you.' Lord Mylt said, 'I was the Immish point of contact for both March Verneth and Tam Rhyl. I was the Immish point of contact for your agents in Alborn. I personally wrote the confession that you were to give before they burned you. So I think I can say with some confidence that all of this is true.'

A bird flew past the window in a flash of shadows. So close Orhan could hear the sound of its wings. Lord Mylt said, '"*The Immish have been occupying Sorlost for the last four years, Orhan. And, actually, you know, things are better now than they were.*" All my life, I have worked to see this. My life's work. My life's goal. I failed and I failed, but I got here in the end.'

What can Orhan say?

'You know the cost of it as well as I, my Lord Emmereth.' A weary little pause. 'I did not work all those years only to see it all about to crumble away.'

'The Emperor is a child who speaks only Immish,' said Orhan. 'I do not think you need have any fears that the people of Sorlost will rebel. Keep the gold flowing, and who cares who rules here? Apart from you?'

Lord Mylt said with his teeth all on edge, 'I have no fear at all of the people of Sorlost, Lord Emmereth.' A pause. 'The sellsword company I recommended to your agents, however . . . with hindsight . . . may have been a mistake.'

Aha. Aha. God's knives. What can one possibly say?

Lord Mylt said, 'After the demon destroyed Bakh, he gave it to the Immish as a sign of friendship. Bakh and all of Cen Andae. A kind gift. We on the Immish Great Council sent him grain and gold and men and horses, acclaimed him as King of Immier and Cen Elora, made him a nobleman of Immish. Gave him most of Cen Andae back again. We planned to rebuild Bakh, repopulate it from Immish. The ground there is so poisoned with corpses that no building will stand one stone on another. Of every ten workmen we send to work there five die of sickness and two go mad with grief. A fine bargain: we have a barren dead wasteland; he has men and wealth and supplies for the army with which he has sworn to conquer the world.'

Orhan said, 'But I'm sure he is as proud of his status as a nobleman of Immish as he is of that of King of All Irlast.'

Lord Mylt ignored him. 'Immish is his ally. Immish kneels at his feet and fawns on him. The greatest desire of the Great Council now is for him to send us even an emissary to stare at us with contempt. My colleagues on the Great Council have already drawn up great plans, feasts and festivities, gifts, wonders, tributes, should he deign to send his pot boy to lord it over us.'

'Perhaps . . .' said Orhan slowly, 'that is the wisest course.' Knew what was coming. Pretended he did not know. I saw the demon's eyes, once. His face was nothing but blood, and he was beautiful.

He thought then: I wonder if he remembers me?

Lord Mylt said, 'The demon gave Immish a dead wasteland. Now Immish will give the demon . . . Well . . .'

Silence. Even great men have some shame buried. Lord Mylt fidgeted with his hands. 'He has burned this very building once already. And, of course, his wife . . .' Looked away from Orhan, at the map on the wall, and then his face went pale and he looked away at nothing. 'As one of my fellow Council members put it, "When a wolf is at the door, rather he eats one's prize sheep than one's own children."'

Silence.

Orhan said, 'Yes. I suppose it is.'

Lord Mylt said, 'I would not tell you this, were I not desperate. I . . .' His hand tightened around his cup, his knuckles white. A fierce look to his face. A disgusted look. 'Your Emperor kneels to me. You great High Lords of the Sekemleth Empire bow down to me. My life's work. I will not see it thrown away.' It's coming. You can say no, Orhan. Refuse and walk out. He won't come here, it is inconceivable that he will come here, this is my life, this is Sorlost, it cannot happen here, to me. Lord Mylt said, 'You wanted to rebuild your city. You wanted to make it great and worthy again. You . . . you have seen the demon's face, Lord Emmereth. So I beg you now: help me.'

For a moment Orhan saw something there behind him, a shadow reflected on the mosaic tiles of the map on the wall. The Sekemleth Empire gold and yellow diamonds, Ith in shadow, Illyr, the White Isles at the far eastern edge.

I promised. I swore to myself. To Dion. To Bil. Great Tanis, can I never be forgiven for what I've done?

'I know – I have a contact,' Lord Mylt said. 'In . . .' He blinked. His hand grasped tight around his wine cup. 'I have a contact in Marith Altrersyr's court. One of Marith Altrersyr's companions, his captains. One of his friends. He has . . . had some thoughts about his own position. He is an ambitious man, could be persuaded to do certain things. But we in Immish are of course the demon's ally, and my contact knows that, does not trust me. Thus I need someone who is not connected with Immish to help me.'

'Why me?' The dull stupid question. 'I failed. I am no one. A poor man who is spat on in the street.' If I am the best you can do, Orhan thought, I will go home now and cut Dion's throat.

Lord Mylt placed a purse on the table. Yellow silk, like the Emperor's diadem. Symbolic. Cruel. No – merely thoughtless 'Here is gold for you to . . . cease to be nothing, Lord Emmereth. Cauvanh will help you, Lord Emmereth. He is a useful man. Very clever. I doubt I have to warn you not to trust him. All of your dealings with my contact in the demon's court . . . he must not know, now, that you are working with me. The risk must be yours alone. Sorlost's alone. Of course you see that.' The certainty returning to Lord Mylt's voice as he held the purse out. Gold is confidence. We are the richest empire the world has ever known, Orhan thought. They say the demon cannot be killed. But there is nothing in the end that cannot be bought.

'My contact and I already have an understanding,' Lord Mylt said. 'He would like to see certain things happen. Aspires to . . . higher things than he currently is.' Lord Mylt rattled the yellow silk purse he held. 'Let us see what my contact will do, then, if you encourage him to dream of higher things.'

There is peace in sitting in this cool green room at the top of a high tower, the breeze blowing, a faint scent of incense from the Temple, so much clearer than the squalor of candlelight and prayer. Two men sitting talking, seeking power, in the Temple they kneel and trust the God, beg Him, in this cool green room we are alive, take some action on the world, plot great things. Here we began all this. Here we shall hope and pretend to bring it to an end. Item: Orhan Emmereth will change the world. Having come so far, sacrificed Darath's love, sacrificed his wife's hands, he cannot now say that he is frightened, that he will not do it. My wife, my son, my life, my heart, Orhan thought. All of these things I will offer up, because I cannot turn away now after what I have already done and what I have already lost. He saw again the boyish face, beautiful, blood-soaked. The voice crying out, 'I'll kill you, then.' The mad grey eyes and the broken glass.

'This is a city built of dreams,' Orhan said.

'I think we are done, then,' Lord Mylt said. 'Lord Lochaiel will see you out. We will talk again soon.' Echoes and echoes of the past where he might once have hoped.

Chapter Nineteen

In the north, they say, beyond the desert, in the demon's lands, in the north the world truly dies at Year's Renewal, the trees put forth no leaves, no flowers bloom, no birds sing, the sun is hidden, the earth is frozen into ice. At Year's Renewal in the north the world is truly dead and reborn. Orhan thought: this is how it must feel, what it must look like. The street children, the hatha eaters, the Immish soldiers marching with bored and boring men's faces, the grandeur, the filth in the streets – so different, so strange. Ghosts. And yet . . . I acted to save this city, Orhan thought. It doesn't matter. It never mattered. Soon we shall die, I think, all of us, whatever I try to do. I will die in pain and all that I love will die in pain, as Darath cursed me. Yet . . . Groping for words, for feelings. Yet . . . I am glad I acted as I did. Look, Orhan! You gave the city . . . a few extra months of violent intrigue, before the Immish turned up. But think of them, just think of them, out there in the desert, hiding in the dust, and then they got the news: Lord Rhyl has failed! Lord Emmereth has won! You'll have to go off home again. Hang your swords back on the wall. Wait a few months.

Orhan thought: could I ask Lord Mylt to write it all down for Darath? Recite it to him? Do you hear this, Darath, do you hear this, oh you people of Sorlost? As you fall beneath the demon's spears, know it to be true: in the beginning, when we were all innocent, Orhan Emmereth was right!

After he left Lord Mylt he had to go back to the Court of the Broken Knife, to look. Fewer people gathered there: a hatha eater scratching bloody eyes in the corner, which was only fitting; a young man with bruises on his hands leaning against the statue's base. A half-naked child flying a scarlet kite.

'A dhol? A dhol?' the hatha eater begged.

'Fuck you all!' the young man shouted. Another man punched at him. The young man kicked and punched back. The two of them fighting, grunting, all sweat and spit and bleeding until the attacker was down and the young man was kicking him.

'A dhol? A dhol?'

The young man ran off. His attacker staggered away.

A woman in the clothes of Immier or Cen Elora knelt before the statue scattering flowers. The statue's eaten face smiled into the horizon, blind and smug. The yellow light of Sorlost framed it. Strained yellow-blue sky, the thrusting leprous grey stone. A gust of hot wind stirring the dust.

Orhan spat in the dust before the statue, petty absurd gesture that made him feel absurd. 'One of your friends is selling you,' he said aloud to the statue. 'You have swords. But we have gold. Ha!' The two purses laughed at the boy from the pocket of his coat. His walk home took him past Darath's house, then down the Street of Yellow Roses. Neither were quite on the way, but not too far off the way, he was thinking, he often walked this way.

Excuses, Orhan?

Darath's house was silent, hunched over itself. The wine shop in the Street of Yellow Roses was open. The shop boy was outside, stacking rubbish in a careful heap. Strong smell of wine and old food. And a flash of patterned colours: someone had broken a cup and a plate. The doorcurtain moved in a gust of wind. Orhan found himself going in. Sat at his table. The two old men sitting playing yenthes, the old woman watching them. Click of the tiles.

Smiles, nodding heads. The Pearl Poet sat in the corner, silent, had never left, was silent there dead and still, a pitiful thing. The shopkeeper had bought a songbird in a cage, since he had been here . . . yesterday. It sat in a wooden cage pecking at the feathers of its breast. The shopkeeper brought him a cup of the wine he drank, a dish of warm bread.

'Orhan.'

Darath came into the wine shop. Came over to him.

Knives in his head.

Loveyouloveyouloveyouloveyouloveyouloveyouloveyouloveyouloveyou

Ox on his tongue. Stone on his tongue. What do you say?

I love you. I'm sorry.

Forgive me. Please.

loveyouloveyouloveyouloveyouloveyouloveyouloveyouloveyou-loveyou

The Pearl Poet raised his head, looked with hatha-blurred blind eyes. Knew and saw. One of the old men coughed. 'Clever play, that.' Bone tiles rattled on the table. Voices murmured, discussing the yenthes game. The old woman said, 'Another plate of bread?'

A man walks into a wine shop. Not the kind of thing you see every day.

loveyouloveyouloveyouloveyouloveyouloveyouloveyouloveyou-loveyou

Darath said, 'Orhan.' Sat down opposite him. Neither of them spoke. The yenthes tiles made circles, spirals, sunbursts.

You're going to die, Darath. We're all going to die.

loveyouloveyouloveyouloveyouloveyouloveyouloveyouloveyou-loveyou

Darath was wearing a green shirt with pearl buttons. The pearls winked milky eyes at him. His hair was greying. Almost all grey. His beautiful gold-black curls. Wrapped a strand of Darath's hair around his fingers once, pulled it tight, Darath had had longer hair then, long curls down his back. Ah, God's knives, the memories of Darath's hair as Darath bent his head down over him.

'Orhan,' said Darath again. The yenthes tiles rattled. Laughter as one of the players made a particularly clever move.

What do you want? Come to jeer at me? See what I'm spending your money on?

loveyouloveyouloveyouloveyouloveyouloveyouloveyouloveyouloveyou

'Selim said you'd be here.'

'Did he?'

'He was . . . worried about you.'

'Why?'

'You mean, "thank you"?' Darath sipped Orhan's wine. Made a face. 'Come home with me,' Darath said.

'You hate me,' said Orhan.

'Fucking bastard, I should slap you. I don't hate you. Great Tanis knows, I should hate you.'

The shopkeeper snapped at the shop boy that he'd left the rubbish too near the doorway, that it would attract beggar children, put off customers. The Pearl Singer was watching them, smiling at them.

'There's a room,' said Orhan. 'Upstairs. Here. Now. Come on.'

Orhan held his hand out.

Darath took it.

Jolt of fire. Clutched tight. Nails dug in. The skin on Darath's hand was rough. *You're dying, Darath. You might as well be dead.* Up the stairs. Through the door. A storeroom, a broken table, a broken chair, dust gathered, a ragged bed.

'I'm sorry. I love you, Darath.'

Darath's hands tugging at Orhan's clothes. Darath's hands around Orhan's neck. Orhan's waist. Orhan's crotch. 'Shut up.'

'You thought I'd slept with him,' said Orhan. 'The demon. You accused me of betraying the city to him out of lust.'

'God's knives, did I?' Darath's hands opening Orhan's clothes. Darath's hair falling over his face as he bent his head down. Black-silver, where once it had been gold-black.

'I love you. I'm sorry, Darath. I'm sorry about Elis. I'm sorry.

I'm sorry. Darath. The Immish have sold us to the demon. We'll all die. I love you.'

'Shut up.'

'I was right. I was right. Everything, everything I did, all the pain, all the bloodshed, the deaths, we're doomed, the demon will bring the fire down on us . . . but I was right. Did Selim tell you that? I was right. I love you. I was right. About everything.'

He came in Darath's mouth. Screamed out tears.

'I know. I love you too. Shut up.'

Later they went back to Darath's house. The onyx gates opened almost joyfully, closed silently with a look almost of peace. Lemon trees in the gardens, the lemons almost ripe, just tinted still with green; an almond tree flowering; a great mass of purple hyacinths as cool as twilight. Gods, the scent of hyacinths, do you remember, do you remember, weddings, grieving, long lonely nights . . .

'You've got a new statue.'

'Yes.'

A young man, carved in white marble, kneeling, veiled.

Darath said, 'Don't talk about it, Orhan.'

The house itself unchanged, but silent. Fewer servants, more unkempt. A beautiful boy with red hair to his waist came out of a doorway and glared at Orhan and Orhan glared back.

Darath said, 'Oops.'

'Doesn't matter.'

'Are you lying to me again already?'

Orhan said honestly, 'No.'

'God's knives, you're still a bloody terrible liar, Orhan light of my life my love.' Darath threw the boy a purse. 'Piss off. You do look so handsome, Orhan, when you're squirming with embarrassment.'

Several doors were closed. Doors to Elis' rooms.

'If I were you, I'd think about having him followed and murdered, then feel overcome with shame at the thought,' said Darath. Pause. 'Mind you, if I were you, he'd turn out to be the last King of Tarboran slumming it.' Pause. His voice cracked. Clutched Orhan's hand again. 'God's knives, I missed you, Orhan.'

'Bil and Celyse and Dion were grateful for the money.' That was so much the wrong thing to say, Orhan thought, as soon as he said it. Darath would think he'd said it out of spite. Heard Darath's breath catch, saw and felt Darath's face change, the stab of it in Darath's gut.

Darath burst out laughing. 'You honestly didn't mean that to sound cruel, did you? You have no idea why you said that, did you? God's knives, Orhan, I've missed you so much.'

They were almost at Darath's bedroom. A servant Orhan recognized crossed the hall in front of them, drew back with bowed head. Orhan was sure she was smiling at them. 'Wine and cakes and armfuls of flowers!' Darath shouted at her. 'Now!' Holding each other, kissing each other, hands gripping sliding across each other's skin. Taste and feel and grasp you tight, drowning. God's knives, Darath. Loveyouloveyouloveyouloveyou. Darath whispering, 'Love you.' Clutch so tight it's hurting, bite and kiss and cry out. After two years it's awkward, like we've forgotten things about each other. Changed, both of us. There's the scar on Darath's stomach, where Tam Rhyl's man knifed him, I remember binding that, praying he'd live. New thinness and flabbiness to Darath's body, the fever wasted him, almost killed him. His hair's going grey. Lines around his eyes, an old man taste to his breath. Love you. Missed you. We're both dying. Never leave you again.

Much later, drowsing, sated, sticky and languid, like children resting in the afternoon sun. Darath said, 'Tomorrow, Orhan, we'll talk about whatever our Lord and Ruler Lord Mylt wanted with you.'

Orhan sipped his wine. 'He wants me to help him save Sorlost from the demon. Conspire with him and others to save us all, save the world from ruin and death. Will you help me do it?'

Darath sipped his wine. 'You mean, he wants you to collaborate with him to preserve our city for the Immish occupiers. You want me to collaborate with the Immish too.'

Darath laughed and laughed as Orhan said, 'Yes.'

Chapter Twenty

Tobias the penniless meaningless washer-woman's assistant
The camp of the Army of Amrath, the insatiable, the murderers, the wolf-men, the beloved of the carrion eaters, more and more he really can't helping thinking of them as his friends

Rumour had it the attack on Turain would indeed be at dawn, because how stupid would you have to be not to follow up the dragon fire with an attack? Not like Marith really planned this stuff any more. Scare the crap out of the enemy. Barbecue the enemy. Throw wave upon wave upon wave of screaming blood-thirsty soldiers at the enemy until there was nothing left. The strict discipline the army was put under the night before a battle would have been a big hint an attack was in the offing, also, once upon a time before everyone gave up on that in favour of celebrating tomorrow's success. One battle near Issykol, half the cavalry including King Marith had had to be tied to the saddle to stop them falling off.

The camp followers tended to divide into two, uh, camps on night like this: (i) join in, party like you too are literally going to die tomorrow, so what if my husband finds me pleasuring his best friend tonight, tomorrow they could both be dead; or, (ii) cower in the darkness hoping you'll survive to see the troops off the next

182

morning, also keeping a clear head means more chance of bagsying something special in the looting; some of the camp followers would be camped out all night near the city walls to be first in line for a bargain. Naillil and Rovi took approach (ii), being sensible sober types. Lenae seemed to as well. They got a fire going, hunkered down, cooked up another delicious feast of slightly pre-smoked blood-stained veg and fruit. After dinner Naillil told the story of the fall of Tyrenae, with added background sound effects, and then for variety Rovi croaked out the story of Serelethe and the birth of Amrath.

Rovi told it well, actually. His rasping dead voice kind of suited the text. Lenae still couldn't cope with the idea that Tobias and Naillil and Rovi had actually been to where it happened. 'I was born two hours' walk from Ethalden, Lenae,' Rovi croaked out, and Lenae's eyes near popped from her head. 'The whole village went up to the ruins the night of Sunreturn,' said Rovi. 'Made offerings in the place Serelethe called the demons to her.'

Always imagined it on the cliffs, somehow. At dusk in the gloaming, clouds all dramatic, Serelethe standing there, arms raised in offering, eyes wide with fear, hair blowing in the wind, the wind blowing her dress against her legs . . .

Fucking hell I'm having fantasies about King Death's great-great-great-great-great etc grandma. Just fucking stop, Tobias, mate. But – looked at Lenae sitting by the fire – always kind of wondered, though, like everyone must, what it had been like when Serelethe had done it with the whatever it was. What it felt like. What it, you know, felt like. Couldn't really not, could you? First thing that obviously came into everyone's head.

Lenae's eyes near popped again, when Rovi got to the bit about Serelethe birthing a dragon. Crossed her legs very tight and winced. It was getting late, the noise from the army was dropping off a bit because date wine was very strong stuff, so Rovi stopped the story with Amrath still in armoured clout clothes and they settled down to sleep. Tobias curled up into the scrap of cloth he called a tent and tried to sleep. Sudden flash of memory of being in the desert wrapping his cloak around his head trying to sleep with King Death and Queen Thalia thinking they were being quiet in their wagon. Serelethe's demon had probably felt: good. It occurred to him that if Marith hadn't pissed him off quite so much pleasuring Thalia ten times a night in ways he'd clearly never managed to please a woman, he might not have fucked the boy over the way he did.

Woke up suddenly.

Sat up.

What?

What the hell?

His tent had . . . exploded.

A horse had just collided with his tent.

Like literally collided with his tent.

Rovi next to him was trying to get up. He could see Rovi, and the remains of the tent, and the horse, because the sky seemed to be on fire. Everything was all lit up white and blue.

Uh . . .

The horse wheeled around. The horse charged back straight towards him. The horse also seemed to be on fire. White and blue flames.

He tried to draw his sword. His arm howled in pain. His sword hung kind of limp. He dropped the sword. Threw himself down flat curled up as small as he possibly could. Godsgodsgodsgodsgods godsgods.

Tobias the hard-bastard sellsword! Oh hell yeah!

The horse was on top of him. Rush of cold. Eyes closed buried in the ground: he saw the dark, the shape of it, the fire burning so cold it hurt his mind. Cold punch in his face, buried there screaming.

Hooves all around him. Thundering crashing roar lasting forever, how many fucking legs did this thing have? A whole godsdamn army of pain pounding over him like he was back drowning in the sea off Morr Town. Colder than drowning. He could see blue behind his eyes. So cold.

184

The crashing screaming roar died away. A little. He stood up and his body wept with pain.

Men were charging towards them. Mounted men. Armed. People were running. Mounted soldiers were cutting them down. Gouts of blue fire. A woman screaming, and her body rang with blue, and she fell into pieces of ice. Soldiers were running. Wrestling on their armour. Gouts of blue fire. Crash of metal. Scream of dying. The riders shouting, pulling their mounts around, surging on.

He'd thought it was some game of Marith's. Like the children dying. Sudden lurch of kingly self-pitying remorse. Camp followers are the maggots that breed in human ruin. Carrion crows that glut their bloodlusts on an army's filth. I hate myself for feeding their hunger. Kill them! Kill them!

No. Gods and fucking demons and fucking fucking fucking fuck, some glorious idiot was actually insane enough to be attacking them.

'Tobias!' Swung around. Lenae, screaming. Terrified. Five men in black armour, rising out of the shadows, striding out of the dark, suddenly so close on top of them, hadn't heard them, hadn't seen them, how can I not have seen? Five swords drawn. Five black faceless helmets, crowned with antlers. Not men but beasts. Rovi had two knives in hands that were dead and cold and rotten. Naillil had a knife that she used to cut meat. Tobias had a sword. A good sword. Tobias's sword was lying in the remains of the exploded tent.

On him. Swords cutting. Trying to fight back. Such pain in Tobias's shoulder. '*So how many years you got left, you think, before you can't do it any more and some younger man spills your guts out in the dust?*' Raeta had asked him at the beginning of it. More than he'd thought, in the end. A blade came down. A wound opened up in him. White, in his mind: how can any man bear the pain of this? This is what I've done to people. Lots of people.

A blade came down. He thought: do it. Just bloody do it, will you? Get this over with.

Died years ago. Stabbed. Drowned. Killed myself.

Do it, then. Kill me.

He thought: fuck but I don't want to die.

Rolled with the sword missing him. Earth in his mouth. Ice. So so cold. Rolled and spat and he was sick, his heart was sick, why am I fighting this? Rolling back one way and another and the swords coming down around him like rain. All over like fucking rain. I'm dying, why am I fighting this? This is what I've done to people. Weak fuck people. So painful, dying. This is how it felt when I killed them.

Sword blade right down over him, like a meat cleaver over his face. Threw up his arm, his arm shook, his elbow caught the blade so that it dragged across his forehead and at least it had missed his eyes and his throat. Rolled and thrashed. Kicked. His vision all grey. Cold. Frozen. The blade came down. Like a door slamming shut.

Crash of metal. Shouting roar. The sky's all light like candles. Warm soft light. The enemy's gone.

'Tobias.' Tobias sat up. Lenae crouched next to him. Her face was covered in blood. Her dress was torn. Her hair was white with frost. Rovi's face was black ice.

More riders galloped past them. Didn't stop. Looked kind of more familiar. Not wearing frigging antlers on their helmets, for one. Ours, thought Tobias. Thank the gods. He watched the horsemen charge off into the dark. Blue light flashed. On the horizon the sky still burned red. A man was lying a little way off from them, bleeding into the earth, his body crumpled up. Tobias crawled over to him. A young man, face hidden beneath his black armour, pink blossom in his helmet wound around the antlers.

'From the mountains,' he said aloud to no one. 'Mountain men.'

So cold. The young man's blood flowed out into the dark earth and froze.

Fighting still seemed to be raging over off to the east and the south, towards the king's tent. So keep away, try to crawl off north and west away from this on screaming weeping aching limbs. After a while, a troop of Ithish horsemen galloped back past them. Lathered horses. Bloody armour. Defeated slumped eyes.

Oh gods and demons . . . fine ladies and gentlemen, girls and boys . . . spoke too soon there . . . Marith Altrersyr King of Death King of Ruin King of Shadows Amrath Return *Ansikanderakesis Amrakane* King of All Irlast Conqueror of the World . . . would seem to have . . . cocked up. Been creamed. Lost a fight.

Didn't I say they were getting complacent? I didn't? Oh. Well. I thought it, deep down, like. Knew in my bones, what with being an expert in this kind of complex military stuff. Under-disciplined over-confident death-worshipping half-cut savages with no battle plan might lose occasionally: old secret sellsword's wisdom, that.

Fuck, Tobias thought, the world can throw some nice surprises at you occasionally.

PART THREE

THE FORGE

Chapter Twenty-One

Marith Altrersyr, the greatest war leader in the history of Irlast
His camp

'What happened? What the fuck happened? How? How?' Marith kicked at a body slumped before him. 'How?'

'They crept up in the dark,' said Osen uselessly.

'Where were the sentries? How did we have no warning? An army! An army rides up over us and we don't see them coming! How?'

'The sentries are all dead,' said Osen. 'Obviously. They came up from the north, from behind us, took the camp followers at our back first. We don't know how they got up so close unobserved.'

'Magery,' said Faseem Meerak.

'I . . . fear Faseem is correct,' said Ynthe Kimek. Who was himself, of course, a magelord. He looked exhausted. Managed to kill some of them, apparently. One of the few with any sense left. 'Magecraft, blinding the men's eyes to their approach.'

'Could they do it again?' said Ryn Mathen. Staring around in panic, as though a thousand screaming horsemen might appear surrounding him, cut him down. Bloody idiot. He who was supposed to be the greatest warrior in Chathe!

'It was pitch black and we were concentrating on the assault in the morning and discipline was bloody lax,' said Osen. 'End of it. I take a share of the responsibility myself, I should have been more vigilant. But we've all been getting slack. Haven't we?'

'Have you?'

Osen looked at him. 'If you'd been sober enough you could see anything, Marith, yes, you'd have seen that we have,' Osen said.

Indrawn breath. Marith felt his face flush hot.

Faseem and Kimek shaking, backing away.

'If you'd been sober enough you could see anything, perhaps you'd have seen them coming yourself,' said Osen.

You bastard, Osen. I hate you. How are you alive and . . . and not . . . and Carin . . . ? You should be dead.

Osen said, 'Where were you when they first attacked, Marith? Unconscious? Puking? Pissing yourself?'

Faseem weeping with fear.

'I'll kill you!' Marith shouted: 'Kill him! Guards! Kill him! Now!' His hand went to the hilt of his sword.

'Don't be so bloody stupid, Marith,' said Osen.

'I'll kill you!' Drew his sword.

Osen hit him in the face and the sword fell from his hand. Pain on his lips.

'Marith.' Thalia put her hand on his hand. 'Stop it. Now.'

'Don't!' He jerked his hand away. 'I'll kill him!'

Her sleeve fell back, showing the scars on her arm.

Stared at the scars.

A dead child. Blood running off her. A dead child. Dead.

He had held the child in his hands and it had moved, very briefly, one hand had moved. Its mouth had opened and closed. Red and brown and blue and pulpy. A girl. He would have called it Marissa. His real mother's name. Its mouth and its hand had moved, he would swear it. My child. My child. Blood dripping around Thalia's thighs.

'Find anyone left alive who was on guard last night, and kill them!' he shouted at Osen. 'Now.'

'You won't have an army left soon, for anyone else to kill,' said Osen.

'They already believe that their king ordered their slaughter last night,' said Kiana Sabryya. Her face was flushed, her voice was angry. 'Are you sure you wish any more of their blood on your hands, My Lord King?'

Silence.

'They what?'

'They believe that you brought the swords down on them,' said Kiana. 'They believe that you ordered the army to turn on itself. The men of the mountains attacked us, my soldiers have been telling them. The men of mountains, cowards and traitors that they are. Their bodies lie there on the earth for all to see. But many of them – many of them do not and will not believe it was not you.'

Silence.

'Not since the dragon, the last time,' Kiana said.

Thalia raised her hand to touch him. Dropped her hand back.

Marith looked down at the body at his feet. Kicked it again. He rubbed at his eyes. His head hurt.

'Kill anyone who repeats such things,' he said.

The men of the Mountains of Pain had crept up in the darkness, their coming hidden by magecraft and mountain skill. The men of the Mountains of Pain fell upon the camp in a frenzy of men and horses and shadows. Broke over the men of the Army of Amrath, shattered into them, felled them. The night so dark they could not see to defend themselves. All was confusion. And so long it had been, since any man dared to lead an army to attack them. They killed others. Fell upon others. They were the storm, the floodtide, the death curse. So long it had been, since any man dared to bring the field of war to them.

The flood had broken over them. Cold liquid fire in waves of killing. A thousand deaths at a sword blade. Then as quickly as they had come the men of the Mountains of Pain had turned and retreated. Disappeared into the dark from whence they came. The sun rose on a killing ground thick with corpses. Trampled bodies, many of them unarmed. Men who had fought their own comrades, thinking them the enemy, and been killed by them.

'To try to be fair to them,' Osen said, 'they probably assumed you'd turn on them at some point whatever they did. Just like you did with Tereen. Just like you would have done with Arunmen.'

'Just like I would have done with Arunmen? Unfair! I left Arunmen alone!' Considered this. 'Possibly I would have turned on Arunmen at some point whatever they did.'

'Possibly?'

'Probably. Okay, yes, very probably. Almost certainly. Yes.'

'Actually, you told me you would have. At the victory banquet after we sacked it.'

'Did I?'

'Yes.'

'Oh.' Pause. 'But the people of Arunmen didn't know I would.'

Osen snorted.

'What?'

'King Ruin King of Shadows King of Death. You think?'

He went back to his tent. Gods. In the main chamber, a table was overturned, he must have knocked it over, running to get out and fight. His cloak lay in a heap where he had been unable to get the brooch fastened, abandoned it. A bottle had overturned. Firewine stained the thick floor carpet black. There was a book on the floor, open. He must have been trying to read it. It had been trodden on, the page it was open at was ruined and black.

Brychan was on his knees sorting the wreckage, a servant girl beside him. 'There's a cup broken, My Lord King,' said Brychan. 'Nothing else. The book's damaged here, but the rest of it is fine. Just this one page.' He held it out to Marith.

. . . *stheone memkabest,*

. . . *Sesesmen hethelen* . . .

. . . love came,
. . . like a flower . . .
The Silver Tree. In the original Literan.

'Thank you.' He went through into the bedchamber, put the book carefully down on the bed.

'Your bath's being prepared, My Lord King,' said Brychan.

'Thank you.' He sat down heavily on the bed.

'Those . . . those horses they were riding . . .' said Brychan.

'Yes?'

'They didn't look . . . Magery, the men are saying. God things. Demons mounted on god things.' Brychan said, 'The men are afraid, My Lord King. I've never seen them afraid before.'

The bath was ready; Marith washed, ate a meal, drank a cup of wine, felt a little better. It didn't happen; it couldn't have happened. A hatha dream. And then a servant would come in to dress him, take away his plate, refill his wine cup, and he would see terror in the man's eyes. And shame.

We will attack them at dawn. Come down on the city in the morning twilight, dragons and shadows and bronze spears, I will break down their gates with my own bare hands, I will kill them. But he did not call his captains to discuss battles. Did not draw up orders for them to march out.

There was a stirring at the doorcurtain. Alleen came running in, alive with nerves. Marith looked up sharply. 'Yes?'

'Marith. They have sent you an envoy. I think you should come quickly, Marith.'

Marith thought: tell the envoy I will come and kill them all. That's it. I don't need to see him, to tell him that. But Alleen looked afraid. Brychan looked afraid, from looking at Alleen. Thalia came in and she too looked afraid and on edge.

'Don't be absurd,' he snapped at them. 'Stop it.'

Thalia fastened his cloak, arranged the folds. Dried blood crumbling off it, filling the air. Marith strapped on his sword.

'Well?'

Brychan said, 'The envoy . . . the envoy's waiting . . . on the edge of the camp . . .'

On the edge of the camp there was bloody chaos. Battered down earth, dead horses still lying where they fell, two of the enemy lying dead. The burned-out remains of one of the war engines. And the envoy.

Marith stopped. Thalia beside him reached out and took his hand.

The envoy was mounted on a black horse. It was vast, taller than a man at the shoulder, but very thin. Like a hobby horse, flayed skin over dry bones. In the daylight, a pale gleam of blue fire played around its mouth and its flared nostrils and its killing hooves. Its mouth was red. Its eyes were red. Its mane stirred and moved and a hissing sound came from it. Its mane was black snakes, flickering out long black tongues, hissing at Marith.

It was saddled and bridled in iron, all studded with sharp spikes. In the saddle sat a woman.

Her hair was the colour of a wheat field in summer and her skin was the colour of the rich dark earth in which the wheat grows. Her eyes were as blue as flowers and her lips were as red as ripe cherries and her body was as slender as a young willow tree. She was wearing a dress of green silk and a crown of green leaves. In her right hand she held a silver sword.

She opened her mouth to speak. Her voice was sweet as music, like the babble of cool deep water or the murmur of the wind in the reeds. 'Marith Altrersyr.'

'Who are you?'

She tossed her beautiful hair. Blur of gold. A memory: the wheat ripe in the fields, the men and women dancing out to the harvest, he and Ti young boys, visiting with their grandfather Carlan in the country, the Murade fortress of Malth Denamen on Sel Island; they had gone out to join the harvesting, played in the corn, got sweaty and weary and joyful, with black soil on their faces; he'd drunk beer and danced with a girl with poppies in her black hair, stayed up very late.

Ti . . . He felt Thalia's presence, tense, beside him. Warm, beside him. Her voice, too low to make out the words, whispering something.

'Who are you?' he shouted at the woman.

'I am the Queen of Turain,' the woman said. The demon horse stamped and snorted. The snakes in its mane hissed at him. 'Will you fight me, Marith Altrersyr? I challenge you for the throne of Turain.'

Laughed, incredulous. 'You challenge me?'

She said, 'I will make a bargain with you, Marith Altrersyr. If I win, you will put down your sword and take your men a thousand miles from here, never return to harm us. But if you win, you may cut off my head and take my place here as king.'

Thalia put her cool hand on his arm. 'Marith. Be careful.'

'That's all? The throne of Turain and your death, or a promise to leave you in peace?'

'That is all. Is that not enough?' She shook out her hair again. Ripe corn, summer fields: lying with his head in Carin's lap, in a cornfield, one morning, there is a lark singing, very high above them, there is a cornflower growing among the wheat just by them, 'Your eyes are that colour, Carin, exactly the colour of the cornflower there.' A breeze makes the stalks ripple and rustle, 'The corn is telling you how much I love you, Marith.' 'I know you love me, Carin.' 'If you love me, Marith,' a kiss, a hand on his chest, Carin must feel his heart beating, 'if you love me . . .' 'I do love you, Carin.' 'My father wants you to kill your father, Marith, after you've married Landra, they want me to ask you to do it, but I can't, I won't, because I love you too much.'

His mouth seemed filled with sand. He swallowed and his throat felt raw. Sand crunched in his mouth. I'd forgotten that. Pretended I'd forgotten that.

'Marith,' Thalia said in a low voice.

The Queen of Turain smiled at him. A long black tongue hissed out through her red lips. A snake's forked tongue. 'Will you fight me, then, Marith Altrersyr King of Dust King of Shadows King of Death?'

'My father wants me to ask you, but I won't ask you that, Marith.' And the guilt in Carin's eyes, the shadow, Carin knew what he was doing, oh he did, Carin had known always. But I loved him and he loved me.

'Marith,' Thalia said. Urgent.

Marith drew his sword. 'I have fought with gods and monsters before, and destroyed them. I will fight you, Queen of Turain. It will be your death. Your death or I will leave your city in peace.'

The snake's tongue hissed out at him. 'When will we fight, then, Marith Altrersyr? Now?'

'Not now.' He looked at Thalia and she was trembling. 'This evening. At dusk.'

'Not at dusk. At dawn. If you kill me before the sun has fully risen, you may have my crown and my city and my people's lives, Marith Altrersyr.'

Marith said, 'At dawn.'

She said, 'We will fight on the banks of the River Isther, where it flows before the walls of my city of Turain, beneath the willow tree that grows there whose leaves make up my queenly crown. At dawn, then. All the birds will sing.'

She turned her horse, galloped away from them. 'An archer!' Osen whispered to Marith. 'Bring her down. Where's Ynthe Kimek, to blast her with mage fire?'

Thalia was staring after her with anger, nodded in agreement. 'Kill her, Marith. Now. Please.'

'Are you a mad fool, my Lord Fiolt?' the woman's voice shouted. 'Look! Look to your enemy!' She laughed like children playing and women dancing and all the happiness in the world, and was gone out of the camp into the burned fields of Turain. Her horse's hooves threw up black ash and white ash.

Look to your enemy. Scouts came in soon afterwards to bring the truth of it: in the plain to the south of the city, with their backs to the bare hills of Mar like an arm cradling them, an army had appeared. It stood silent, in perfect order. Not a man moved there, the horses stood silent, every spear and sword was frozen still. Their shadows were still. Only the pennants they carried danced in the wind, to show that there were real men there, not an illusion born of fear. Black armour. Antlered helmets, through which dark eyes stared. In the armour, with the antlers, they did not look like men. Their mouths showed red beneath the shadow of their helmets. Their armour was spiked, like teeth. Infantry, shields locked together. Archers, their bows made of sweetwood and human bone. Cavalry, mounted on huge black horses with living snakes for manes. They were armed with axes and knives. Golden-winged eagles circled above them. The air above them glowed. The men of Turain and the men of the mountains, rank upon rank, filling the plain. Like the plants in a wheat field, said one of the scouts in wonder. Rooted in the earth, silent and still and numberless. Too many to see them individually, or to count. Never, the scout said, had he seen so many men gathered, they made the Army of Amrath look like boys playing in the roadside, he had not thought, truly, that there could be so many on all the face of the earth.

Marith rode over to see. The man's exaggerating. He is. Obviously he is. Took a role as a scout because he's too much of a coward to stand in the front ranks and fight. We'll see, this mighty terrifying army, we'll see . . .

Saw.

Rode back.

The men of the mountains. Bloody traitors. '*Oh Dragon King, Great Lord of Death, Master, King of All, here, take these gifts, a toast to your glory, take our oaths of fealty and love. Truly are you called Great Lord and Wonder and King.*' Bastards. Just like Arunmen.

'They swore me their loyalty. Crowned me.'

Osen said, 'You just can't trust people, can you? And size isn't everything, isn't that right, Alleen?' Osen tried to laugh at his own joke. Alleen Durith tried to laugh, as did Ryn Mathen. It came out of them like dogs barking. Died off. A servant girl pouring wine spilled some over the table. Gasped and muttered while she mopped it up.

'Leave it,' Marith said to her.

'You shouldn't be fighting this woman,' Osen said. 'Let me fight her, Marith.'

'Don't be absurd.' He slapped his hand on the table, spilling more wine. 'I said leave it.'

'She's a demon, Marith. A god. Something.'

'So I can fight her, Osen. You can't.'

'But I can be spared to die, Marith,' Osen said.

People shifting in their seats. Don't say that word. Impossible word. The serving girl gasped.

'I can't die. I cannot die.'

'I'm sorry,' said Osen. 'I didn't mean that. I don't know why I said that.'

'She is not a demon,' said Thalia. 'She is what she says she is. The Queen of Turain.'

'How do you know?' Alleen Durith shouted at her. 'Did you see her? Her tongue? That horse she was riding on? She's a demon or a sorceress.'

'How could I not know what she is?' said Thalia. Her face looking at Alleen was filled with disgust.

'You can't bloody fight her, Marith.' Osen said, 'You've barely slept, you spent last night fighting gods only know what, you can't fight her now. You should never have agreed to it. I should never have let you agree.'

'I didn't have much choice, did I? What could I do, tell her to go away? And the bargain she made was absurd, I could hardly refuse that, could I? A woman offered me her death or my retreat and I refused?'

'You need to be careful of her promises, Marith,' said Kiana. 'You cannot trust her to keep them. The mountain men have betrayed their promises, she rides one of their horses, she summoned them.'

'Betrayal is something you, of course, know all about, Kiana,' said Alleen Durith.

'What?'

'The mountain men swore us fealty, and broke it,' said Alleen. 'The mountain men got into our camp somehow. Did that man not say, back in Arunmen, that someone was betraying the king? Before Lord Fiolt your great admirer killed him.'

'Are you saying that I am a traitor?' shouted Kiana.

'You take that back, Alleen,' Osen shouted. 'Take that back now.'

'It was your men, Alleen, who had the watch last night,' Kiana spat back. 'At the place where the enemy came in.'

'My men died! Fought them off!'

'Didn't notice them coming. Men on horses, and they didn't hear or see them . . . ?'

'Magecraft!' shouted Alleen.

'Or treachery?'

'Stop this.' A quiet voice. Angry. Weary. Thalia stood up. Something in the way she stood, the look in her eyes . . . the others fell silent, looked down at their hands in shame. 'It will be dusk soon. Perhaps it would be best if you had a rest and prepared yourself, Marith. If your friends will leave us in peace.'

She was terrified, Marith realized. She was more afraid of this creature he must fight than she had been of anything.

When the rest had gone, he lay down on the bed holding Thalia next to him, put out all the lamps save one. This hateful false dark, here in his tent, the light picking its way in through the seams in the leather, dark even in the sunlight of a day. Only a little while to rest, dozing on her shoulder. Then Alis came to fetch him. All was ready: now they must bury the previous night's dead. The Army of Amrath set to work hauling the bodies. Set up the funeral pyres and the marker stone. Marith sacrificed five horses, calling down vengeance. The soldiers processed beneath, shouting his name. The dragons came, flying low over the pyres, hissing out smoke. They settled themselves on the peak of a mountain, and fire could be seen there. The King's Star shone very bright for a while, then the clouds came over and it was hidden. The sky grew very dark. Every man in the camp waiting now for dawn.

The bodies of the enemy lay in a pile. The Queen of Turain had not asked for them to be returned to her. The men of the Mountains of Pain had not sent a messenger to ask for them. So they lay where they were left, stripped naked, stiff and hard and cold, dead and dying, horses and men. The crows and the flies and the vultures came down. A last few camp followers picked over them, searching for any scraps. The air was very cold, the ground was very cold, where they lay. A shimmer in the air, over them, the cold visible. It was said that a woman had placed her hands for too long on one of demon horses, and that her fingers were now numb and black. A woman was heard shrieking in pain, later, off on the edge of the camp.

A funeral feast was laid. Roast meat and wine and spirits, on tables set beneath the dead bodies of the horse sacrifice, beside the stone.

'I will have a great monument built, after Turain falls!' Marith shouted. He poured wine on the stone in offering. 'Our hallowed dead! Always, always we will remember them! Avenge them!' It sounded thin and bitter. Absurd. Useless lumps who were hacked open in their sleep.

'Once, we would have cut a man's throat here,' Osen said.

'We will cut the throat of every man, woman and child in Turain for them! Raise a vast monument, of gold and iron, capped with the Queen of Turain's head!'

The men roared their approval. Gulped down their cups of drink. The sword dance started up, the clash of bronze, the stamp of feet. Wild and fast. Some of them will die tonight, fighting each other, Marith thought. And indeed, he saw men fighting already, on the edges of the feasting place, wrestling and cutting at each other with hands or with knives; in the shadows at the edge of the feast near where the enemy dead lay he saw two men fighting and a man forcing a woman down, a knife at her throat. This will be a bad night. An evil night.

'Come to bed, Marith,' Thalia whispered to him, clutching at his arm.

'Should I not drink and shout and dance? Like my men? Mourn the dead?' He thought: you think that woman may kill me. Shall I try to get another dead child on you, Thalia my love, before I die?

'She cannot kill you,' Thalia said fiercely. 'Come away.'

'Go to bed, Marith,' said Osen. 'Please. This is not a good place to be, tonight.'

He turned to go. The flames of the pyres roared up higher. The flames danced against the black sky looking like antlers and snakes' heads. The dead men there burning seemed to writhe as if they were in pain. The flames spat and hissed, the fat spitting, the bones cracking. As if the men were screaming there as they burned. A great shower of red sparks went up.

Chapter Twenty-Two

In the grey light before dawn, Marith and Thalia and Osen and
Alleen Durith rode out to meet the Queen of Turain. None of
them had slept. Marith rubbed his eyes. He felt sore and heavy,
very slow, his eyes were gritty, stung him as they did when he had
been in battle smoke. Two nights now with barely any sleep. He
felt as though he could fall off his horse. He probably looked as
though he had fallen off his horse. The rest of them were as bad,
Osen's eyes were red-rimmed, Alleen itched at his face and shook
his head to try to clear it, Thalia's shoulders were stiff and hunched.
Brychan and Tal, riding behind them, looked grey like dead men.

A long ride, down the foothills of the Mountains of Pain, onto
the plain where the river ran fast and cold with snowmelt past
the thick walls of Turain. The clouds had cleared, as they prepared
to set out, the world was glowing with the blue luminous light
before dawn. Black trees and black rocks against the morning
twilight. The sky glowing waiting for the sun. The Fire Star was
clearly visible, though the rest of the stars had set. The King's Star,
I mean, Marith thought. My star. The moon was huge on the
horizon, a full moon shining very white.

'If it were a sacrifice night,' Thalia had said, 'a woman would
die, tonight.'

'Marith!' He blinked. Dozing in the saddle, lost in his thoughts.

The sky was turning pink in the east before them, the moon had set. Birds were beginning to sing. The silver line of the river. There beyond it in the distance the walls of the city of Turain. At this distance the city was very still. The air smelled very sweet suddenly, heavy, sensuous: he looked down and saw that they were riding through a field of white hyacinths, crushing the flowers beneath the horses' hooves. They were glowing white. The smell was like the taste of Thalia's skin.

There were torches burning, on the banks of the river. They rode closer. Came to a stone bridge. He could hear the water lapping around its pillars. Beside it a huge willow tree was growing, silver-green leaves brushed the surface of the water. A woman's hair hanging down ragged. A gust of wind made the tree shiver, the leaves whisper to the water beneath. A beating of wings and a pigeon flew up from the tree making it shake and the water splash. Ripples on the water, the leaves splashing it. How lovely it would be, to swim in the river, in these warm southern days, swim in through the green leaves as into a green cave, float there. The leaves would shiver and whisper and the water would ripple and sing.

The Queen of Turain was waiting for him before the bridge. She was crowned in hyacinths. Her armour was burnished gold. The bridge behind her burned blue.

'Marith Altrersyr. The sun is rising.' She held up her silver sword. 'Will you fight me?'

Marith dismounted. Awkwardly, his head was so heavy, his foot almost caught in the saddle. The horse was skittery, shied as he dismounted. He had to step back quickly.

'Careful!' Osen had dismounted, was grabbing at his horse's head.

'I'm fine. Leave it.' Gods, this was a farce. Thalia dismounted, squeezed his hand.

'Come,' the Queen of Turain said. 'Let us begin. The sun is rising. Kill me and be King of Turain. Or leave here and do not return.'

205

Marith drew his sword. Joy, he had named it, after the sword he had once owned that had been called Sorrow, that had killed Carin. This sword Joy had killed his brother and his mother. Made him king. Thalia, he thought, had once thought about using this sword to kill him. He could smell the sea, the cramped ship, Thalia's hands on the hilt, her face thinking. A little room in a tall house by Toreth Harbour, gulls screaming, a candle flickering into light.

'Stop it.'

'Stop what, Marith Altrersyr?' the Queen of Turain said in her beautiful voice.

'A kindness, Marith,' he thought he heard Thalia say. 'But I didn't do it, did I?'

The Queen of Turain strode forward, squared up facing him. She was very tall, as tall as a great green tree. Far, far taller than he was, she reached up to the sun as it rose. The earth smelled of crushed hyacinths and her breath smelled of fresh-mowed hay. Her hair was loose and it was the colour of ripe wheat, and her armour was gilded and patterned with flowers and leaves. She held up her sword, and he saw that the blade was worked with pictures, etched in green fire, women and children bringing in the harvest, men hunting and fishing and tilling the fields, and then the river ceases to run down from the mountains, the earth dries, the men and the women and the children starve, there is murrain in the fields, there is plague in the city and the people fall sick, the river runs in flood and drowns them, the ground is rent in earthquake. They all die, the people, all of them, in the end.

'Stop!' He tore his eyes away from the woman's blade.

'Stop what, Marith Altrersyr?' She tossed her beautiful hair. 'You think that you are stronger than I am? You think that you alone can kill?'

He came at her. Their blades clashed. He struck and she warded it off and the shock of her strength, like striking a tree trunk, went all up Marith's arm. He struck again. She warded it off. He struck again. The ground was slippery under his feet. Crushed flowers, he thought, and then he glanced down and the ground was slippery with blood.

The Queen of Turain laughed, and attacked him.

Crash of sword blades. He blocked it, stepped back, his body was ringing from the blow. Their swords met again and again. She struck him on the shoulder, wounded him. She struck him on the thigh.

I cannot be harmed! I cannot die! I am as a god, he thought. Nothing can harm me.

Pain there, in his body. She laughed. There was blood on her sword blade. She had wounded him.

He redoubled his attack, slashed at her, the swords rang, she moved back. There was blood on her face. A strand of her hair was stuck to her cheek in a smear of blood. She was sweating.

The ground beneath his feet was liquid with blood. He slipped, stumbled backwards. His shoulder hurt. His thigh hurt. Lashed out and maybe he had her, his sword met her armour, the metal rang out. She leapt away from him. She was so fast. She came at him. He shouted, because she was huge, and all gold and shadows. Lashed out at her; his sword did not even touch her. She slipped away from his blade. Like catching water in his hands, he thought. She jabbed at him, he felt her sword go past him, so close, he did not try to block it but only moved back. He drove at her. She warded it. He tried to close with her. She danced away. Drove at him. The weight of her stroke was like a rock. He slipped backwards, his body screamed out. He flailed with his sword, met her arm at the wrist. Grazed her. Perhaps. He felt her sword go into him. Deep in. Red pain, white pain, black pain, black in his eyes, his mind was blank and roaring, couldn't hear, couldn't see. Hurt him. He was down in the mud, scrabbling, he was holding his sword over himself to shield himself. The mud stank of blood. There were hyacinth petals stuck mushy on his face.

She looked surprised. She too was bleeding. She spat blood at him. He kicked out, his foot caught her leg. She swayed, her leg buckled.

He scrabbled backwards in the mud. Hurt. The sword fell from his hand. Tried to push himself away.

She raised her sword over him. The blade there above him. Hanging there above him. Very close to him. And then it would come down. His blood, on the blade. It would cut him open. It was the strangest thing he had ever seen.

He rolled, scrabbled in the dirt. Rolled. Crawling. Began to run. The sky was pale and pink and clear. He thought he could see a bird, very small, black in the sky. There was a great noise of crashing and shouting. Thalia's voice was shouting. A voice screamed, 'He's dead! The king's dead!' He could see the hyacinth flowers crushed up beneath him. His shoulder hurt.

He ran from her and ran from her. Please.

Arms were lifting him, holding him, he was hanging face down over a horse. The smell of the horse was in his face. The horse was galloping. Voices were shouting. His shoulder hurt. His thigh hurt. He closed his eyes, behind his eyes his head was white with pain. The feel of the horse galloping made him feel sick. He was back in the camp, and more voices were shouting; he was being carried into his tent. The sky again, he could see the sky. His body felt very odd and sticky. They were carrying him and it took forever, he was floating. He was lying on his bed. Thalia was bending over him. Hands were pulling and cutting his armour off.

'What happened?' he said. They got the armour off him. A voice screamed. A voice swore. 'I lost,' he said. 'I lost. Didn't I? I lost. I ran away. How can I have lost?'

Thalia said, 'Hush. It will be well.' There was a light in her. He turned away from her, afraid.

Chapter Twenty-Three

Tobias, briefly happy
The camp of the Army of Amrath, very upset

Bloody hells.

I mean – obviously you kind of expected him to lose at some point – I mean, nobody wins all the frigging time, 'even, um, that poet, you know, that poet whose name I can't remember, wrote that dirty poem the boy's so keen on, even that poet nods occasionally' as they say in Sorlost. But bloody hells. As ways to fuck up go, that was a fucking triumph. Get creamed overnight, rumour had it the buggers came fairly close to setting the king's own tent on fire before the king almost fell over his own sword fighting them off, then get thrashed by a girl in a remarkably impractical gold breastplate. Glory to him! The king being carried off face down over the arse of Lord Durith's horse like a sack. And that was frankly fucking cheating. She'd been whipping him. If he hadn't run like a frightened rabbit, the boy would have had his head taken off. Wonder if you can come back from having your pretty head taken off, Marith, you little shit? What's it going to do, grow back?

The camp and everyone in it were in shock. Grown soldiers openly weeping. Three women were said to have miscarried at the news, another two had given birth. Two old blokes and five injured soldiers had died straight out. They said three people had committed suicide, but that was less convincing and if they had the army was probably better off without them. If they had, they would have been feeling pretty stupid if they could still feel anything, seeing as there'd been three proclamations in the last hour that Great King Marith Altrersyr *Ansikanderakesis Amrakane* King Ruin King of Dust King of Shadows King of Death absolutely categorically cross-my-heart-and-swear-it-till-I'm-blue-in-the-face wasn't dead. No one making the proclamation looked like they'd noticed the irony of announcing that the King of Death wasn't dead.

'He'll be fine,' Tobias said to Lenae. She was crying. He killed your fucking baby, Tobias wanted to yell at her. Only except he felt . . . if Marith had died . . . did die . . .

'They say he's unconscious.'

'They say all kinds of things. He's Marith Altrersyr *Ansikanderakesis Amrakane*! He'll be fine.'

Gods: Thalia, widowed. Four unborn babies and a husband. Someone Lenae knew knew someone who knew someone who'd seen her going into the tent. She hadn't been crying, they said. But you wouldn't want to have looked into her face.

Someone who knew someone who knew someone said Osen Fiolt had been crying, when he went into his own tent. '*Marith, Marith, Marith. My life for yours. Marith.*' Less romantically, perhaps, they also said that Alleen Durith and Osen Fiolt had screamed at each other and Alleen Durith had broken Osen Fiolt's nose.

'*Mawifff, Mawifff, Mawifff. My vife vor vours, Mawiff.*'

'He can't die.' Lenae looked genuinely quite terrified. 'What will become of us all, Tobias, if he dies?'

I've been wondering that myself, girl. Shit, I should think. A glorious new golden era of peace and prosperity, with us here in this army really not on the receiving end. Tobias moved a little closer to Lenae, thought about taking her hand. 'I've got a sword, Lenae. I'll protect you.'

She rolled her eyes a bit but looked slightly more reassured. Maybe.

Good if she was, because he really wasn't. A whole fucking army, and no one in command?

'You'll be okay, yeah?' he said to her. 'You've got money and that. And I've got my sword.'

Rovi sat down beside them. Talk about timing. Death stink that made Lenae gag and that's that. Off sex for life.

'They've set up a shrine,' Rovi said. 'To make offerings for him. Beg for healing.' Rovi laughed.

'I'd like to go,' said Lenae. 'Make an offering.'

Make an offering for his life? 'He killed your baby,' said Tobias. Flushed with shame as he spoke.

Lenae wrung her hands. 'We'll be dead and lost,' she said, 'if he dies now.'

'We will,' said Naillil. Tears running down her cheeks. 'Gods, Amrath and Eltheia, our new young king, his beauty, what he's done for us.'

They'd set the shrine up on a hillock, a green mound topped with a grove of sweetwood trees, looking down over the plain, close to where the Army of Amrath had sat to watch the dragons break the city open before the army sacked it. From the top of the hill you could see the city clearly, the scorch marks, the shattered buildings, the charred ruins of towers and houses. The massive bloody walls. It was still, seemed to be largely deserted. Most of the inhabitants gone to join the huge army waiting further south. The river was very clear, and there was the bridge, currently surely the most famous bridge in all Irlast. Gods, if Marith was dying, that bridge'd be sung about for a thousand thousand years.

'What's the bridge called?' Tobias asked. 'Anyone know?'

'The Turain Bridge,' the answer eventually came back.

Epic name.

On a rise in the middle of the camp, a scaffold had been set up. Ten heads staring out. Neatly arranged facing forwards and

211

backwards alternately, someone had put some thought into it. Tobias was in perfect time to watch a crow peck a woman's eyeball out.

Dumb sods who had said Marith was behind the night attack. Everyone had thought it, even if only briefly. Logical thing to think. But the sheer stupidity of anyone saying it was enough to make your eyeballs bleed.

Boom boom. You're on form today, Tobias, mate.

The shrine itself was kind of . . . don't know what the word is, 'earnest' might be one way of describing it. Couple of stakes looking remarkably like the stakes with heads on them he'd just been admiring; ribbons and leafy branches and flowers woven around them; couple of strings of bells and stones and bones rattling in the wind. A branch of a willow tree, which might be a tad insensitive. A pile of objects building up at the base of it – coins, knives, arm-rings, necklaces. Splashes of wine and milk and honey and blood. Lenae bent down to place a posy of red flowers. Rovi snorted loudly. Tobias wondered if pissing on it could count as a libation.

'My life for his, oh gods and demons, all you powers, my life for his, my life, my life.' A young soldier, probably Marith's own age at most, kneeling, his face creased up with grief. Slashed the palm of his right hand with his sword, splattered blood. 'My life for his.' A much older man, older than Tobias, his knees creaking alarmingly as he knelt down but still dressed as a soldier. Placed a crude carved image of a horse beside the blood. 'My life for his.' A very young girl in a white dress, long dark hair falling down her back, her eyes puffy with tears. 'He cannot die, he cannot be harmed, oh gods and demons, oh gods, he cannot be harmed, my life for his.'

Lenae took out her knife, cut a lock of her hair, twisted it around a sprig of green stuff. 'There.'

A shadow. The dragons came down low over the shrine. Cried out, and Tobias could almost, almost understand what they were saying. Felt the wind of their wing beats on his face.

212

In the camp of the Army of Amrath, trumpets began to blow. Over and over, loud, calm but urgent. Silver music. Voices shouting, soldiers moving, the people of the camp churning, flowing, pulling themselves into place. The army moving into ranks for war. A voice shouted, 'March!' The dragons shot up into the air screaming, spewing fire. The drums began to beat. Voices howled, 'Vengeance for the king! Vengeance!'

Chapter Twenty-Four

Marith Altrersyr the King, the Lord of the World, the greatest conqueror in the history of Irlast
His camp

Opened his eyes. A woman's voice was whispering around the tent: 'You lost, Marith Altrersyr.' Thalia's voice whispered in his ear: 'A kindness. But I didn't do it.' The sound of leaves shivering in the wind. He sat up. Screamed in pain. Brychan was beside him suddenly, holding him. The pain in his body was the worst thing he had ever felt.

'You need to lie down,' Brychan said. 'You shouldn't try to move, My Lord King.'

Brychan held a cup to his mouth. He gulped down water. It was cold and sweet, tasted of mint. His mouth was full of dirt and soil. He choked as he swallowed.

His shoulder was hurting him. It felt very heavy. He tried to move his head, to see. The bed beneath him felt gritty, rough on his skin. He was naked, his left shoulder and his left thigh were bandaged. There was blood spreading over the bandages. Like spider webs.

Wounded. He'd been wounded. He couldn't be wounded. He couldn't lose.

'He's awake, My Lord,' Brychan called. Alis Nymen came in, sat down by the bed.

'My Lord King,' Alis said.

'What's happening?'

Alis said, 'Nothing of importance.'

'No. Where's Thalia? And Osen? What's happening, Alis? Tell me.' He tried to sit up again. His body screamed again. White pain. Blind and dumb. Gasped and breathed, tried tried to make it go away. I cannot be harmed. I saw a knife cut my skin and crumble away to rust. I have fought and won a hundred battles. I have fought gods. I cannot be harmed, so I cannot be in pain. 'Tell me. I need to get up, I need to know. I need to lead my army.' He tried to stand. Fell down. The pain screamed through him. He vomited up water soiled with blood.

'Where's Thalia? Where's Osen? I have to get up.'

'Lie down, Marith,' said Alis. 'Please.'

'Marith? Am I not king any more? Where's Thalia?'

'Later,' said Alis.

'I'll die,' Marith screamed, 'if I have to lie in this bed in the dark not knowing what's happening.' The tent was very dim: I want to be in a room with windows, he thought, I want to look out and see the sky, see trees and houses and clouds and the sea, I want to see the sunrise, the moonlight, the stars, I want to feel the breeze, I hate this tent. Tried again to get up, got himself on his feet leaning on the bed, his body howling at him in pain, red lines scrolling over his bandages. Brychan came to help him.

In the distance, he heard a ring of trumpets.

'What is going on, Alis? Tell me now.'

Brychan said, 'You've been unconscious for most of the day, My Lord King. Lord Fiolt is leading the men into battle against the army of Turain and the Mountains of Pain. The queen is with them.'

Battle? Without me to lead them? The men, my army, fighting beneath another's command. No. No. They cannot. They must not. He tried to walk to the doorway, looked around for his sword.

Turning his head made his shoulder hurt. He had almost forgotten what it felt like, physical pain like this. He cried out in pain; Brychan and Alis took his arms, helped him back into bed. Brychan held the cup of water to his lips.

'Rest, My Lord King,' Alis said. 'Please.'

'They attacked us, then, the enemy, the Queen of Turain and her soldiers? She did betray us, then, as Lady Sabryya feared?'

Alis fidgeted with his robe. Brychan didn't say anything. Coughed.

'Brychan?'

'Lord Fiolt . . . Lord Durith . . . The men . . . The men were desperate, My Lord King. Half the camp thought you were dead, the state you were brought back in. The witch woman, the demoness, who murdered you . . . The men were mad to fight. So Lord Durith announced he would lead them out to attack the enemy.'

'What? What gave him . . . ? The queen and Lord Fiolt: they command, in my absence. Not Alleen Durith.'

Alis said after a little while, 'Lord Mathen tried to reason with Lord Durith. Told him it was too dangerous. Lord Mathen knows the mountain men, how they fight. But Lord Fiolt could see, in the end . . . I could see . . . We had to attack them, My Lord King. If we hadn't . . . the men were going mad, knowing you were harmed.'

Alleen Durith. Gods. But a sweet shameful pleasure at the men's grief for him.

'And . . . Thalia?' He was unsure what he wanted them to say.

Alis said, 'She agreed with Lord Durith. She told them to attack the enemy in all strength, My Lord King. She has gone with them.'

No. Thalia, encourage this? She would, I suppose, he thought then. She is their queen. She will want to lead them.

Marith said, 'Help me to get up.'

'You need to rest now,' said Alis. 'Please, My Lord King, Marith.'

'I have to know what's happening.'

'I don't know,' said Brychan. 'They marched an hour or so ago. We have not heard anything yet.'

Osen might die, he thought, without me there. Osen, Alleen, Ryn Mathen, Kiana – and what if Thalia has gone too close, what if she is caught up in it? She followed the men into battle once. Or what if she despairs, thinks that I am dead? I have to go to them.

These are lies, of course. The real reason they must not march without him . . . he cannot face himself if he speaks it, thinks it.

'Leave me,' he shouted at Alis Nymen. 'Leave me, now.' Brychan went to go out as well, taking the lamp with him. 'Not you, Brychan.'

Thought he heard the sound of metal crashing on metal, voices yelling out the paean. Thus the endless battle is joined again, the Army of Amrath against the men of Turain and the men of the Mountains of Pain, who stood as numberless as the stems in a wheat field. The Army of Amrath mad and raging, half believing their king to be dead. Swords and spears and axes, the music of bronze and iron, the swirling dust kicked up by ten times a thousand feet. Men struggling, stabbing, the voices screaming out 'hold' and the voice screaming 'forward, go forward', the voices sobbing as they died. The thunder of horses' hooves in the charge, the arrows loosed to block out the light of the sun. The dragons, the shadowbeasts, the god things, wrestling.

I have to be there. Struggled to get up, fell down in pain. 'Brychan, I have to get up, I have to.'

A long silence, Brychan standing in the bedchamber doorway holding the lamp.

'You swear to me,' Brychan said, 'My Lord King, you swear you won't try to fight.'

'You're my servant, Brychan.'

'I won't help you if you don't swear it, My Lord King.'

Gods, he remembered this man crying in terror when he questioned him, once.

Marith winced and gasped as he finally made it back onto his feet. 'I swear I . . . won't try to fight.'

'I'm the queen's servant, as well, My Lord King,' said Brychan. 'I have to think of her, also.'

Oh, you do, I'm sure. Often.

Stood up very slowly, Brychan helping him. Together they managed to get him dressed, a knife at his belt, his blood-spattered cloak fastened at his throat. His crown on his head.

'I need my sword,' he said to Brychan.

A pause. 'You just promised me you wouldn't fight, My Lord King.'

'I need my sword, Brychan. Now.' He looked at the bed he had been lying in, the sheets soiled with sweat and blood, they looked dirty, as though the bed had been made up unwashed. He brushed his hand over them: they felt rough with dirt.

Black sand, he thought. He gagged and gasped for breath.

His sword was fetched. His horse was ready, waiting beside the tent. Brychan gave him a cup of firewine. Helped him walk to his horse, lifted him into the saddle. His hands shook when he tried to take up the reins. The world spun and he thought he was going to faint; Brychan had to grab at him, hold him upright, to stop him falling. But when the people in the camp saw him mounted they shrieked for joy.

Brychan took the horse on a lead-rein. As they went through the camp people came rushing up trying to kiss his boots, the hem of his cloak. A woman threw flowers over him, one caught in the horse's mane. A white flower, in the white horse-hair: he shuddered at it. Reached out to flick it off. Why, he thought, why should I do that? It's a flower a pretty woman threw at me in delight. Another woman grabbed at Brychan's arm, gave Brychan a posy of white flowers. The pleasure of it flushed through him again.

And a new feeling. Something like grief. Not a new feeling. He looked at Brychan, looking ahead smiling as a girl blew kisses, dropped a pretty scarf in the dust before Brychan's horse; head nodding as a trumpet blew and a voice shouted, 'The king! The king!'; sitting up so proud as a burst of sunlight came down on them and the camp people cheering around them. A familiar feeling. Grief and pity, Marith thought, for all of them. Fools, all of them.

* * *

They rode through the foothills of the mountains, skirting high above the burned plain where the enemy sat. A rich, golden evening, very warm: it should be pleasant. Night-flowering lilies, gardenia, glasspetals, their scent drawing the first moths. Groves of wild peach trees in blossom. Birds circling, calling, swirling in the darkening sky, drifts of lace. The melancholy of them, the grief of them. And he himself with a few guards around him, no one speaking to him, no one to think about, gazing at the sky and the trees, seeing patterns in the birds' flight. Washed away in it, dreaming. He stared at the sky and the longer he looked the more colours he saw there, shifting into one another, he saw them changing, the sky changing colour, becoming huge and every colour in his eyes. Blue as Thalia's eyes. This is peace, he thought. A memory of something, peace like this . . . and the pain and the shame came rushing back, wearying, because he remembered walking in the dawn, in the silence, feeling this, and then feeling grief. Riding in the dust, feeling this, with Carin. Standing by his window in Malth Elelane, in the dusk, alone, feeling this, a few days before Carin . . . before Carin was dead. His heart in his chest singing. Long caressing fingers of sorrow and pain. Knowing, feeling, hoping it would come.

They have betrayed me, he thought. It has come. He looked around at the guards: Brychan, the others whose names he did not know. Expected to see the swords coming for him, blades trying to cut him down, stabbing at him, forcing him from his horse. So clear. He could see them doing it. See the evening light flashing on the swords and in their eyes. Hear the horse scream beneath him, maddened, the crashing of birds overhead. And he would lie in the earth, in the evening flowers, in the silence, breathing in the flowers' perfume, listening to the birds calling overhead. And he would lie there until he died, or if he could not die he would lie there alone until the world ends.

The guards on their horses kept going. Did not look at him, or speak to him. A horse whinnied, another tossed its head hard, made its trappings ring. The lovely creak of the leather, the smell of the leather, the jangle of the bronze bit. The ground became stony, a patch of white rock thrusting bare through the black earth, so that the horses' hooves rang with a good hollow sound. It was almost dark now. The glow of the sky in the far west. The stars rising. An owl called. The men did not speak. They were not going to kill him. The creak of leather saddles. The sound of horses' hooves. The jangle of a bronze bit. The last plaintive song of a bird. They came around a shoulder of land, looked down into the plain, and they saw his men dying.

Chapter Twenty-Five

The Army of Amrath draws up in long rows stretching away into the horizon. Rank upon rank of them. Gleaming armour, gilded bronze over fine white cloth. They carry the sarriss, the long spear, its barbed point a thing to rip flesh going in and coming out. A short wide-bladed sword that will stab and hack and tear. A broad cruel knife. Their helmets cover their eyes. They wear red horsehair plumes that nod in the wind. Seen from above, standing on the walls of a city looking down at them, they must look like a great field of flowers. Like the Rose Forest of Chathe must have looked, before we burned it. They stand in perfect silence, still as standing stones, still as teeth in a dead mouth. Perfect order. Perfect discipline.

The infantry have the centre. The men in close formation, shoulder to shoulder, tight-packed, a wall of bronze. A solid block. A hammer. A single, deadly blade. On the left wing, the light cavalry under Faseem Meerak and Alleen Durith. There also, the magelord Ynthe Kimek and two war machines hurling banefire. On the right wing, the heavy cavalry under Osen Fiolt.

The enemy fill the plain like an ocean. A surging tide of men and horses, black horses, black-tempered iron axes, black armour that sucks down the light. Black antlers on their helmets, reaching like clawing fingers. Like dead bone hands clawing out. Above them, circling, golden eagles with wing spans wider than a man. Snakes in the horses' manes. Blue fire in the horses' mouths and beneath their hooves. Gold fire flickering around the eagles' wings. Rank upon rank of them moving, swirling, no order to them, the horses buck and rear, the infantry twine around them, the mass of them is like the ocean, restless, formless, a dance that is blurring to the mind, soothing almost to the eye as I watch them. One of the great pleasures of my life now, to watch the sea. They do not have drums or trumpets, as we do, the men of the Mountains of Pain and the men of Turain. The snakes in their demon horses' manes hiss, the snakes' scales rasp together, the eagles above them shriek. They fly pennants of gold silk hung with horse tails, and there are whistles set in the pennants to catch the wind. They make a low moaning sound, like the sound of a cold wind. It reminds me of the silence of the Small Chamber, the breath of the victim waiting there for my knife.

A good omen, then, surely, I try to think.

The Queen of Turain rides at the head of them. Her face is bruised, a red wound runs from her mouth to her forehead. Her right arm hangs limp at her side. The willow leaves in her crown are brown and withered. Her golden hair is ragged and stained black.

'Like a field of ripe wheat after the blight,' Osen Fiolt says. There is the same desperate kind of hope in his voice. He looks at me. I look back at him. We will do this, our eyes say. We must. Curse Marith, our eyes say. All the trust we placed in him. The world, he promised us. We did not, any of us, we did not think that he could simply lose.

'We are outnumbered,' says Ryn Mathen.

'We have been outnumbered before,' Alleen Durith says. 'The Army of Amrath was outnumbered ten to one on the plain of Geremela, as I recall.'

'Let's hope someone gets the same brilliant idea as you did, then,' says Dansa Arual, 'and changes sides early.'

'Let's hope,' says Alleen, glaring at her. He licks his lips nervously.

Frayed, all of them. So on edge it hurts me to watch them. 'You surrendered after the battle at Balkash, with ten of your soldiers left alive around you, Dansa. Of the soldiers I led at Geremela, two thousand survived,' Alleen says. 'Ask them if I betrayed anyone.'

Osen Fiolt moves his horse away from them. Reviewing the lines once and again. Our lines, and their lines. Looking, trying to see something. Whatever it is that Marith sees, when he looks them over and knows how to win. 'We kill them before they kill us,' Marith says, before a battle. 'Our men and our horses, we go at them, we kill them all, we win. That's all there is. There's nothing special I do.' Osen looks at the lines of soldiers, our lines, the enemy lines. Again and again. Trying to see it. I ride over to join him. Tal, my guard, follows me, as he always follows me.

'We can defeat them,' I say. 'You believe it.'

Osen laughs. 'We have to defeat them. We suppose we could see what happens if we try to slip away overnight.'

'We can defeat them,' I say. I think so clearly of the Small Chamber and the knife. 'Death to the dying,' I say to Osen. 'We can defeat them.'

We look down over the great lines of my soldiers. So beautiful. So perfect, lovingly carefully turned out, their swords and spears clean and sharp and hungry, their armour polished, the crests of their helmets nodding in the wind. A horseman stroking his horse's neck, whispering into its ear; an infantryman with his hand resting gently on the hilt of his sword; an infantryman rubbing fretfully at a smear of dirt on the pole of his sarriss.

Marith's words come back to me, shouting, his voice slurring drunk: 'Kill them all! Onward forever! On and on until the world ends!' Weeping, drooling, he disgusts me, I want to strike him, I am repulsed by him, I wish I had never seen him. 'Never stop! Never stop! On and on! Kill them!' Brychan has come running to wake me and fetch me, because he thinks that as the king's wife I can do something. Marith is crawling through his vomit, sobbing, cursing, I wish with all my heart that I had killed him. 'Never stop! On and on! On and On! Again! Again! Kill them!' Marith's words come back to me, lying beside me in the cool green of the mountain slopes, his hair damp from swimming in a stream, he is weaving a garland of white flowers for my hair, in a glade of lilies and woodstars and wild honeysuckle they are setting a tent of gold silk for us to sleep in, laying our bed with rose petals, preparing honey cakes and wine, guards keep anyone from coming within a mile of this place, he is sad and kind and beautiful, his hands rest on my pregnant belly, delighting in the child's kicks, but he says again in grief, 'But what will we do, Thalia, when we have conquered the world?' And there is fear, deep in his eyes, he twists the stem of a woodstar flower and it snaps between his fingers, its juice on his fingers is red, he says fearfully, 'What will the army do, Thalia, once it has run out of places to conquer? Go home? Live at peace?'

Once, when I was a child, I put my hand into a silver box, drew out a little piece of painted wood. If it had been painted black or white, I would have died that evening. Because it was painted red, I was enthroned as the Beloved of the God Great Tanis. If we win this battle, I am the Queen of All Irlast still. If they defeat us, I am nothing. How very simple that is.

The army crackles with readiness. Eager. I can feel their hope and their love.

'Marith swore we would retreat,' Osen says. 'If he lost.'

'I know that.'

Osen says, 'Shall we attack?'

When a child in the Temple reached the age of five, she put her hand into the box. If she drew black or white, I killed her. If she drew red, when she was grown to adulthood she would kill me.

I say without a pause, 'Yes. Attack.' The two armies facing each other. The enemy clashing their swords on their shields. I raise my left arm. In my hand I am holding a knife, the sun flashes on its blade. I remember . . . The smell of it, the taste of it. I drop my arm down.

The whole army before me breathes a great gasp.

A shout from off to my left. The war engines loose. Barrels of banefire crash into the enemy ranks. The bubbling voiceless cries of men dissolving away in fire as they die for me. A shout from the enemy. Answering crash of their war machines, loosing black rocks.

Rocks! It is pitiable. The King of Death looses banefire, commands dragons, and his enemies defend themselves with rocks!

A shout from the enemy. A hail of arrows, thick ripping barbed poisoned iron points. Slamming into the Army of Amrath's front lines. Punching through the soldiers' bronze. Piercing through to the bone. Among the killing arrows, whistling arrows that sing as they fly. An eerie howling sound. It reminds me of a prayer chant.

Both armies are champing their teeth waiting to get going. Desperately hungrily ears pricked for the signal to advance. The enemy loose another arrow-storm. A shout from our men and our war machines loose again, all four of them, hurling banefire. Osen looks at me. I draw a breath. Raise my arms for the dragons. Rehearse the words in my mind, once, twice, they come out with a sweet hot taste: '*Ke kythgamyn!*' Kill! Kill! At my voice they rise together. Their fire bursting out of them. Ah, Great Tanis, my head spins with it, I raise my hands and the dragons come at my command. *Ke kythgamyn!* It is wondrous. Yet, even as I had expected, dark shapes rise from the enemy lines to match them. Shapeless, shifting wing beats, the old things of ice and darkness that walk the high peaks of the Mountains of Pain on cloven-footed legs. Wild terrible god things.

The war engines loose. Ours and the enemy's both. Banefire and dead black stones. Ynthe Kimek the magelord looses out a blaze of mage fire. That, also, is matched from the enemy ranks by lightning bolts of silver and black. Mage fire searing through the front ranks of both armies. The war engines loose and loose.

Ke kythgamyn! Osen draws up his horse for a charge. He looks strange, his teeth gritted, his eyes fixed not on the enemy but on the head of his horse.

Opposite him, the men of the Mountains of Pain charge first.

Red shrieking lips, black helmets with antlers nodding, black horses with cold fire hissing from their mouths and beneath the tread of their hooves. I call out to the dragons that spiral in the air fighting the mountain gods.

Osen charges. The spear point, where Marith should be. The men behind him shrieking, foaming-mouthed with rage, kill them kill them kill them. The war engines loose over them. A black stone crashes towards them, brings horses down. Men scrabble in the dirt before they are crushed beneath the charge. A wash of mage fire. Horses and men burning. The earth rising as steam. Bronze rising as steam.

Osen smashes into the enemy's charge. Horses breaking. Men breaking. Everything red and dust and screaming. Nothing but sword blades coming down. The two armies face each other. Swords and spears. Aching for this. Starving men coming to sate themselves. Drums. A peal of trumpets. The massed lines of the Army of Amrath begins to advance. The men of the mountains stand waiting. Faceless iron helmets. Cut off from the world of the living. Dead, iron men. Ah, Great Tanis. I see it. The thrill of it, the beauty of it, for this alone all that he has done is worth the cost. To see it, to see men die in light and fire, falling like stars, tearing all the world apart as they die. This is what Marith sees. What they all see. It is like light. I who was the High Priestess of Great Tanis the Lord of Living and Dying, she who alone was permitted to shed blood for the God – I thought that I understood death and killing.

Meet them! Kill them! Take them! The killing ground. The two lines moving. The two armies meet.

The infantry lines push together. The massed ranks of the Army of Amrath, a wall of flawless bronze, pressing forward, advancing, crushing, their feet trampling down the earth. The thinner line of the men of the mountains is pushed backwards at the centre, its battle front curving, a thin crescent of black iron like a waning moon. Weaker, surely? I had faith in our army, I knew that they could do this, they who die for me, fight for me, they cannot be defeated, they will be triumphant. Yet the crescent holds them, pushes back. Hold them! Hold them! Break them! Break them! The two sides pushing and grappling. Everything utter confusion, pressed so tight, everything shattering. Crushing too tight to breathe. Everywhere swords and spears and metal grinding remorseless against metal and skin and bone. Push. Hold. Hold them! Break them! The lines wavering. The weight of the Army of Amrath bearing down. The enemy begins to move back.

On the left wing, the light-armed cavalry under Faseem Meerak struggles to engage the enemy. Repeatedly, the mountain men charge towards them, eagles flashing down above them, talons ripping at their horses' heads. Repeatedly, Faseem screams to his men to be ready. Repeatedly, the mountain men break off short, wheel away left or right, reform, make to charge again, again break off. Confused and maddened, Faseem Meerak's men begin to lose cohesion. Their formations begin to break up. Faseem can be heard cursing, his face flushed. The mountain men jeer. Shake their axes. They have bells strung on the handles of their axes that ring with a jingle of child's bells. Osen Fiolt comes riding towards them, his sword the Calen Mal shining. The Eagle Blade. Faseem Meerak's horsemen cheer him. Faseem Meerak can be seen to grind his teeth.

In the centre, the infantry push forward. The men of the mountains are staggering back. Their lines folding, their centre crumbling, the Army of Amrath surging through them. Water eating its way through sand. The red dragon tears apart the mountain gods.

Faseem Meerak shouts. Readies his cavalry for a counter-charge. Swords flashing. Polished bronze reflecting killing light. The mountain men on their demon beasts retreat back. Clearly, in the melee of the battle, I can see Kiana Sabryya, strapped to her horse. Alis Nymen, who was once a fish merchant in Toreth Harbour, hacking away with his one good arm. Dansa Arual, wounded, her face so bright. The enemy riders swarming around them.

A shadow crashes into the melee. A dead god falling from the sky. It breaks over horses and men, mine and my enemy's; blue mage fire cold as wanting, surging in waves, rising as mist, eating flesh and bone and iron and bronze. An enemy sword takes down Dansa's horse. It falls and she falls with it, crushed beneath its bulk. Blue mage fire rips two of her men apart.

A wall of mage fire sears across Faseem Meerak's advance. His light-armed troops fall back panicked and burning. Shadow creatures with eyes of stone. Faseem Meerak screams and curses and burns and dies. I see it, so clearly, through the melee. Alleen Durith pulls his horsemen into some kind of order. Mage fire seethes over them. They too break, flee with the fire burning them to ash even as they run. The ground around them is strewn with corpses. Ice freezing over faces black with cold. Faseem's horsemen are pulling back, terrified. Defeated. They are not used to defeat. The men of the Mountains of Pain on their demon horses shriek with laughter. Wheel away. Charge the infantry lines. At the flanks the enemy surge inwards. The horns of the crescent drawing together. Enveloping the army. Closing like a mouth.

Above the battlefield, watching, I see it. All of it. I cry out to them to warn them. I am powerless to do anything to help them. I watch uselessly, helplessly, I am their queen and I can do nothing to save them.

The Army of Amrath tight-packed. Shoulder to shoulder. Their long spears are tall as a man, heavy, difficult to manoeuvre. Their minds soaked with blood. The enemy lines are closing from the flanks, encircling them, closing up behind them. They are unable to turn to respond.

The green dragon comes down rending fire, the gods it fights claw it and hurt it, fight it and it comes down tumbling in shadows, the demons clinging to it devouring it, its blood sprays out, but it turns and burns the ranks of the enemy, burns them, destroys them. But it is too late. Our infantry lines struggle and are surrounded. The enemy lines close around them. Discipline is lost.

Weapons are flung down. A slaughter. A choking crush of bodies. Sword blades and spear points and mage fire and mage ice. Their own bodies. Dead men trampling on dying men.

This is not like light.

There is a song the men sing, sometimes, when they are tired and maudlin and the lamps are burning dim.

> *You who were strong as mountain streams,*
> *Warriors, lion-men, storm-bringers, spear-clad.*
> *You drank wine in the feast hall,*
> *Boasted, wrestled, your fathers were proud,*
> *Your wives loved you, women loved you,*
> *The bright-faced ones, shining sword-men,*
> *'Be as he is', mothers bade their young sons.*
> *Joy you brought to all in the feast hall,*
> *You sang the songs, the maidens sighed when you danced.*
> *Handsome-faced, gold-wearing,*
> *Your renown, your valour, your glory,*
> *Pleasure to all, we sang of the strength of your spear arm.*
> *On the grey hill you lie now.*
> *Food for crows.*

The old songs, the glories and the tragedies, let us sit now by the fire and tell sad stories of the death of kings. The enemy is defeated. The hero conquers. Evil is vanquished, the world turned to rights, good men stand victorious, the shadow is cast out. The rout of the enemy who came to rape and slaughter and pillage and must be destroyed and must be cast out. And the enemy were men, as we are. And the enemy were husbands and fathers and brothers and mothers and children and sisters and wives. The enemy loved and hoped and sorrowed and wanted. The enemy raped and slaughtered and destroyed. And those who loved them weep.

* * *

A hundred thousand men we have in our army. Loving us. Following us. They have conquered half the world for us. They fight for us. They die for us. A hundred thousand men who have grown to love fighting and have done nothing else for four long years but fight. They have made me Queen of the World. They delight me and disgust me. I stand and watch them dying, and I want to bury my face in my hands for shame. But I will not look away.

If we lose, I am nothing.

Chapter Twenty-Six

The whole battlefield is burning. There is no battlefield. Huddles of men fighting and dying. Lying wounded, staring up at the sky. The sound of men dying, gasping for breath. Horses' hooves again, thundering like water, black horses rushing down like water; golden hair like a wheat field rippling in midsummer breeze. Blue cornflower eyes. A scent of flowers. A woman's laugh. Swords and axes, metal crashing against metal, skin ripped open, the crack of bones as they break. All eternity, fighting. Nothing, nothing left but to fight and die. The shriek of murder. The hiss of breathing. The gnashing of men's teeth. A horse runs past without a rider. Two men fighting together cursing each other, each blaming the other for their wounds.

A voice screams on, 'The army is destroyed! The Army of Amrath! Destroyed! We lost! We lost!'

Tal curses and curses and curses. Soldiers dying. More and more of them dying. Cut down unarmed. Trying to flee and there is nowhere to flee. Their bodies are frozen. Blue lips rimed with ice. The ground where they lie is white with ice. Horsemen coming closer. Smash of iron axes. Taste of cold.

Ashamed and betrayed. Humiliated. Knowing ourselves for fools. All is confusion, soldiers running here and there, blood stink, death stink, bronze and iron, rank sweat dirt smell. The men collapsing on the damp earth, cold and filthy, bleeding; they sink down, stretch out exhausted, trembling. Dry voices calling out for water and bread. On the edges of the fighting the camp women are already picking their way forward, women with knives, and their hands move, and occasionally their hands come up flashing with gold. A woman comes up to a wounded man weeping and shrieking, begins to mourn him as already dead. The shadows come down to the dark earth to lick at his bright blood. His mouth and nose and eyes are grey with dust. The look in his eyes is the look of a man who knows that he is dead.

And I remember, suddenly, then, something I have not thought of for years, buried away in shame. Ausa, my friend, one of the priestesses in the Temple, leading her small nothing life in service to the God. I remember leading Ausa away to punish her for her crimes against the God Lord Tanis, and Ausa cried out, 'Look at the sun, Thalia! Look at the sun!'

The bronzesmith works for days, forges a great sword for a king or a mage lord, sets its hilt with jewels, weaves it around with spells and charms, makes sacrifices to its forging, whispers rune words over the molten bronze. Men die in the dark to mine the metal, crouched beneath the roots of the mountain, scrabbling mouthing like worms in the rock. The closest a man can come to being a dragon, bronzeworking. *Ca deln*, Marith says they are still called in the old rune tongue of the White Isles. 'Dragon men'. Sacred men. The work breaks the body. Leaves the bronzesmith crippled and in pain. Destroys him.

Marith's voice, stricken with grief, screaming. '*On and on! On forever! Killing till the world ends*!'

We have unleashed it. We cannot stop. We must go on. A ravaging beast, my army. Its hunger is eternal. Its hunger grows and grows. So many other things we could do indeed, Marith and I. But – I think . . .

This is why he let the Queen of Turain defeat him, I think. Because he wanted to lose. Because he wanted . . .

A man comes crashing towards me, one of our own soldiers.

In front of us, screaming. In our way. Tal cuts him down. Cold blue ice flames. Tal is panting: 'Run! Run!'

Fear pouring off Tal, and I am terrified. But we must go, get out. Ride through cold fire. The Army of Amrath is dying, Marith is dead or dying. I have lost everything. But I must get out. Crawl out of here on my hands and knees. Down on my belly, if I must.

The dragon's shadow, the dragons coming down. I hear voices screaming in fear of them. Riders coming up behind us. The sound of horses' hooves. I run. Like trying to outrun the waves of the sea. Five men in black horned helmets, going past us, cutting our men down. They swing around. They are facing me. They stop still, their horses trampling red gore. Hold up bloody axes. The absurd sweet ring of silver bells.

I will not die. I refuse to die.

Silence, suddenly. We are cut off from the world. Standing waiting, the horsemen waiting. I can hear the horses' breath. The hiss of the snakes in the horses' manes.

Five pairs of eyes staring at me from black iron helmets. Eyes as terrible and empty as Marith's own. I will put the fear on them. Fear and dark and light. From the fear of life and the fear of death, preserve us, Great Tanis, Lord of All Things.

The horsemen come closer. Perhaps four spear-lengths away. Behind us, distant, the roar of the battlefield, my soldiers being torn apart. A single scream cutting through all the rest, a woman's voice in pain beyond anything.

Crackle of ice. The woman's scream is cut off.

One of the horsemen comes still closer. Black eyes in a black helmet. Black armour. He could be made of black iron. He smells of iron. He does not look alive.

'You will not harm me.' I can hear my voice very clear, very cold, like a mountain stream.

This is how Marith feels, I think, when he kills.

I can make him fear me, I think. His horse snorts, stamps, tosses its head. I see the man tremble. He moves his horse a step back.

One of his companions shouts something in their language. He shouts in reply.

The world closed down to this, I am staring and the man in his black helmet staring back. I feel the ghost of my dead child kick inside of me.

I will not let him kill me. He will not. He must not. I did not do it all to die here defeated. I also take a step back.

A long time, I think, since I killed a man. I remember it. The way it felt to kill. The feel of blood on my hands. I can feel it, on my hands. He is my enemy, I think. He wants to kill me. Thus I must kill him first. It is a sweet thought. Of course it is.

I am unarmed, I look at him, I feel him fear me, he chokes out a cry. With his left hand he takes a knife from his belt. It reminds me of the knife I used in the Small Chamber. It is long and sharp.

'Do it,' I say to him. My voice sounds clear and cold and unreal. My mouth feels filled with blood. My hands feel sticky with blood. My dead child kicks in my womb. His companions cry out to him in horror as he raises the knife to his throat. He is crying with fear.

He slumps dead in the saddle. The knife falls from his dead hand. His horse bolts away. His companions flee from me.

The rain is coming down harder, washing the blood on the knife away. It is made of iron, it is colder and heavier than bronze. It lies on the trampled earth gleaming clean. My hands are sticky with blood.

Tal cries out, 'We must go, we must flee.' He is so afraid. The enemy comes at us again. My guards' pathetic swords, against these demon men. Butcher men. I am trapped. And I am afraid. One man I can break with fear, still, I can put fear into him, fear of death, fear of living, he falls away from me weeping in fear, shaking. But there are so many of them. So many. My guards are dying or dead. My horse shrieks, wounded, and I scramble from its back before it runs and then it crashes to the earth, dead. Tal, my guard, falls dead.

I am so alive. I am nothing. I don't want any of this to stop.

Twenty years dead, if I had chosen a different lot, if another child had chosen a different lot. I don't want to lose this. The sheer futility of my life, if one day I must die. I who knew life and death. Make it stop, take it away, make me not a mortal woman, say I will not die!

Marith shouting in his sleep, '*Mother, Father, Tiothlyn!*' Say you will not die. Say you are not dead. It is impossible to conceive of it, that you are dead and will not return. Say I will not die as you are dead. I stand looking at the enemy soldiers before me. They stare at me. They will not kill me. They cannot.

'Thalia!'

Absurdly, mockingly, Tobias is standing there. His whole body is soaked in blood.

'Thalia!' Tobias cries out. There is blood and sweat and spittle on his face His face when I turn to him . . . it is like a light has settled on his face.

'Run!' he screams to me. 'Run!'

Always, always, he follows me. I should kill him.

The sun is setting in a sky the colour of rotting wounds. Dusk coming: s*eserenthelae aus perhalish*. We will. Oh my love, we will. Too dark now for shadows. The cold seeping in. Chaos and murder: they do not know, the soldiers, they do not know what to do, they have no words for this, no thinking, they march and they die and they kill and they are victorious, and now they are like children, and they do not know now what to do.

The sky is full of death things, walking, calling. I touch the scars on my arm. Sacred words of life and death. So many have I killed. But I wanted . . . all I ever wanted was to live.

I take his hand and we run.

Chapter Twenty-Seven

Marith
Fighting

And in his head all was crimson. The filth of blood covering him. Peace inside him. I never wanted this. Remember? Never. I meant it and meant it and it's all too late. I thought there was a way out. There's no fucking way out. There never was. There never is.

An enemy horseman came up against him, drove his mount against the flank of Marith's horse. Chill of cold down to the bone. A mage blade lashed out. Blue fire flickering down its length. His horse shying, stamping, maddened, the snakes in the enemy horse's mane goading it. Biting at it. Couldn't get straight. Horses wrestling. Blue mage fire cold as love. Hacked and hacked, got the man, his sword twisting on the man's armour, blows so hard the sparks rose. His horse's legs going, skipping, stumbling. Shrieked in pain. The mage blade thrusting itself into his face. Marith drove his sword in. Killed him. The air rang with the crash of it, his blade hacking at the man like an axe against a tree. And he was killing.

Hacking and stabbing. Stinking press of men and horses and demons. Black mage fire. Killing. Killing.

The battle was lost. The men were dying. His army was crushed, scattered, torn away on a cold wind. Alone, Marith rushed down to them, wounded, his sword shining in his hand. The Army of Amrath parted before him, drew back knowing he was coming without needing orders, felt him, knew him, and he was there and their lines parted in wonder to see him charge through them, cleave his way into the enemy ranks. As a dog knows its owner is approaching, lifts up its tail, trots eagerly to the doorway, waits there, so the Army of Amrath knew their lord their king their god their master, parted for him, surged back after him to follow him as the sea parts and breaks and surges onwards when a fast ship races on bringing plague and death. And he was killing. And he was killing. And his sword and his sword arm were soaked through with blood, and his eyes were filled with blood, and his head was sweet with blood.

'Marith!' Osen Fiolt was staggering towards him, on foot.

'They're dying,' Marith cried to him. 'My men. They're dying.'

'I know. We're losing. We need to retreat.'

'Retreat?' No, Marith thought, no, no, but I'm killing them.

'Marith!' The blood on Osen's face was new and fresh. Osen was holding his body wrong, his shoulders, his leg; gasped and winced, cursed, breath hissed out of him, his face screwed up, his body shook.

'Osen?'

He's hurt he's hurt he's hurt. Not Osen. Osen can't be hurt.

His own body hurt, still. His sword was very heavy. His head felt heavy. Fall off his horse and sleep . . . Men running past him, bloodied, shrieking. Stinking of fear. Some of them had dropped their weapons. A sword fell at his feet as a man ran. The blade all bloody. The man's face all bloody. Gone and ran on. Breaking from him. His horse moving backwards, pulled back by the men. Rout. Slaughter. Those that stood firm, their swords hungry, fighting, brave men, men who loved him, who loved war, who would not break, fighting on, their swords hungry, their spears hungry, hacking, pressing, they stood firm and he watched as they were butchered and swept away. He thought, suddenly, of digging

237

channels in the sand on the beach on a hot summer's morning, the sea would come in, sweep over, the sand would hold in places, little islands, the sea would eat away at it but it would stand, and then . . .

'Sound the fucking retreat!' Osen shouted. Screamed.

'No! Kill them!' Osen looked so small, on foot, all hunched up in blood.

Trumpets sounded. Osen had not been asking him.

Osen pulled at Marith's horse, mad, trying to drag it. 'Fucking get out of here.' The horse reared, almost struck Osen's chest. Osen screamed, 'We've lost, Marith, we need to get out.'

The enemy was boiling up around them. Cutting them. Bringing his men down. His men retreating. 'Hold them!' Osen screamed to someone, 'Hold them while we get the king out, get back, oh gods gods—'

Through the enemy ranks a figure was coming, huge, towering over the men around it. She was wounded and bloodied, as Marith was. Her hair was filled with black blight, her skin was cracked like soil in a drought. She brought down his men around her, felled them. They died like children at her hands. She rode her black horse that poured out cold blue fire, frosted the earth beneath it, its eyes were blind wounds where they had been hacked out, its ears and its lips had been cut off. The snakes of its mane dripped venom.

'Hold them hold them hold them while we get the king out oh gods oh gods oh gods oh gods—'

And Marith thought: is this how men feel, when I come at them with my sword drawn?

'Get out get out get fucking out.' Osen pulling at his horse his horse shrieking and bucking. 'Get out cover us get the king out.' Two men throwing themselves before her his army crumbling like sand running like the tide going out running like clouds. 'Get out, Marith.' The men came running. Screaming. Shouting. Blind dumb dead broken crushed. Their voices called out the despair of the end of all things. The dragon came over them. The red dragon.

Flying very low. Marith raised his face to it. *Ke kythgamyn maritket!* But it swept over them to the south, flying fast, and was gone.

'Osen!' he shouted, because Osen looked as though he might be going to stay, to try to fight her, to cover him fleeing. She killed one of his men with a sword stroke that cut his body in two. Red madness. Rage. Scent of sunlight and wet earth and fresh baked bread. The men dying. All dying, shrieking, falling, the green dragon wrestling in the sky with gods that overcame it, tore at it, stifled its fire, the shadowbeasts broken down fleeing, his army eaten up by the enemy, consumed in black iron jaws, oh my army, my beloveds, you who fought and died and lived for me, you who would follow me forever, my loves, my companions, oh you who were true to me, who trusted me, who cared for me and placed your lives in my hands . . . you see? You see? What I am? What you are? Rotting flesh, my army, men marching who are a long time dead.

Didn't I promise you death? Death and ruin and killing without end?

You wanted it! You wanted it! All of you!

The swords came down, the axes came down, teeth and fists and knives and down to the bone. His men were scattered, fleeing, dying, the earth was slick and liquid and scented with their blood.

The Queen of Turain, laughing. The enemy lines are solid as the mountains. Perfectly ordered, shields locked to shields. Black armour sucking all the light out. Cold fire plays around their helmets, runs down the black iron, dances on the antlers they wear that make them monstrous beast things. The blades of their iron axes burn blue. They are not men. They cannot be men. A shower of arrows, whistling. There are long ribbons tied to some of the arrows, brilliant red and silver streamers that snap in the wind as they fly. Beautiful. Terrifying, somehow. Ribbons and whistles. They run like the dragon runs in the sky, they come down on the Army of Amrath and the tips are poisoned. Like the dragon's blood. The sound, like rain on water, of the arrows striking the

Army of Amrath in retreat. Cold fire in the sky. Old gods. The shadowbeasts twist and flee in panic. Shatter into grey ice.

He thinks: I can father no living children. My father hated me, he was right to hate me, he didn't hate me. I killed him. Thalia is dead. Carin is dead.

The ground is churned-up mud. It catches in his horse's hooves, drags at the horse, slows it. This is my soldiers' blood, he thinks. The horse snorts and shrieks. Black horses coming towards him. He draws his sword. The horse goes forward in the mud. On the edges of the killing ground things crawl towards him in the earth. Blood and bone. Hungry maggot things. Consuming his men.

This is what they were born for. What all men are born for. What is life, Marith? Life is a lie. Life is death. He screams out to his men.

His men remember this as they stumble backward in retreat in fear, and their hearts beat. He screams to them to rally. They steady themselves. Become themselves. Their lines reform around him. They shout out his name. 'Marith! Amrath! Death!' They pull themselves into order, grasp tight their swords, grit their teeth. A bloody sweeping howling tide. 'Marith! Marith!' They charge the enemy ranks.

This is the Army of Godsdamned Amrath. Some of these men, they butchered their own mothers to be here. Some of these men, they'd drag themselves along by their bloody fingernails to kill. There are men fighting with maggots eating their faces. Grinning, stroking their swords, and you can see them rotting away, their skin going black and green as they fight. The crows come down. Peck at the wounds. Pretty little songbirds up overhead twittering, swirling clouds of them, beautiful like smoke, gorging themselves on maggots and flies. The Army of Amrath regroups itself, steadies itself strong. The Army of Amrath fights joyfully, singing the paean, pushes on. Kill them! Kill them! The *Ansikanderakesis Amrakane* leads his horsemen forward. His sword shines in his hand brilliant with rainbows, rainbows dancing on the ground around him, dancing in the air, like snow falling, like coloured stars. Drums pound out a rhythm. Silver trumpets ring. Crash of metal and flesh. Slaughter. Death like the world's end.

It is too late.

Alleen Durith turns to the enemy, throws up his hands in surrender, calls out to them, 'I am with you! Kill the demon! Destroy it, the plague, the King of Ruin and Death!' Some of his men join him, merge into the ranks of the enemy, rush down onto the Army of Amrath from behind, tearing down on them like a sudden flood. Some stand in confusion, while the enemy goes past them. Are overwhelmed and dragged on. Some few of them shout out in rage or in horror: 'Betrayal! Treachery!' Die as they stand. Ynthe Kimek the magelord blasts out power, lost and panicked, hesitant to destroy his own men. 'To me, to me, Army of Amrath!' The men do not listen, to him or to his magic. A man comes up behind the magelord, runs him through. Blood spurts from his mouth. A glorious thing, magic. A wonder. A marvel. But it can't stop a man dying in pain. Ynthe Kimek the magelord falls dead. Alleen Durith shouts, 'Destroy the monster!' Leads the men of the mountains and his own men down on the Army of Amrath. One of your own generals himself plots to betray you. Conspires against you. Thinks you nothing but filth and death. The gods run with them on cloven-footed legs.

Lord Ranene the weather hand swings his sword, wounded. Blood is pouring from his chest, his arms, his gut. An old man, now. Tired. In the last years, as weather hand to the *Ansikanderakesis Amrakane* the King of Ruin, his black hair has turned white. Standing on a beach looking down into the wine-dark sea he could raise a tempest, drown every man here fighting, blast them with lightning, call up a wind so strong every tree in a hundred miles would be torn down. Here, in the mountains, he is an old man with a sword he does not know how to use. He screams, reaches out for his power. He falls and his mouth is filled with grey dust.

His entrails lie spilled in the dirt for the crows. His death closes over him.

Ryn Mathen and the Chathean allied troops break. Run in panic. Stampede down toward the river, their eyes wide and wild. The enemy does not follow them. They throw themselves into the water, some are drowned there, the water is churned up with men's limbs. They get across, trampling on the drowned. The enemy leaves them to run. 'Betrayed!' the men of Chathe scream, 'We are betrayed!' And others scream, 'Destroy the monster! He will lose this battle! What is he to us but bloodshed? Why should we fight for him?' Across the mountains and across the plain, in every direction, like autumn leaves on the storm wind, the men of Chathe run.

'Alleen!' Osen Fiolt screams. He is weeping with rage and grief. 'Alleen!' Osen Fiolt screams, 'Alleen!' The enemy breaks over him like a wave. The shock on his face – and Marith realizes, dimly, that Osen truly did not expect this. 'Marith!' Osen Fiolt screams, 'Marith! Please!' Osen's eyes roll from side to side, waiting for another of his friends to turn against him. Confused and lost. 'But you were my friend,' poor Osen screams.

A man with an axe comes charging at him, a huge black horse with red demon eyes, blue fire in its mouth. Its hooves strike blue flames as it runs. The axe is raised at him; he sees as it comes down that the man recognizes him even as he strikes him, checks his arm with a cry of fear or wonder or triumph. He feels the blade of the axe on him, the weight of the whole horse and rider behind it, it bites into him through to the bone. The axe blade crumbles. The metal eaten. Fallen to rust. Blood comes out of his wound dry as rust. The horse rears up in terror. Black hooves shod in iron. It writhes and twists itself, a thing of shadows, a mass of shadow dirt writhing together, like the white horses riding the waves of the sea. Its hooves strike him, send him reeling, they hurt him. He goes down under the hooves and he sees the rider's face staring at him in disbelief. The horse rears again, the hooves come down. His blood running from the iron-shod hooves. Thrashes away from it, its shape is changing, it shrieks out in a human voice. Dead and alive and never-living, a shadow horse, this is a dream, he thinks, a dream a nightmare I am dreaming about horses riding horses being a child before all of this when I was alive when the world was a real place for me. He strikes it, kills it, kills the rider, the rider falls crumbling corroding eaten away. He can't remember how he killed it.

He can hear the scream of horses. Children's voices screaming as the enemy butchers the camp followers of the Army of Amrath. His eyes sting him, blurred and swimming. He staggers to his feet. Gods, he's so tired. His hand shakes on the hilt of his sword. His mouth tastes of blood. Make it stop. It twists in his head. Like fingers. Tangling themselves, all entwined together. Hands clasped. Light and sound screaming heat and blood smell. Hatha dreams: I'm lost, it's not real, I'm far away back somewhere, in my bedchamber at Malth Elelane, in the desert, none of this is real, all of this is a dream. Carin. Carin. Help me. Father. Ti. Mother. Not real. Not real. None of this is real. My father is alive and my mother and Ti and Carin. I'm a nameless man in the desert. I'm a child in a castle by the sea. Birdsong in the orchards. Running in the gardens. Reading a book by a winter fire. The smell of a summer stream. That's real. Not this now. This is a lie. This is a dream. His sword is in his hand. Red jewel at the hilt winking at him. Glittering. Red light like the red light of the Fire Star. The King's Star.

'Marith,' Osen Fiolt is screaming, 'Marith! Marith!' He can hear it so clearly. 'Marith. Please.' And a voice there in his head shouting, laughing, this can all end, he thinks, he can stop soon, he can be free of it. The swords come down around him. His sword sings in his hand. His enemies' swords are bright as fire. The blades come down and come down. His wound hurts him. His enemies' swords are numberless. His head is white and empty. His sword sings, but it is growing heavy in his hand. His wife is dead. His captains, his companions, all of them are dying or dead. His army is dying. His army! His heart sings.

Five men. Ten. Twenty. A pile of corpses. Kills and kills and kills and kills. The swords come down. So many of them. He strikes and kills, and another rises up in its place. His head is spinning. He cannot see. All there is in his world is blood.

'Marith!' a voice screams.

Die and become nothing. End it.

Pain. Blood. All I am. All I ever could be.

Cool dark. Like Thalia's hair. Thalia's skin.

Make it go away. All of it. Please. Yes.

Pain.

Light.

And the world ends.

Chapter Twenty-Eight

Landra Relast, the gestmet, *the* gabeleth, *the bringer of justice*
Sailing to the White Isles on the ship *Palle*, that is the smooth
sheen of a calm sea

In her mind again and again she saw her triumph. In the blue of
the sky, in the dark water that moved beneath the hull of the ship.
A man in armour, a red cloak and red-black hair, a sword shining
bright as starlight, his face is buried in the filth and then he raises
his head. He is smiling as the shadow of a sword falls over him.

Her fingers dug into the ship's timbers, her skin catching on the
rough wood.

Forgive me, Marith, she thought.

I'm sorry, Carin.

PART FOUR

THE KNIFE

Chapter Twenty-Nine

Orhan Emmereth the Lord of the Rising Sun, the Dweller in the House of the East, the luckiest man in the Sekemleth Empire
The Golden City of Sorlost

Coarse sunlight spilling through the shuttered window, making patterns on the wall. Swirls and spirals, a game of yenthes, catching all the floating dust motes. The shutters carved as a trellis of flowers, the shadows they cast hands and smiling mouths. Afternoon. Peaceful. Orhan sitting reading. Darath sprawled on the bed reading. A distant sound from the gardens that might be Dion playing an ivory flute. The flute had been a gift to the boy from Darath. Darath had realized very quickly that it had been a mistake.

'I had no idea about children. No idea. God's knives, I nearly bought him a tin drum. Would he be upset if I accidentally trod on it, do you think?'

Darath had been living in the House of the East for weeks now. Since the news came of Arunmen's sack. If the world is mad, hang on to the few things one can love. 'There was no one left alive in Arunmen,' Bil had said. 'This is your son's house, and I don't want you to leave your son, and I know you don't want to leave him. So bring Darath to live here with you.'

Dion called him 'Uncle Darath!' with a breath of happiness, because that was how Orhan had said it the first time Darath and Dion met. Even that, Darath seemed to rejoice in, embracing the child tenderly, teaching him to play knuckle-bones, running through the garden with him in games of hide-and-seek.

'Where's Aunty Cese?' Dion asked once in a while. 'Why did she have to go, when Uncle Darath came? Did they swap?'

'She still comes to visit,' Bil comforted him. 'Soon she'll have her own son back again. That will make her happy, you see.'

'Happier than seeing me?'

Bil would laugh, tousle the boy's hair. 'Maybe even happier than seeing you, my baby baby boy, my lovely thing.'

Celyse had gone to live in the House of Flowers. A somewhat irregular arrangement, not received with enthusiasm in all quarters of society, but one couldn't have everything. A man, his lover, his wife and her son, his sister and her grief – too many relationships to keep track of there in one household. So throw the sister out and be done.

Celyse hated it, everyone else frowned on it. But, as Bil said, 'Being frowned on means they acknowledge we exist.'

Indeed: the Emmereths had some kind of status again now. The other high families could walk past without having to pretend they did not recognize Orhan's face. Orhan had no longer done whatever it was he had been accused of doing. A good man again. A loyal man. A true servant of Sorlost. The Immishman Lord Mylt had said so himself, and what could be higher praise than that? The Lord of the Rising Sun, the Warden of the Immish Marches, the Dweller in the House of the East: men with titles such as these cannot ever really have done bad things. And money: Lord Emmereth had been seen publicly spending money; Lady Emmereth went every day to the Great Temple, wearing a new dress each time, offering a purse of gold to the God. No one could ignore the sound the coins made each day as she put the purse down.

The past is like sand, shifting, changing, the wind blows and the sand moves and one cannot remember how it looked before it was changed, as a shiny bright new poet brightly said. And the metaphor is perfect, because it looks just as it looked before, it looks like yellow sand, and no one remembers because no one cares, because it is so dull.

This city is a dream city. Thus, as in dreams, there is no thought for the future, no memory of the past.

Philosophical musing interrupted by a particularly shrill noise from the garden. Orhan winced. 'If you don't tread on it, Darath, I will.' A howl that, if the Great Tanis was merciful, was Bil confiscating the damned flute.

The book Orhan was reading was a good one. A new one: he was enjoying getting to understand it. In Pernish, a long tale of the old kings and queens of Ith. Pernish literature, Pernish poetry, White Isles style clothes – anything with a connection to Marith Altrersyr suddenly quite the thing. 'Romantic', 'exotic'. These mad kings, their scheming wives, their ungrateful children, their endless cycles of rage and pain. Half the city must dream of savages with red-plumed helmets, huge spears raised erect . . . The more Orhan read of it, the more sensible the Empire and the Emperor seemed, in contrast; celibacy in a ruler very clearly a good thing. Which was in itself a very good reason to read a book.

The book's pages were perfumed. The scent varied: a few pages might have a faint scent of lilies, sweet and sad, to match a scene of love and heartbreak; the next page might smell of pine resin, bracing, clearing, when the story turned to a hero king come to restore his people's pride. This too was new and fashionable, a flippant new little wonderworking. The page he was reading now was a genealogy of the kings of Bakh, shocking in its lack of scandal, incest and murder, and smelled of green leaves.

The most sought-after book in Sorlost was the three volume *True History of the King Marith Altrersyr Amrath Returned to Us*, the pages of which were said to smell alternately of blood, semen and human excrement.

Janush the bondsman knocked and paused for a while outside the door and finally came in. Weeks since Darath moved in here, still everyone tiptoed around in terror in case they walked in on Lord Emmereth and Lord Vorley doing it. We're both almost forty, we've been together for . . . longer than I care to acknowledge. We don't actually do it very often. We should probably make the effort to do it more, in fact. I bet Darath thinks of savages with sweaty spears. There'd really be nothing to see, if anyone did walk in on it. Two middle-aged men having uninteresting, 'usual brief bit of foreplay, usual standard position, be back reading your book again before you know it, barely broke a sweat, do you have to fart like that immediately we've finished?' sex.

The joy of it, after everything. A dull married couple are Orhan and Darath, and God's knives it's sweet.

'My Lord Emmereth?'

Orhan put the book down. 'Yes?'

Darath sat up. 'What?'

'My Lord Emmereth, My Lord Vorley . . . Lord Lochaiel is downstairs, waiting for you. He says it's urgent.'

Ah. Darath said, 'He wants advice on toddler tantrums, perhaps? Tell him never, ever to buy his boys any kind of musical instrument.'

Selim Lochaiel was in the courtyard garden. There too the scent of green leaves, less real than in the pages of the book. He was standing running his hands over the lip of the dry fountain, seemed deep in thought. Heard them approaching and turned around. His face was lit up.

'Selim? You have something . . . good?'

'I have news from Turain,' Selim said. His voice was shaking with excitement, which certainly made a change from voices shaking with grief. 'The demon has overreached himself. His army is destroyed. He is dead. Dead!'

Dead! A lot of time and planning and bribery and begging and hope and . . .

'You're sure?' said Orhan. 'I was rather under the impression he kept boasting he couldn't die.'

252

'The great thing about immortality as a drinking boast,' said Darath, 'is that you're never going to have to go through the embarrassment of admitting you were wrong.'

Selim said, 'A messenger arrived an hour ago, his horse dying under him. There was a great battle south of Turain. The demon lost. There were almost no survivors. The demon's men would not surrender, the messenger says, fought on long after it must have been clear all was lost. Not, of course, that the men of the Mountains of Pain would have accepted a surrender. By the end, the messenger says, the demon's men were throwing themselves onto the mountain men's spears; the bodies were piled ten, twenty deep. They did not count the dead, they counted the survivors. And then they killed the survivors, and left them with the rest. The king's tent, his treasurers, all of it has been taken. The Army of Amrath has been wiped out as though it had never been. Every last trace of its pestilence has been cleansed from the face of the earth.'

'Apart from the huge pile of corpses,' said Darath. 'And I hope they've got a plan for cleansing that.'

'But him,' said Orhan. 'Marith Altrersyr. He is dead?'

Selim said, 'The messenger assures us that he is.'

'"Assures"?'

'They could hardly send us his body,' said Selim. 'He is dead. Alleen Durith saw it.'

Darath coughed. 'Alleen Durith is well?'

'As far as he says in his letter, yes.'

'Typical. We'll have to find the rest of the cash, now. He couldn't have gone and died a hero, could he? No, no, selfish bastard has to stay alive.'

'Darath.'

'*Turns on his king, his beloved friend, his trusted companion, his kin* – related, aren't they, somehow? – *his kin, blood of his blood, brother of his sword, cries out "Die, monster!", cuts him down. Dying, Marith Altrersyr the demon the enemy cries out "Traitor!", stabs him, the two fall together, their blood mingling, their filth mingling where they've pissed and shat themselves in death, white hands entwined . . . The demon and the hero, the demon's murderer, together in death.* Written on shit-scented pages. Now there's the best ending for us.'

'That's the other one,' said Orhan. 'Osen Fiolt. Alleen Durith's just a man he drinks with.'

Darath looked at Orhan pettishly. 'Yes, yes, I know. Anyway. Hurrah, rejoicing, Irlast is saved, children still unborn shall praise our names, thank the God Great Tanis. So now we have to pay Alleen Durith off?'

Selim said, 'Yes. Unfortunately we do.'

'Three thousand gold thalers. God's knives. What possessed you?'

'It wasn't me,' said Selim. 'It was Lord Mylt.'

'Lord Mylt! It's not Lord Mylt's money,' said Darath.

'Alleen Durith originally asked for four thousand,' said Orhan. 'Be grateful I bargained him down.'

'God's knives. Remind me again what we paid to have the Emperor killed, Orhan?'

'Darath. Please.'

'Alleen Durith writes that he will arrange to collect the money shortly. He will be passing through the western desert, of course, on the way back to Ith. It is possible . . .' Selim looked thoughtful. 'He will be wanting men, of course. Supplies, weapons and so forth. There are any number of things for sale in Sorlost that might be of interest to the new King of Ith with two thousand thalers to spend. Perhaps we should encourage him to come here.'

Orhan thought also. Interesting possibilities. A grateful young man with an army behind him, only too eager for our gold? 'Yes. We should certainly encourage him here.'

Selim laughed. 'Indeed.' Darath was looking a bit lost.

'If the demon is dead,' said Orhan, 'I think we need to start talking about Lord Mylt.'

'Wait. Wait. What about Lord Mylt?' Darath was looking very lost. It suited him.

* * *

Letter from Lord Durith of Ith to Lord Emmereth: 'I want Ith and Immier and the White Isles and Illyr.'

Letter from Lord Emmereth the Lord of the Rising Sun to Lord Durith: 'Ith, and that's it.'

Letter from Lord Durith of Ith to Lord Emmereth: 'Ith and Immier and the White Isles. Or the deal's off.'

Okay. Okay. Seeing as I have absolutely no authority over any of these places anyway and frankly never will, and, even more frankly, neither will you. Letter from Lord Emmereth the Lord of the Rising Sun to Lord Durith: 'Ith and Immier, and five thousand men from Immish to help you hold on to them for more than a week.'

Letter from Lord Durith of Ith to Lord Emmereth: 'Ith and Immier and the men and four thousand thalers in hard cash, my Lord Emmereth, I'm throwing away being best friends forever with the Lord of the World here, don't forget. I want something worthwhile back.'

'Two thousand thalers, Lord Emmereth,' *Lord Mylt saying,* 'and Sorlost pays it. And he can hire his own bloody men. Who does that treacherous little shit think he is? He's nothing. Drinking-friends with someone.'

Lord Emmereth the Lord of the Rising Sun to Lord Durith: 'Look, just bugger off, won't you?' *I won't write that down, obviously, in case someone accidentally rides the length of Irlast to deliver it.*

God's knives. How difficult should it be to get people to rise up against the King of Death? Dion was less demanding than this.

The rumour ran around the city in hours. Marith Altrersyr *Ansikanderakesis Amrakane* was dead and his army dead around him. He rode into the Mountains of Pain on a white horse with the light shining from him, and the mountains claimed him. Stories of starving men in the Nor Desert, lips black with thirst, wounded, screaming, babbling of gods and demons, cutting their own throats with bronze swords. 'All dead. All dead. Everything's dead.' White-robed merchants who had made the long journey from Mar across the Nor Desert told of vast battles, the sky over Turain turned to silver with mage light, the very air reeking of dead meat. 'All dead. All dead.'

'And yesterday a woman drunk on firewine stood up in the Court of the Fountain and screamed that King Marith was dead, that the world was ending, that all would fall in ash and blood,' said Darath. 'When she'd finished speaking she cut her own throat. If I hadn't heard it from Selim Lochaiel, I'd certainly believe it after that.'

The streets ran with wine and honey, celebrations from dawn to dusk to dawn again. A great weight that the city had not fully realized it felt lifted away. This is Sorlost the Unconquered, the Unconquerable, we had no fear of Marith Altrersyr's little wars, they were far away, unreal absurd things. We're safe! We're safe! Toasts drunk to victory over the demon, any one in Sorlost who could claim to be from Turain or the mountains feted, personally thanked. The owner of the wine shop in the Street of Yellow Roses suddenly announced Arunmenese ancestry, embraced Orhan, gave everyone a free drink. Poems describing the final battle could be bought on every street corner. Were sung every night. The whores offered a new position called 'the enemy in defeat'.

Three days after the news broke Orhan came down to breakfast to a strong smell of burning from the gardens. 'What's that? Is something on fire?'

'Bilale ordered her new White Isles-style dresses and Pernish scented books burned,' said Darath. 'If I hadn't heard it from Selim Lochaiel, I'd certainly believe it after that.'

In the Court of the Broken Knife a shrine was rising, a monument to the dead king. At the statue's feet refugees from half the world piled flowers, lit candles, cut locks of their hair in offering. The statue was weighted down with crowns of flowers, crowns of ribbons, crowns of silver and gold. The Immish soldiers did nothing now to remove them. Some of the soldiers, indeed, stopped there themselves to lay offerings, stood or knelt before the statue with a drawn sword, wept for the new dead war god. After a few days, a rumour flew around the city that drinking wine mixed with flowers from the shrine would cure impotence, help a woman conceive, ward off fever and weakness of the limbs. A few days later again, a woman left a dead ferfew bird there in offering, claiming that the bird's death would give her long life. A few days later again, a man opened the veins in his left arm, let the blood pour out at the statue's feet. The Imperial guard had to take some action, then, to stop the whole square stinking of rot.

The Emperor decreed a ceremony of thanksgiving in the Great Temple. They went by litter, the curtains closed, Orhan and Darath in one, Celyse, Bil and Dion following. Dion was still crying when Orhan and Darath left. Bil had refused to let him take the ivory flute with him. Even in a bag. Even if he promised not to play it.

'Can I take my red ball, then?' Orhan heard Dion saying as he left. 'Please? In a bag, and I'll carry the bag the whole time.'

'He's getting worse since you moved in, you know,' Orhan said to Darath. 'You're a terrible influence. Spoiling him.'

A warm dry wind was blowing through the city. Up from the south. I wonder what's blowing on that wind? The curtains of the litter flapped close, brushing against Orhan's legs.

All the high families gathering on the steps of the Great Temple, filing slowly in through the single narrow door. Nods to Darath, nods to Orhan; Orhan and Darath nodded back. Holt Amdelle and his son Symdle, their nods particularly stiff and formal, Symdle's eyes searching the crowds for his mother Celyse. I will beg Lord Mylt tomorrow to let her go back to them, Orhan thought. One last favour after everything I have done for him; it will go better with Holt if it's an order from Lord Mylt. Aris Ventuel, The Lord of Empty Mirrors, Dweller in the House of Glass, and his wife, the first of the high families to invite Orhan to a party after his return to favour; he threw the wildest parties in the city, he was at heart the kindest of all the High Lords of Sorlost. He stopped and greeted Orhan and Darath, smiled at them, they talked briefly of nothing, Aris' last party ('the first time in ten years I've had a two-day hangover, thank you, Aris'), Aris' wife's new dress. Eloise Verneth, Selim Lochaiel and Elolale, servant girls carrying their infant sons. Furious, raging anger still boiling off Eloise at the sight of Orhan. Orhan thought: look at Bil's hands, Eloise. You did that. You tried to kill my son when he was a baby: he will be here any moment, with his mother and her maimed hands, how can your hatred of me not turn to shame then, how can your hate not break you, when you see that? Elolale swept past them not looking, Selim nodded to Darath and Orhan but did not speak.

A voice shouted, suddenly, a woman pointing, sunlight flashing on her jewelled sleeve. People turned, staring. More shouts. More pointing hands. 'Look! Look!' A godstone had been set up in the Grey Square, in the very shadow of the Temple. As tall as a man, and as broad, a rough column of dark crumbling stone looking rather as though it had been stolen from an abandoned building site. It was leaning over, had not been set up straight.

A child screamed, looking at it. Orhan himself felt a chill. One could almost see a form in it, a woman, wide mother's hips, a shadow suggesting a face. A pattern carved into it, running lines that might be flowers or simply a mason's chisel marks. It was near enough to where the bodies of the Temple rioters had once been stacked – where he had once ordered the bodies stacked – that might or might not be coincidence.

Orhan thought: the people who erected it have lost their homes, their families, their lives had been torn to shreds; we can probably allow them some comfort in their misery, some show of thanks for the demon's defeat. But no, we'll have it thrown down immediately because either it's a useless lump of rock or it's a real genuine god.

Darath beside him muttered, 'Blasphemy. I only hope they find whoever did it.'

Another murmur. Eyes swinging from the godstone to the entrance to the Street of Flowers. Equally loud whispers of outrage.

Lord Tardein the Lord of the Dry Sea, Dweller in the House of Breaking Waves, the Emperor's Nithque entered the square in a vast purple litter, carried by ten bearers in purple robes. The litter was almost, almost dark enough purple to be black. Only the Asekemlene Emperor is permitted to use the colour black.

Orhan said, 'God's knives. What possessed him?'

'I'm told . . .' Darath lowered his voice. 'The Immish Great Council gave it to him. He could hardly refuse it.'

Cammor Tardein got out carefully, his hand pressing down on a bodyservant's arm. Orhan could see the servant wince. Splendidly dressed, a coat of gold brocade, a diamond arm-ring, more diamonds at his throat. But his face had a looseness to it, his cheeks were unshaved. The beautiful clothes seemed to hang off him. His body moved stiffly as he walked through the staring crowds. His clothes did not match each other, Orhan thought watching him. Magnificent but awkward. As though he had put on all his brightest colours, to compensate for the black litter. Cammor went up the steps into the Great Temple, through the narrow doorway and was gone. The rest of the high families began to file in again behind him. There were Bil and Celyse, a servant holding Dion tightly, Dion looking sulky, Bil flushed and cross. There was Symdle staring over at Celyse as he followed his father into the Temple.

Soon, thought Orhan. Soon.

Through the narrow doorway into the darkness. The clawmarks on the door mere scratches: he hardly noticed them, they cannot have been made by the demon, for rejoice the demon is dead. The dark, the long corridor so crowded it had no mystery to it beyond the common fear of being crushed. Pressing forward close beside Darath, breathing in sweat and perfume and flatulence, oppressive, and his foot caught someone's heel making him stumble and the person in front of him spit out a breath. Through into the Great Chamber, the heat and the light, blinking, screwing up his eyes, the light was brighter, somehow, more blinding, more frightening, for his not having been afraid.

'Orhan?' Darath took his hand.

'Nothing.'

There enthroned before them the child High Priestess in her gown of silver. She sat perfectly still, in the way a grown woman would sit, staring at nothing; she could have been dead and embalmed there. The blankness of her face was unpleasant. Even Darath found it unpleasant, now he spent time with Dion. Everyone seating themselves, adjusting and readjusting glorious clothes not made for sitting squashed in together, the hot smell of them all, the rumbling chatter, high up beneath the ceiling a flock of pethe birds danced. Then the trumpets, the voices calling, 'The Emperor! All kneel for the Ever Living Emperor! Avert your eyes and kneel and be thankful! We live and we die! The Emperor comes! The Emperor comes!' The assembled congregation knelt carefully. All but the child in silver who sat stiffly on her throne. The Emperor walked down through the Great Chamber, blank as the High Priestess, a little boy of five years old. He seated himself in his throne, facing the High Priestess. Two little dolls facing each other. The priestesses of the Temple began to sing the hymn to light and living. Dion pointed up at the pethe birds fluttering. Bil reached out her maimed hand to quiet him.

Chapter Thirty

And when this is over, the real work begins.

He had explained it to Darath, and Darath had looked astonished; for a horrible moment he had thought Darath would tell him not to do it.

'You're insane, Orhan.'

'I've dedicated my life to this, Darath. I'm so close. Why else do you think I did all this?'

'Out of compassion for the wider world, I naively thought, what with you being a good man. One apple for two plums, or whatever it was. And that was far away. Just money. This is . . . not. You made a promise, didn't you? To Bil?'

'I did make a promise, yes.' But . . . After everything we've suffered, Darath . . . To be so close . . . We can't draw back. We can finish it. Achieve everything I ever hoped for.

As I've said before. As I'll probably say again. And again. And again.

Darath said, 'You should have left me in sweet ignorance, Orhan. God's knives, I almost wish you had. Bilale and I, sitting at home wondering where you've gone, "That's strange, Bilale, there seems to be some shouting in the streets, I hope it doesn't wake Dion up." Greeting you afterwards with wondering joy.'

'You can stay at home, yes. I wish you would.'

'When you love someone, Orhan, you stay with them. I'll never leave you again. I swear.' Darath kissed him. 'Thank you for telling me, Orhan.'

The early morning sunlight made pools on the bedroom floor like spilled water. A great glorious burst of birdsong. Darath yawned, 'Why must things begin so early in the morning? Why not a civilized hour of the afternoon?'

'The last "thing" we did began at dusk. Look how that turned out.'

'What thing was that?'

'Umm . . . ?'

'Oh, when we attempted to assassinate the Emperor? That thing?'

'That thing.'

Darath pulled a shirt over his head. 'Uncivilized hours for uncivilized work.'

The jasmine was in bloom in the morning room. A servant girl brought fresh figs and dried apricots, bread, honey, cold meat. The best gold plates. If it was early for Lord Emmereth and Lord Vorley to be awake, she was careful not to look surprised at it. Dion was already awake, naturally, shouting from the gardens behind the jasmine. Bil came in to join them. Her white face was flushed with nerves.

'Have a fig?' Darath asked her innocently, holding out the plate.

'How can you eat? I feel too nervous to eat.' She gestured to her servant girl to serve her fruit and some bread, pour her a cup of soured milk.

'Did you sleep at all?' Orhan asked her.

She shook her head. 'Not well. Dion didn't sleep well, either. Cried out, wouldn't lie down unless I came in to him. It's almost as though he knows.'

'He knows something's happening,' said Orhan. 'Picks it up.'

'Are you ready?' Bil asked him.

Darath said, 'No.'

They ate, and washed, and went upstairs to arm themselves. It was easier strapping armour on than it had been. Curiously. Orhan's hands didn't shake this time, as he remembered they had the night they did that thing. In his memory his hands had trembled so you'd wonder how he'd ever managed to get everything on. It should be worse, not easier, knowing everything they were about to do, already hearing it and smelling it in his mind.

'Your shirt's crumpled,' said Darath.

'It hardly matters, does it?'

'Yes.'

Actually, yes, it probably does. The look of the thing. We are civilized men, we who do this.

He felt so much more . . . so much more self-belief, this time.

At the door Bil waited to see them off. Janush the bondsman stood beside her, gave them each a cup of wine, a mouthful of salt and honey on a white dish.

'Bit early in the day, isn't it?' Darath said. They made an attempt to laugh. Great Tanis, Lord of Living and Dying, we stand away from you now in the place between light and darkness, between life and death. Protect us, Lord Tanis, hear our prayers and give us life or death according to our due.

'Where's Dion?' said Orhan.

'I had him sent to his bedroom. I didn't want you to frighten him, dressed like that.'

'That was wise,' said Darath. Still trying for levity as he always did. 'Orhan would terrify me, dressed like that, too, if I hadn't been the one who helped dress him. As it is, I'm insulted, Bilale. I smoothed the crinkles out of his shirt and everything specifically to stop him frightening little boys.'

'You should go,' said Bil. She kissed Darath's cheek, then Orhan's. Dry lips. Rasp of scar tissue against Orhan's skin. Smell of dried apricots on her breath. 'Good luck. I shall pray to Great Tanis.'

'Better to stay at home and lock the doors,' said Orhan.

'Did you send word to Celyse?'

'Of course.'

Darath said, 'If she hasn't locked and barred the doors of my house, I'll never forgive her. I told her to push tables up against the windows. Have buckets of water standing by just in case.'

We can be so flippant about this now, Orhan thought. Is it because it's more real than it was the first time? Or because it's less real?

Just the two of them. Different from last time there also. Easier. Simpler. Worse. No ranks of puzzled followers, the guilt of their deaths already pressing down. Darath and Orhan, two grim uncomfortable middle-aged men. Unlike last time nobody looked at them, walking the streets like this, armed, afraid. In Sorlost once real men did not need to go about in armour, flaunted themselves without fear in fine silks and brocades.

There are so many things the people of Sorlost can be accused of. But that should be to their credit. Always.

Selim Lochaiel, Lord of the Moon's Light, met them at the palace gates. The gates opened. There was Cauvanh, with a contingent of Immish soldiers at his back. Chief Secretary Gallus was there also. More frightened even than Bil. Darath gave him a dark look. Never forgiven the poor man for being Orhan's type.

Here we are again. Let's see if this time we can have any better luck.

Cauvanh licked his lips nervously. 'I was uncertain you would do this,' he said. 'I was half expecting you to turn back.'

Darath said, 'It would have been the better course not to, yes.'

The Immish guards were edgy. Do they know? thought Orhan. They went quickly through the palace; Orhan found himself walking next to Gallus, noticed the smell of drink on Gallus's breath.

'Gallus?' Looked weary, his eyes pouched, the lovely golden curls in his hair had turned grey. Gallus shook his head. The highest official in the Imperial Palace of the Asekemlene Emperor of the Sekemleth Empire of Sorlost, dancing at the feet of the Immish, who were the allies of the demon the King of Death, who had just died betrayed by a friend who was paid by the Empire's High Lords at the behest of one faction of the Immish. Yes, Orhan thought, I suppose it would drive one to start the day with a cup of something. The cost of intoxicants had gone up noticeably in the last few months, come to that.

'He's in the Pearl Chamber,' said Gallus.

'Alone?'

'There's a man with him, talking about the work on the road to Reneneth. He arrived very suddenly, there's been some problem with the work, I tried to put him off.' Gallus ran his hands through his thinning hair, scratched at his eyes. 'I'm sorry, My Lords.'

'And guards?'

'Three or four.'

'They will not be a problem,' said Cauvanh.

No. I'm sure they won't. 'Where's the Emperor?' said Orhan suddenly.

Gallus paused. Confused. 'I think . . . in the gardens.'

'Don't worry, Orhan,' said Darath.

Then all of it again, going through the palace, servants pulling back out of their way. The swagger of men walking with swords and in armour, trying to feel like great heroes, feeling self-conscious trying too hard to be swaggering with a sword. What fools we feel. Walking beside Darath, sweet nostalgia, back where it all began, my love, my love, you still here beside me. Cauvanh threw the door wide, they walked into the Pearl Chamber as though walking into a room of water, rainbows shimmering on the walls and the floor.

Lord Mylt was indeed talking to someone, the two of them deep in discussion over a map. They both started around. Lord Mylt's mouth fell open. 'Cauvanh?' Angry, and alarmed: 'Guards!'

'Kill him,' Cauvanh said to the guards.

A moment, just a moment, when the guards hesitated.

They killed the man Lord Mylt had been talking with as well. The only possible thing to do, but one had to feel some pity for

265

the poor chap. Come to see Lord Mylt about a problem with a construction project, end up dead on the floor. What was that about one life for the greater good of many, Orhan? One apple for two plums? Every time, every single time, you say it's just one life for the greater good, just one or two innocents for the greater good.

Which it always is. That's the worst thing. One life in exchange for twenty, thirty, a hundred – is there anyone, anywhere, apart from the man who's dying, who'd say that the cost isn't worth it? A hundred people will die because you were too squeamish to kill one innocent? I think I know what those hundred and all who love them might say. Two people will die, even, if we don't kill one innocent – are not two lives more precious than one?

'I don't know. I don't bloody know. How should I know?' That's the only human thing anyone can say.

It was quick, at least. Two sword thrusts, blood on metal, blood on bright silk cloth, done. The road builder had fallen face down but Lord Mylt lay on his back with his chin jutting up in an expression of astonishment. No time to feel fear, one could only hope.

'Thank you,' Cauvanh said neatly to the guards. The one who'd killed Lord Mylt nodded. Gallus rubbed his face, his whole body slumping. Selim Lochaiel choked, clamped his hands over his mouth.

'A little girl will stab a man in the heart this evening,' said Darath, 'so that your children will grow and live. Take your hands away from your mouth, Selim.' He rolled his eyes at Selim. 'Oh, God's knives, yes, it's horrible, one day you shall be as he is, blood smells vile, far worse than it does when it's on a plate as your dinner, it's a profound mystery the change from living man to slowly rotting corpse, you and Orhan can have a long philosophical discussion about guilt and eternity later once we're done. Here.' Passed Selim a silk handkerchief. Selim held it to his mouth, gulped, choked, managed not to be sick.

'Thank you.'

'God's knives, I don't want it back. Keep it. Burn it. Dump it with them.'

Cauvanh was already making a search of Lord Mylt's robes. 'A coin pouch – eight talents, five dhol. A letter . . . from his mistress. A letter . . . from his wife.' He crumpled the letters, dropped them. Flicked through the papers on the table. 'The poor innocent road builder here seems to have been embezzling half the cost of the road building.' Read a particular paper in more detail. 'Oh, and splitting the profits with Lord Mylt. The road should be built more quickly also now, which is an unlooked-for bonus outcome.' Gestured to the guard who had killed Lord Mylt, his sword blade now clean again. 'Get these . . . things out of here.'

A proclamation was issued on the steps of the Great Temple at midday:

'*A new time of peace is upon us, the city is saved from the demon, Lord Mylt praised be his name is to leave the city, return to a life of peace on his estates as befits a man who had worked so hard and with such dedication to the glory of Immish and the Sekemleth Empire; Lord Cauvanh will take his place on the Great Council as the Immish representative in Sorlost. Lord Cammor Tardein the Lord of the Dry Sea the Dweller in the House of Breaking Waves the Emperor's Nithque is retiring from his post also, having guided the city back to security and peace; Lord Darath Vorley Lord of All That Flowers and Fades the Dweller in the House of Flowers is appointed Nithque to the Emperor in Lord Tardein's place. A new age of peace will be upon the Sekemleth Empire, let us hope and pray. Two thirds of the Immish troops will be leaving Sorlost in three days' time: this should not be taken to mean that Immish is withdrawing its aid to the people of Sorlost or its friendship with the Emperor, indeed, the bonds that tie Immish in loyalty to the glorious Sekemleth Empire, so firmly forged, so precious, will not, cannot, be broken, cherished as they are by the glorious Asekemlene Emperor, the Ever Living, the Eternal, so fond in the hearts of every man, woman and child in*

267

Immish, even from Telea in the west to Immerlas on the far-off shores of the Bitter Sea, cherished as they are by the Immish Great Council, the wise and just rulers of that fair country; no, the withdrawal of these troops means only a restoration of balance in the honour and care that Immish feel for the people of Sorlost their allies. The demon is dead and his army destroyed: it is time for a new age of peace, for men such as Lord Vorley, who has suffered much grief, who can share the longing of the people for quiet times, not for soldiers.'

And so on and so on. It's meant to be confusing, yes, obviously. Says absolutely nothing and nothing and nothing and nothing; methinks those involved in drafting it may protest perhaps a little, a tiny bit, too much.

'But if that's what Cauvanh wants to say,' Darath said with a shrug, 'let him.'

Ragged cheers at Darath's appointment as Nithque. Also a few laughs. Little real interest apart from at the mention of the Immish troops leaving. At that a group of street women groaned aloud. When the proclamation was finished a small crowd milled around for a while uncertainly before dispersing.

'They know it's lies,' said Orhan to Cauvanh. 'Look at them.'

'Everyone knows it's lies,' said Cauvanh. 'But you have what you want, and I have what I want. Thus what does it matter?'

'It doesn't matter,' said Orhan.

Cauvanh said, 'Your city is liberated. Congratulations, Lord Emmereth.'

Some soldiers. Taking a walk. That's hardly the worst thing in the history of Irlast.

Orhan thought: so many years, I've worked for this.

A crowd had tried to put a crown of roses on the statue of the demon at around the same time as Cauvanh's proclamation was being read out. Another crowd had gathered a little later, tried to bind the statue with ropes and tear it down. Fighting: knives, stones, new-forged new-bought swords; the beautiful pouting stone mouth smiling down at the bloodshed. The Immish soldiers did nothing, the Imperial army did nothing, the fight dragged on, ten people left dead or dying, over thirty injured, it had looked, briefly, as though a more general riot would start up. More people involved than had been there to listen to the proclamation.

Darath had his things moved into the Nithque's chambers in the Summer Palace. He looked genuinely sorry for it. 'God's knives, I'll miss Dion. I won't spend much time here,' he told Orhan, 'I'll come back to visit him.' The rooms were as beautiful as Orhan remembered them, jewelled mosaics, silk hangings fine as breathing, the balcony with a view of gardens lush with flowers and bright water, the House of Silver winking in the sun. Sweetmeats, wine and tea waiting on an ivory table; a servant boy with golden curls pouring him a drink with a movement of the arm as elegant as dancing. 'We did well kitting it out, didn't we?' said Darath. 'Masters of the Sekemleth Empire! I'd forgotten just how nice it all is.'

Servants carrying Darath's things in crossed with servants carrying Lord Mylt's things out. 'Distribute it to the poor and the starving,' Orhan ordered. 'Tell them it's a gift from the new Nithque.'

Selim Lochaiel came into the room, looking pale. There was still a splash of blood on the toe of his left shoe. 'They've got rid of . . . of Lord Mylt's body. And Cauvanh . . . has got rid of the soldiers who killed him.' Selim sat down, chewing at his hands. 'I should get back to Elolale and the boys,' he said. Cheer up, Selim, Orhan thought. In a few years it will all feel fine. Just another sordid palace coup, Selim. In a few years' time you'll be doing this without a second thought.

'Cauvanh's sending the Immish soldiers to Cen Elora,' said Selim. 'Poor men.'

Darath said, 'Poor men?'

'From a nice warm posting here doing less than nothing to march across the world to wage war?' Selim shuddered. His eyes still full of Lord Mylt dying, you could see Lord Mylt's blood in his pupils. 'So yes, poor men.'

The whole of Irlast was in uproar. The demon is dead, the cities of his empire have declared themselves free. The Immish Great Council hears the word 'free' as a challenge. Forty thousand men under arms and an empire has fallen? You'd be a fool indeed not to seize that opportunity with both hands. Famine and pestilence, ruin, desperation. Every village declaring itself a kingdom, turning on its neighbours, every man with a sword dreaming of cutting himself a throne. The Immish with forty thousand trained men under arms looking on. Smiling.

Cauvanh himself was so happy he might be dancing. 'Ith . . . The White Isles . . .' Orhan had left him in his rooms pouring over a map of Irlast, his fingers tracing out cities' names, thinking how best to break them to his will. 'Immier . . . Chathe, even . . . If we can raise the men . . .' Part of the agreement was to pay the Immish ten thousand gold thalers upfront, plus two thousand every year indefinitely. Orhan could almost hear the coins clinking in Cauvanh's mind. As had already been established, two thousand thalers that could buy a lot of very useful things.

'That fool Mylt with his fixation on your city.' Cauvanh lisped out a parody of his former master. '"*Keep it, hold it, make it ours, make them bend to accept our rule.*" Idiot. Milk it for all it's worth and move on.'

'Like Marith Altrersyr did, you mean?' Orhan had almost said.

'So now we just need to raise the money,' said Selim.

'We can sell the Imperial furniture and fittings,' said Darath. 'The Emperor is barely out of clout clothes. He doesn't need gold cups. Also, Cauvanh can't possibly be expecting us to honour the agreement in full.'

'Of course he isn't,' said Orhan. 'Five thousand upfront, a thousand a year for maybe the next two years. If that.'

'Almost a bargain,' said Darath. He sipped tea from a tea bowl so fine his hands showed through the porcelain. 'If I sold this bowl for a talent, how many deaths could I buy?'

'And we'll need to get the Emperor tutored so that he can actually understand Literan,' said Selim. Trying not to hear what

270

Darath had just said. 'Apart from the money, that's the first thing we must do, surely. It was absurd, seeing him unable to understand a word of the Temple ceremony. Then . . . The Imperial Army needs strengthening. The guard house at the Maskers' Gate needs to be rebuilt. The streets damaged in the rioting . . . I thought we could rebuild them, improve them. Some of the buildings . . . disgusting. Rancid. And people still live there! I thought, the other day, in the Grey Square while we were waiting for the ceremony . . . we could use this as a chance to tear them down, rebuild them as something people could decently live in . . . Improve things.'

All of this sounds oddly familiar. 'We could,' Orhan said.

A servant came in, bent and whispered in Darath's ear. Handed over a note. Darath read it, burned it in the flame of a lamp. 'Good. Thank you.' Turned to Orhan. 'Well, then. Lord Tardein the Lord of the Dry Sea the Dweller in the House of Breaking Waves, ex-Nithque to the Ever Living Emperor, the Emperor's Counsellor and Friend: what do we want done with his body? Disposed of quietly so nobody knows anything, or publicly and ceremonially displayed?'

Selim said, 'What?'

'I don't know.' Orhan put his head in his hands, closed his eyes. 'I don't know. Why ask me? What do you think we should do?' His hands were dry, calluses on his fingertips rubbing on his face. Need to put something on them. Almond oil, Bil uses, I think, to soften her skin. 'Put it out that Lord Tardein the former Nithque slipped on the stairs, fell, broke his neck. Have them take the body out on a litter, bury it publicly somewhere near the Maskers' Gate. Send someone to offer prayers in his memory in the Temple tonight.' A thought occurred. 'I'll send a message to Bil, telling her to go too, with Celyse. To bring Dion with her, give him an offering to make. Tell her to get him to say something nice about Cammor Tardein in a loud voice.'

Darath nodded. Sipped tea.

Selim looked at them. Two grim weary middle-aged men scrabbling

271

for power. Playing the game for the sake of playing the game. Nothing more.

Selim said, 'You didn't have to kill him.'

Darath said, 'Probably not. But it's done. So, now: you were talking about your ideas for rebuilding the city and restoring the army. Orhan was about to ask you about the cost . . .'

There on the desk sat the treasury ledgers, written in gold ink, said to be bound in human skin. Orhan pulled one over to him. Oh look, all these years and there's the stain where Darath got honey on the cover, reading it in bed. There's one of my hairs, still stuck to it. He flipped through it, found an entry for Cammor Tardein's stipend as 'Watcher and Warden of Enia Beyond the Mountains', wherever that might have been. Crossed it out. That's, oh, two talents saved. How many deaths can we buy with that, do you think?

Darath signalled to the serving boy to refill their tea bowls. 'And the excitement's all ended. Back to ledgers and balance sheets and work. God's knives, I'd forgotten how dull this all is.'

Chapter Thirty-One

Landra Relast, the vengeance demon, who will destroy all who serve him
The White Isles, the island kingdom of the Altrersyr the descendants of Amrath and Eltheia, the dragon kin, the demon born. Her home

There was the headland. There, the grey rocks, a tiny smudge on the horizon, grey against the grey of the sky. Only her eyes deceiving her, and she stared, her eyes watering with the effort, and it was real, the cliffs of Fealene Isle the most northern of the White Isles, bare winter woods at their heights, and there, to the west, surely, that must be Morn with the smaller islets behind it, 'the sow and the piglets', small islands off Fealene Isle's coast. Ah, Eltheia, you are merciful, to let me see my homeland again. And yet, Landra thought, all I can bring here is death. Thus am I punished for everything I have done and failed to do.

They had followed the ragged coast of Illyr, the blank coast of the Wastes, around the long spits of land that the sailors called the Blades, all of it almost as new and unknown to the sailors as to Landra, 'the fourth time,' they said, 'the fourth time we've made this journey,' 'my father,' one of them said, 'he refuses to believe I have sailed to Illyr, says I'm joking with him.' The tracks of the water, even the stars, were new to them. Making a new road across the water: it was true, as the fishermen had said, that the sea creatures came up to the ship out of curiosity, fish in vast numbers visible as patches of darkness beneath the surface, dolphins and whales nosing up in the ship's wake. For the first few days, many seals seemed to follow the ship.

Landra slept on the deck, wrapped in her cloak, the spray soaking into the cloth around her head, making her scalp itch. In the day she stood and watched the coastline spooling out. Saw Marith's death in her mind over and over. Smiled at it and grieved at it. Wondered what would be happening in the great expanse of his empire. How long the news would take to spread. It could take years, she thought, for the certainty of his death to reach the far ends of his empire. Men could go on for long months, for years, thinking themselves his subjects, praising him and worshipping him. An impossibility and a certainty, that a war leader will one day be brought down by war. In the White Isles, even now, people would be sitting talking in smug satisfaction of their mastery over the world as a certain unarguable thing. She thought then of course of Ethalden, the silver tower falling, breaking – how many of them are left alive there, she wondered sometimes. Did all that live there die? Did any of them escape? The innkeep's son, the boy in the harbourside inn's stables, the man who had sold her the blanket. Are they alive there still? And what do they think, if they are alive? Do they understand? Long ago under the first Amrath the people of Illyr rose up, sickened by their bloodshed.

Tobias's voice, clear in her mind: '*What do you think they bloody think, Lan?*'

I wonder what Tobias is doing now, she thought. I hope that he is somehow not dead.

Two weeks into the journey they had put in at the Halien Islands to take on food and water, the three lonely islands that humped out of the Bitter Sea like the whales for which they were named. Barren, empty islands, wretchedly poor; so battered by storms the few houses were half-buried in the earth like the burrows of animals. Like Ethalden the air smelled of stonedust and sawdust, new buildings were rising around a new harbour; the people were dressed in White Isles-style finery, loaded with new wealth; children ran to greet the ship, eager to practise speaking Pernish, shouting for news. In the centre of the new town, a half-built temple to the new god Marith, decorated with whale skulls. They sailed again the same evening, 'Dangerous, at night,' the sailor with the black beard told Landra, 'the people here never had money, never had anything, now they have money to spend . . . In ten years' time, gods willing, this will be a great city, a staging post on the great sea road from Malth Elelane to Ethalden. You can see it, if you squint at it. But at the moment, it is merely not a safe place.' Muttering among the crew, Landra gathered, that everything in the town had doubled or tripled in price. How strange it is: great battles are fought, the clash of armies, cities are sacked, a hundred times a thousand lives are shattered into dust, and because of this a child on the other side of the world has a new house to live in, new clothes, better food, a new chance at a different kind of life.

From hugging the coast in safety they must risk the last run out into the open sea. Landra's heart had leapt, to be on a ship looking out over the Bitter Sea, but she had shivered with fear as the lights of Halien Town fell away from them. The sea has no bottom. The sea has no end. Drop a coin into the waters out here and it will sink forever. Sail a boat north or east and you could live and die a thousand times and never reach land. 'Hail to the sea!' the sailors shouted. 'Sea and sky, have mercy! Sea and sky and wave and wind!' The ship's captain threw a cup of sweet water into the sea from the prow. Sailors did drop coins down. In cold winter sunlight Landra sat on the deck watching the sky. Other journeys, other homecomings, other desperate flights away. *'Pretty.' 'Pretty enough. Not much different to yesterday. Bit more cloud.' 'One of nature's wonders, the sunset. Never the same twice.'* The delusion of hope. She saw the people of the White Isles dying, Matrina Fiolt, Alis Nymen's wife and children, saw Morr Town in ruins, Malth Elelane burned down. Suffer, she thought. You who can bear to live through this. You who sit in peace at home and do nothing, you who profit from this. My brother and I, we plotted, we sought to profit from cruelty and another's pain – look what has become of us.

There was the headland, the grey cliffs of Fealene Isle the most northern of the White Isles, the yellow cliffs of Morn and its children. The wind dropped, they crawled at oars down the coast of Fealene. The sailors eager to be home. Landra twitching and fearing to be home. We will not go near to Third Isle, she told herself over and over, it will be all right. She thought of Ben and Hana in their cottage by the sea on Third Isle, Ben's fear that he would be taken for a soldier in the Army of Amrath. If he has gone off to war, she thought, I will go back there and I will kill Hana and their son. The ship passed Fealene Isle and the north shore of Seneth rose before them, they curved west around Tha Head. 'Hope', in old rune tongue of the White Isles. The first point of land that Eltheia and Serelethe saw when they fled across the Bitter Sea from the ruins of Ethalden, 'which suggests they took a very odd course,' as Marith had once said, 'terrible sailors, my ancestors, obviously.' A pillar of bronze there as a marker, set with a shard of mage glass. Landra could see it as a smudge of green and a flash of light. The coastline of Seneth closing in on them, golden coves, winter fields flanked with winter woodlands, smoke from the village of Pelen Tha, on the water ahead of them the red sails of a fishing boat. So close to the shore here she could almost reach out and touch the cliffs. A spit of rock drawing out into the water, and beyond that a beach of shingle and yellow sand.

Now was the time for it. Landra looked at the ship and the sailors bent over the oars. They are carrying cargo that was stolen in war, she thought, they are merchants of the White Isles and Illyr, they are profiting from Marith's wars, they must know this. She placed her hands on the ship's rail. Bent her head. On the sea the waves began to rise. An oily, rotten smell, rank sweet. The sea was bubbling white, boiling white, waves ripping at the sides of the ship. The temple of Amrath, falling, crumbling, the side of the ship crushed, giving way. Grinding of teeth beneath the surface. Shapes moving deep down. White foam. The sailors at the oars went on, blind to it, the sailor with the black beard was humming as he rowed, the captain watched them and urged them on. Spray broke in their faces, they shook it away. Spray stinging Landra's lips. Her hands were hot and red. Puffed up like a dead man's hands. She felt the *gabeleth* and the *gestmet* inside her hiss. The ship's timbers crunched open. The sailors did not move from the rowing benches as the ship went down. Teeth in the water. The water stained red. The bundles of goat hides split apart and gold coins poured out in the water, they shimmered like a shoal of fish as they went down.

Landra kicked in the water, her wet clothes heavy and dragging at her. The waves pushing her towards the shore. Dead hands holding her. Her burns stung. Washing clean. Salt taste of tears and iron taste of blood. Her feet dragged against the bottom, she swam and stumbled, hauled herself up onto a beach. A single plank of wood floated beside her, marked at the end with tooth-marks. Her dress was leaking blue dye into the water, she noticed, and that made her laugh with memories. When the tower of Ethalden fell, she thought again, I wonder if the cloth-seller survived it? It is only a shame, she thought, that I could not curse the whole city to fall. But when the tower fell the rotting flesh beneath it was revealed, the ground beneath their feet is rank with dying, and so perhaps sickness will come and devour everyone who lives there. Let us hope.

She walked up the beach, her wet clothes leaving a trail behind her. She should be cold, she thought, the air should be chilling her to her bones. She should be cold and hungry and weak. Dead voices stirred inside of her, the dead the never-living that never grew weak. She had to scramble up to reach the cliff top. Grazing her damaged hands on the rock. At the top there was woodland. Some of the trees were already fuzzy with yellow catkins, which made her blink in surprise. A first sign of coming spring. Purple irises were in flower beneath the trees, and yellow aconite. Leaf litter crunched under her feet. Tattered skeletal leaves, fading to grey; hazel shells. Her hands ached. They were puffed up huge, the skin dry. The feel of the air on them hurt.

After a long time walking she came to the edge of the wood and a village beyond it. It was late in the day now. On the still air came the clang of a cowbell. Cows being brought in for the evening milking. Landra stood in the shelter of the trees watching them come down the track, three of them, brown and mud-spattered, swinging their big heads, slather trailing from their mouths. She breathed in hard as they passed her, the muck smell and the smell of their mouths chewing. 'Kie kie kie kie kie,' the boy bringing them called to them. They went in through a tumble-down wall into the milking yard. Perhaps the farmer would sell her some milk to drink.

The village was poor and small, poorer and smaller than most of the villages she had seen in Illyr. A few huts huddled around a barn and a farmhouse. The boy noticed her, nodded. 'You all right, miss?' His broad Whites accent made Landra shudder. Echoes of so many things.

'I . . . Yes. Could I buy a cup of milk, perhaps? Is your master at home?'

The boy looked at her sodden dirty clothes, at the cloth slipping awkwardly around her head. 'The mistress is at home. Maybe . . . maybe if you stay here, miss, I can bring you out a drink? If you've coin for it?'

Landra handed him a gold coin from the ship's drowned treasure, stamped with the King of Balkash's head on one side, long curling beard and the ram's horn crown, on the other a winged horse rearing up. The boy turned it over and over. 'What's this?'

That is the face of the man the magelord Ynthe Kimek burned alive with mage fire on his own throne. And that is a god spirit of the Kara Kol desert that King Marith Altrersyr beheaded with the sword Joy. 'A gold coin,' said Landra. 'That's what it is.'

The boy looked more closely at her. 'Wait here, then,' he said. She leaned against the wall and breathed in the smell of cow manure until the boy came back with a clay cup of milk and a heel of bread.

'Thank you.' The bread felt horrible in her swollen hand, dry and rubbing. The cup also, the outside was unglazed and seemed to suck at her dry skin. She drank the milk with a long gulp.

'You've got a milk moustache,' the boy said.

Landra wiped her mouth. 'Thank you.' Asked, 'Who is lord hereabouts?'

'Lord Ronaen, up at Malth Pereale. He's an old man, though,' the boy said. Dismissive child's voice. 'Didn't go away to war.'

'His son did,' said Landra unthinking.

'And died there,' said the boy. 'They sent his bones back in a leather bag. Everything but the head.'

Landra thought: someone's bones, certainly. 'Could you point me in the direction of Malth Pereale, then?'

'How do you know?' the boy said. 'That the young lord went off to fight? If you don't know where Malth Pereale is?' He looked at her coldly. 'Why's your dress all wet?'

'Which direction is Malth Pereale?' Landra said in her old half-forgotten Lady Landra Relast voice. It was stronger here, came out without catching in her throat. And perhaps other voices, behind it, because the boy looked straight at her face and pointed. 'Take the road, there, when you get to the crossroads turn left, keep on. An hour or so, it should take. But I shouldn't bother. Lord Ronaen's a coward, like. His daughter's mad to go off to the war, but he won't let her go.' And then he blinked, as though he was surprised he had said this last thing.

'Is he now?' Landra said. 'Is she?' She paused. A sick feeling, looking at the boy. Things uncoiled within her. She said, 'Do you want to go off to war?'

Shrug. 'Maybe. Not sure I want to come back in a leather bag, though. And not sure the mistress would let me.'

And for that, Landra thought, you will live. She might feel relief. She did not stop at Malth Pereale, looked at it from a distance hunched and grey and so poor-looking, now, compared to the world she had seen. Sheep grazed beside its walls, there was an orchard like the orchards at Malth Salene, with pigs grubbing beneath the bare trees. She went on through the night, not needing to sleep, walking south down the coast road slowly slowly towards Morr Town. And then Morr Town would be destroyed, and all the people there would die. At dawn she came to a village, stopped at the inn there for a meal. The place was poor and ragged: but the White Isles are rich, she thought, rich in timber and fruits and grains and herds, the whole world knows it.

As she sat in the inn three young men with bundles on their backs gathered in the street together just outside, a woman embraced one of them, an old man shook another's hand. The third stood and watched with a sad, scornful look on his face. They were going to war, Landra the *gabeleth* the *gestmet* the dead thought. The people of the village came out to see them off with shouts for good luck. So. She reached out her hands for them. A little later Landra walked down the road with the village dead and gone behind her, walking slowly slowly towards Morr Town.

Chapter Thirty-Two

Tobias

The Mountains of Pain. Very, very aptly named and the world's best ever funniest joke

A trail of wounded staggered through the mountains. Wailed like seagulls. Crows big as vultures coming down in their faces picking at them. Like flies. Wounds oozing in the heat. Pus and sweat.

Got really bloody hot suddenly. Like proper southern heat. And raining: it barely ever rains here, they say, should be grateful, the locals must be out jumping up and down singing with happiness. Knee-deep in mud full of insects. All the world rushing up alive, plants and insects and animals, gods, you could see it and smell it, that lush living rain-damp hot-air scent. Swelling all the streams, glutting the mountain slopes, nourishing the fields. Ideal breeding ground for wound rot. The lost and the wounded, hiding in the wooded valleys, in the mountain caves, digging in trying to make any decision, frightened, defeated, uncertain which way to go or what they would find, soldiers and camp followers all mixed together, scattered, all of them stinking of bloody wound rot.

Mountains. Valleys. Rock falls. High passes. Enemy soldiers. Pissing it down.

Got up higher, where the mountain slopes were barren. Huge outcrops of black rock rearing up out of grey soil, that had to be scrambled up or around. Hidden gullies overflowing with rainwater, overgrown with dark scrawny trees. Tamas birds shrieked and called, sounded like they were speaking. Was sure, briefly, that one of them was shouting 'Hail King Marith!' Which was creepy and freaky and stupid and way too frigging weird as an insight into the state of his mind. There were enemy soldiers moving down in the valleys, harrying the survivors; they had heard fighting ahead of them in the early afternoon and again at dusk, from a high slope they looked down to watch horsemen skirmishing far below. Impossible, from that distance, to tell which side won. They had to stop for the night shortly afterwards, sat down in the shelter of an overhanging rock face on soaked grey earth you could almost see growing, and the rain had even briefly stopped. Still had some dried salted meat stuff that everyone pretended was dried salted pig. Tough, gristly, bled-out-in-the-mud-after-marching-a-thousand-miles pig.

It's pig! It's just pig. If you don't ask you don't know. If you don't know you're not guilty. Shut up and chew. What will become of us now he's died? Better things, maybe, like no longer thinking it's normal to eat "salt pig".

'I might even have some rock-hard soggy crusts of mouldy bread,' said Naillil. 'If you're lucky.' Rovi wheezed at her in a way that made Tobias feel sick. Gods, half the Army of Amrath slaughtered, half the camp followers slaughtered, but Rovi the walking dead man goes on and on.

'We should get on,' said Lenae. She was jumpy, twitching. 'Might be more soldiers around.' They had their backs against the rocks, facing the way they had come. Camp followers of the Army of Amrath: think we might know something about what will happen if the enemy happens on us.

'No way. We stay here. There is no way we're bumping into anyone or anything in the dark.'

Thalia sat alone, staring off at the sky. Her cloak was pulled

close around her. She did not take the bread when Tobias offered
her some. Or the pig. She had walked with them all day without
speaking, just going along close to Tobias. She needed to eat and
drink something, he thought. Say something.

*'Eat some bread, Thalia. Drink some water. Speak to me. Hey,
look, I promise, it's not laced with hatha, if that's what you're
worrying about. I wouldn't do that to you.'*

Okay . . . no. Maybe, you know . . . leave it to someone else.
Lenae. Naillil.

Nudged Lenae. 'Do me a favour? Offer her a waterskin and a
bit of bread? Like . . . talk to her a bit?' Thought: talk to her?
About what?

Gods knew who or what Lenae thought of her. On the one
hand, she was dressed in midnight blue silk sheer as cobwebs,
diamonds around her neck, her fur cloak trimmed in silver thread;
how many impossibly beautiful women with strong Literan accents
and scarred left arms was a man likely to come across in one army
camp? Lenae had seen the queen at a distance: call him biased,
but she wasn't exactly someone you'd easily forget. On the other
hand – the Queen of All Irlast wouldn't be wandering around with
mud on her face in the company of Tobias and especially of Rovi
because that would be stupid. She'd be . . . thought back to
yesterday . . . dead somewhere. What was remarkable was just
how quickly it had taken for everyone else in the whole Army of
Amrath to be dead.

*'I do like your dress. Very nice. Where'd you get it from?' 'Top
tips for getting your hair so shiny?' 'Which do you prefer, a cup
of wine or a piece of honey cake at the end of a long hard day?'*
Yeah, that was going to work wonderfully. But Lenae, bless her,
went over to Thalia and said something. Thalia even said something back. They spoke very low so he couldn't hear what they
said, annoyingly. Thalia's cloaked head moved a little. Tobias saw
her arm move up to her throat. She took a crust of bread and the
waterskin from Lenae. Further quiet talking. Strained his ears hard,
pretty sure he heard Lenae say the word 'widowed', that being

the kind of word people can't help but say louder whether they mean to or not. Or he could be making it up completely to make himself feel better about sending Lenae to talk to her, it's all going to be all right, they'll be two women together burdened by adversity but drawing strength from each other determined to go on, right.

The two women spoke a little longer. Lenae took the waterskin back and came over to Tobias.

Awkward pause.

'She's not anything like I thought she'd be.'

Well, that settled that one.

Didn't ask the obvious.

The sun had set completely now. They didn't dare get a fire going, just sat in the dark. Curled up in their cloaks and tried to sleep. Alarming sounds in the dark that might be enemy soldiers wandering around, or their soldiers, it was almost certainly a bit past caring what side anyone was on when it came to a bloke with a sword versus a woman with a crust of mouldy bread. Couple of alarming sounds and then fuck it. Crawled over to where Thalia was lying. Could tell from her breathing that she was awake. People don't often cry when they're asleep.

'I'm still sorry,' he said after a long time sitting beside her. 'For . . . whatever.'

'For my children dying? For my husband being a drunk and a monster?'

'Yeah, well . . . I did warn you.' It was still raining. Warm, gentle rain. Her cloak was all wet with rain and her hair was wet. Raindrops on her eyelids. He thought: we'll die out here in the wet.

She said, 'I suppose I should be glad, now, that you have been following me across Irlast. Since I would rather be alive than have died there.'

'You could try going back and looking for him.' Pointed off into the dark. 'It's that way, I think. Just follow the smell of death. We can spare you a water bottle and a crust of bread for the journey. Two crusts, if you ask nicely. Walk fast, you might make it back by dawn. Bury him just as the sun comes up.'

Silence.

Hurt her. Hurt her! Yeah! Do it! Feels good, doesn't it? Shocked him, seeing her close up, even in the darkness: shadows under her eyes, her shoulders bent under a weight.

'So where do you want to go now, then? Assuming this is it? Just tell me and I'll take you there. Don't bother asking me.'

She said after a long time, 'I don't know. Where can I go, do you think? Where can I go, what can I do?'

'In all honesty? Fuck knows. I'd say all kinds of things, anything you want to do, if it weren't for all the other things. You're beautiful, and clever, and there's power in you. Oh yes. But, in all honesty, Thalia, girl, I'd suggest hiding away somewhere for the rest of your life under a different name.'

She made a funny noise in her throat. He realized after a bit that she was trying to laugh.

'I have a temple in the Eternal City of Sorlost the Golden, where I am the holiest and most powerful woman in the world, the Chosen of Great Tanis the Lord of Living and Dying Who Rules All Things, I am the only person in all Irlast who may shed blood for the God. I have a fortress and a temple to myself, in Ethalden, my bedchamber there has walls of diamond, my bed is made of pearls, my throne is solid gold. My temple there is made all of solid gold.' She shook her head. 'What can I do with my life, Tobias?'

'You could learn, Thalia. Most people do.'

Dreamily, almost: 'I could sail away perhaps, find an island somewhere in the Bitter Sea, like Eltheia.'

Kindly, trying not to laugh out loud: 'Worse things I can think of, yeah. I could maybe even find you a ship. Not made of gold, but it was once called the *Brightwatch*.'

No reaction. She didn't remember the name, or more likely never knew it. He was probably glad of that.

'I was a queen.' She stared out into the dark. 'If I had drawn a different lot I would be twenty years dead.'

'You could have been a priestess in the Temple,' he said pettishly. 'Don't be too dramatic. Worn a grey robe and a mask, lit candles, sung songs.'

No reaction to that, either. Dreaming into the darkness. Self-pitying. You can see why Marith and her got along.

She said, 'You were the third man I ever spoke to, Tobias. Did you know that? Tolneurn, the Imperial Presence in the Temple; Marith; you.'

What? Really? No. Gods. 'That . . .' tried to think about how to phrase it, 'that . . . must have had an interesting effect on your view of the world.' Found himself saying: 'Rate must have been the fourth man you ever spoke to, then, and you killed him.'

Choking sound. Like a dying man's breathing. Oh fucking hells. 'But he would have got himself killed one way or another.' Trite wisdom. Possibly true.

She said, talking to herself as much as to him, 'Or perhaps there were others, before Marith, that I could have spoken to, who would have protected me from danger, asked me if I needed helping, offered me kindness, but who did not stick in my mind the way Marith did. I wanted to be free. Marith – and you . . . He seemed to offer that. He seemed to offer so much . . . I looked at him and I saw . . .' She shook her head. 'Beauty and hope. All the dreams of a glorious romantic life. His hope for me.'

Hope? Hope? A hollow laughing sound, and then some. He said crudely, 'And why is he such a bloody pissing sack of shit, then? Why was he, I mean.'

Thalia didn't bother moving herself to reply. Stared past him into the night, her hand twisting over the scars on her arm. In the dark he could see the shadows in her face, under her eyes.

'That man Robi—'

'Rovi.'

'Rovi, I'm sorry. What . . .' She knew, of course. And he knew why she was saying it. 'What happened to him?'

'Nothing special.'

'He wants to die,' said Thalia.

'Probably, yep.'

'He's from Illyr. His family were killed?'

'His family were killed, yeah. His village was destroyed. He killed some people and saw some other people die, he almost got killed himself. Now he's here, following Naillil around, depressing her.'

'He—' Silence.

'Like I say, nothing special. Not compared to having a crown on your head. You should get some sleep,' he said awkwardly. 'Long walk tomorrow. I should let you get some sleep. Try to get to sleep. You'll need it.'

'Yes. I should.' She lay down. In the dark, he saw her cradle her beautiful head on her beautiful arms, hunch herself up. 'Tobias?'

'Yes?'

'Marith . . . I remember Ninia telling me a story, when I was a child, in my bedroom in the Great Temple. In the dark, like this. About a queen of Allene, during the Salavene Wars, when Allene was sacked by the Immish. Her baby son was torn from her arms and killed in front of her. She killed the man who did it, tore out his throat with her hands and her teeth. The gods of Allene turned her into a dog to reward her for her valour, let her spend the rest of her life howling over the man's grave, worrying at his dry dead bones. Ninia told it to me to frighten me. She was cruel like that. It was a reward for the queen. I remember so clearly Ninia saying that.'

The next morning the cloud had sunk lower over the mountains, and everything was grey and hidden in mist. Colder, with the strange heavy silence. Water droplets gleaming on everything, furring everything, wearing away all the edges; the rock felt softer, swollen with water, the rock and the sky blurred into each other, a stream of water ran down the mountainside. Tobias tried to get his head clear. Make some decision about something.

'Right. Lenae. Naillil. Rovi. Right.'

Lenae stretched and groaned. Her hair was sticking up full of dirt. She looked awful, like the rain had soaked into her and puffed her up like it had the rocks.

'We go south-west,' said Tobias. 'Away from everyone that's left of the army.'

Lenae said, 'South-west? There's nothing south-west of here. Mountains. Then the sea.'

'Exactly.'

'We need to find shelter, food . . .'

Lenae, defenceless and rich and pretty; Naillil, kind of hardened but. Rovi, rotting; Thalia, her face puffy like she'd been crying half the night. Surprise surprise she'd been crying half the night. Odd smell in the air, every so often, when the wind changed: weird and freaky, what the fuck's that now, that odd smell? And then the realization that sometimes, when the wind blew from the south-west, the odd smell was that they weren't smelling death.

'What we need is to get out of the way of everything with a weapon.'

The mist lifted, as they were walking. The mountains rising out of it, mist and cloud in the valleys at first like the peaks were islands in the grey sea. Find you a place to live, here, then, Thalia girl, a kingdom of your own up here? It burned off, as they came down the mountain, the clouds fading away as they walked. A narrow valley, folded away into the mountainside, giving them some cover; its sides were high and wooded, the sky a thin pale strip hidden by leaves. They followed the course of a stream. Once they had to stop, when Naillil held up her hand and gestured to them to be silent, Tobias had heard nothing but she glared at him, finally there was a splashing in the water ahead of them, a sound that might be metal on stone. Thalia and Lenae stood together clutching each other's hands. The sounds went on a long time. Silence a long time afterwards, before Tobias held up his hand, nodded, and they went very cautiously on. There were rocks in the stream bed a little further on, a crossing place, and the rocks had wet footprints on them.

Surrender to them. Whichever side they're on.

A little further on again, the stream fell away in a waterfall, singing, and the valley closed in, became a ravine. High steep stone walls. The way the water ran down was beautiful. A silk veil, strung with rainbows, sewn with tiny bells. Could almost forget everything, watching it, listening to it. It went on down the ravine fast and white.

They were about to begin to scramble up out of the valley when Thalia said, 'Stop.' A shape in the sky, very high above them, moving slowly. It shone in the sky. It looked like a bird, except that it must be huge, to seem to move so slowly in the sky.

'The green dragon,' Thalia said when it had gone.

Wanted to say no, it wasn't, just a big bird, a trick of perspective. Didn't. They'd made it up out of the valley when they heard it scream.

'We should go back down there, hide in the trees,' said Lenae. 'Wait until it's gone.'

'Travelling at night would be worse,' Tobias said.

They went on very cautiously. Blue lights high in the sky off to the north of them that morning, a cold wind. Not just scouts harrying camp followers. Soldiers under attack and fighting back. A roar in the air, a brightening of all their hearts, and then a crash that made the mountains ring out and a flash of red light. A shriek. The sky seemed to swallow up the red light. Thalia looked to the north, trembling. A column of smoke rose up in the north, thick and black. Fire in the sky, rolling in heavy waves.

'Come on,' said Tobias. 'Stop looking at it. Just don't look at it. Please.'

An hour or so later they had to crouch in the undergrowth while horses' hooves galloped past ahead of them, heading north. A voice shouted in Pernish, with an accent of the White Isles, Thalia's face lit up and fell back into shadow. She could try to run to them, Tobias thought, shout to them, stand before them radiant in her glory, order them to kneel at her feet, fight for her, rally to her. Saw her thinking it. Saw the thought die away. After a little while there was silence again, and they went on.

* * *

'I don't like it here,' said Lenae. They had stopped to rest in a copse of yellow-leaved trees. A short rest, then a final hour's walk, then stop for the night. A mountain between them and where they'd started that morning. The curve of the mountain between them and the column of black smoke. The trees were sickly. Withered. The leaves looked dried-up. Made Tobias itch. There was a dead tamas bird lying at the foot of one of the trees, its wings spread open black and red. It too looked dried-out, mummified, as if it had died of thirst.

'Protection against death by drowning, death by starvation, death by thirst in the midst of the sea,' Thalia whispered, looking at it. She shuddered. Tobias took out his knife, went to flick it away from her. 'No,' she said, 'leave it there. We can sit away from it.'

'I don't like it here,' said Lenae again. 'I don't like it.'

'I don't like any of this,' said Tobias shortly. 'But I need a rest. Rovi needs a rest.' Rovi stank of rot and bad water, he wheezed and gasped and his wounds opened, he was grey like the earth, like he was crumbling away. Thalia looked at him with horror, couldn't stop staring at him. 'He's fine. Stop staring. Got his throat cut by a soldier in the Army of Amrath, that's all, like I said.' Thought: why do I have to be so cruel?

They drank some water, ate a little more dried meat. Need to find some supplies, soon. Find a village or somewhere where the inhabitants wouldn't fall on them with drawn swords. Get to the coast . . . and then maybe Thalia was serious about the sea.

If we survive all this to do something, Tobias thought, I'm going to ask Lenae to marry me.

She'll say no, obviously. But I'll ask her.

'We should go on,' said Naillil. 'We need to rest but now we need to go on.'

Lenae nodded. 'Yes.'

Thalia got to her feet and looked away to the north behind them. Walked after them reluctantly.

* * *

The trees ended. A stretch of grassland rising, another damned mountain to climb. More peaks behind it. On and on until the sea. A lake, perfectly circular, reflecting blue sky and the mountain top. Birds reflected in it. An island in its centre, grown up with tall silent reeds. Far off on the horizon, far to the east, more smoke. Tiny figures moving on the horizon, black like insects. A troop of horsemen, riding fast. A moment's flash of shining bronze. Then gone. And that look of fear and longing on Thalia's face. Walk on. Come on. The dusk is coming. An hour or two more of light. We must go on. Get on further. Up into the high slopes of the mountain and hide. Have they seen us? Ah, gods, pray to all gods and demons they didn't see us.

Tobias the bastard-hard sellsword. Oh yes.

'Look,' Lenae moaned. 'Look.'

There, on the other side of the round lake. A god bird. Its body sprawled over the grass. The weight of it had broken the earth open as it came down. Silver and gold, draining the light away into it. Great wings unfurled, as the dead tamas bird's wings had been unfurled to show the beauty of its feathers even in death.

In the sky, the enemy, it had been vast. Sprawled here, it was smaller, weaker, so fragile, like a thing of cloth. Tobias thought of the kites he had seen children flying, in Sorlost, in the evening as they walked to the palace. One had caught in a tree branch, he could see it still, a bloody omen, this little scrap of pitifully bright cloth. But in the sky it must have been like watching a dream.

There was not a mark on it. They crept up closer, all but Thalia who stood back from it watching the distant smoke. 'Look on your works!' Tobias felt like shouting to her. 'Look at it. What you did.' In one of its talons it clutched a long curl of red and black scaled skin.

They came very close, all but Thalia. The right eye was open. Tobias bent over it, saw himself reflected in it. Dead heavy black, like a night sky thick with cloud, or the choking dark of a windowless, lightless room.

'Is it dead?' whispered Lenae.

'What do you think, woman? Maybe it's just having a pleasant snooze?' His voice sounded awkward and heavy: why do I keep saying these crude things? He said more gently, 'Yes, it's dead, don't worry.'

As he had once before, so long ago now, he put out his hand. Touched it. It was cold, of course, it had lain out all night dead in the rain. It felt no different to any other dead thing. Feathers, like any other bird feathers. Its body soft and hard together, like the meat of a man's thigh. No different to dead cattle, or dead men, or dead dogs.

Lenae touched it also. Put both hands on it, ran her hands over its feathers. Drew her face up very close. Naillil did not touch it but looked at it with tears in her eyes.

Piss and pain and grief. Curse Marith, for doing this. Like the dragon's death had hurt him, that the boy could be so careless of something as terrible and beautiful as a dragon. What the boy must feel about other things, if he could destroy wonders such as this.

My mum and my gran were weavers, Tobias thought, and we all valued beautiful things, everyone in my village valued wonderful things. Gar the dyer, he was a small thin man, nothing to look at, grumpy old bugger, no manners, he had terrible wind – but he made dyes so beautiful, blues and reds and greens so vivid, cloth dyed in his vats looked more real than the world itself. And we all treated him like a king and a magelord, because of it, because he could make beautiful, wonderful things. And then after he died we didn't make the cloth any more, I gave up the weaving, because the colours wouldn't be right.

Hope, Thalia says Marith felt. Hope!

Thalia took a step towards it. Stepped back. The horror of what it must feel like, Tobias thought, to know that you did this. Bile rose in his throat.

No scavengers, no insects or carrion birds. The body would lie here slowly rotting, years and years, the bones erupting out of the wound it had made in the mountainside. This would surely be a haunted place. A fearful place. 'A god died here,' the people of the mountains would say. 'The gods fought, and our gods won, but a god died here.'

'Look at this.' Lenae pointed to a spray of waxy red flowers, carefully arranged near to one of its wings. There was a battered helmet beneath the flowers.

'Offerings,' said Lenae.

Looked at them for a while. Finally, to his own embarrassment, left a couple of iron pennies beside them.

They walked on past, looking back. The round lake gleamed like an eye. Reflected the sky and the mountain peaks and birds in flight. Thalia looked away the whole time until they had left it far behind them.

When they finally stopped for the night it was already growing dark. Walk on, get away from the dead god. Who could sleep with that near? It must light up the darkness. Pouring out shame into the night. Thalia walked on very fast. The evening came and her eyes were wide, Tobias saw her lips move, her hand close again around her scarred arm, a pulse beat at her beautiful throat. *Sereletha . . . Sesesere . . . seserenthelae aus* however it went. Marith's voice, dreamy and longing: 'Night comes. We survive.' The ache in his voice for these distant strange things.

A dangerous time. 'There's a place just up ahead, see it? There, where the trees are. We can stop there.'

Fuck, my feet are aching, Tobias thought. My legs are aching, my chest feels like shite. I could have gone twice as far twice as quickly, only a few years ago. Trotted along with a frigging tent on my back. No sloggers on the job! You, new boy, green boy, keep up, speed up! Gods, my leg aches and my shoulder bloody aches. What in the world I wouldn't give for a hot bath and a bed with clean crisp sheets. Gods, the smell of clean linen, slipping into it, the feel of clean bedding, the smell of clean linen when you bury your nose in it, stretch out, roll over, pull the sheet up. Sleep.

Woken by voices. Thalia's voice. Been dreaming about Thalia. Not . . . like that. Just seeing her, in his dreams, as she might have been, if things had been different, if the world could be changed back. Her voice must have made him dream.

'. . . dead,' Thalia was saying.

'My baby died. Six months, he lived.'

'We killed him. Didn't we? That night.'

Silence. 'Your husband killed him. Yes.'

'How do you go on?' said Thalia.

'Sadly,' said Lenae. Her voice sounded different. More real. 'With my heart screaming all night and all day.' Her voice came out in a rush, choking: 'I remember – one day, maybe a month, two months after my baby had been born – I remember putting my hands to my face, rubbing my face because I was tired, and I noticed the smell of my hands. They were all dry and spoilt, from washing clout clothes, washing and tending the baby, not getting any sleep. And they smelled like my mother's hands had. Like I remembered her hands smelling, when she held me, when I was a child. I used to take her hands, hold them to my face. And they looked like her hands, all red and gnarled and worn.

'A proper mother's hands, I thought, that's what I have now. But now my child is dead.'

Silence. 'And your husband? You said that he was dead.'

Silence. 'My mother arranged the marriage. I don't miss him like . . . you know. But he was a good father to our son.'

'Marith would have been a good father.' A pause. 'No, Marith would have been a dreadful father. But he would have loved our children.'

'You might find another man,' Lenae said. A pause. A nervous rush: 'Any number of them, I expect.'

Silence. 'I should think that bedding the High Priestess of the Lord of Living and Dying, Eltheia Returned, the *Ansikanderakesis*

Amrakane Amrath Returned's widow might . . . put most men off
their stroke, don't you think?'

A laugh. 'Perhaps.'

Thalia said, 'Ryn Mathen hinted that I should marry him . . .
should anything happen to Marith. He's not as bad as some.'

'The Chathean war leader?' Another pause. 'He's gorgeous.'
Another laugh.

'I should think he is dead by now. Or running back to Chathe.
His cousin is the King of Chathe. His cousin is also unmarried,
I've been told. I don't know what he looks like.'

Silence. 'I don't think I can have a child. I don't think – I don't
want to endure that again.'

Silence. 'What do you want?'

Thalia said, 'I don't know.'

'I have a purse with two thalers left in it,' said Lenae. 'I could
give you one thaler. That's enough to buy a farm somewhere.'

'Somewhere my army hasn't burned and sown the soil with salt
and human ashes, you mean?'

Silence.

'I – I mean – I—'

Pause.

'I'm sorry. That is a kind thing to offer. Thank you. But I can't
take it. I will go – wherever I go, whatever I do—'

Silence.

'That was a kindness. Thank you. Thank you, Lenae.'

'I could come with you, even. If you wanted. I'll ask you . . .
You think about it. Tobias is right. There are so many things you
could be and do.'

'Are there? Really?'

Both women fell silent.

On through the mountains. Day after day. Getting confusing, sometimes, the ache in his legs and his shoulder, his chest hurting him,
limping along hungry and tired. Alone in the wilderness. Am I
walking with Raeta and Landra, are we back in the Wastes, can I

still make it all go right? Time has stopped, time has gone back-wards, there's still a chance to make it right. Or before that, before everything, walking with Rate and Alxine and Marith through the desert, and Marith's the pretty new boy in the Free Company, cries at night sometimes, Emit's running a book on how long he lasts before this breaks him, starts crying for his mum, he can't make tea to save his life. I should feel anxious, knowing what we're going for; I should feel guilty, knowing they won't be coming back. We stop for a breather and he's sitting on the grass eating an apple, legs drawn up before him looking fresh as new cotton, sweet and young and innocent apart from his eyes. He smiles. Alxine's hoping he might smile at him. Rate says something and we all laugh.

Once they almost ran into a troop of soldiers, mountain men in their black armour, heading home after the victory. They had a man's head on a pole. A woman walked with them, her hands bound. There was a rope around her neck like a horse's bridle. A tall man with an antlered helmet dragged her along. They were going slowly and leisurely. The woman was stumbling. Very slow. A child with the same skin colour and hair colour as the woman trailed behind them. The men laughed, one brandished the pole with the head on it, one threw a stone that struck the child in the leg. The child cried out, but kept on following them. The woman turned to look, cried out also, and the man leading her jerked the rope around her neck, made her choke. The whole company of them went on out of sight.

'I would have jumped them. If there'd been twenty of me.'

Lenae said, 'Yes.'

'The child,' said Naillil.

Thalia said nothing. Put her hands to her throat.

They went on, and none of them spoke for the rest of the day. That night Tobias lay awake trying not to close his eyes. The woman's face was there in the dark with his eyes open, and there close up with a face like his mother, or like Lenae, or like Thalia, when he closed his eyes. 'You could at least have killed my child,' she said when he closed his eyes.

The next day they saw smoke rising, a village appeared perched high up on a crag of white rock, looking down over a river that must run on to the sea. The village looked well-made, strong houses of stone, cut into the living rock. Between the houses there were trees heavy with unripe fruit. Wheat grew in terraces on the slopes below, was already turning from green to gold. It was a very warm day, thin clouds over the sun giving the world a gentleness. Everywhere there seemed to be the droning hum of bees. Around midday, they came upon the child's body. His throat had been cut.

Thalia stopped by the body. Knelt. Very straight and proud, with her hair falling over her face. A river, Tobias remembered Marith saying about her hair. A cool river to swim in on a hot day. Not that Tobias was supposed to have heard that.

Said: 'Nice chaps, aren't they, the conquerors of the Army of Amrath that is the pestilence, the plague, the killing tide, that all good men must strive to wipe out? These heroes the conquerors of the monster the King of Death.'

Thought: yeah, yeah. Point made. What do you want anyone to say?

'Bury him,' said Thalia.

'The blokes what killed him might come back.'

'Bury him,' said Thalia. 'Please. Please, Tobias. Please, Naillil.'

Naillil said, 'Perhaps you should bury him yourself.'

Tobias said, 'Have you ever buried someone you killed before? Any idea how long it takes to dig a hole that big?'

'Shut up, Tobias.' Lenae knelt down beside Thalia. 'We can't bury him, Thalia. It would take too long, it's not safe. Tobias is right, they might come back. But . . . look.' Lenae took off a bracelet she wore, a pretty thing of silver and pearls she bought after they sacked Issykol. She fastened it carefully around the boy's thin wrist. Broke off a long stem of yellow grass flowers and laid them carefully over the body. Adjusted the head, arranged the long dark curls, until the wound was almost hidden. 'There,' Lenae said. Rovi watched her do it. Perhaps envious.

Naillil also placed a spray of flowers on the body. Thalia drew a ring from her finger and bent to put it on the boy's hand.

'No!' Panic in Lenae's voice. Lenae's hands reaching out over the corpse in a gesture to ward off ill-luck.

Thalia froze. Recoiled. Her hand clenched around the ring.

'I . . . I mean . . .' And Lenae's face too was filled with fear and grief.

'I know what you meant.' Thalia got up, very slowly, very graciously, carefully brushed the dust from the skirt of her dress. 'I'm sorry. I should have thought.' She put the ring back on her finger. It had a blue stone that caught the light.

'We should get out of here now,' Tobias said. 'They might come back. All this noise.'

It got hotter and hotter, dusty and sticky, a warm wind was blowing making Tobias's skin feel dry. His eyes felt sore, full of dust. After the village the landscape got wilder again, the mountains they walked through steeper, sharper, harsher. They seemed to cut at the soles of his feet with every step. His knees ached. His back ached. His shoulder ached. His head ached. But the sound of their feet on the stones of the mountains was almost calming, a pleasant dry sound. The sound of my life, he thought.

Another conversation in the dark that night, voices whispering:

'That was cruel. I—'

'I should have thought about it more carefully.' A long sigh. 'He gave me that ring as a Year's Renewal gift.'

'I didn't mean—'

'You did. You were right. It – he – he hacked it off a dead woman's finger, I should think. Or someone did, anyway, for him. I will throw it away, when we get to the sea. I should have thought.'

'No – yes – but . . .'

Four bloody years, Tobias thought, and you finally realized that. Come on, Lenae. Say it.

Thalia said, 'It doesn't matter. Thank you,' she said, 'for refusing to let me do it.'

Lenae said, 'Are you thinking about my offer still?'

Tried to block up his ears to them. In the day, he noticed, they largely ignored each other. Lenae walked with him. Thalia walked alone apart from all of them.

Skirted wide around a couple more villages. Another party of soldiers, dragging along two men as prisoners. A group out hunting, young men and women, who might be nothing to do with anything, but must be avoided because this was an enemy place.

Crested a ridge one morning and there suddenly before them was the sea. It was silver, gleaming, so near already that Tobias could see white froth where the water was stirred up over hidden rocks. Joy, wonder, thankfulness, various things. They walked right on to the very edge, where a cliff tumbled down sheer like a face looking out, staring at nothing, for there was nothing beyond to see.

Because you would, wouldn't you?

Walk to the end.

Lenae shouted. 'Look!' Below them, where the water broke against the grey cliff face, a disturbance in the water. Thrashing, splashing sound. In the sky, back shapes of birds gathering. The water churned white. Foamed and frothed. The birds wheeled across the sky shrieking. A neck like a dragon's neck, rising from the Sea of Tears. A beaked head, hooked and curved. Glistening wet flaccid as seaweed. All red and black. It roared. It sounded like the waves that the boy's weather mage called up. The sea beat with ripples. White waves crashed against the grey cliffs. A smaller creature rose up beside it, flashed silver in the water. The head came down all raw, it looked like it had been hacked out of rotten driftwood, worm-eaten, the rotting figurehead of a rotting dead ship. The beak opened. All lit up inside, rainbow colours, the inside of the thing's mouth glowing. The water, glowing.

Foaming, thrashing water. Churned around itself. Tobias saw somewhere in his mind the dyeing vats, the dyer's pole trampling the cloth into the water, the water boiling with it, waves and foam, twisting shapes. Lenae cried out wildly, 'They are fighting? They are fighting. Why are they fighting? What are they?'

'Creatures,' said Rovi. 'Sea things.'

A red sea dragon and four huge silver fish with long teeth. The sea dragon surfaced, screamed, dived in a rush of water, a wave that broke so high against the cliff the water stung on Tobias's face. The fish dived down after it, flashing beneath the surface of the churning water. Like the dyer's vat, a growing patch of vivid red.

Slowly the sea calmed. Red foam sinking away. Birds landed on the water, fighting over shreds of red and silver skin.

The map that Skie had owned, the Company Map, beautifully drawn, greasy and tatty and used to buggery, had a border of real gold leaf until some former commander of the Free Company of the Sword picked the gold leaf off . . . that map had pictures of sea dragons and sea beasts on it. Only nobody had believed in them. Fancy artistic messing around map-maker's touch.

Thalia said, 'A red dragon. Red-black.'

Tobias said, 'Yeah. Talk about omens.'

Chapter Thirty-Three

When the sea beasts have gone, we find a path that leads down to the shore. A narrow valley, a gorge where a stream runs down to meet the sea. We walk in the bed of the stream over wet stones that shine like glass, that move and rock beneath my feet. My shoes are sodden. We walk down where the water runs in a miniature waterfall, holding onto the rocks with our hands. The gorge is very narrow, it reminds me of the corridors in my Temple. Of course it does. Where the sides are less steep there is earth and green grass and white flowers. The air smells of salt water, soft, clear, soothing. Very suddenly the gorge opens out onto a beach and the sea and the sun. As I knew it would. The sand is perfect gold. The sea is deep brilliant blue. Where it meets the sky there is a haze, a film of white cloud, and then the sky is blue as the sea. Everything is bathed in light. So much light. Not harsh like the light in the desert. Clean on the eyes. Soft.

I walk down to the shore and the sea is warm, I had no idea that the sea could be warm. On the White Isles the sea was cold as ice, Marith swam in it, danced and shouted because it was so cold. Now I bathe my feet in warm water, wash off the dust of the mountains, I sit with the waves breaking over my skirt. The sand is warm like it is alive. The air is warm. I close my eyes and my vision is all red and golden, and it is warm behind my eyes like nestling under a thick blanket to sleep. The waves break very soft and gentle. Sleepy. Shushing laughing murmuring sound on the sand. A woman's voice whispering a lullaby to a child. I dig my hands in the warm sand. Beneath the gold, where my hand moves the sand grains, the sand is black and wet. For a moment, the clear water looks black.

I have missed the sea. I remember the first time I saw the sea. 'You'll like it,' Marith said. 'You'll like the sea, Thalia.'

These things are the way of the world: betrayal, pain, suffering, grief. My life. And others' lives. Others' pain. Others' grief. I have done terrible things, and I have done wonderful things. I feel nothing but shame, and I feel nothing but joy in it. It was glorious. No one can say it was not that. Yet I feel also as though a weight has been lifted from me. A relief that it is gone.

So many died for me. On and on forever. Never stop.

I am glad, I think, that he is dead. I hope that he is at peace. I . . .

He wanted to die.

He was so very afraid of death.

I was the Queen of the World. Eltheia Returned to Us. Feared and loved. I was the Chosen of Great Tanis Who Rules All Things, child-killer, the holiest woman in all Irlast. If I had drawn the black or the white or the green lot, I would have died as a child. If I had drawn the yellow lot, I would have spent my life lighting candles, gathering flowers, singing hymns to the rising sun. A dull life, my friend Helase always said.

I bathe in the warm ocean, sit on the yellow sand in the clean light, washing it all away from me. Today we saw the sea beasts fighting. Tomorrow we will walk up the coast, back north, and I will find somehow some other way to live. If I cannot be queen, I would like, still, to live.

Chapter Thirty-Four

Landra Relast, the destroyer, she will dance on their graves in triumph
Seneth Isle, the King's Isle, where she once felt something that was almost happiness

In a cold spring rain Landra stood at the gates of Morr Town, looking up at the walls.

Still it caught in her heart, to see the high stone walls, the open gateway, the red cloaks of the guards, the central tower of Malth Elelane shining, Eltheia's diamond blazing at its height. The Tower of Joy and Despair indeed. A long time, since she had last seen these walls. A great deal had happened in the world. And yet it felt as though she had never left. She went in through the gates quickly, her heart beating very loud. The guards looked at her without interest.

What do you want in Morr Town?
Nothing. I want nothing.

The town was bustling, crowded with people even in the rain. But, like the villages she had passed through, it had a ragged look to it. Stretched and thin. Like Ethalden it was filled with new building, the first thing that met her as she passed through the gateway was a building site, the foreman cursing his workers for

303

slacking off in the rain. But the man's voice was forced, as though speaking from a script, the workmen in their rags ignored him, shuffled on slowly without looking up.

They are slaves, Landra thought. War captives. All they had in their lives is dead. When they die here, they will be glad. As she watched, a worker's hand slipped on a wet rope and the beam she was hauling fell. A scream and a crash. The foreman and two workers lay dead. The woman whose hand had slipped began to shriek.

Good, thought Landra. He deserved it. Dead voices inside her whispered: kill them and set them free. The scaffold the workers were standing on began to tilt. The rain, so sudden and heavy, soaking the earth beneath, turning it to mire, the building had no foundations, had been thrown up in haste, the struts of the scaffold, the stones of the wall, slipping, slipping, the wet earth was opening sucking the wood and the stone down and sucking the workers' lives down. The rain, turning the earth to mire; like the temple of Amrath in Ethalden the building was cheaply and badly made.

The whole town will come down. All of them must die. Fall in the streets vomiting where they have gorged themselves on human blood. Let their bodies wither, where they have not risen up to stop this. Let them be struck dumb and witless, where they have not spoken out. Let the pain they have unleashed consume them.

Landra walked through the town looking at them, the townspeople's worn faces, narrowed eyes, the new buildings, the traders' stalls overflowing with looted wealth. A slave auction was taking place in the courtyard before the gates of Malth Elelane. This was a new thing. A young woman was dragged up before the crowd, beautiful, black skin and black hair falling loose down her back. She stared furiously out at the crowd. 'Five in gold,' the slave dealer shouted, but the woman's eyes were so full of hate.

'Look at her!' the slave dealer shouted, tearing the woman's dress to show her naked body. 'Five in gold! A bargain!'

In a place where all the men are off at war, Landra thought, who wants a woman for five in gold? And look, there behind her another waiting her turn, a girl still barely out of childhood with long red curls and a pretty milk-white child's face. The woman sold for three in gold in the end, the child for two in gold and an iron piece. The child's buyer was a man with half his face missing, his left hand a ruined lump of meat. He wore a brocade cloak fastened with a jewelled brooch, that must be worth more than the girl's life and the woman's life.

I wonder, thought Landra, if he would give up the cloak and the brooch and the girl to get his hand and his face back? He walked quite near her, leading the child, who was whimpering, and Landra thought: no. I do not think that he would. He would say that he would, perhaps.

She smiled as the child walked past her. The child looked back and opened sea-green eyes very wide. Their eyes met. Then the child was gone. The woman went past with her hands bound, her new master pulling her on a rope like a beast. Her eyes stared left and right. From her, even Landra drew back in fear and sickness.

There were slaves everywhere, now she looked. Their masters dressed in an absurd jumble of wealth from everywhere in the world. But the poor folk of the town were yet poorer, she realized, because there were slaves now to do the work.

She spent the day walking the town, remembering. The harbour, where Marith had lost a battle and then sailed in in triumph to be crowned; the rich houses with their backs to the sea; the hovels dirty and tumbled; the inns where Marith and Carin had drunk themselves stupid; the market place. Remember it all, she told herself. Etch it into your heart. The shadows of Malth Elelane's towers falling onto the water of the Heale river; the sweep of Thealan Vale where the fields were churned from the ploughing, but where she noticed that many of the trees had been cut down; the vista across the town to the Hill of Altrersys that was the burial ground of the Altrersyr kings. Dark mounds, cairns scattered all over the hillside, all the way back to Altrersys and Eltheia.

Landra craned to see it clearly: there, that patch of newer, rawer stone – that must be the grave of King Illyn. She had travelled the world, she thought, but this place would always be the most beautiful place.

From one of the rich houses near to the Thealeth Gate, a man's scream came up and was suddenly cut off. Then another scream, shriller, angrier, a child's shriek not of pain but of fury and triumph. Then it too was cut off.

Landra smiled. Yes. Good. These people who lived here their smug lives on the spoils of war and bloodshed. Guilty. All of them. She pressed her raw red hands onto the stone of the town walls. Deep within her a dead voice began to sing. In her mouth was a taste of fresh sweetness like apples. Her hands felt as though she held a sword. The heat from her hands was painful.

By nightfall the whole of Morr Town was burning. The flames rose higher than the town wall. Higher than the towers of Malth Elelane, perhaps, had the air not been so choked with smoke that they could no longer be seen. Stone burned like dry tinder. The water of the Heale itself burned. It was not the violent red of dragon fire, not banefire green or maggot white; it was not the same as the fire that Marith used to destroy. It blazed up with the flames reaching to the stars, the light of the fire stained the moon golden-red. Purifying fire. Cleansing. Like the fire that the men brought around at Sunreturn, the luck fires that burned away evil spirits, cleared the air of curses and malice things. Like the fire in the fields when the stubble must be burned out before the new corn is sown.

'Burn,' Landra whispered to the fire. Her voice croaked in her throat from the smoke. Her hands hurt her. The skin on them was almost black. The burns on her scalp and face felt very raw. Hurt her as they had when they were first made. Her home burning, her hair burning away, the skin on her face burning, her sister Savane screaming in terror as her dress caught fire, her sister's silver dress and silver pale hair burning up in a column of flame. 'Burn,' Landra whispered. It is not the same, it is not, she thought.

People were dying in the fire, she could hear them, shrieks of fear, faces thrust at the windows of upstairs rooms, shrieking, pleading, gasping. Sometimes one of them would jump. She thought she saw the face of the slave woman, very briefly, at a high barred window, clawing at the bars. So the woman had not had to endure slavery for long. People flooded out of the town, half naked, some of them, in their bed robes, stumbling under the weight of their possessions, throwing their burdens down to run on as the fire leapt. Sometimes someone would fall, be trodden down by those running behind them. At the gate there was a great crush of people fighting to escape, though the gate itself was burning, a mass of people churning and pushing, she saw people go down under the trampling feet.

Those that got through were running into the fields of Thealan Vale or up the slope of the Hill of Altrersys. Strange feelings, watching them.

Some of them must be good people, she thought. Some of them must have wept at what he did. Cursed him, in the depths of their hearts. Tried not to be part of it. Perhaps that is why they are spared.

It came to her, briefly, hesitantly, a memory came of the fisherfolk Ben and Hana bent over their child's cradle, frightened of what would happen if Marith's soldiers came. 'Ben's young enough and strong enough to go for a soldier, My Lady,' Hana had said apologetically, 'so you . . . you can't stay, see?' A poor household, and the man must go out every day in his boat on the cruel sea, and the Army of Amrath paid an iron penny a head . . .

No. Do not think on that. Watch the flames. Watch them cleanse it away. The fire rose in a great sheen of gold. It billowed like a sail. It swelled like muscles flexed beneath golden skin. The towers of Malth Elelane must be fallen, the grey towers of Joy, the golden tower of Despair. Eltheia's jewel that shines at the summit of the tower, winking out to call home the fishing boats and the war ships . . . the tower burns like a torch in the darkness, the jewel is cast down. The earth beneath opens molten to swallow it up. Sheets of fire. Skeins of fire like long hair. Eddies and currents of fire, drifts of fire, walls of fire; a new cityscape rising, towers and domed rooftops, great trees, figures, vast beasts. They writhed like dreams. Like watching clouds on the wind. Landra's hands ached and her heart ached. She wept for joy and grief. The town is burned and the pestilence is purged from one small corner of the earth. It is gone, all of it.

Benth, that is safety from disease,

Anneth, to ward off the lice and other parasites.

Eth, that is destruction,

Tha, that is hope.

Bel, for love,

Ri, for hate.

The moon disappeared behind a cloud. It began to rain. Hard and heavy, very cold. Beating the fires down. The stone hissed and steamed. The flames fought with the rain. Landra threw back her head so that the water soaked into her burn-scars. The rain spat and steamed on her red raw hands. Soothed them. The sea and the sky were lost in smoke and mist. She stood alone in the world in the blind darkness. This, she thought, is how the world was before the earth rose from the waters, before all that is real was made. Before men's poison came. Ah, gods, she trembled before it. Inside her, dead voices rose in glorious song.

It's worse. It's worse than he is.

No. Do not think that. They have to suffer, she thought. All of them.

The fires were quenched. The town sat blackened, damaged, the towers of Malth Elelane rose up proud, the town's walls were strong and unharmed. People stumbled about in the wreckage. Those who had fled where beginning to turn, go back to their homes. Voices called in joy, as people recognized each other, embraced family and friends and neighbours in the streets.

'Look, look, the house is still standing! Eltheia be praised!'

'The Gate Inn's survived! Mostly! Gods, I hope the beer's not too singed . . .'

'Our house is gutted. But Mum and Dad's is fine, just a bit of smoke damage, nothing they can't sort out.'

'Gods, I'm sorry. We're fine, the fire never got near us. If you need anything, do please say.'

'The house is salvageable; we got the valuables out with us. But Dan's forge is rubble, ironically.'

'And to think we'd only finally got everything straight after the storm four years ago. Finished painting the children's bedroom, like, literally last week. Gods. Gods.'

'Praise be to King Marith, the money lender's shop is cinders!'

'That's a cheap and tasteless joke.'

A kind of party beginning, people in their nightclothes in the cold and the wet, laughing, crying, hugging, bewailing their losses. Taking each other in, fussing over lost children, sharing blankets and hot soup. Lining up burned bodies. Rejoicing over how few there were.

'Praise the king! Praise the king!'

'Eltheia is merciful!'

'We survived! Oh, oh, the world is a good place!'

A sickness in Landra's heart. She felt herself drained, wearied, broken down. Futile. Pointless.

The dead of Illyr, laughing. The gabeleth, licking bloodied lips. The *gestmet* Raeta crying out in fury, as Marith stumbled unharmed to his feet, in a tent on a mountainside in the Empty Peaks, while a dragon looked on and laughed at the absurdity of it. Bile rose up in her throat. It struck her cold in her heart so that she put up her raw red hands, cried out.

She had seen Marith fall, seen him jerk and then lie still. She had seen his face, smiling, peaceful, dust in his teeth. But she had not seen him die.

In her mind, she saw it. Osen Fiolt with tears running down his cheeks, his heart breaking in his breast. 'Marith, Marith. No. Please. No.' The swords coming down, bronze and iron, black iron axes, an ashwood spear with a cruel barbed iron tip. Arrows overhead, clattering, a rain of arrows, they have bright ribbons tied to their shafts, coloured streamers like god spirits dancing, they whistle as they come on. There is a red mist over the battlefield, blood mist from the bodies trampled there. The air is filled with metal dust where iron has ground against iron, bronze against bronze, metal against living bone. The magic of the killing, the alchemy that translates love and joy to bitter death. Ryn Mathen running, kicking his horse faster, faster, get away, get away, flee; Alleen Durith casting around him, lashing out at those he so recently had laughed and drunk and joked with, 'Kill the demon, cast it down, put out its filth'; Kiana Sabryya wounded and crying, killing, killing, 'I have sworn him my loyalty, I have turned my coat once, I will not do so again, I am a good and loyal soldier, a woman of honour, I swore him an oath and I will not be forsworn now when the end comes.' Soldiers of the White Isles and of Ith, whose homes Landra has burned, whose loved ones she has destroyed, they fight and fall dying, and they will never know what she has done to punish them. And they die. And they die. And the darkness comes for them.

But Osen is running towards Marith, as Marith lies in the dust his body bloodied from the crest of his helmet to the soles of his boots. Marith's hands scrabbling for his sword, even as he smiles up waiting for the release of his death. His eyes are lover's eyes, welcoming, delighting, as the sword blades come down and down at him. He is soaked through with others' death. Drowned in others' deaths. But Osen is running towards him, weeping, screaming, snot and tears streaming down his face. 'Marith. Marith.'

Marith's lips moving. Whispering, 'No.' Osen with his sword raised casting about him furious, a storm of love and fury, single-handed he cuts them down more and more and more, their bodies fall like a wall to shelter Marith's broken limbs. Marith whispering, 'No. Please.' The arrows fall like rain, swords, axes, the thrashing hooves of a black horse as huge as a mountain, its mouth and its hooves pouring out blue fire that freezes the blood-mire around it to black ice. And Osen kills them, and kills them, and a wall of corpses grows to shelter Marith Altrersyr from his enemies' blades. Dead men forming a cradle to rest and shelter him.

Osen pulls at Marith's body, drags him upright. 'Marith, Marith, come on. Come with me.' Carrying Marith's body. The ranks of the enemy part before them. Fall back in fear at the look on Osen's face. There is Kiana Sabryya, her girl's face happy and smiling, reaching down slender fingers sticky with blood to receive him. Pulling him up onto her horse. And they are riding, with Osen running beside, still lashing out with his sword to ward the enemy off.

The enemy hold the killing ground. The Army of Amrath is cast down and slaughtered. But Marith Altrersyr is not dead.

PART FIVE

THE RUINS

Chapter Thirty-Five

Marith
The Mountains of Pain. A sick joke

This is not a good place.

They had found him a hut to sleep in. Crude stone walls, the roof so low he had to crouch. No windows, but the gaps in the walls and under the door let in a bit of light. It reminded him of being in the hold of the ship dragging him back across the Bitter Sea to Third: sometimes, lying trying to sleep, he seemed to rise and fall as though moving through waves. The feeling was pleasant, until he thought of being on the ship. Beams of light came in through the cracks in the walls, and that made him think of something too, another memory, light moving in long fingers across a wall, raising his hand to stir up dust to watch it move in the light. Couldn't remember where that had been, or why, or why the memory frightened him. He closed his eyes, rolled over to bury his head in the pillow they had made him. It had been made out of a horse blanket, and stank. The bed beneath it was made of dried leaves. His shoulder still hurt like fire, constantly, endlessly, sometimes the skin seemed to be crawling, the pain got down into his back, his ribcage, strained all the muscles in his body as he tried to hold himself to avoid the pain. Sleeping rough like this wasn't helping it and wasn't helping it.

It was still very early, he'd guess from the light and the sounds. You can always tell, somehow, the feel of early morning. Birdsong. People trying to move silently, outside the hut, not wanting to wake him. Then someone dropped something, very close to the wall of the hut; a voice shouted, 'Be quiet! You'll wake him! Come away from there.' 'What does it matter now?' another voice, Kiana's voice, said.

'Because it matters,' said the first voice. It might be Brychan.

He pushed back the cloak he was using as a blanket – Brychan's cloak – groped around in the gloom for his jacket and his boots and his sword belt. A spasm of pain across his shoulders. Bit it back, clenched his teeth. No one can know. No one must know. The jacket was too disgusting to wear, as it had been the previous morning, and the previous morning before that. The boots were lying on the floor, and he thought of Rate finding a scorpion in his boots one morning and shrieking. The ruby in his sword's hilt winked at him. Joy! He wrapped the blood-clot cloak around himself, his hands trembling on the brooch as he fastened it. The ruby in the brooch winked at him too as he looked down to do the clasp, the dark flaw at its heart jumped. He pricked his finger on the pin, as he often did. He took up his knife from beneath the pillow. It occurred to him that he should have taken it up first, before anything.

You see, Marith? Go outside and enjoy it.

It was indeed only early morning. The grass outside the hut was wet with dew. It made a lovely pattern on his boots, like a flower pattern, black wet on the scuffed black leather. He kicked his foot back and forth on the grass, enjoying the sheen of the dewdrops. Should have gone out in bare feet. The morning warmth was bringing the dew up as mist, hazing everything pale golden. Under the trees a cookfire was trying to burn, all smoke and no heat because the wood was too damp. The smoke did not rise, mingled in a pool with the dew mist.

Over the door of the hut Osen Fiolt's head stared towards the fire. It had been hung in wood smoke to keep it from rotting but a crow had pecked at it, giving it a lopsided look. Stupid. Comic. Grumpy couldn't give a toss. Sort of like Osen sometimes looked when he was very, very drunk. The eyes were sunken, withered up, the lips cracked and peeling back from the teeth. Actually, it looked more the way Osen did when he was very, very hungover.

'Good morning, My Lord King.' Brychan was sitting neatly beside the hut doorway, a drawn sword in his lap. Shadows in his face, grey, stiff, the dew soaked into him. Got up, stretched; a crack from his knees like dry twigs snapping, another crack from his back. Leaned on the wall of the hut bent over.

'Careful you don't knock the hut over,' Marith said.

Brychan coughed. 'I'll try not to, My Lord King.'

'Go to bed, Brychan.'

Brychan looked around them. Fading mist and wood smoke and the trees pressing in close around the clearing, and maybe ten men. Gods, the man looked dreadful. Grey-skinned, red-eyed, his shoulders hunched, he moved and his knees cracked again.

Alis Nymen came up close beside Marith. A sword on his hip, two knives at his waist, armed. He looked slightly better than Brychan, except for the dirt in his hair from sleeping on the ground. Nodded at Brychan.

'Thank you, My Lord King,' said Brychan. 'I'll go to bed.' He shuffled off behind the hut.

'Brychan?'

Stopped, looked back, looked . . . frightened? 'My Lord King?' Sounded frightened. Looked down at the ground as he spoke.

Marith said, 'Take your cloak, Brychan. It's in my hut, go and get it. You can take the pillow, too.'

Brychan seemed to hesitate. Looked at Alis Nymen, at the hut door, at his feet. 'Thank you, My Lord King.'

There were twenty of them, camped in the clearing around the woodsman's hut. The King of All Irlast, the World Conqueror in

317

His Glory, the Light of the World, the King of Dust, the King of Shadows, the King of Death; Lord Nymen the wealthiest fish merchant in Toreth Harbour; Lady Kiana Sabryya; the guardsman Brychan; fifteen soldiers; one terrified camp boy. Three horses, one of them lame and they really should kill it like they should kill the camp boy and at least three of the soldiers. Sixteen swords, ten helmets, thirteen wearable cloaks, no alcohol. Osen Fiolt's severed head.

Osen Fiolt's body was buried off in the woods somewhere. He'd ordered Brychan not to tell him where. Made Brychan swear it. Even if he begged the man later on.

Stupid.

'Some breakfast?' Kiana asked him. Badly roasted woodrat. Yum. You could live very well out in the wilds in the summer warmth, on fresh meat and wild plants and fresh meat and wild plants and that's it. How happy I am: I'm free of it! I've put down my burden, taken off my crown, my empire is fallen, my army is slaughtered, all that I built is thrown down in the dust. Here I sit beneath the vault of heaven, myself alone, stripped, scoured, naked before the darkness, I have nothing no burden no weight. All I ever wanted, to be nothing. Such longing! How I waited, how much I yearned for this. I do and I did I did I did.

Three kingdoms I had that were mine, and I sat by the fire like an old man like my father, Osen was going to grow a beard, we could have sat growing old while our children and our grandchildren played on the floor at our feet. I had a father and a mother and a brother I loved, I had a lifetime stretching out ahead of me.

I'd give all five fingers of my right hand and the lives of every single one of these useless fuckers around me for a cup of something. The thing about being the lord of the world is how quickly you miss it once it's gone.

He sat down next to Kiana. One of the fifteen surviving soldiers of the Army of Amrath passed him a lump of badly roasted woodrat. It was skewered on the blade of a knife. The tip of the blade had snapped off. That was somehow almost the final insult.

'Do we have anything to drink?' he asked no one in particular. No. Obviously. But there's this thing called deluded hope . . . If you've based your life on it, you can't help still hoping. *It's all right, Marith. Everything's all right*: so why shouldn't someone have found a barrel of firewine and a dozen vials of hatha abandoned under a tree?

'No,' said Kiana. If Brychan and Alis looked bad, she looked indescribable. Hard as stone. Her eyes huge because her face had grown so taut and thin. 'There's water, in a wineskin.' She passed it over. He drank. The water tasted of leaves, a metallic aftertang, it had a brown tint to it that they were trying not to see. The nearest stream was probably tainted with something. Blood. Piss. Pus. But it was the nearest stream.

Kiana said, 'Please let me bury it, Marith.'

'What?'

Kiana pointed. 'Osen's head.'

Marith said, 'No. It stays with me.'

It struck him suddenly that he owed poor Valim Erith an apology. Valim Erith might even have been telling the truth when he swore blind it wasn't him who was betraying them. Thus justifiably upset when he was accused of it all. Those hate-filled eyes, the rage in his voice: 'Curse you, Marith. You deserve this.' Well, now, actually, thinking about it, Valim Erith just being upset about being accused for no reason . . . that was almost a relief. Valim hadn't hated him at all, hadn't schemed against him, hadn't wanted him dead. Just half-asleep and confused and understandably upset.

Alleen Durith that treacherous bastard didn't hate me either, he thought then. Certain of it. Alleen just wanted to be king of somewhere for himself. He'll be King of Ith by now, if he's really unlucky. Planning his own wars, raising his own men. If he'd asked me, I'd have warned him. Don't do it, Alleen. Look at me. Think about it.

'We should move on,' said Kiana.

'Why? We have the hut, the stream, woodrats . . . Yes.' Marith sighed, itched at his eyes. 'Give the order, then.'

Kiana looked at him oddly. Snorted with laughter. She clapped her hands: 'We are moving on. Get everything ready. An hour till we march. Get everyone awake.' Ten weary faces blinked at her.

They marched perhaps two hours later. Kiana and Marith mounted, the rest on foot limping. The third horse was dead. One of the men was dead. 'I did it quickly,' the dead man's friend said, when Alis asked about it. The wretched camp boy trailed at the back in silence. Alis said he hadn't spoken since they encountered him. Brychan walked beside Marith's horse with a sword in one hand and a knife in the other, his shoulders hunched up, yawning. Kiana looked happy, at least, now she was back on the horse. Osen's head jolted along in a bag hanging from Marith's saddle. He could feel it knocking against his left leg. Marith took a last look at the hut in the clearing. Three nights.

'Where did you bury him, Brychan?'

Brychan looked pained. 'You made me swear not to tell you, My Lord King.'

'I know I did. Where did you bury him?'

Brychan sighed. 'Back there. In the other direction, a hundred paces from the clearing, maybe. Near the stream.'

Looked over his shoulder. Goodbye, Osen.

'There was a young tree near where I buried him,' said Brychan. 'Looked like it might flower soon. I dug a good deep hole, don't worry.'

The ground here was soft, good to walk on, trees for cover and shade, dappled light; they kept to the lower ground where streams ran west to the river Essern or south to the river Isther, through belts of pines that left the earth bare and dusty beneath them, glades of wild myrtle and star flowers, sana trees heavy with poisonous red fruit. Marith rode on absently, the horse chaffing under him. It had been one of the soldiers'. Seemed to dislike him. One of the soldiers, whom he was beginning to imagine was the soldier the horse had belonged to, hummed occasionally as they walked, one of the Amy of Amrath's favourite marching songs. It was warm, almost but not quite too hot, almost pleasant in a cool breeze. Marith rubbed his eyes. Itching. He thought: should I send someone out to look for Thalia again? The last man he sent had not come back.

That night he had to sleep rough under a tree, wrapped in the horse blanket, twigs poking into his back. Amrath slept rough with his men, didn't the stories say that? I think they may have been lying. His shoulder was screaming; he had had to fight to hold himself upright, keep himself from twisting and slumping over in the saddle. His whole body was stiff. They brought him water in a helmet to wash his face; cold going-off badly roasted woodrat to eat. They couldn't build a fire: too dangerous, the trees weren't thick here, the light would show, Brychan looked sick at the thought. Brychan looked sick anyway, after a night's watch and a day tramping at his king's side. Marith gave him his cloak. Brychan gave it back. Marith gave it back again.

'You'll be cold,' said Brychan.

'Give it to Kiana, then.'

Brychan took the cloak, wrapped himself up.

A wind stirred the leaves of the tree. Black, and the sky behind them was deep black-blue. Clouds moving, covering the stars, shredded away by the wind. Hard to tell what was sky and what was cloud and what was the leaves dancing. No moon tonight. So the stars were brighter. Thalia hated moonless nights. Did not often want to make love on moonless nights. It seemed understandable why.

I'd happily never even touch her again, he thought. Just look at her, have her near me; no, not even look at her, just hear her voice. Just know she was alive. In another man's bed, falling in love with someone else, never thinking of me, as long as she's alive somewhere.

The clouds grew thicker. Even the branches of the tree above his head were lost in the dark. The men around him black shapes in the black. Tricks of his eyes, his eyes wanting to see something in the dark. A weight crushing down over his face. The darkness was like a stone.

My shadowbeasts, he thought. Come to smother me. Wrapped all around me. Ti blindfolding me with a velvet scarf playing blindman's catch, trying to make me run and grab hold of him. It occurred to him suddenly that he would be dead in a few days. He should try to get to sleep. It would be nice to get some sleep before he was dead. Thought: I can't die. Stupid. What made me think that? I came so close to dying, and I cannot die. I sit in the filth in the dark and I cannot die and I cannot live. If I could die, oh gods, I would be long long dead.

Ha. No. I wouldn't. I'd be here just as I am, trying to hang on with every last fibre of my being. Possibly I wouldn't have let my army get slaughtered around me, though. Try to get some sleep. It's so late. Perhaps the sun will rise soon. I would like that. The comfort of falling asleep in the dawn. These maudlin self-pitying dreams banished. I—

A noise, in the dark.

Off to the left.

An animal noise. The night is full of animal noises. An owl, a deer . . . A mountain god, prowling on cloven hooves, coming to kill him . . .

A noise again. A horse's nicker, the jingle of a bridle, the horse rapidly hushed. A snap that might have been a twig breaking. Hard to tell in the dark where it was coming from. The whole camp, if you could call twenty men a camp, must be awake now, surely. Sat up, heard a twig snap under him, had to bite back another howl at the pain in his shoulder. Reached for his knife and his sword.

The dark got suddenly darker. Black shape beside him, close to him. 'My Lord King,' Alis Nymen whispered in his ear. 'Horsemen, over towards the next ridge. Danger.'

Really? You think?

Quiet rasp of metal that was swords being drawn. All of them lying in the dark, trying not to breathe, trying not to move. One

322

of their own horses neighed, unnerved by the tension licking around it. A bird called, off to Marith's left. Rustle of leaves. A wild desperate animal shriek. So many things are awake tonight.

A soldier crept over to him, whispered close: 'There are a lot of them, My Lord King. Forty, at least. Most of them mounted. Further off than the noise suggests, and the land falls and rises again between us and them. If we're lucky . . . There's nothing we can do, My Lord King, except hope they don't hear us. I'm worried about the horses making a noise. But I can't see what to do else.'

One might, if one were feeling unkind, suggest not creeping around whispering like a little boy sneaking out of bed. 'Yes. Thank you.' And now we lie and wait. A horse neighed, and it sounded further off. The clouds were thinning, a single star visible through the leaves of the tree. Black clouds black leaves black sky, layers of darkness. Thank the gods it's a moonless night. One of their horses neighed. Gods. Gods. His whole body aching to jump up, run; a shout hammering in his mouth. More stars visible, a pattern of them like open hands. A fox barked. So much noise in the darkness. The clouds thickened. He felt as though he would choke on the dark.

This is all so familiar. Lying in silence in the dark. When the dawn came he might have been dozing. He was wet with dew and the blanket he was wrapped in reeked of damp. There had not been any noise of the horsemen for a long time.

The clouds were low, the dawn came very gradually, setting the world soft warm pink the shadowless milky first light. A bird burst up from the tree above him in a clap of wings. A leaf drifted down onto his face.

A soldier crept over to him, moving in the stiff way that men do when moving silently. He put his head very close to Marith's face. 'My Lord King.' Marith recognized his voice and the smell of his hair as the man who had spoken to him in the night. Grey-haired, a lean sharp face. 'My Lord King, the horsemen are gone. Do you want me to scout out their tracks?'

'Yes. Do it. Carefully.'

The man smiled, 'I think I can be careful, My Lord King.'

'He could be going to betray us to them,' Alis whispered.

'He could. He should have reported to you, not directly to me. He could have yelled for them to come and butcher us last night.'

An eternity, waiting. In the light now they sat and looked at each other. None of them looking at Marith. He went over to Kiana, who was checking her sword, turning it over and over, polishing the decoration at the hilt with her cloak.

'My Lord King.' She frowned. 'Marith.'

'If they'd come on us in the night, you would have been defenceless.'

'Yes. I know.' She turned the sword over and over, the blade very close to her face. It was almost black, and then it was bright silver, and it was grey and cold.

'What's the man's name?' he asked Kiana. 'Do you know?'

'Selerie,' she said. 'The same as the old king. He's one of my captains.' She looked at Marith, daring him to flinch. 'You used to know all the officers' names, Marith.'

The man Selerie came back. Moving less cautiously, almost a smile on his face. Marith said, 'Yes?'

'My Lord King. I was right, forty of them at least, horses and men on foot with them. There's a gully, on the other side of the ridge, they were on the other side of that, they went off to the north-east. Same direction we're going in. I followed the trail a little way, there's smoke, I think they may be camped somewhere up ahead. But, My Lord King . . . I found this.'

The man Selerie opened his hand. On his palm was something dusty, metallic-looking. A copper brooch to fasten a cloak. A cheap, badly made thing. The pin was bent, it must have fallen from a cloak, been lost in the dark. It was stamped with a crude picture of a rose tree.

'Chathe?'

The man Selerie nodded. Grinning. 'Chathe. Could be prisoners, but . . .' He looked straight into Marith's face. The first time he had done so. 'Lord Mathen of Chathe broke and ran from the battle, My Lord King. His horsemen with him. He must be some-where. Him and his men. They would be heading north-east, I should think. Back home. I would bet a lot this is him.'

Gods. Ryn Mathen.

That cowardly useless treacherous bastard Ryn Mathen. If he is still alive, he deserves slow killing.

Ryn Mathen the Chathean war leader, and his horsemen. Cousin to the king of Chathe, the new young one. Good with his sword: I saw him cut a man in half once, when we took Ander, rode up at him, cut his body straight across the middle, the man's legs stood up straight on their own for a moment after his body went flying, rooted in the mud, Ryn didn't so much as blink. Looks at Thalia sometimes. Popular. His men are very loyal to him.

Marith felt a great sickness come up over him.

Good soldiers, too, Ryn's men.

'It can't be. It's a trap. The man's wrong.'

'I can think of better ways of setting a trap than wandering around in the dark dropping a cheap brooch, hoping we find it. If they had any idea we were here, they'd have fallen on us last night.'

'It was a prisoner. Someone dropped a looted brooch. The man's lying.'

'I would trust Selerie with my life,' said Kiana. 'He is not lying. He may be wrong.' She looked at Marith. 'We have very little to lose.'

'Only our lives,' said Alis. 'The king's life.'

What she just said. Walked into that, didn't you, Alis? They started out immediately, over the ridge, a nasty scramble down the narrow gulley the man Selerie had mentioned, a stream trickled down so they refilled their waterskins, splashed their faces, a nastier scramble up the other side. The land beyond was the same scrubby woodland, rising to bare mountain peaks. Marith tried to remember distance on the map, how much further the mountains lasted before the great dry plain that stretched away to the city of Elarne, the capital city of Chathe.

'Here, My Lord King, you see?' The man Selerie was crouching, pointing to marks on the ground. 'Horses, and footprints, you see? I found the brooch further on, near those rocks there.'

Horse shit, horse piss, a bit further on what might have been man piss, up against the rocks near where Selerie had found the brooch. Definitely people on horseback, definitely heading northwards. Could be anyone going anywhere. Could be a bunch of people heading south and getting lost.

But he knew. Knew and felt sick. 'This is too easy,' he'd once said to Tobias inside the Summer Palace in Sorlost.

Not exactly moving stealthily, Ryn Mathen and his men. Going fast. Eager to get on. The mountains must end soon, Marith thought, the plain of Elarne there stretching out before us, grasslands and flat fields; they'll be pushing on, trying to get home. Their wives and children waiting for them, sleep in their own beds, sit before their own fires, try to go back to a pretence of their old life.

She could be alive, there with Ryn, he thought then. Up ahead, and I'm coming for her, and she doesn't know. Be happy, Thalia! Don't mourn me! If it is Ryn Mathen up ahead of me, I hope you're in his arms every night with him telling you he loves you, pregnant with a child that will live. Let it be for that that Ryn and his men were spared, to lead you to Elarne in safety, settle you there to live in peace.

'Marith?' Kiana nudged her horse over to him. 'You look . . . Is something wrong here? It could be a trap. My captain Selerie could be wrong. We could turn off from following them.'

'No. Nothing. It's Ryn Mathen and his men. I know it.'

Thought: it's too easy. I was dying. It was ended.

They caught them at dusk. The very edge of the mountains: they had travelled more quickly than Marith had realized. Remembered approaching the Mountains of Pain from the north, the endless flat grassland and then suddenly on the horizon the mountains, bare blue sky with the mountaintops tearing it apart. Mount Trianor the tallest peak in the Mountains of Pain. The tallest peak in all Irlast outside of the Mountains of the Heart. Its name meant 'the Needle'. A sacred mountain, god-haunted, snow-girt in the heights even in the heat of the south, any man who climbed it would be accursed. And they called it 'the Needle', after a woman's embroidery tool. It stood as a guardian, the first and greatest of the mountains. Seen from the north, riding south at the head of a vast army . . . it looked like a needle. Seen from the south, running away . . . it looked like a needle.

He strained his eyes, staring, the mountains too dark against the sky, the contrast too much to see. A tiny thing, wheeling in the air, near the very top. A flash of light. Moving, moving . . .

No. A trick of the eye, the sky almost purple from looking, the grey mountain, the white snow catching the sunset, making his eyes hurt, him staring until he could no longer see. He rubbed his eyes angrily. There are no gods up there now. I know. Kiana pointed. 'There.' A column of smoke, so faint in the evening, a ghostly thing. Like the peak of the Needle it was half-illusionary, there and not there, his eyes were itching and it was gone. Could be a village, a camp of axe-wielding savages on demon horses, picking their teeth with his soldiers' fingerbones.

Ha. No. They went on over another rise, a fold in the flanks of the Needle's foothills, and there they were. Horsemen and horses and banners, even a few camp women had survived with them. The rose tree standard of Chathe snapping in the wind. A thousand of them. At least. A hundred horses. The noise of it; the smell of it, after days alone in the mountains, the reek of it. Shit and blood and hurting, and mostly blood. Familiar thing. Pulled his horse up short, whipped his head back with a hiss of pain in his shoulder, the noise and stink hitting him. Thought of the first time he'd seen an army hungry for the killing time, his father's men lined up before Malth Salene's walls. *They did not fear to ride out to slaughter* . . . Shock of it, running through him. So familiar he'd forgotten the way it felt.

'Yes!' Kiana cried out beside him. 'Safety. Eltheia be praised.'

Three mounted scouts came up to meet them. Recognized him from a great distance, too great for sight, surely, as though they already knew him. Felt him coming, as a dog feels his master.

Recognized his outline against the darkness, the shadow he cast. Blood stink, hunger stink. Thin pinched faces. Their horses all thin and sick.

Hesitant. Confused. 'My Lord King . . . My Lord King . . .' Marith looked back at them in silence. They were fully armed.

'It is the king,' said Kiana. 'Take us to Lord Mathen.'

The camp was nestled in a river valley at the foot of the mountain, a steep wall of rock rising behind it, a high bare ridge shielding it to the east, the river cradling it in the west and the south. Well-protected against attack from all sides. But easy, Marith thought, to surround and pen in. He looked up into the sky towards the Needle's peak.

They had to cross the river, which was high and cold from snowmelt, biting at the men's chests. Marith's horse stumbled on the further bank, slipping on a loose stone; in the end he had to dismount, splashing heavily into the water, leave it for the men to lead up. Almost fell himself. When they got it up the wretched thing was lame. Kiana got her horse over easily. None of Ryn's men seemed to think of lending him their horse, so he had to go on foot. His boots were soaked. Squelched when he walked. His cloak felt revolting, dripping around him.

There was a rough fence around the camp, barely enough to call a defence against anything, a shallow ditch scratched in the earth, a row of stakes behind, piles of brushwood. Quite a few tents, though. Cookpots, blankets, a line of men's shirts hanging to dry after washing, even a couple of carts. Useful things. Ryn seemed to have gathered up quite a number of useful things, when he fled the battlefield in panic running for his life.

Ryn's soldiers surrounded them. Silent faces, more voices murmuring, 'The king . . . The king . . .' Well-armed. Few obviously wounded. A woman in the ragged finery of a courtesan, silk flowers in her hair. Even a child, clutching his mother's skirts, peering out at Marith. Hands moved in luck gestures and in warding signs. A gasp, a shriek. A man spat for luck.

And there ahead was Ryn's tent, green and red leather, a rose tree banner flying at its height. It was looking a bit battered, pleasingly. Like it had got wet and not properly dried out again. Wrinkled. Old man skin. The rose tree banner was ripped, so that the rose tree looked like it was diseased. Like the trees of the Rose Forest had, when his men got to work on them. Torches thrust into the ground at either side of the doorway, smoking heavily, giving off a strong scent of pine. A guard with a sword, his helmet making his face a shadow, a nice thick warm cloak, a great rent in his armour where something had ripped it apart.

The tent curtain moved aside. Ryn Mathen came out. For a moment Marith thought Thalia would come out behind Ryn. Almost saw her in the way the curtain moved.

Ryn stood. Looked at him.

'Marith,' Ryn said. Not 'My Lord King, My Lord *Ansikanderakesis Amrakane* Amrath Returned to Us, our god'. Not 'my friend, my comrade, my heart leaps with delight to see that you live'.

'Marith. Gods.' Ryn's clothes were soiled and crumpled, battered like the tent. His coat had been mended with a patch of gaudy yellow cloth. But his hair was clean, his beard clean and oiled, he wore a silver chain at his throat, a jewelled brooch at his shoulder, a gold ring. His left hand had a new wound on it, a fat scab running from his thumb to his wrist, disappearing into his coat sleeve. He was otherwise unharmed.

'Marith. Gods.' His hand moved in a warding gesture. There was a long string of stones hanging beside the tent doorway that rattled loudly in a gust of wind. Ryn blinked at the sound in fear. Distant ripple of laughter. The torches flickered and the flames seemed almost like golden hair.

Ryn's hand was on the hilt of his sword, jerking there, pulling against the sword as a horse pulls against a bit. The guard held his sword level, his face was black nothing beneath the helmet, the rent in his armour ran where a man's heart is. Half the plumes on his helmet were torn off. The soldiers came crowding up behind Marith, and they were all as silent as the guard was. Ryn's sword rasped in the scabbard.

'You were dead,' said Ryn. 'Alleen Durith said you were dead.'

Marith's hand also on his sword hilt. 'I'm sure he did.'

Kill him.

Kill him.

Could already taste Ryn's blood in his mouth.

Horse's hooves. Kiana rode up to them. Marith heard her sigh deeply.

'Kiana?' Ryn called out. 'I thought . . . you would be with Alleen Durith.'

Kiana snorted. 'As I have already told you, I am not a traitor, Ryn.' She pushed the horse right up to them, so that Marith had to step back. Looked down at Ryn from the saddle. Her face was a picture of disgust. She looked at Ryn the way Tiothlyn had sometimes looked at Marith.

'I am exhausted,' she said dryly. 'My whole body hurts, I'm half-starved, my clothes are falling apart on me. And, yes, I am vulnerable because my legs are damaged and hurt like murder, and I need help to walk. So you, Ryn Mathen of Chathe, traitor and coward, will give me help.'

Ryn felt her look. Flushed. Marith thought: delightful thing about betraying friends, Ryn. Putting a proper face to it.

Ryn's hand tighter on his sword hilt. Eyes fixed now on Kiana. Armed men all around them. Full night, suddenly, the last of the light gone, and it was impossible to see their faces. Even the torchlight dimmed.

'Don't,' said Kiana. 'Don't, Ryn.' Her hand, too, on her sword hilt.

Her horse stamped its front hooves. An accident, perhaps. Shook its head, mouthed at the bit. Kiana jolted in the saddle.

Ryn shouted. Drew his sword. Kiana drew her sword.

Marith grabbed at her horse's bridle.

'Please, Ryn,' he said.

Chapter Thirty-Six

Ryn's face was unreadable. He sheathed his sword very carefully. His eyes never left Marith's face.

'Help her down,' he ordered his men. 'Lady Sabryya, help her. Bring her into my tent.' He half-knelt to Marith. His head was bowed, showing the skin at the back of his neck. Marith's eyes were itching. Shut them, and when he opened them Ryn was standing upright, the two of them very close face to face.

'My Lord King,' said Ryn. 'Be welcome here.' He drew back the doorcurtain of the tent and Marith walked in. Could feel Ryn's sword behind him as he went. Sat down very carefully with his back well away from the tent walls, facing both the doorcurtain and the curtain through to Ryn's sleeping place.

She could be in there, he thought. Sleeping. Or awake, afraid. Ryn followed him in, sat very carefully facing him. Kiana was helped in, sat facing both of them. Ryn gestured and one of his men went into the sleeping place, brought out a cloak and placed it over her. Alis Nymen followed her; Ryn gave him a look of contempt. Lord Fishmonger.

There was no furniture in the tent; they sat on the floor. It felt unpleasantly damp, smelled of mould. A girl came in, also smelling of damp, served them wine in cups of gold and ivory set with rubies and emeralds and black pearls. The scent of the wine! Gods.

331

Gods. Marith's hand shook, taking the cup. Gasped it down, held it out for more.

'That's almost the last we have,' said Ryn as the girl refilled it. He held out his own cup. 'You can have this one, as well, Marith.'

Ryn's cup was enamelled silver, yellow garlands around a scene of fighting birds. It looked familiar. As did the gold cups.

'Fine things you have here, Ryn,' he said.

'Four cups and a few barrels of wine,' said Ryn. 'Oh yes. Little else, mind, but at least the wine is good, not goat's piss, anyway.' Reaching for it, itching to say it, nervous, desperate. Say it, Ryn, Marith thought. Come on.

'You recovered it from the enemy, I'm sure,' said Kiana. 'All you could salvage.' Desperate. She was terrified Ryn would harm them. No, wait, she's not stupid, she was terrified Ryn would throw them out to sleep in the wilds again under a tree. I'll walk out, Marith thought, before he throws me out, I won't beg again. Only one person I've ever begged for, and one person I've ever begged to. So come on, Ryn, speak. Kiana, and you really should thank her for it, Kiana has just given you a way in to it. Speak. Ryn swallowed, mouth opened, mouth closed, swallowed, come on, Ryn, you coward, you'll have to say it, I'm sitting here with a cup of good wine in my hand after a month of bad water, you have to say it and there'll never be a better time. You really don't want to wait and say it tomorrow, when you've run out of drink; my shoulder hurts worse in the morning, Ryn, you coward.

Ryn swallowed, closed his eyes, opened his eyes. 'I didn't know,' said Ryn. 'I didn't know what Alleen was going to do. We were fighting, it was all going wrong, you know it was, Marith, my men were dying, and when Alleen . . . when Alleen . . .'

'When Alleen betrayed me,' said Marith.

Dry, rasping voice. 'Yes. When Alleen . . . betrayed you . . . I didn't know he was going to . . . to do it . . . but we were losing, you know we were, and I . . .'

'You ran,' said Marith.

'My men were dying. I was . . . I . . .'

'You were afraid,' said Kiana.

'Of course I was afraid,' said Ryn. 'We've never lost before. I thought I was going to die. Weren't you afraid?'

Marith said, 'No.' Of course not. No.

The wine was finished up. Gods. Four whole cups of it, gods, the taste of it, licked at his lips hoping there was a last drop of it there. Something to eat, also, that might have been venison or more woodrat; Kiana seemed to enjoy it, whatever it was. Hot, tasted of meat. Marith yawned hugely. It must be getting late. Ryn seemed nervous again, awkward, glancing at Kiana and then at Marith and then at nothing. Alis trying to make himself small in the corner, sensible man who shouldn't have followed them in here at all except he was sensible also not to leave Marith's side here.

'If you're still planning to kill me, Ryn, I should thank you for giving me a drink first.'

'I'm not . . . I was never . . . Marith . . .'

'Gods, never mind, I know you're not. Does your lack of furniture include a bed?'

Ryn looked so bloody awkward. 'No . . . I mean, yes . . . I mean, there's no bed frame, but there are blankets and things, you should be able to sleep.'

'Good. For blankets and four cups of wine, Ryn, I forgive you everything. I mean that.' The girl drew back the curtain to the sleeping place in the inner room of the tent; Marith's eyes caught her face and he recognized her. Osen's pretty acrobat, who had showered silk flowers over him. Raised his eyebrows at Ryn, who flushed. I'll have to break it to her tomorrow, Marith thought, that Osen's dead. I'm sure she'll mourn him. There was indeed a bed of a kind on the mildewed floor, blankets and coverlets in a pile, splendid as a cloth merchant's shop: one of the coverlets had gold embroidery and looked suspiciously like it had come from his own tent. A chest that must contain Ryn's clothes. Or Marith's gold, thinking about it. A lyre, one of the strings broken. I never knew Ryn played the lyre, Marith thought. He struggled out of his vile clothes. Pricked his finger on the damned brooch. 'Burn them,' he ordered the girl. 'I'll wear some of Ryn's tomorrow, unless you've got a chest of my clothes looted here somewhere. In which case I'll wear my black coat with the silver trim at the neck. I always liked that one.'

In the main chamber of the tent, the last thing he heard, Ryn was talking to Kiana, discussing finding her a healer and then somewhere to sleep.

A noise woke him the next morning. A murmuring, it sounded like starlings, no, like water, like a river, no, like rain, yes, that was it, like rain falling on the sea, rain drumming on water – he must be in Malth Elelane, his bedchamber there with the scarlet hangings, that faced east into the rising sun into the sea. *It's raining, Ti, curse it, that means we can't go out riding; it's raining, Carin, curse it, that means we can't go sea-swimming – no, we can, I'm sure, in the rain, it will be fun.*

Sat up, kicked off what was very obviously one of his own coverlets, he remembered the gold embroidery very clearly, that flower pattern, there was a tiny flaw in it, just . . . here, yes, where the thread had snagged. There was mildew on the coverlet, the whole wretched tent smelled mouldy, sweaty. His cloak and his sword were hanging on a hook on the tent wall. He burst out laughing, because on the floor next to them the girl had laid out a shirt and leggings, boots, and his black coat with the silver trim.

There was also a basin of water for washing, a towel, the enamelled silver cup, a jug of wine. The wine wasn't half as good as that he'd drunk last night. Nothing could be as good as the wine he'd drunk last night. He washed himself roughly, splashed his hair wet and rubbed it dry. The water in the bowl was black just from that. Dressed – gods, the feel of clean clothes! As good as the wine. The feel of clean skin and clean hair! Stepped out into the main chamber of the tent. Almost fell over Brychan lying on the floor in the doorway asleep. A drawn sword next to him. That could have been unfortunate, if the poor man had rolled over the wrong way. Marith coughed politely. Brychan sat up with a start, clutching a knife as well as the sword. 'My Lord King!'

'I'm still alive, it's fine. Look, they've even found me my favourite coat.' Brychan fastened his cloak for him, adjusted his sword belt. Wanted to feel he'd been helpful. Marith finished the last of the wine, pulled open the doorcurtain, stepped out into Ryn's camp. Two soldiers stood guard outside. A cookfire was burning, a woman was bending over it stirring a pot. She broke off when she saw Marith, dropped the spoon, cried out.

'The king . . .'

The murmuring noise broke over him.

'. . . *The king . . . the king . . .*'

Men came running. Knelt at Marith's feet, their faces pressed in the earth. More of them. More. Soldiers, camp followers, the woman with her child, the courtesan in her silk rags. There was a tree near the tent, thick with new green-golden leaves, a few last flowers, white petals fading to brown. The soldiers began to break off branches, pull down the flowers, wave them, scatter them.

'The king . . . the king . . . the king . . .' Like a lover's voice: 'My beloved!' A man's voice, almost forgotten: 'My son! My son!'

There is no way out. No, indeed. Always the hardest part, getting out, Tobias had once said. There is no way out and there never was.

A pipe struck up, men dancing, garlanded in branches, clapping and stamping out the beat. Clash of swords. Men embracing. The cook woman darted through the crowds kissing every soldier she could reach. They crowned Marith with flowers. Crowned him with leaves. Embraced him, as a child clutches its mother after a day's absence, when it has been sad and alone and its mother sweeps it up into her strong arms. Crowded around them, cheering until they were hoarse. Bronze rang out in triumph. Armour crashing. Swords crashing on swords. Hearts beating out the war dance. The world was radiant. Warmth like midsummer. Golden sweet-scented sweet soft warm wind. The tree seemed to burst out in new blossom. All the birds of the air burst out in song. *Saleiot*:

to shine. To sparkle. To dance like the sunlight on fast-flowing water. To live. Light, flowers, glory. There was Osen's pretty acrobat, crowned in leaves, dancing; Marith caught her hands, swung her around to the rhythm of heartbeats, shouted in her ear, 'Thank you for the coat!' She giggled. Kissed him with soft lips. He thought about kissing her back. The woman with the baby squeezed her way through to him, held her child up: 'Bless my child, My Lord King. A blessing for him, please, My Lord King.' Marith found himself holding it. A pain, inside. A scream. The smell of it, the feel of it, the noise it made, its grave strange face. The mother's face terrified suddenly, reaching out to grab it back, he thought: she's afraid. Held the child up, kissed it. It began to scream, which made him laugh. '*Nane Elenaneikth*,' he said to the mother. *Joy to him.* 'May he grow up to be a strong and glorious soldier in my army.' The baby cried and lashed out little red fists.

'See, he's a warrior already, My Lord King.'

He kissed the mother. 'He is! Brychan: give this woman your sword, for her son when he grows up!'

The mother kissed Brychan, too, as did the woman who'd been kissing everyone. The pretty acrobat grabbed Marith's hands and began to dance with him; someone pushed a cup of drink towards him. Everyone was dancing, singing, clapping, pounding their swords on their shields. The sky was full of birds, singing.

'*Why we march and why we die,*
And what life means . . . it's all a lie.
Death! Death! Death!
The king! The king!'

Ryn Mathen appeared, pushing his way through the crowds, trying to reach Marith. The cook woman kissed him. Soldiers dropped a garland of leaves askew on his head. He swam through his men to Marith. Stood face to face. Marith was taller, Ryn broader in the shoulders. Marith clapped his hand on Ryn's arm. Ryn bowed his head. Knelt. Held out his sword hilt. Marith raised him up. Kissed him. The men near enough to see cheered. Embraced

Marith, embraced Ryn, Marith kissed them, clasped their hands. The dancing grew wilder. Faster. Trumpets and pipes, drum beats. Marith threw back his head as he danced and there, brilliant in the sky over the very peak of the mountain the Needle, hung the Fire Star. The King's Star. His star.

A flicker of light, on the mountain.

'The king!'

Chapter Thirty-Seven

Orhan Emmereth, the closest confidant of Lord Vorley the Emperor's Nithque. Said to be the most powerful and most dangerous man in Sorlost
Sorlost

'The demon has taken Elarne!'

Orhan said, 'What?'

Darath was sweating. Had been running. 'A man . . . in the Court of the Fountain . . . a man from Elarne . . . he said . . . Orhan, God's knives, Marith Altrersyr . . . He has taken Elarne. Sacked it. Destroyed it. Destroyed it.'

'Marith Altrersyr is dead,' said Orhan. The letter confirming it is on the High Altar of the Great Temple. Across the city, new rumours: a friend had a sister who knows someone who met a soldier in the Army of Amrath, staggering out of the Mountains of Pain to confess the atrocities he had committed for the demon's pleasure, beg forgiveness before he killed himself out of shame. *'Kill me. Kill me. I cannot live, thinking of what I have done.'* Stories of men in the desert who had put out their own eyes, cut off their own hands, to stop themselves doing again what they had done at the demon's command. *'I enjoyed it. That's the worst thing. I did as he told us. Gods, Eltheia have mercy, I'd do it again.'*

'Sit down, Darath, calm down.'

'Secretary Gallus said . . . the man has been arrested . . . they're questioning him, I should be there questioning him. But his story . . . half the city must have heard it by now. Orhan. Orhan.'

Darath was crying.

'A host calling itself the Army of Amrath came out of the Mountains of Pain like a storm wind. They flew red banners. They flew banners of bloody human skin. At their head was a man on a white horse, crowned in silver, so beautiful it hurt the eyes to look upon him. His skin was pale as moonlight. His hair was red-black silk shining curls. On his back he wore a cloak of bloody tatters. His shadow came before him, and his shadow was as blood. He shouted a great shout and the walls of Elarne fell in rubble. Single-handed, he put every man, woman and child in Elarne to the sword. Rainbows danced on the ground around him as he killed them. He killed them a hundred with each sword stroke.

'That's what he said. That's what I heard him say.'

But. But . . .

Orhan said, very slowly, clinging to the words, 'Marith Altrersyr is dead, Darath. His army is destroyed.'

Darath said, 'Like the High Priestess Thalia was dead? Dead like that?'

'Alleen Durith—'

'He has destroyed Elarne, Orhan. He has killed every man, woman and child within its walls.'

'But—'

Darath screamed, 'The city of Elarne is destroyed. The city of Elarne, the seat of the Kings of Chathe, the city that is our nearest neighbour, the city with nothing between us and it but dust, the city of Elarne is taken and sacked and everyone who lived there is dead. Go out into the city, Orhan,' said Darath. 'There are no crows and no flies left in Sorlost the Golden. They have flown west to Elarne, to glut themselves.'

* * *

It's not true. It can't be. It isn't. I went to Elarne once. A fine city. The demon is dead.

Orhan and Darath, huddled in each other's arms, pleading with the world. Great Tanis, please, please, make it not be true.

'We could take poison,' said Darath. 'Die here together, your cock in my arse.'

Even under torture, the poor wretch refused to change his story. Orhan watched him, begging, praying, until the man was too damaged to speak.

Thus in one of the great state rooms of the Summer Palace the Emperor's Nithque Lord Vorley summoned Lord Cauvanh the Immish Great Council's Representative in Sorlost. Cauvanh had a sick look to him as he entered, his pale hands drumming at his sides.

He knows, Orhan thought. He has proof. He knew before this.

'The troops we paid to leave,' said Darath. 'How much do we need to pay for them to come back?'

They couldn't be more than a few weeks' march away. Six thousand men in black iron armour. A mage in a silver robe. A general in the Immish army who had once hanged the Telean nobility from their own city walls. That should keep the ravening hordes back for an hour or so, at least.

'No preamble?' said Lord Cauvanh. 'No glossy flatulence first? How much do you have, Lord Vorley? Remembering that if you don't offer it to me now, Marith Altrersyr-returned-from-the-dead will very soon take it.' He tried to smile. Failed. 'My men are marching back to Alborn, I have just sent a messenger ordering them to march twice as fast. Every Immishman in Sorlost will be gone by tomorrow at first light. I will certainly be gone at first light.' He had the decency to look ashamed. 'A hundred wagons of corn and iron weapons is even now setting out from Alborn to greet his army. My only regret, My Lords, is that I cannot tear down the walls of your city in preparation for his army's advance.'

Darath said, shocked, 'What? What?'

'We are his allies,' said Cauvanh.

Quiet, embarrassed pause.

Cauvanh said, 'Lord Vorley, Lord Emmereth. You have failed to kill the demon Marith Altrersyr, despite paying one of his most trusted lieutenants a quite astonishing amount of money to ensure his death. You have conspired to overthrow the Immish rule here in the Sekemleth Empire, when the Immish Great Council would have given your city to Marith Altrersyr the *Ansikanderakesis Amrakane* the man you just failed to kill as a loving gift.'

Quiet, embarrassed pause.

Cauvanh said, 'If we in Immish once harboured any other ideas about our alliance with him . . . I'm not sure what else you think I should do now, if you were in my place?'

'He'll come for you too,' Darath cried out. Orhan thought: oh Darath, I love you for your innocence just as much as I love you for being the most jaded old roué in Sorlost. 'Chathe was his ally. He'll wallow in our blood up to his eyeballs and then he'll come for you. Of course he will. You heard what they say Marith Altrersyr did to Elarne. He'll do that to us. He'll do that to you. He was defeated in the mountains, he must be weakened, everyone thought he was dead for Great Tanis's sake!' Pleading. Almost running around the room. Trying to get out. 'If we stand against him now, while he's still recovering, if you help us now, we can raise an army together, fight him in the desert, his army can't be used to the desert as we are, they'll run out of water, they'll struggle in the heat, if you help us, if we—'

Orhan put his hand on his lover's arm. 'Darath.'

You sound like my father when he was dying, Darath, Orhan thought. *I can't die I can't die I can't die not me not me do something do something there must be something all this power this money there must be something I can't die not me not me.*

'Chathe was the demon's ally,' said Cauvanh. 'Yes. Chathe's King Rothlen went to Ethalden in state, brought tribute of gold and jewels. Knelt at Marith Altrersyr's feet and kissed the soles of his boots. He went so hastily that the walls of Ethalden were still being raised when he arrived. Before even the Immish Great Council reached Ethalden, which says something indeed. The blood of the people of Illyr was still wet on the demon's hands. Rothlen kissed it off. Swore fealty, offered troops, grain, tribute. All he asked in exchange was that the demon leave Chathe in peace. Which the demon agreed.

'Rothlen died soon after arriving home. As soon as he was crowned in his father's place, King Heldan also set out to offer homage. Knelt at Marith Altrersyr's feet and kissed the soles of his boots. The blood of the people of Cen Elora was still wet on the demon's hands. Heldan kissed it off. Swore fealty, offered troops, grain, tribute. Sent Ryn Mathen the king's cousin to serve under him, at the head of five thousand Chathean troops.

'We Immish at least only offered fealty once. And we have never fought for him.'

Cauvanh placed a letter on the table. 'This is from my agent in Elarne. She was there to see it, is now a part of his army, indeed. Marith Altrersyr came out of the mountains at the head of his Chathean troops. Ryn Mathen rode beside him, his eyes shining with love. He turned the Chathean troops on their own people. Burned the land, destroyed whole villages, killed every person who would not join him. King Heldan sent an army to hold him a little while, buy the people of Elarne time to run. They must have known that it was hopeless. Dead men knowing they went to die to buy their children an hour or two more of life.

'A sensible decision. Who wouldn't die, to buy their children an hour or two more of life?

'Nor did the men of Elarne. They fled at his advance. The demon sent his shadowbeasts after them. Turned the Chathean troops with him on their own city. Elarne is razed to ashes. King Heldan and every man and woman and child in Elarne is dead.'

He put the letter down on the table. Carefully folded it up.

'Chathe is a plague-ridden wasteland. She writes that the Army of Amrath is already eager to march on. They are full of new-found energy, she writes. Like children. They are shouting for glory and plunder and revenge on the world that briefly dared to thwart them. She writes that they are now preparing to march on Sorlost.'

Darath said, 'So help us. You have twenty thousand men under arms. Strike now, while he's still weak. Where will he go, after he has destroyed the Empire? He will destroy Immish, he will kill you. You fools.'

'Of course he will,' said Cauvanh. 'The White City of Alborn is filled with treasure and beauty and wine and women, his troops will I am sure greatly enjoy themselves there. Immish has deep clear rivers that he can poison, wheat fields longing for him to burn them, sweet green woods crying out to be uprooted. Towns and towns of people, thousands and thousands of people to kill.

'But the men of the Immish Great Council will be sailing across the Bitter Sea by then, a hundred miles out to sea, our ships laden down with gold. Heading for Ae-Beyond-the-Waters. If it even exists as a real place. Or perhaps we will all be drowned.'

Cauvanh stood and bowed to Darath and Orhan. 'Thank you for everything you have done for me, Lord Emmereth, Lord Vorley. Thank you. And . . . I am sorry. Truly. A part of me . . . a part of me thinks that we should stand with you and fight.'

Cauvanh walked out.

The city was filled with screaming. *It can't . . . It can't . . . Do something . . . Do something . . .* People fighting to get into the Great Temple to make offerings. People fighting to kneel in prayer beneath the statue of the demon in the Court of the Broken Knife. The godstones, the heathen shrines and holy places were soaked in blood and milk and wine poured in offering. One man had crawled into the city crying and the whole city was pissing itself. Oh Sorlost. Oh my city. Beauty and wonder and old sorrows, the dream memory of golden childhood, the desire for a lost beloved never truly known. To see the end come like this. Bil went to the Temple, used all the wealth in their house to push her way through the crowds, throw herself weeping before the low altar where she had once made offerings in thanks for Dion's life. Celyse came and sat with Dion, sat and stared at him. She was back at her own house, reunited with her own son and with her husband at the Nithque's written order. But she sat and stared at Dion, her hands clasped.

It is impossible to imagine. Conquering the world. Conquering a city . . . that is hardly a notion we are unfamiliar with. But the question comes suddenly to a thousand lips, that had not occurred before when it was a far-off unreal thing. Why? Why does he do this? Why do they do it? An army marched from Illyr in the north a thousand thousand miles, suffered injury and sickness and weariness and defeat, each man in that army risked death a thousand times, saw friends and comrades wounded, dying, screaming, went on themselves wounded, hurting, so that they could . . . do that.

'Why?' Bil whispered, dry-lipped, when she returned, her eyes filled with the stories. 'Why did they come all this way, to do this?'

'They are poor,' said Orhan. 'They are angry . . .'

Darath could only shrug and say, 'Because, Bilale. I am going out to buy a new toy for Dion.'

Just before dusk the gates of the Summer Palace opened, and the last of the Immish soldiers marched out, Lord Cauvanh at their head. They looked as shocked as the people of the city did. They must know, also, what had happened. Perhaps some of them felt guilt. Orhan watched from a high window of the palace. Cauvanh raised his head, looked back, raised his arm in a wave. He can't see me, Orhan thought, he might guess I'm watching but he can't see me, obviously he can't.

Voices drifted up on the wind:

'No.'

'No.'

'Please.'

A crowd had gathered – people knew, how did they always know? The street whores, the sweetmeat sellers, the beggar children

344

with their hatha sores, they knew what was happening, what it meant. People gathered at the palace, in the streets, at the Maskers' Gate. Odd silence. Then moans, wails, a woman's sobs. Then a rush, a howl like a dog, people rushing forward, wrestling with the Immish soldiers, begging them to stay, begging to go with them.

The Immish soldiers pushing their way forward. Cauvanh at their head, trying to keep looking ahead of him, like this was all perfectly normal. Like he wasn't a man to feel shame and grief.

Some soldiers. Taking a walk.

'No. No. No. No. No.'

Behold. We are liberated!

The crush was growing. A woman screamed. The Immish soldiers pushed forward, people pushed against them, not quite a riot, almost a wrestling match between the Immish and the city people, a flow of water grinding against a wall until the wall breaks. This must be what a battle looks like, thought Orhan. A real battle. Absurdly, he thought of Bil in childbirth, Janush shouting, 'Push, push, Bilale, push,' Bil's body straining almost tearing itself apart. A woman went down under the soldiers' feet. A soldier shouted something in Immish, tried to grab at her, someone mistook his action, a punch was thrown, a sword blade flashed.

Orhan screamed uselessly over the turmoil, 'Cauvanh! Get them out! Get them out!'

The gates would be shutting soon. If the Immish soldiers were shut in overnight, they and many others would be dead before morning.

The soldier's blade was red. More people were screaming. Cauvanh was looking around him, had stopped moving his men forward. Great Tanis, his face. He was enjoying this. There was a look of something like hunger on him. He had had the same look pouring over his maps after killing Lord Mylt, planning where to march his men off to next. '*Cen Elora . . . Cen Andae . . . Immier . . . Chathe, even, if we can raise the men . . .*' He does not crave power, thought Orhan. All of this, he did it all only because he craves chaos and blood. Enjoys playing these games. We are well rid of him.

No, we aren't. Don't be an idiot, Orhan.

'Gallus.' The Chief Secretary was watching Orhan, trying to pretend he wasn't. 'Gallus. The palace guard – get them out. Get them to clear the square, clear the Immish route out. Now.' Should have thought of it before, Orhan thought. Gallus hesitated. Already blood on the street, a riot starting. 'Get anyone you can find, out there between the Immish soldiers and the crowd,' Orhan shouted.

Thus we come to it again already, the soldiers of the Sekemleth Empire killing their own people to save them from themselves. The people are righteously angry, are suffering; they are stupid children and the wise must use force to control them. Kill a few of them for their own greater good.

One day, Orhan thought. One day of power, without this. Was that too much to ask? Must everything be born and made in blood? The Empire's soldiers marched into the square, cutting their way through to the Immish. Orhan watched from his high window, tiny figures shifting, the crowd moving like cloud shadows, from here it looked like a dance, like Dion's toys, like watching ants around a spilled drink. Could not see or hear anything. The Immish soldiers marched on through the violence to the Maskers' Gate.

More riots when the gates closed behind the Immish soldiers at sunset. In total perhaps a hundred dead. The bodies were piled up by the gate waiting to be buried, under guard. Three bodies and three of the wounded turned up in the Court of the Broken Knife, piled beneath the statue's feet in offering. Fires were lit there, people danced around them singing, dropped flowers and coins into the flames. Soldiers were sent to retrieve the bodies. They stopped at the edge of the square. Refused to go further. 'The knife,' one of them said when questioned, 'the knife had a blade to it, if I had gone into the square to take His tribute, He would have struck me down with His knife.' Orhan thought of going to the Court of the Broken Knife to make an offering himself.

'I saw your face, I looked into your eyes, once. Why do you do this?' He and Darath trying to settle who should tell the child Emperor he was going to die again shortly. *'You've died so many times, you must be used to it. Does that console you? It can't be worse than when you died of plague.'* He's five years old.

This city is unconquerable, and will be till the end of the world. Bronze walls encircle us, five times the height of a man, they have no seams or joins, a perfect ribbon of metal twisting around the city, punctuated only by the five great gates. They have never been breached: even Amrath himself dashed his armies to pieces against them to no avail and gave up in despair.

(Also, we paid him his army's weight in gold to go away, we have no idea how things would have gone if he'd been bothered to exert himself, he'd have broken through our walls in a week, I suspect, but let's not talk about that, let's not think about that.)

It's like a challenge. Like a street whore touting himself to a client. Even if we hadn't done the things Cauvanh listed to me.

'We could negotiate,' said Selim Lochaiel. 'Surrender. Beg him to spare us.'

'I suppose we could. It might briefly amuse him.'

'Pay him. Beg him. Open the gates, welcome him.'

Darath said, 'Give him our wives and daughters to play with, offer to massacre every tenth person in the city in front of him, send him my head and your head and Orhan's head on gold plates?'

Orhan thought: my life for a hundred lives. For twenty. For ten. For one. But it's pointless. Isn't it?

Isn't it?

Hang on to that. Go home and kiss my son, and say it wouldn't make any difference if I offered to die for him.

The whole city, he thought. The whole damned city, the whole world, I'd sacrifice, for Darath and Dion. My life for Dion's life, if my dying in agony bought him another few moments. But it won't. So I won't consider it, and I won't feel guilt for not considering it.

'Darath's right. We lock the gates, arm everyone who can hold a weapon, stockpile food, wait,' said Orhan. 'Like everyone else has done. Hope. Pray.'

'Things might go differently for us than for everyone else,' said Darath. 'You never know. He might take one look at our walls and give up. I mean . . . he won't. But he might. Let's just try to hold on to that, shall we? You never know until it happens. And then if you're lucky you die before you really have to get your head around it.' He wept and he wept.

Chapter Thirty-Eight

Marith Altrersyr who may or may not still be the Lord of the World the King of All Irlast
The desert west somewhere of Sorlost

The bag containing Osen Fiolt's head banged against the saddle. Ryn Mathen, riding next to him, was humming. The Army of Amrath sang as they marched. The desert sand was almost pleasant after the hard mountain stones; they had a fine train of provisions, ate bread and meat and drank wine every night. The wind blew from the east, dry and dusty, but bringing with it the distant scent of the Sekemleth Empire, spices and incense and gold gold gold gold gold and revenge. Marith chewed a handful of keleth seeds, wiped sweat from his forehead. Turned to Ryn.

'Want a race?'

Ryn grinned back at him. 'Yes.'

They kicked their horses, galloped out across the sand. Soldiers having to leap out of the way. Yells and cheers. Marith caught a man shouting, 'Five in gold on the king.'

The new horse was a marvel. Beautiful, naturally: pure white; clever limpid blue eyes; a perfect arch to its neck; it had been brought to him decked out in red and silver, red plumes, red saddle, silver cheek pieces studied with rubies, silver-gilded hooves, it quite obviously enjoyed its finery, knew how splendid it was, pranced for him to display itself. Strong. Clever – it had been trained for war, it had carried him and understood him. And so gloriously absurdly breathtakingly fast. Shouldn't be riding it outside of the fighting, should be resting it. But it was so fast and it loved to march and show itself off as the king's horse and it loved to play and race.

He kicked his heels in again and it was almost flying. The glorious sound of its hooves pounding into the sand, his breath and its breath, the men cheered their heads off behind them. Gods only knew where they were racing to, until the horses gave out under them or beyond that. Marith pulled around to the right, Osen's head banging against the saddle, rushing past the ranks of the army as they marched. Ryn followed him, whooping; the men cheered and cheered. Marith pulled the horse up, sweating and blowing, stroked its neck. 'Good horse.' Ryn pulled up next to him, gasping like the horses. 'One day, Marith, one day I'll beat you.'

'You should have kept the horse yourself,' Marith said, 'you'll never outrace him.'

'Oh no. He was born and bred only for a king.' The horse snorted. Ryn said, 'And he knows it. He was bred for you.'

Gods knew if he was a king still. The men around him called him 'My Lord King', knelt to him, Ryn and Kiana Sabryya did him deference, Alis Nymen arranged the cook woman and the woman with the baby as his household servants, and beyond that, only the gods knew. He wore his crown. His army had destroyed a city. He had sat on the throne of Chathe, apparently, and Ryn had held up King Heldan's severed head to him and acclaimed him king. And I thought it would be a good thing, Marith thought, if my army was destroyed. That it could be ended.

The nights out in the mountains, free, the darkness pressed on him, soft and heavy, it was all the same whether he looked out into the dark of the world or in into the dark of his own mind. All that he was running wild in his thoughts, crushing him; his mind crawled, like there were things crawling inside his skull eating at him. His body shaking, things pulling at his body, inside him. No peace. Never any peace. Filth tearing up inside, making him shake and weep. The desert, here, now, yellow dust, yellow sky, yellow light. I failed: I am a king still. Thank the gods.

There were other things, once, he thought then. I remember . . . I used . . . I . . . Other things. But I can't remember . . . I thought, if the army was destroyed, if everything stopped, if there was an ending, I hoped, I thought . . .

I was wrong.

He made the horse rear up with a shout. A king's horse. Drew his sword and saw the light flash on it. The army cheered.

A girl's voice called out to them. They'd ridden right back to some of the baggage wagons: there was Ryn's pretty acrobat, riding on a pretty ribbon-decked cart. She cheered and waved. Blew kisses. They rode up to her, dismounted, Ryn shouted for someone to take the horses. They both scrambled up onto the cart while it was still moving, just to show off further. She laughed and kissed them both. She could do this amazing thing balancing on her hands on the back of a moving horse. Naked. Not that it should be any more impressive than doing it fully clothed, but.

Ryn was a simpler man than Osen. Marith had the feeling she was happier with him.

'Shall we have a party tonight?' she said to Marith.

'We could.' Scouts reported an oasis up ahead, they should reach it well before sunset. A local guide reported it also, but local guides were not to be trusted. A muddy well, a ruined cara-vanserai, a chance to stop and replenish their water supplies, so why not have a party? We're running over with wine and hatha and all the good things. Elarne had been poorer and uglier than Marith had imagined. The magelord Nevet burned the place to ashes with a single word: it wasn't worth more than a single word. Six months ago, the Army of Amrath would almost have turned their noses up at sacking the place. The one thing it did

351

have in great quantities was hatha. He'd had a very good few days, after Elarne fell, Ryn assured him.

The acrobat prodded her new servant girl. 'A party. See to it.' The girl nodded. Got down from the cart to run back through the columns, talk to people, start getting things prepared. She limped as she went. She'd be almost as pretty as the acrobat, when her bruises healed, poor thing.

A lot of new servants in the trail of camp followers. Tired, grey-looking women. Men carrying soldiers' baggage like pack mules.

The people of Chathe had no love of magecraft. Feared and hated magery, since the day a thousand years ago and more when the first Amrath came down upon them, ordered the magelord Nevet to burn the city to ashes. The men of Elarne fought before the gates of their city, throwing rocks and spears. Nevet spoke a single word and the city burned and every living thing within it burned up into dust. That was a thousand years ago. But not a thing one can easily forget. So the people of Elarne banished magecraft. Punished mages with death. Stupid, really. Given the only thing that can hold off magecraft is another mage. But one could perhaps sympathize with their desire to make a point. They must have learnt something, anyway, from the whole experience: they did not accept Amrath as a god, the heathens, but when they raised up a new city on the congealing remains of the old one they built temples to the god Fire, and to the god Pestilence, and to the god Grief. The people of Sorlost gave thanks each night that the sun had set without them dying. The people of Elarne gave thanks each night that the sun had set without them dying of fire or plague or heartbreak. And when Marith Altrersyr was crowned king in Ethalden, they did him homage. Gave him troops and money. Burned the Rose Forest at his command. Knelt to swear fealty to him.

They had crowded into their temples when he came for them. He had cut them down like the corn in a good harvest, sweet plump golden corn in the sweet fresh breeze of summer warmth, and the farmer comes with his scythe to cut it down. Blue fire on his sword glowing. It lit up their skin blue as they died. They had crowded into the temples. He led his men to the temples. Fire and Pestilence and Grief. Fire is wonderful. Divine, glorious; Thalia had asked him if the people of the White Isles worshipped fire, once. Pestilence is a terrible thing, carries off whole villages, kills in long-drawn-out ways that a sword can rarely match. Grief is grief, and worse than fire and worse than pestilence, grief is a knife in a man's mind, ruining him. But fire and pestilence and grief are not gods. He led his men into the temples. They killed and killed there until there was no one left. They took the city apart stone by stone with their bare hands, ripped the buildings into rubble, ground the rubble into dust. They had been nervous and reluctant at first, on edge, uncertain. Their homeland, their families, their friends. Ryn had reassured them. Then they had done it eagerly.

And then a few days' rest, and a few days' gathering themselves, and they went on. Defeat had shown them the truth of themselves. We have not come to conquer a kingdom. We have come only to kill. They marched into the sunrise, while behind them the air was so thick with flies they blocked out the sun.

The party was a good one, given the circumstances. The oasis was indeed a muddy well with a ruined caravanserai looming beside it, an immense thing still painted with fading birds and flowers, the central courtyard tiled in blue to look like a pool of water, some of the rooms around it even had the remains of roofs. Alis Nymen got Marith's things set up in the best of them. The well was reached using a wheel and a pulley, the well shaft so deep that the water couldn't be seen; when the buckets came up the water was brown with sand, but ice cold even in the desert heat. Once the goat shit had been cleaned out of the caravanserai court-yard, it was a fine place for a party. Marith's beautiful white horse was brought in and the acrobat did her handstand trick on it.

They were all a bit drunk by then and Marith had a vague worry the horse wouldn't understand what was happening, but it came off well. Kiana's leg seemed a little better, her pain a little less obvious; and like the acrobat she was more relaxed without Osen moping over her trying to look down her dress. Even the ache in his own shoulder was somehow more bearable since Elarne fell. After the girl had finished her act Marith stumbled over to the doorway to look at his army feasting, the flicker of their campfires, laughter and song. It was strange thinking that only a short while past they had been fleeing in terror away from him, broken and afraid that they would lose, cursing him.

'*I should bloody kill you, Ryn.*'

'*I know you should. Give me a chance to make it up to you. Please.*'

'They look fine, don't they?' Ryn came up to lean beside him, looking out at the army also. Singing and dancing; men in full armour fighting mock-duels; men naked and wrestling with each other, showing off the strength of their arms and legs. Some simply sitting quiet in the dark, looking out into the east, dreaming of what was to come. 'Elarne was good for them,' Ryn said. 'Gave them their confidence back.'

'Yes.'

'Gods, it was splendid, wasn't it? I haven't felt that good for years. That first charge, riding down on them, and they just ran, gods, the look on them, when they ran! And then going through the gates, when the gates gave way, going in, and the noise they made, when they saw us, and the feeling inside me, when I saw the first of them go down to me . . .'

'Yes.'

'Yes. Anyway.' Ryn frowned. 'Yes.' Tried to brighten: 'I've sent for some more of that rosehip spirit you were so keen on. Drinking game, Marith: can you down a drink for every city you've sacked?'

'I could the last time we played it.' It was boring then. 'I don't recall having sacked that many cities since.'

Ryn would be loyal forever, now. Could see it in Ryn's eyes.

'Let me take Elarne for you, Marith. Let me march the army on Elarne, show you my loyalty. I'll kill everyone in Elarne for you, Marith. I swear. I'm so sorry. Gods, Marith, I'm sorry. I don't know why I abandoned you.' I'm at your mercy, Ryn. I have a handful of men and Kiana Sabryya with her wounded leg. You have an army. But you're down on your knees, grovelling to me.

'And Callisa wants to show you another trick she's been working on. Just for you. She's very proud of it.'

Callisa? Oh, yes, that must be the acrobat.

Ryn leered. 'Her servant girl takes part in it, too. Two of them.'

'Two of them.' Two women. Imagine that.

Down in the camp someone was playing a flute. A faint little tune, the same few notes repeating, like a young boy might play. Someone down in the camp was sober and clearheaded and feeling melancholy. Looking up at the stars and the endless dark of the sky, feeling the desert pressing around them, empty, vast, grieving over it, turning it into music.

I should find them and bloody kill them, Marith thought. Get a few more drinks down me and I probably will. He went back to join the party. Callisa and other girl did their new trick. They played the drinking game. Marith won. Twice.

The flute player's brother complained loudly the next morning about how upset he was. Alis Nymen gave him a bag of gold and exempted him from latrine duties. The flute player's brother went off with a spring in his step, whistling.

There were other things, once. I remember. I thought of . . . of other things. I used . . . when I was a child . . . when . . . And with Thalia, sometimes, I thought . . . when I looked at her . . . I hoped . . .

Beyond this, fuck it.

More and more soldiers drifted in to join them as they marched. A handful of desert people, a trickle of them every day, looking for anything more than sand and goats and sand again. Familiar, isn't that, somehow? Sure he'd heard it before. They were scrawny and ignorant of soldiering, but tough as anything, could march for days on bad water and worse food, bloody good with a knife. Survivors from the Army of Amrath, creeping out from hiding; they had thrown away their weapons along with their pride, came meek and fearful of the welcome Marith might offer them, half-expecting, all of them, that he would have them killed as traitors, frightened now of their own weakness. 'You were dead . . . We thought you were dead . . .' Hollow little voices. Astonished at themselves, ashamed of themselves. The army embraced them delightedly, welcomed them back as old comrades. 'How could the king be dead? How could we lose? Look at him! Look at us!' Every night came the sounds of song and laughter, another man found, welcomed home. Newcomers, men from all over Irlast who had heard tell of the miracle, came running to offer themselves. Immishmen; men from Medana and Maun, eager to tell of the riches of their own homes, how easy the conquest would be; thin, bitter-eyed survivors from Calchas, Tarboran, Eralad, tired of starving in the ruins, forced at last to embrace their rightful king. A well-equipped cavalry troop from the White Isles, even, that had been half a year on the road and had never heard the story that King Marith was dead; they were welcomed with wild rejoicing, stared in wonder as they heard the tale, roared and screamed at the absurdity. And, one glorious morning, fifty men from Alleen Durith's forces, weeping with shame, kneeling to kiss the lowliest camp servant's hands, they had killed their commanding officer, turned and run back across the desert going day and night, when they heard the rumour that Marith was still alive. The Army of Amrath, reborn in glory. We have merely been tested in the fire, we have been remade stronger, more determined than before. We know the taste of defeat, now, we know what it is the vanquished must endure. We will enjoy it more than before, now, when we inflict it, for we know what it is our victims feel. The *Ansikanderakesis Amrakane*'s sword is made of iron, it was forged and cooled and heated again and again, it was tempered in blood. Bronze is brittle, blunts, shatters: iron is made stronger each time it is plunged into the fire and the blood. We are men with hearts of iron. We doubted once. We shall never doubt again.

It rained, the day after Alleen's men had come, and that felt like a gift to welcome them. Gods, gods, he remembered the desert in the rain. The smell of the water. The life there, so suddenly. Men dancing in the rain. Marith lay in the acrobat girl's cart listening to the raindrops beating on the canvas covering it, drumming hard and fast, dripping in through a hole somewhere in the canvas and that sound, too, was musical. Distant shouting and talking. The motion of the cart changed, the horses splashing through the water, the sound of their hooves changed. The cart must be going slower. The men were laughing in the rain. The light in the cart was different. Clouds blocking the golden sun. The dim light was moving, he could feel it spreading around him. There was a damp mark on the canvas, where the water was coming in: it looked a little like a tree, he could see the shape in it like looking at a cloud. It rippled, there were colours in it, flashing and fading to the rhythm of the drips coming in. It was green, a forest spreading, he stared at it and saw tall heavy trees, their leaves rustled, a bird flapped pale pink wings in time to the rhythm of the water, now the bird was in a golden cage, and the bars of the cage were moving and trembling, the bird flapped its wings, the bird was in the forest again and the forest was changing into a wild dark sea, he was moving up and down with the waves, floating. He was falling through the night sky, tumbling over and over, and the waves were silver stars. He was looking up at the ceiling of a huge building, and the ceiling was painted with flowers and trees.

The hatha in the vial tasted of rainwater. The flowers faded and he could no longer see anything. He had a hangover worse than he'd had for ages the next day, and Ryn looked at him blankly when he asked about the rain.

'This is a bloody desert, Marith, My Lord King.'

357

They were getting very near now, Ryn and Kiana told him. They needed to make proper plans now. The journey seemed to have gone much more quickly than he'd realized. 'You said it would take a month, at least,' he said to Ryn, and Ryn looked at him in astonishment again.

'Marith—'

'Ryn?'

'Nothing. Never mind.' Ryn shrugged. 'Plans.'

'Plans. Yes.'

That afternoon it really did rain, and the men really did enjoy it, laughing and whooping for joy, and there were insects, suddenly, and pink flowers, and the smell of the rainwater, and the light was changed. And it was beautiful. He set out his plans: sack it and burn it and kill everyone. That done, he sat in the cart with the cover open to the rain. But today the hatha didn't taste of rainwater.

Chapter Thirty-Nine

'The scouts say there's a town about an hour up ahead.'

Marith sat up groggily, rubbed at his eyes. He seemed to be in a baggage cart. He banged his head on the side of the cart and winced. The cart seemed to be moving. Ryn Mathen seemed to be speaking to him.

'What?' Thought that was what he got out. It sounded strange. Echoey. Might be his head or his ears or his mouth. His mouth was very dry.

It was Ryn, wasn't it? Blinked. Yes.

Ryn passed him a bottle. 'A town, Marith. You wanted to be informed. The scouts say that it's larger than anything we've come across for weeks now.'

Reached out to take the bottle. He was holding something. He squinted at it. A hatha vial. Empty. Sadly. Took the bottle from Ryn, had a long drink. Sat up again, more carefully. Managed to stay upright. 'Good.' He crawled past Ryn, poked his head out of the canvas, blinked and cursed at the light. Yellow desert. The tail end of the army, marching, the baggage train and the camp followers stumbling along. There, if he squinted, surely, on the horizon, a flash of fire that must be the sun catching the bronze walls of Sorlost.

'What time is it?' The shadows suggested late afternoon. Or

early morning, if they'd turned around and were now marching back west. Which would be stupid. He shook his head. Late afternoon. Definitely. And there was a town up ahead. Ryn had just said that. I think?

Ryn said, 'I was about to give the order to stop for the night. The town is about an hour further on, north-east of here. Give the men a rest and a meal first.'

'Yes.' Marith thought about jumping down from the cart while it was moving. Ryn must have just clambered onto it while it was moving. Decided that might not be the best idea in the history of Irlast. A town. Yes. 'I'll lead them.'

Ryn looked at him, said, 'Of course,' in a commendably unperturbed voice.

The wine was beginning to clear his head a bit. 'I'll take – did the scouts have any thoughts of how big the place is? Walled? No, not walled, the towns and villages around here aren't as I remember. They're small places, as I remember, piss-poor, defenceless, all of them, locals can barely speak their own language, no taste in clothes or drink.' I'm rambling. Shut up. 'Yes. I'll take . . . a hundred horsemen, and as many again foot. The men from the Whites among the horsemen, the new ones. Test them. Kiana can come. You stay here with the rest.'

Poor Ryn looked most disappointed. Marith jumped down from the cart, almost ended up in a heap in the sand but Ryn caught him and held him up.

'All right, all right, you can come. Tell Alis he's in charge while we're gone.'

They got settled on a stretch of rockier ground that dipped and then rose again, a low hill between the army and the town. Someone had lived here, once: there was a ruined wellhead, the remains of a house and garden, a withered copse of cimma fruit trees. The well still had water, when they could find a rope long enough; they put Marith's tent up next to the largest of the trees so that he could see it from the doorway. There was time for a bath while

the camp got settled. Luckily. Wasn't sure how long he'd been . . .
enjoying himself, but it seemed to have been a good few days.
Distinct impression he must have developed an unpleasant smell
from the way the servant girl reacted when she came to wash him.
Tried to eat something, but between the excitement and the hangover he couldn't manage it. A few cups of wine and a handful of
keleth seeds to take the hangover away. The men were buzzing
excitedly, he could feel the happiness in them; the sound was like
the droning of honeybees. Peaceful: drinking wine in a hot bath
on a warm evening, while the rose of sunset paled and the shadows
fell long behind him. He dunked his head under, leaned back and
closed his eyes as the servant girl rubbed his hair with oil that
smelled of jasmine.

After the bath he dressed and armed himself slowly. This was
the worst part. Perhaps it was the last of the hatha . . . the ghost
of her, he could see her there in the tent, helping him dress himself,
belting on his sword, fastening his blood-clot war cloak, her slender
fingers on the silver, her eyes reflected in the dark ruby, serious
look on her face as she adjusted the brooch and the cloak just so,
her fingers cool as they brushed the bones at the base of his throat.
The people of Chathe say that the seat of the soul is there, at the
base of a man's throat. Used to say, rather. And then she'd smile,
as she always did, and sigh, and kiss him, and tell him to stay
safe. He had to fasten and refasten and refasten the brooch of the
cloak to get it to hang right.

'*My heart, is it?*' A brilliant red ruby, with a great flaw running
down the centre of it, like a scar. '*Did you mean it to be quite so
symbolic, Thalia?*'

'*If it was your heart, Marith, I'd lock it away in a chest and
bury it in a pit a thousand miles deep in the furthest corner of
the desert wilds. If it was your heart, Marith, I'd sail out a thousand miles over the Bitter Sea and cast it away into the waves
where no one would ever find it. No. I didn't think of any kind
of symbolism. I just thought you'd like it.*'

'*I do like it.*'

361

'*I knew you would.*'

He came out of the tent. It had got full dark now. The people of the town would have sat in silence listening to the twilight bell, in the Great Temple of Sorlost a child who was not Thalia might have sacrificed a man to their cursed god. I'll tear that bloody temple down and melt the twilight bell to make myself a new throne as King of Sorlost, Marith thought. And I'll stand in the Small Chamber, the sacrifice room, and I'll curse their god in every language for what Thalia had to do there. I'll break the altar stone to bits with my bare hands and spit on it and curse the god.

Memory: a great gobbet of yellow phlegm on a gold-painted dais. Smell of shit. A wild man's eyes and an empty hate-filled croaking voice. 'Filth. Pestilence. Poison. Better all the world died in torment, than lived under your rule.'

Ha! Set up a Temple to himself, in place of one to Great Lord pissing Tanis. Keep the altar and the priestess and the knife.

Kiana Sabryya's voice cut through his dreaming: 'Marith. We're ready.'

The camp was alive with torches. Horsemen. Kiana rode up, eyes glittering.

'We're ready, My Lord King.'

'Good.'

Brychan led up the white horse. Gods, it really was a beautiful creature. It too looked excited, on edge and happy, it seemed to know what was to come. Marith swung himself up, spread his cloak out behind him. In the torchlight the horse looked red, his cloak looked black. The horse pranced joyfully. The bag with Osen's head in it bounced up and down.

Ryn rode over to them, smiling. Looked at the bag briefly. He'd never asked. Kiana must have told him? He'd never asked about Osen, so he must know. He'd never asked about Thalia either, come to that. Unless he thought it was her head in there.

'Ready?'

Marith smiled. 'I think so.'

* * *

A hundred horsemen, as many again on foot. He kept them in better order than Ryn had; they went on very quietly, even the new ones from the White Isles. The sand was lovely to ride over for keeping quiet. And then, very suddenly, the sand was growing up with crops, poor wretches trying to farm here, and there ahead were trees and houses. The town. Many of the houses still had lights burning. Noises. Midden smells. The smell of goat-dung hearth smoke. In the house nearest to them a window was lit up and a baby was crying and a dog was barking at the cries.

Kiana took twenty of the horsemen off, skirting around to the other side of the town. Marith chewed a handful of keleth seeds, took a gulp of wine. Drew his sword.

A bell began to ring in the town. Marith almost fell out of the saddle at the noise. More dogs began to bark. More windows lit up.

'Amrath and the Altrersyr!' Marith kicked the horse into a run.

The baby stopped crying. He remembered that very clearly. The town was alive with panic, but the baby stopped crying.

The townspeople, crazed, all of them, came running out of their houses. Shouts and wails. Most of them weren't even armed. Marith cut them down one after another. Blood. Blood. Blood. Blood. Blood. They tried to run, he came after them. They threw themselves at him, he broke them. Through the streets, crashing down killing as he went. On the horse he towered over them; the children especially made him laugh just how small they were, he had to bend forward in the saddle to reach them. They scattered before him, like birds flying up. There was no resistance to him. Men, women, children dying before him, so easy, simpler and easier than it had been for so long. A slaughter: he thought of the men who went out on the rocks on the north islands of the White Isles, killed the seal pups as they lay there on the rocks. No fear in him, or in the men: how could they be afraid, killing unarmed children, weeping women, screaming weeping shaking men? In his head all was calm and certain. Peace in him. Killing that does not need doubt or thought. A woman with two children in her arms was running, he pushed the horse after her. One of the children fell from her arms. Wriggled out of her arms. Purple-faced with fear. It rolled on the ground screaming, Marith rode the horse up to it, stopped over it, the horse raised one gilded hoof, stepped down. The woman ran on with the other child in her arms, had not tried to go back. Marith rode after her and killed her, and killed the child that she held clutched to her breast. She held it like a shield, over her heart. Gods knew if she was trying to protect it or use it to protect herself from him. He had to cut through it to get to her, either way. She dropped it, dying, as she died and he rode the horse over them both. The horse's hooves were covered with blood. The blood was quickly covered in sand.

A man came at him. He cut the man down. The man died. A woman came at him. He cut the woman down. The woman died. It blurred. Became nothing. One shapeless mass of bodies, that he was cutting at. People were trying to run, and he chased them down, and he killed them.

A yell. Looked up. A woman leapt from the roof of a building, screaming; it was a tall building, three storeys, she made a gasping sound as she struck the ground. One of his men was up on the roof behind her. Disappointment on the man's face.

The building was a caravan inn. Large and crumbling, painted façade all rubbed away by the desert wind. Leprous, like a man with rotting skin. Marith recognized it. 'The Seeker After Wisdom'. Its sign showed a dead man hanging suspended from a dead tree. He'd stayed here, with Thalia and Tobias, after they'd left Sorlost. He'd first slept with Thalia here.

He looked up. There. There was the room.

Two soldiers came out of the inn laughing, swords in one hand bottles of drink in the other. Marith called to them and they fell over themselves to pass him the bottles.

'Your health.'

'Your health, My Lord King.' The wine tasted of ripe fruit.

Kiana rode up with two of her men behind her. Her sword was

brilliant with blood, there was a smudge of blood on her face. 'I think we've got most of them,' she said triumphantly. 'There are still some people clinging on hiding in a couple of the houses. I've given the order to burn them. Other than that, we're done.'

'Good.'

Even as he spoke, he saw flames beginning to rise from the window of the inn.

Oh.

Kiana said, 'It's been stripped clear, don't worry. Not that it had much to strip. Ryn has got men loading a couple of carts up.'

A shower of sparks as the shutters caught fire. Burning wood spiralling to the ground.

A scream. A man leapt from the burning window. Unlike the woman, he survived it, lay scrabbling on the ground like an insect, staggered to his feet. His nightshirt was on fire. The soldier who had given Marith the bottle wandered over and killed him. Blood pooling out into the sand. A fine thing.

Marith turned his horse around. 'Call the men together. Let's get back to the camp, then.'

Columns forming up, men flushed-faced, laughing, shouldering bags of loot, hurriedly refastening their clothes.

Chapter Forty

They lost four men in the attack. Two were killed by the towns-people, one fell off his horse during the first charge, one got knifed by his best friend over something or other of no monetary worth. Marith had the friend killed as well, as an entirely futile warning to others, 'Try not to knife your best friend to death; or, if you do knife your best friend, try not to get caught'. So five men. To balance it, two townspeople had surrendered and begged to join the Army of Amrath. A young couple, a boy and a girl. The girl looked delighted to be among soldiers, her eyes followed Kiana as though she was in love.

'They gave her a sword and she held it like she'd been born to it,' Ryn told Marith. 'Said she'd never held one before. Real find, there. Sadly her man's useless, terrified: they gave him a sword and took it away again quick. But she's wanted this her whole life, she said.'

'Yes.' Thought about this suddenly. 'I'm . . . delighted I've given her a chance to fulfil her dreams, then. I hope it all works out well for her.'

I wonder if anyone here remembers me? he thought. The joyful young man buying clothes and food and horses, eyes bulging out of his head because the most beautiful woman in the world somehow agreed to sleep with him.

He untied the bag containing Osen Fiolt's head from the saddle.
Held it out to Brychan.

'Brychan—?'

'My Lord King?'

'This . . . I . . .' Tied the bag back to the saddle. 'Nothing.'

Brychan nodded.

His shoulder was hurting again. Throbbing, itching, he wanted
to tear his armour off, rip out the maggots that must be crawling
there. It was alive with insects, it must be, running with filth down
all over his arm, his back, it was torturing him, and they would
spew out, everyone would see and be revolted. But when he finally
got to his tent – Ryn's tent – and Brychan helped him get his
armour off, the skin was white and perfect, only the faint silver
traceries, like lacework, where the wound had been. He felt the
skin itch and ripple, poison moving beneath it, maggots gnawing
at it. Had a bath and washed it clean.

A war council, the next morning, after a good long night's sleep.
He had gone to bed almost sober. Woken with a clear head. 'It
went well. The men enjoyed it. Good new supplies. A few of them
got off towards the city, as you wanted, My Lord King. But now
we ourselves are less than a day's march from Sorlost.'

Marith thought: we are? I thought it was further. I thought I
still had another night away from it, at least. I remember . . .
that night with Thalia, when she sat by the stream, she'd never
seen a stream before, I remember that, it was like a gift she gave
me, her face, when she saw the stream running, heard the sound
of it, we sat beside the stream in the dusk and I told her about
myself, and she seemed not to care about it. And I . . . yes, that
was it, yes: I thought I had a day, a night, at least, before we
reached Sorlost.

Dryly, at the back of his mind: she slept with me the next night,
so she can't have cared about it. And it occurred to him suddenly
to wonder what she'd have done if he hadn't told her who he was.
Told her he was a goatherd from Belen Isle, where the soil was

so poor even the lords ate grey bread off clay plates. He'd never
. . . never thought of it like that.

'The men are rested,' said Kiana. 'Give the order now, and we
could be at the gates not long after sunset.'

'They know we are here,' said Alis Nymen. 'Why do they not
send out a messenger to us?'

'What would they say?'

'We march,' said Marith. He got to his feet. 'Give the order. I
wanted them on the move by noon. Kiana. Ryn. With me. Have
our horses saddled.'

'With you?' said Ryn.

'I want to be the first of the army to see it.' I want to remember
it as I was. Alone. I have put this off for a long time. I hesitated,
I let the men of Turain harm me, because I was afraid of reaching
this place. That was why I lost. Yes. That was why. Not because
of Alleen Durith betraying me. Not because I thought, I wanted
. . . I made myself lose because I did not want to come here. I
will stand before the bronze walls and I will see too many things.
Did I think that I could come here and not be changed? I will cry
out and the walls will shatter before me. I will speak and the walls
will open to welcome me in. City of death and dreaming. Had
every man in my army sunk down into death and nothing, had I
been left to crawl through the desert on my hands and knees, I
would have come back here to destroy it.

He rode like the wind for hours. Ah, cliché. But in the desert, on
a horse bred for kings, it was almost true. Yellow air yellow dust
yellow sky, and the horse flying, his hair and his cloak flying out.
He kicked the horse and it gasped beneath him, running with its
hooves throwing up the sand like they were running through water,
its trappings were hung with silver bells and they chimed as it ran.
On and on, it was dying, its heart would burst, foam and blood
were pulling around its mouth. On and on, and his own body was
exhausted, clinging on to it, kicking it to make it run. Like the
wind. Tearing across the desert, trampling the earth, almost like

riding a dragon, I should have tried to ride one of the dragons, he thought, Thalia and I, together, ridden a dragon into the sky up into the stars and gone.

The horse pulled up, blown and shaking, lathered to the eyeballs. Covered in sand. Marith pulled himself from its back, also shaking. Wiped dust from his eyes. All grey and green, scrub plants, withered grasses, dull life clinging on. A village, off to his right, distant, a single column of smoke rising. A stream cutting through rocks, dirty and choked with rubble – Thalia's stream? Empty ground before him, where the people of Sorlost buried their dead. Barren soil. A few grave markers, a patch of new-turned earth, a thorn bush.

The bronze walls of Sorlost. Golden as fire in the afternoon sun. Blinding. The Golden City, ringed round with a wall of golden flame.

As long ago as tomorrow, beneath the brazen walls of Sorlost. They had no seams or joins, a perfect ribbon of metal twisting around the city, punctuated only by the five great gates. Thus they had no beginning and no end. A snake swallowing its own tail. On and on and on.

The horse gasped and stumbled beside him. He'd ruined it. Broken it. It shied away from his hands. It sighed, bent its head to him as the dragons once had.

He had dreamed of seeing this place. Dreamed, often, as a child, like every child on the White Isles must have dreamed, of sacking it. He and Ti had played games with walrus-ivory toy soldiers, sacking it. Heaping up their mother's jewellery to make the shining walls. A golden city, so it must be made of their mother's gold. 'Your soldiers in at the main gate, Ti; mine round the back; trebuchets – loose!' and the gold piles fell with a wave of his hand, in a sparkling jangling crash. He had first seen the bronze walls of Sorlost lit by the sunrise, the metal turning from inky dark to blazing fire, more beautiful and vivid than the dawn itself. The moment the light hit them had been like watching someone thrust a touch into a bowl of pitch. Dragon fire. The feeling in his heart when he first saw Thalia's face. Now the setting sun caught the walls and made them burn darker, harsher, a savage brilliance, not dragon fire but dragon's eyes. He thought then of the mage in the Court of the Broken Knife, bathing a weeping woman and her child in mage fire, and the woman had not even seen that she burned with light.

Brilliant as all the stars and the sun and the moon and all the gold and silver in the world, a city of pure blazing screaming raging light. He shouted aloud. Screamed. The sun sank away behind the horizon. The shadow fell over the walls. The walls were dead cold killing bronze. The sand in which they stood looked black. It was full dark when Ryn and Kiana finally rode up behind him. A full moon shone down on the city. The walls were black and pale together. Within the walls a hundred thousand lights burned. Numberless as the stars in the sky . . . and indeed the stars were half-hidden by the city's light. Ryn and Kiana checked their horses and stared.

'There,' said Marith. 'Sorlost. Easy, don't you think? One day, do you think, our armies will take to destroy it? Or two?'

Ryn closed his eyes. Opened them. 'No army in the world . . .'

'Except ours,' said Kiana.

Marith clapped him on the arm. 'Except ours, Ryn.'

He sat out in the desert alone that night, drinking firewine, taking hatha, thinking. The world spinning over him, breaking over him. Blind. Floating. Crawling. His body writhing with insects.

Hatha rips your mind apart. Some people drink firewine to see visions. They are fools. Piss-puke-sweat-spit-shit. But oh gods we've seen so clearly that there's a truth in that. He was swimming in the darkness, sinking. Onwards forever. On and on. And it was morning, he was lying in the dust, with the walls of Sorlost rising before him. They looked dark and cold against the pink dawn sky. His shoulder hurt. He felt as though he was swimming deep beneath the surface of a great sea in glorious sunshine, looking up at the world above. He had crawled somehow into the midst of the city's burial ground, the earth was raw in places over new graves, he was lying huddled in the shelter of a grave mark.

A city built on dying. Tear it down, shatter the Temple into the dust. Look what they did, what they made her do. Look what happened to me there. Their death god, the child-killer they worship. Put up in its place a temple to myself as King of Death.

For a little while, he thought, I was a man again. Briefly. Nothing and no one.

'Marith.'

Thalia was standing over him.

Her dress was ragged, her hair was full of dust. Her skin was dry and burned by the sun. All the light in her, like the first time he had seen her, offering up hope to him.

'I knew you'd come back,' he tried to say. 'I knew you were alive.' He coughed and swallowed, spat into the sand. 'I knew,' he said.

She looked at him in disgust.

Chapter Forty-One

There are so many things I can be and do, I am certain. Good things. Joyous things. Kind things. Pointless things. *From the fear of life and the fear of death, release us.* Humble, mundane things.

What I want is to live and to live and to live.

He is drunk and a monster. He is not worth a moment's thought. But I have had wonder and glory. And I want him, in the end, I want him also to live.

I know him. I care for him. Therefore I want him to live.

Chapter Forty-Two

Tobias, the most naive man living
The desert west of Sorlost

Fool girl. Bitch. Moment the rumour goes around that he's still alive after all, her eyes bloody fucking lighting up.

Tobias, man, you're a bigger fool than she is, for thinking it might go any other way.

One defeat, and she's going to change her mind about everything? Really?

'I have to go back to him, Tobias. I have to.' Staring out into the desert, like she could see him if she looked hard enough. Half-feared she'd leap up and start to run to him right then.

'*The things you said, Thalia, girl . . .*' That was then. Don't remind her. She looked at him challenging him to think it.

And Lenae, too. '*Will you marry me, Lenae? I know I don't love you, I know you don't love me, but: a house, a garden, children, normal, peaceful things.*'

'*Uh . . . Uh . . .*' Astonished look on her face. Revolted look on her face. Tries to hide revolted look on her face. '*Uh . . . no, Tobias. No offence [No offence? No offence?] but . . .*' Her eyes roll: '*I've only been widowed a year, Tobias. I'm not that—*' Cuts off the word 'desperate'. '*I just mean . . .*' Her eyes glaze over:

373

'*Look! Over there! The Army of Amrath! Glory and fun and loot and glory and fun and loot and loot and more loot!*' And that's not fair. That didn't . . . quite happen. And it's her free choice to do what she wants if it did. It's just him being bitter about it.

Rumours running all over the bloody world, that Marith Altrersyr isn't dead, the Army of Amrath isn't destroyed, who in the world would be stupid enough crazy enough to believe that? '*That bloody bastard got what was coming for him, overambitious deluded power-drunk sick fuck cock?*' Ahem. Not me. I never said that. Gods, no. I might have . . . passed on a rumour that tragedy had befallen us, lamented that the joy of the world the wonder of all human hearts is brought low, but, I mean, only as an example of the kind of idiocy some people will believe, some people will believe literally anything, yeah, but me, personally, me, I never believed a word of it. Marith Altrersyr's dead? How can Marith Altrersyr *Ansikanderakesis Amrakane* the King of Death be dead? Lies and the liars who tell them. Hurrah hurrah three cheers and all hail the king!

Boy's like a damned cockroach. Like trying to get rid of a wart on your dick.

When you realize you're the only optimist left in Irlast, Tobias, man, really might be time to slit your own throat. Or swallow your pride, escort Queen Thalia back to her true love, wish her and everyone else luck.

They had been sitting around a campfire in the cold desert night, when they had learnt that Marith was still alive. Tobias, Thalia, Lenae, Rovi, Naillil. Travelling east towards the city of Pen Amrean along the coast where the Sea of Tears beat against the barren sand of the Nor Desert. Water, water, everywhere, and not a drop to drink. But a few people clung on to living, even here. Built shelters of whale bone and driftwood, ate raw fish and seaweed. Swam in the sea until their skin was wrinkled like a newborn baby's, their hair bleached white by the sun and the salt; sang of far distant countries where men walked the land without fear, tricked by the demons of the earth into thinking the land a blessed thing. They had never heard of rain or rivers: they harvested water from the sea mists that rolled in with the dawn, hanging out great nets of dried seaweed in the evenings, squeezing them out in the morning drop by precious drop. Tobias kept the party well clear of them. But one evening they had heard the jingling of bells, the sound of horses, came over a sand dune to find a group of merchants from Pen Amrean come to trade jars of water for green and yellow pearls. By the light of the merchants' fire, half-dazed by hearing other men's speech, they had listened to the story: Marith Altrersyr the demon the King of Death is alive still, he is marching his army on the city of Elarne, his army is destroying everything in its path. Even the fish-eaters are afraid of him now, the merchants said. The corpse of a great sea beast had been washed up on the shore, a red sea dragon four times as long as the largest whale, torn in a thousand places by jagged teeth. The fish-eaters would not touch it, the merchants said; it lay on the barren sand a mountain of meat and fat, its bones would be worth a kingdom, its hide the same, but the fish-eaters had forbidden them to go near it. Brandished clubs of whale bone and sharks' teeth. It was one of the great god-powers of the sea that gives all life, the fish-eaters said, its destruction is an omen of the ruin the demon will bring.

Thalia nodded her head in agreement at the fish-eaters' words. Sat, looking up at the stars, after the merchants had finished speaking. Lenae and Naillil watched her, awed. Rovi made a noise that might have been laughing in his dead hollow voice. Thalia asked then begged Lenae to buy horses, water, supplies from the merchants, pay double, triple the asking price, quickly, that she could go back to him. Tobias sat with his head in his hands. Don't do this. You're free of him, girl. We're all free of him.

'I will walk there alone, if I have to,' Thalia said. 'I am begging you.' She said, not looking at Tobias, 'I will reward you all, when we get back to my army. Gold, jewels, whatever you want.'

'Can you bring Lenae's baby back to life, then? And her husband?'

Thalia said, 'My husband, it would seem, has come back to life, Tobias.'

'That island you were talking about? Sailing away?'

'Don't be an idiot, Tobias,' Lenae said. Stretched out her arms. 'Look at where we are, Tobias. She's the queen, Tobias,' Lenae said, Naillil clucking in idiot agreement. 'She has to go back.'

'We can go on east, we can go back west, we can go north all the way back to Illyr.' Found himself shouting, 'We don't have to go back. You don't have to go back. We can go away and never bloody well think about him again.'

It cost almost the whole of Lenae's two thalers, to buy the horses and the supplies. Merchants could see a hard bargain when it was there begging them. 'I'll stay here,' Tobias said. 'I'll go east or west or north. Go home to Immish. Still got some coin of my own, for that.' Then the ride across the desert, Thalia pushing them faster and faster, staring day and night ahead of her towards him, riding east with the sun blinding their eyes in the mornings, burning on their backs in the afternoon. Nightmare memories of the desert the last time, like he was certain that his ruin and his guilt was out there waiting for him. How will you betray her this time, then? Hey, Tobias? Do you remember her face, before, the first few days she was with Marith, how happy she looked? Do you remember, Tobias, how happy Marith looked? You had never seen him look happy before then. Never seen him look happy like that since. Do you remember his face, Tobias, when you destroyed him? And do you remember her face?

I'm going mad, he thought.

Or I was mad back then. That dream I had, so sweet and brief, when I was fighting for him and I believed in him and we were winning everything and it was the most glorious thing in the world because I believed in it so much. But dreams can never come back. *'I can't let you get to Ith, boy. You know that. Can't let you have power and command. I know what you are. What you'd do.'* Ah ha ha ha ha. Laugh so hard you bloody piss yourself. I'll stop you, boy, I'll make you so fucking unhappy you want to break the world to shreds, yeah, to stop you breaking the world into shreds.

'Why?' Finally got up the courage to ask her, something like the tenth evening out in the desert, she was brushing sand out of her hair with her fingers. Dry and hot and thirsty. The sand scoured her face, her knuckles were grey and cracked. She would not let them rest. One of the horses looked like it might be dying. He really thought Rovi might be going to die. Naillil and Lenae seemed almost unbothered, 'Come on, Tobias, get moving,' Lenae would stress at him, glaring at him as he hauled himself up onto his horse with both his knees ringing out. Infected with the need to get Thalia back home to the king her husband, because that's . . . that's what people did. 'I'm coming. Gods.' His knees when he stood up now sounded like a trebuchet missile hitting a wall.

'Why, Thalia, girl?'

Thalia carried on brushing her hair out. It was so dry out here in the desert that it crackled with sparks.

'Don't tell me, Thalia, it's because you want to go back to him.'

She stopped her brushing. Lenae and Rovi and Naillil were listening, and Tobias thought somehow that they somehow knew and understood what she was going to say.

Rovi stank worse than dead, in the desert. A few brief glorious days, by the seashore, he'd been free of the smell of death.

'You're hurt. Yeah. I can get that. Your life was shite before, in your Temple, and it's been quite a lot shite since. Four pregnancies in four years. I—' Looked at Lenae. 'I can't imagine how that feels, Thalia, to be honest. You want to punish the world. You want to punish yourself. I think—' Looked at Naillil. 'I think I might know a bit about that. You think?'

A smile, almost, on Thalia's face. 'Yes. I think you might know.'

'But you don't need to do this.'

Thalia said, 'I do, Tobias.'

377

The dying horse died. If Lenae rode with Naillil they were still all right. They travelled mostly at night now, it was getting hotter and hotter, the earth more and more parched. Huddled for shelter in the day from the sun's merciless relentless hateful heat. No surprise it hated them, going back to the King of Death.

'It can't be out of love,' Tobias said to Thalia in the morning, as they collapsed down to rest. 'And you can't want power and wealth that much.'

'Why not?' Thalia said. 'Why shouldn't I? I am their queen. I am the richest and most powerful woman in the world. That's a hard thing to give up.' She sounded so gentle. Reasonable. 'What if Lenae found out her husband was alive still? Or Naillil, or Rovi? What would you say, if they went back to find someone they cared for? Or if they didn't go back?'

'I didn't go back,' Tobias said. 'Ever. I wouldn't go back to him for anything in the world, if I was you. And you can leave Lenae out of this.'

They had maybe three days' water left, and Naillil's horse was very obviously dying. They hadn't found a stream that day, they hadn't found a place to put the tent up until well into the day when it was burning hot. Thalia sat in the day's heat looking at the shrivelled dried-out skin on her hands, the finger joints all grey and cracked.

'You saved my life,' she said to Tobias, 'back in the camp, when the horsemen came.'

'I didn't save your life. You probably saved mine.'

'No.' She laughed, a dry laugh in the dry heat. 'You didn't. Thank you for saying that. But when you didn't save my life,' she said to Tobias, 'why did you do it?'

'Why?'

'Why?'

Thought: because you were there, Thalia, girl. Because you were standing there and I couldn't bear to see you. Because I feel so fucking fucking guilty because so many things.

'I want you to live, Thalia. Don't you understand that?'

'Perhaps,' she said, 'perhaps I want that, also, Tobias. For myself and for Marith.'

Tried to spit with a rank dry mouth. 'Marith doesn't deserve to live.'

She said, after a long silence, 'My child died. My children died. Marith—' Shook her head. 'I need to get some rest, before we go on.'

Naillil's horse died, and they had one day's water left, and only Thalia was riding still, and they had gone on all night finding nothing no streams no shelter, and now the sun was up again pale pink dawn evil bastard hot hates us, when they reached the camp of the pathetic remnant of the Army of Amrath. *Glorious they sailed, a mighty host in golden ships. I alone came back.* There, in the distance, you could feel them, sense them, the air was different, a creeping feeling on the back of the neck, eating at you, Tobias felt his heart getting hot beating in his chest.

'Come on, come on,' Thalia had cried, pushing her horse forward. The poor thing was dying, gasping, its mouth all foam, 'Come on,' she shouted to it. Then she started in the saddle, and pulled the horse up, and she was dismounting, running across the sand. The city walls looming up in the distance, a metal cliff. She's running off home? No. No way.

She stopped running. A dark figure, very small, huddled there. Raised its head.

The other four of them went on to the camp. Just about managed it before Thalia's horse finally gave out. Lenae went running on to join our boys. Wild with excitement, shaking the sand out of her hair, chattering about the gold she'd been promised. 'Some of my friends might still be there. I'll get us some things. Wine, blankets, pillows, horses. Some of the people I know must be there, my friends.'

Naillil watched her go. Started to walk after her. Rovi paused, then limped after Naillil. 'It's familiar, isn't it?' Rovi wheezed at Tobias. 'What else am I going to do?'

'Nothing, Rovi.' Only place in the world you could be at home, death-stink walking-dead-man. King Marith should make you his standard bearer. I'll ask him to, shall I, Rovi man? He owes me one.

'Someone's going to be bloody king,' Rovi wheezed. 'Aren't they? Lead the army to murder. Might as well be him.'

Tobias walked on and now the camp was spread out before him, well-ordered, professionally done, and now he was walking through it, and it was slowly swallowing him. Neat rows of tents, horse lines well downwind of the tents, latrine trenches well downwind of everything. 'Bloody fucking lying cock-sucking untrustworthy shifty pox-on-him bastard,' one of the blokes digging over the latrine trenches kept shouting. 'He bloody well promised me.' Weird place, an army camp. Just ignore the swearing nutters. Old secret sellsword's wisdom, that. Smell of breakfast drifting over towards the blokes practising sarriss drill in the dawn sunshine. Sarriss – up! Sarris – lower! Sarriss – up! Sarriss – lower! Sarriss – up! Like they were waving at the rising sun. One or two of them moved their heads in the general direction of the breakfast smells. The drill instructor yelled at them. Stop thinking about the bacon, our lads! Sarriss – lower! Sarriss – up! Nice rhythm to it.

Two figures, small and fragile, coming out of the desert. Going very slowly, haltingly. One of them lit up gleaming in the sunlight. One of them dark as night. The whole camp halting. Turning. Knowing. The murmur rising around the camp. 'The queen.' 'She's come back to him.' 'He will be happy again now.' 'She's come back to us.' Men scrabbled to the horses, grabbed at swords and spears. An honour guard forming, rushing up to greet them. The drill instructor abandoned her soldiers, rode fast towards the approaching figures, shouting behind her to the soldiers to follow with sarriss raised in salute. Cheering cheering cheering.

Yes. Well. Remind me why anyone would put up with a drink- and drug-addled fuckwit like Marith Altrersyr? Cause I haven't got a clue.

Marith stopped, raised Thalia's hand in his. The two of them together, hands raised, triumphant. 'Your queen has returned!' Marith shouted. His voice was hoarse. 'This forthcoming victory shall be in her honour. Soon, she will be seated on the throne of the Sekemleth Emperor as Queen of Sorlost.' He kissed Thalia passionately. Loud cheering. She melted into him, her hair enveloping them both. Whistles and cheers, at that. Gods, felt randy watching. Take a heart of stone to point out the stain on the boy's crotch where he'd shat himself.

His shit and her sweat from weeks riding a horse through the desert. Nice.

They made their way together to the tent at the very centre of the camp, set up on a hillock so everyone could see it looming over them. Some poor sods probably spent the previous night digging the hillock. The tent was green and red leather, battered-looking, like it had got wet and not dried. Odd runny look to it, also, like someone had tried to colour it all red and it hadn't worked properly. It was flying a dark red banner that wasn't human skin because even Marith Altrersyr had some common sense seeing as there was a hole in the tent roof. The happy couple disappeared inside, to violent cheering. At least Marith would now be taking his shit-covered trousers off. The guard Brychan stood up straight and stiff (snigger) directly outside the doorcurtain. Blank face that screamed, 'I'm listening like no one ever listened before and dear gods it's good.' Various other chaps hanging around giving him the death-stare, like, 'What did he do, what noble achievement, to be overhearing all that?'

Okay, let's calm down a bit. Probably they're just having a very thorough wash.

Whichever, give them a couple of hours. She'd missed the boy. Kept saying she was fine, wasn't heartbroken, would manage fine without him, which she obviously would. But she'd missed him. So sit in the shade a while, find someone here selling fresh bread, shake the worst of the sand out of his hair, wait. Let them have a few hours together first.

'Haven't finished the sarriss drill, you buggers get back here now, right now,' a good loud voice rang out. 'Twice more, we're going to do it, for the king and the queen.'

Rather less than an hour later, Tobias marched up to Marith's tent. The guard Brychan held up his sword. Eyes boggling: who in all hells is this chap and how's he got this far in life with this much of a death wish?

'Brychan.'

The guard Brychan was silent. Looking straight ahead, silent scream on his lips '*ignore him, ignore him*'.

'I need to see the king.'

Brychan's eyes went big as bloody cart wheels. Just . . . ignore him. He might go away. Please? Head moved a bit, looking off to one side, like: 'someone help, make this nutter go away.'

'I need to see Marith, Brychan, mate.'

Two servants came trooping up with buckets of water. Gods, warm water smell in the dust . . . A bath . . . Tobias took a step closer. Brychan twitched, staring around frantically: I have to let the blokes with the water in so King Marith can wash the shit and cum off but if I let them in this madman will try to get in after them.

Tobias thought about it. Looked at poor Brychan. Not his fault. He's a guard. He guards the king's tent. 'All right, all right. I'll leave him in peace a bit longer. I'll come back in a bit. Tell him an old friend is waiting to see him. Tell him . . . tell him I'm proud of what he learnt from me about camp hygiene.'

The man Brychan was trying to ignore him as he stamped off.

The summons came an hour or so later again. Just as the nervous terror of every moment waiting was wearing off. Ten men in red-crested helmets, drawn swords, the breeze blowing their blood-red cloaks. Their leader had gold trimming to his armour, a pattern of leaves and flowers, ivy, daisies, roses. A jewelled brooch at his throat fastening his cloak. A jewelled sword hilt.

Flashy. Posh bloke. Or good at dice and tavern fights.

Ominous/gratifying, that the boy had sent all this lot. Ominous/

gratifying/fucking what possessed me?/what kind of inferiority complex do you have to have to send ten men and a flash git in gold armour to escort one old bloke with a bad leg through a heavily guarded military camp?

'You're to come with us. Now.'

'I'd guessed.' Played up the limp a bit as they went, made them all walk slow. Everyone staring as they went past. Stared back. Wonder if there's anyone I know still alive somewhere here? Acol. That kid with the bowl of porridge . . . Clews, wasn't it? Odds are . . . well, there's maybe eight thousand men here, tops, I'd say with my best professional years of experience finger in the wind guess. Accepting the claim that the Army of Amrath numbered a thousand times a thousand, as many battle-hungry soldiers in the Army of Amrath as there are grains of sand in the desert, that's . . . [looks down at the sand in the desert] not great odds anyone I know survived, really, is it?

They reached Marith's tent. Brychan was still standing there, rigid, sword in hand, sweat dripping down his face. The flash git nodded to him as they went in.

As they went in.

Oh fucking hell. What possessed me? Terror. Skin went cold. Doorway like a bloody wound into something. Gaping gnawing mouth. Don't go in. Don't go in. As he crossed the threshold, the shadows came up to meet him. Pus pain hate rage trauma bloody murder my fault my fault. World screams at him.

Marith was sitting on a camp chair, dressed in a loose shirt and leggings, bare-headed, unarmed. His hair was still damp from his bath. He looked so bloody young. Thalia came through from the sleeping chamber at the sound of them entering. Her hair too was wet, tracing a pattern of damp lines like foliage down her dress.

'Hello Tobias,' said Marith. Sounded so young, too. That gentle soft lilting voice.

'Hello Marith, boy.' His own voice sounded less shaky than he'd feared. The space between them seemed vast, he felt vast, dizzy, as though he was falling. Hard to keep looking, like none of this was real, like he should be looking at something else beyond this. 'Mind if I sit down? My leg's never been the same since that night in Sorlost. And as for my arm after that night in your tent with Raeta—'

The man in the gold armour hurried to bring up another chair. Then slipped out. Just the three of them. Thalia standing, Marith and Tobias sitting face to face. Long, long time since they sat face to face. *'I want a straight answer out of you, Marith.'* Blinked and looked away. A trumpet sounded in the camp outside. The army readying itself for battle. Tobias swallowed. Rotten taste in his mouth, maggots and bad meat. Why? Why? Why the fuck any of this? Why can't any of us just be happy with what we've got? Why do we have to do this? Come on, then, Marith, boy. Draw your sword on me. Curse me. Spit in my face. Just bloody say something. Do something.

Thalia said, 'Will you fight for us, Tobias?'

Uh.

Uh.

All the questions in the bloody world.

You wouldn't expect bloody that.

Thalia said, 'Will you?'

Trying to be casual, like. Tobias said, 'I can't fight any more, if you hadn't noticed. I can barely use my bloody arm, after what your husband there did to me. I'm in constant bloody fucking pain. If you hadn't noticed. I'm—'

Thalia said, 'You don't need to fight yourself. You could lead a troop of men.'

'I just rode through a desert to bring you here, Thalia. You damned well near killed me doing that. You begged me to bring you back to him. So I brought you bloody well back to him. Act of kindness. This is how you thank me?'

Marith just sat in silence, staring. His hands were clasped in his lap, very still, every now and then he'd raise his right hand to his face, make to scratch at his eyes, flinch and drop his hand back down.

What? I mean . . . come on, Marith, boy. Come on here. Say something.

'I brought her back to you, Marith. Yeah? So say something.'

Thalia frowned at him. Bit her lip, shook her head.

'Come on. I could have been anywhere else in the bloody world but here. I've spent the last four fucking years dreaming about trying to kill you. And here you are and here I am. You've got your sword, your army, you can kill me right here right now. So fucking well say something.'

'You trusted me,' said Marith finally. 'Back then.'

Uh.

'Back then. Before. You trusted me.'

Fuck off. Right? But I did. Gods, Marith. You could've been . . . What you could have been. What I saw in myself, when I looked at you. Fucking hope, like Thalia said. Tobias said, 'I've dedicated years of my life to trying to kill you, Marith, boy. You out of your tree on hatha again?'

Admit it. Confess. Said slowly, 'I did fight for you in your army, once. At Malth Salene, way back in the beginning. Not sure you ever knew.'

Marith looked almost surprised. 'You did?'

'I saw you kill your own father, Marith, boy. I cheered you doing it. I sailed into Morr Town with your war fleet and almost got disembowelled and was almost drowned and was almost eaten by a thing with too many teeth. I swore to all the gods and demons, I swore on my mother's soul that I'd never bloody fight for you again.'

The boy's face twitched. 'You must be the only other person who was there who's still alive, then.'

'I saw you crowned in Ethalden and I swore it again. And swore again that I'd kill you, in fact.'

Thalia said gently, 'So go into Sorlost and fight against us.'

Oh, yes, right. That's why I came back here with you, girl. Not. 'I'm not fighting at all. I told you.'

Thalia said, 'I can give you a bag of gold thalers, as I promised you, thank you, send you away alone into the desert. Or you can fight for me. Or I can give the order and men will come with swords and kill you, as my enemy.'

Oh. Oh, you bitch. Oh . . .

Tobias thought: gods, Thalia, girl, I thought . . . I thought you were better than that. All those days riding in the desert. Talking, being honest. You bitch.

Thalia said, 'Well?'

'One company,' Tobias said slowly. 'Swordsmen, not those stupid sarriss blokes, I wouldn't know what to do with them.' Voice got faster, he could hear himself gabbling. 'Blokes with swords. And not anywhere near anything involving your shadow-things or dragons. I'll need a new sword, armour, new boots, I won't fight in the lines, but I'll lead them, give them orders and that. And I want a servant of my own, and a tent, and all that. A doctor, to have a look at me. Lenae and Naillil and Rovi get their bags of gold you promised them. Big bags. Very big. Like, they can piss half of it away on rubbish and still never have to worry again big. And—' Sudden brilliant idea. 'And I want you to introduce Lenae to your friend Lord Mathen, tell him what a fine nice young woman she is. And I want you to find Naillil and Rovi and Lenae a fine tent as well, and horses, and servants, and all that.'

Thalia nodded. Like she'd had it all planned for days. Marith said, very quietly, 'Thank you, Tobias.' His hands dug at his eyes. Thalia pushed his hands away from his face.

The bloke in the gold armour found Tobias a tent, and a sword, and a pasty-faced servant boy. And he had a bath himself (cold water, but) and a change of clothes, scrubbed himself down and felt the sand run off him. His skin beneath the dirt was yellowed, cracked, stained with age. Moisture seeping back into him, could feel himself plumping up, swelling like dried fruit. After the bath he sat with a warm wind blowing his wet hair. Cold and warm together, delicious feeling, like he'd been crying a long time or exhausted himself fighting, his body languid now, a piece of taut thread that had snapped, stretched out now resting in the sun. He was half-asleep in the pleasure-ground between dreams and thinking when the bloke in gold armour came back, embarrassed, turned out the bloke in gold armour and all of his men were now Tobias's squad. Marith boy had obviously thought long and hard about Tobias's skills and where they could best be of use to him. They called themselves 'The Winged Blades'. Had had to turn his laugh into a cough.

'Right. Right. Okay. Get them lined up, let's have a look at them.' They blinked back at him, 'who's this loser?' written in every pair of eyes. Tobias walked down the line studying each face. Grown men, grown women, an old codger wheezing into his helmet, a boy with a face full of spots. But . . . gods and demons, there at the end was Clews, here, one of his men.

'Clews, man! Remember me?'

The boy shook his head in confusion. On second thoughts, maybe that was for the best. Got introduced to the rest of them and the gold-armoured bloke, thought the latter's name was 'Dyrk' but could be wrong.

'Right, you can fall out now, lads,' Tobias told them. 'Relax and that.' They had a nice little circle of bed rolls and knapsacks, no tents or anything fancy but some branches and a spear shaft rigged up with cloaks to keep off the sun. A big canteen of water, a girl with a thin grey face to fetch the water for them. The whole lot of them squatting around a horse-shit cookfire drinking tea.

'Another cup, lads?'

'Gods, this is good tea. The best tea.'

'Put the leaves in when the water's proper boiling, that's the secret. Thirty years soldiering, I've had, to perfect making a cup of tea.'

'Worth it, worth it. What's thirty years and your left eye and half your nose, when you can make a perfect cup of tea?'

'Just what I tell myself every morning, Clews, boy. What's my left eye and half my nose, when I can make a perfect cup of tea?'

'They should give you some special commendation, services to tea making above and beyond.'

'Somewhere out there, there's a gorgeous blond, his heart's desire's a bloke who can make the perfect cup of tea.'

'Oh, I think I killed him in battle just last week. Fell down to the black earth, his teeth in the dust and the dust covering his shining hair, the light dying in his eyes, and his final words were, "If only, if only I'd ever loved a man with half a nose who could make the perfect cup of tea."'

'Here's the new squad commander. Look lively.'

'Hello, lads. Sit down, sit down, no formalities here. I'm just coming to sit here and join you. Let's have a cup of this famous tea, then.'

There was that time way back when, when he was a sane man. *I kill people for money. That's it. That's what I do.* And then there was the madness, killing and fighting to make Marith king, blood-soaked to the eyeballs, still no idea what all that was about, don't ever want to know. And then there was the time afterwards when his heart was so fucked up mad with hate and all he could see was his fury, the world was a bleak terrible place not worth living for and maybe he could die lying to himself that he was doing something good. The boy's a fucking sick-in-the-head killer. So . . . I'm going to kill him to put things right! Right? Makes sense?

And now there was this time when he felt sane again. Just plodding on. Live and let live.

'Got the money to buy your dad a farm yet, Clews, lad?'

Clews's face lit up. 'Soon. Really, really soon.'

Thought: tried the whole martyrdom resisting thing, tried as hard as I could, yeah, four fucking years, you know I did. Not complicit. Fighting from the inside. There was a night once after a battle when I gave water to one of his enemies who was dying, stuck a knife in the throat of one of his soldiers who would have lived. That's got to count for something. In the grand great scheme of things? But I'm so fucking tired now. And Clews is going to buy his dad a farm with his soldiering money, and I'm going to help him. What's wrong with that? We're a bit past 'let's all try to come to an amicable arrangement here, chaps': kind of guessing Clews's dad and a lot of other people would be happier if I kept their loved ones alive, than if I helped their loved ones to die a horrible death.

Helping someone stay alive rather than helping them die, because they trust me and I promised them I would. Helping someone feed their family, do well for them. These aren't excuses. These are the root of human things.

PART SIX

THE GLORY

Chapter Forty-Three

Orhan Emmereth the Lord of the Rising Sun, the adviser to the Emperor's Nithque, the Emperor's Counsellor and Friend, trying to keep himself from weeping until his heart breaks
Sorlost

And they awoke one morning to find the Army of Amrath camped beneath their walls.

How fine it sounded, how stirring to the blood, when it happened so long ago it didn't really happen at all.

So few of them. This is absurd! A village of them, raddled barbarians waving bronze-tipped sticks. In the blazing sun, in the desert sands, they have a muddy stream to drink from, at night they must be cold as ice. Look, the wind is rising, blowing sand into their faces as they march about. Tiny, tattered figures. See one bend its head, imagine it blinking and spitting as the sand blows in its face into its teeth.

'You can almost count them,' Darath said. 'Look.' Held his hands up to the window and the whole camp of them was blotted out. 'If they linked their arms to make a chain around the city walls, they'd stretch perhaps between the Gate of the Evening and the Gate of Dust.'

Never had the city felt such fear. Worse than deeping fever.

Worse than the Immish coming. Worse than the night the palace burned and for a moment there might have been civil war between Orhan and March Verneth. Writhing at the heart, eating at the mind of every man, woman and child in Sorlost.

After long hours the Emperor's servants bethought themselves to meet to consider. There must be . . . something. Between them, they have killed and betrayed and lied a thousand times, they are lucky that they do not believe in the soul to fear their souls being judged. They sat in one of the great state rooms of the Summer Palace, on chairs of ivory and whale bone dragged a thousand miles across the desert, drinking wine from porcelain cups. Their eyes moved, again and again, to the window. It looked out over a fine courtyard garden, fragrant almost to rank excess with jasmine. They tried to see, through it, beyond it, the tents of the army of the enemy, the dripping bloody red banner of the King of Death. As a newborn baby looks again and again to its mother, knows her face before it can see more than the flickering of light and shade, so they looked again and again out to the west, as if they could see him.

'We should . . . send a message?' said Darath. The Nithque to the Emperor, the Emperor's Beloved Counsellor and Friend, the most powerful man in the Sekemleth Empire.

'Oh, I'll just get Gallus to draft one, shall I?' said Orhan. 'There must be a standard letter somewhere for what to say.'

'We will have to go out to meet him,' said Selim Lochaiel.

Orhan said, 'Yes. I know.'

'Not a thing to say,' said Darath. 'That's an obscenity, Selim. Go and wash your mouth out.'

'Darath, obviously,' said Selim. 'Orhan, of course. Who else?'

'The Emperor. He gets down from his palanquin and prostrates himself in the dust. The High Priestess. She gets down from her palanquin and prostrates herself in the dust.'

Selim said, 'The Emperor is forbidden to leave the palace except to visit the Great Temple. The High Priestess is forbidden to leave the Great Temple. In the whole history of the Sekemleth Empire, neither of them has been beyond the city's walls. It is the word of the God.'

'There's a first time for everything,' said Darath. 'Two young children between me and the demon sounds better than nothing. You're serious, aren't you?'

What did you expect, a gnashing of teeth? The gates were sealed, the city was silent. Even the Great Temple was almost deserted. The people of Sorlost sat in their houses in stunned silence, mouths opened but no words came out. Like the whole city was drugged with hatha, Orhan thought, their minds so numbed they could not see or think. After the frenzy of the last few years, murder, fire, plague, heresy, murder, the death blow comes pitiful and silent. In the palace a few servants wandered through the corridors, changing the oil in the lamps, mopping the floors, dusting, washing, picking up the child Emperor's toys. At home, maidservants would be trying to play with Dion. A few shops were open, the owners trying to pretend. People still had to eat, do things; a wedding procession moved through the streets to the accompaniment of walnut shell rattles, the dancer at the front crowned in gold ribbons shouting 'Joy to the bride!' in his rich well-trained voice. In the groom's house the cooks would be bent over the feast, shouting at the underservants, cursing as a pot boiled over on the hearth. In the bride's house the women would be making the last arrangements of the flowers, pinning and repinning a jewel just so on the bride's dress. These things were still somehow important things. And still, in the back of the mind, the little voice that said that everything would be well, this was not happening, death and ruin and fire would not come to pass. Because. Dion won't die, and Darath won't die, and I certainly won't die, not ever, really, not really die, because. None of this can come to pass. Not in my life.

The Court of the Broken Knife was crowded, one might imagine. If one could bear to go there.

* * *

They got the Emperor dressed and ready. A black shirt crusted with black embroidery and black gems so heavily he could barely move his arms. Black leggings the same, black jacket, black boots. Around his head the yellow band of cloth that marked his status, shining even in the sunshine, lit like mage glass from within. In the dark, it glowed with its own light as bright as a candle. No one knew how it was made, or where. Dragon cloth, cloth-of-the-sun, woven light. The demon Marith Altrersyr would doubtless soon be using it to wipe his arse.

The Emperor yelled and knocked the comb away when they tried to do his hair. Managed to get a damp stain on his jacket because they somehow had to wash his face again after they'd got him dressed. Silk-velvet, treated with oil of roses, itself getting rarer every day now, the Rose Forest being years' burned: there was a permanent mark there, a blotch in the fabric's pile. Wretched boy. But, as it turned out he only had two jackets that fitted, he'd have to meet the King of Death as he was.

Dion, Orhan thought proudly, never made a fuss about having his hair combed or his face washed.

They got the boy loaded into his palanquin, an absurd thing of onyx and dragon bone and more black velvet carried on the shoulders of twelve bearers in black robes and hoods sewn all over with white seed pearls, their bodies strangely humped and twisted, two lumps like horns, surely, rising beneath the cap of their hoods. 'It's too hot,' the Emperor moaned as they got him into it. 'Ugly. Too hot.' Bowls of incense burned sending up a thousand different heavy scents. The Emperor coughed loudly, started to moan that the smoke made his eyes itch.

'Look, God's knives, here.' Darath snapped his fingers and got someone to give the boy a bag of sweets.

Orhan and Darath walked behind. Selim Lochaiel. Aris Ventuel the Lord of Empty Mirrors, Dweller in the House of Glass. Mannath Caltren the new young Lord of Weeping, Dweller in the House of Shadow, a gangly youth of fifteen. Ishkan Remys the Imperial Presence in the Temple. Chief Secretary Gallus. At the rear, in a litter hastily borrowed from Eloise Verneth, the High Priestess of Great Tanis the Lord of Living and Dying in a dress of pure silver and a veil of copper thread. Surrounding all of them like an honour guard, thirty servant girls of surpassing beauty all dressed in white samite, crowned in diamonds, garlanded in lilies, each one carrying a casket of wrought gold filled with precious gems.

'No guards?'

'No guards. If he wants to kill us, he will kill us. No matter how many guards we bring.'

Finally, the people of Sorlost came out of their houses to watch the procession pass through the streets. Still silent. Baffled. Dazed. The wind blew the incense smoke in people's faces and they coughed, and that was a wonderful omen. There were guards at the Gate of the Evening – oh fitting name! The sun is setting on our empire, it is the evening of our lives and the lives of all who long only to dwell in peace, the shadows fall long behind us, the light fades, the light fades . . . We could have chosen the Gates of Dust, I suppose, would that not have been yet more fitting? But some things cannot be borne no matter how fitting they might seem – forty guards at the gate, a good proportion of the soldiers of the Asekemlene Emperor of the Sekemleth Empire, they wore gold breastplates and gold helmets and they carried long spears of sweetwood gilded in gold. The Emperor's palanquin stopped, the velvet curtains moved, the pretty boy's face looked out at them grave and steady.

The gates opened, and the procession moved on. The day was very hot, even for the desert, the wind that had blown the incense smoke and made the crowds choke had dropped. Though they said the demon had a weather hand, whatever that meant, so perhaps he had brought the heat and the wind and now he brought the calm dead air.

Walk on and walk on through the sand through the burial ground where a thousand years of the city's dead lie unmourned and unremembered, until we reach the figure standing there before us, a tiny thing still in the distance, but we cannot look away from him, he draws us nearer, trembling, broken, sick with fear, desire for our death beating sensual in our hearts. I see him, I feel him, the tension before a storm breaks, two lovers coming together walking together up the stairs to the bedroom. It would be undignified to seize Darath's hand, Orhan thought.

And there he is.

He was alone. Orhan had not expected that. Serried ranks of soldiers, fully armed, their eyes hidden beneath their helmets, blood already glittering around their parted lips. The woman who claimed to be the High Priestess Thalia, weighed down in jewels – he liked giving his wife jewels, everyone agreed, all the stories had repeated it, hence the caskets and caskets of gems, God's knives, Orhan thought with a panic, what if that wasn't true, or she'd died, there were some confused stories about her, what if they'd brought out caskets and caskets of jewels for her and he was upset, angry, if she had died and he was left looking at piles of woman's jewels . . . Stop it. Calm. God's knives, Orhan thought. Try to stay calm.

They came a little closer. He stood there, quite alone, waiting for them. Like the Emperor he was dressed all in black, his skin looked very white against it. The wind picked up again, blowing sand in Orhan's face. It carried his stink with it. He reeked like a corpse. Fishy, bloody, sweet. He reeked like Orhan's father had smelled dying of fever, lying in his own bloody excrement. Like the city had when the deeping fever was at its height and bodies lay abandoned in the streets. The wind blew and it wasn't sand that was blowing in his face, Orhan realized. Dried blood was flaking off the demon's cloak, blowing around him.

They came closer. The beautiful white face stared at them. He was exquisitely beautiful, pale and fragile like the lilies the girls wore. Thoughtful grey eyes. A tired look to him.

They came closer still. He had too many shadows around him. There was darkness around him, you couldn't quite see it but it was there like the blindness that comes in bright bright light. He moved his head slightly, tilting his head to one side and a little up. His hair rippled prettily in the breeze. A slight smile on his full red lips. Look at him another way and he was a pile of rotting bodies, one of the towers of carrion his men were said to build. He had died that night in the palace, he had been rotting here in the desert for years.

They knelt down at his feet, Orhan, Darath, Aris, Den, Ishkan, Gallus. Right down flat on their faces, arses in the air, eyes pressed into the hot bloody dust. Breathing in the dust and the blood that flaked off him, taking his disease into themselves. He was wearing a sword, of course, his famous sword Joy, Orhan could feel it see it smell it taste it hanging near him. Pus and semen dripping off its blade.

The litter bearers came forward. The twelve Imperial bearers shuffling their strange awkward gait. Hobbled men. Cloven hooves stumbling in the sand. Nothing, just sand and dust beneath their pearl-encrusted robes. The Emperor's litter came to rest, you could hear the awkward sound of the boy clambering out in his stiff clothes; Orhan tried to look without raising his head to see the Asekemlene Emperor place his immortal foot on the sand of the desert, hesitate, prostrate himself at his enemy's feet. The little figure of the High Priestess Sissaleena followed. Her veil made a noise like paper tearing as she knelt.

'We bring you a gift,' the Emperor said in Pernish. Four hours, that morning, getting him to repeat it over and over until it sounded half-intelligible. 'My Lord King Ansikander . . . Ansik . . . Ansikand . . . We bring you a gift.'

A rustling, as the women came forward, piled the gold caskets at his feet. There was a pause, and then a soft voice said in perfect Literan, 'Thank you.' A further pause, and then he said, 'And . . . the women as well?'

The Emperor was trying to work out what to say. Being five. Oh, God's knives. They should have thought of this. The sound of feet shifting on the sand. 'If . . . if you like . . .' the Emperor said, 'if you want them . . .'

'My men would, I should think,' the soft voice said.

'You can have them, then,' the Emperor said, puzzled.

'Thank you,' the soft voice said again.

'I am begging you to,' the Emperor said haltingly in Pernish. 'Spare. My people.'

The soft voice said, 'You can speak to me in your own language. I have studied Literan since I was younger than you are.'

'Please don't hurt us,' the Emperor said in Literan in a kind of squeal. 'Please. Please. They say you will kill everyone in the city, they say you will kill me, take all my things, pull my palace down, please don't hurt us, look, look, I've given you the women, and the jewels, look, you can have this coat I'm wearing, if you want it.'

'I don't want your coat,' the soft voice said.

'Please!' A boy's sob. The rustle of cloth. A shriek. 'You can have it. But I can't get if off.'

'Here, then, let me help you. What stiff buttons. There.'

'So will you leave us alone now? Please? They said you would, if I asked, if I begged you. They taught me to say it in Pernish, to please you.' He tried the phrase again, getting hopelessly jumbled now: *'Beg you people gifts'.*

The soft voice said, 'You want to come to terms with me? With my army?'

'"Terms"?' Even the Literan word, the boy did not know.

Orhan got up on his knees. Felt Darath gasp and flinch beside him, have to restrain himself from pulling Orhan back down on his belly in the dirt. He himself felt sick, the ground spinning under him as he raised his head. 'Any terms, My Lord King *Ansikanderakesis Amrakane* Lord of the World. Any terms you wish.'

The demon's beautiful face turned to him. The soft grey eyes opened wide, like moth's wings. A single curl of red-black hair slipped forward over the left eye. The demon raised a hand that was scarred and deformed to push it away. The demon said, 'I recognize you.'

The Emperor cowering on his throne. A bright figure, sword

raised, bloodied from head to toe. *'I'll kill you now, then.'* A boy's face, falling backwards in a shower of coloured glass. A boy's eyes meeting Orhan's eyes a moment, before he fell. Marking each other in that moment as two murderous things. Orhan vomited yellow bile into the sand. The Emperor cried out, 'Lord Emmereth!'

He will kill me now, for that. But to Orhan's confusion the demon flushed red and lowered his eyes away.

'I . . .' His throat was burned. He choked on fear vomit, his chest felt tight like it was crushed. 'I was in the Emperor's throne room, My Lord *Ansikanderakesis Amrakane* Lord of the World. That night.'

'Yes.' The grey eyes narrowed. 'Take the women and the gifts back to your city. I will send you a list of my demands. I will give you a day, to comply with them. Go.' The demon bent down, gave the Emperor back his coat. 'One of the buttons has come loose,' the soft voice said. 'You will need to get it sewn back on.'

'He's offering terms! He's offering terms! Dance! Sing!' Darath grabbing Orhan's hands like a child, hugging Selim, hugging the child Emperor, even hugging Gallus. 'Terms! Terms!' The city was dancing and singing, every wine shop open offering free food and free wine, merchants handing out their wares for free in the streets. This madness, that they had survived another hour. They danced and sang like men who had won a great victory. And perhaps, in their own understanding of the word, they had. 'Terms! Terms! Whatever they are. Whatever he wants! Every last coin in the city, every last trinket, every last grain of gold! The Emperor's head on a gold plate! Terms!'

At dusk, of course, of course, a messenger rode up to the Gate of the Evening. The gates cannot be opened. The gates are sealed and sealed from dusk to dawn. It is the law, the word of the God. We do not know, Orhan thought, if the gates can be opened once the sun has sunk below the horizon, they were not raised by mortal hands, who knows what enchantments were wrought within them?

The Gate of the Evening was heaved back open. A great crash as the gates fell back. Every soldier in Sorlost lined up in the square beyond. Each carried a torch, besides their weapons, to light up the dusk, pretend it was not twilight. *Seserenthelae*. Night comes.

A very ordinary woman, riding a very ordinary horse. She had pretty curling brown hair, a fresh young-looking face. She did not speak. Rode out of the darkness. Dropped a curled scroll of parchment at Darath's feet. Turned her horse and rode away. The soldiers stood waiting uneasily. People waiting helpless for someone to give the order to close the gate. Gallus reached down and retrieved the letter. Handed it to Darath. They had agreed to take it back to the palace, open it there, alone, not let the people of the city see. It might yet be something they could manage. Darath opened it. Read it. Handed it wordlessly to Orhan. Gave the order to close the gates.

Flawless, perfect Literan, elegant turn of phrase worthy of a poet, every inflection correct, the symbols neat and well-shaped. Very carefully written – though one might note that the secretary's hand had a slight shake to it. The Emperor's head and the head of the High Priestess, one in five of every man, woman and child in the city, every soldier in the Imperial Army, every inhabitant of the Great Temple, the Great Temple itself to be torn down. If they did these things by dawn, they would be spared for ten days.

'He has an army of six thousand soldiers. He was defeated in the mountains. Turain held out against him, is standing proud and untouched. We can hold him. We need only to close the gates.'

'This is the city that defied Amrath. Unconquered. Unconquerable.'

'I would rather die tomorrow, than live for ten days knowing the cost.' A nervous twitch of the head. 'But . . .'

'In ten days,' said Darath, very slowly, looking at Orhan as he spoke, 'in ten days we might be able to . . . do something.'

'They will all die anyway. Longer, slower deaths, even, perhaps.'

Orhan thought: they expect me to tell them to do this. They

are waiting for me to give the order. That is what they think of me. And then it shocked him, that he might have hoped they would think otherwise.

Darath said like a child, 'Wouldn't we? Orhan?'

They were all waiting for him to give the order. Orhan licked dry lips. Opened his mouth to speak.

Chapter Forty-Four

Marith Altrersyr Who Is Amrath Returned to Us, the King of Ruin, the King of Death, the Lord of the World
The camp of the Army of Amrath

Dawn. He had not slept, eager, terrified, pacing back and forth in his tent. Ryn's tent. Thalia had not slept either, sat in the sleeping chamber with her hands clasped in her lap. He had not taken drink or hatha: since penning the letter, he had not felt the need for it. Three times, he had come out of his tent, sent the order for them to saddle his horse; three times, he had told them to take the horse away when they brought it up. I will not go out there early. I will send Ryn or Kiana in my place. I must not look too eager. And then would stare at the sky, see the first false ghost light in the east, he would order them to ready his horse.

'Bury Osen's head,' Thalia said to him as he paced. 'Please.'

He ignored her.

'Dawn is coming,' she said at last. 'It's time.' And the darkness was no different, but of course she knew.

Are you coming? he wanted to ask her. Ten thousand men. Bronze walls that even Amrath did not breach. She looked at him with clear blue eyes and smiled at him.

He took Ryn Mathen and Kiana with him, and a guard of forty men. It was cold, riding in the pre-dawn in the desert. The sand was very cold.

The rising sun was in his eyes suddenly. Tearing at him. A rim of light on the horizon, like the rim of a shield, and the city black against it. The sun must be reflected brilliant on his face.

If they've done as I asked, yes, I'll bury Osen's head. There's a bird there, look; if I see another, they'll have done as I asked and I'll bury Osen's head. Osen's wife might want to mourn him. I'll send him back to lie next to Carin, perhaps. Or Tiothlyn. Or the midden where they buried my last child.

The city was there right before him. The sun had risen. The gates were closed. There was nothing outside the city. No messenger. No pile of waiting dead. The smell of cold metal. A stretch of pale sand, delft grass in bloom before the heat of the day withered its flowers. Two crows, pecking at the sand where beetles crawled over a pile of dried horse dung.

They hadn't done it.

He felt an obscure sense of victory.

Ten thousand men. Get them drawn up. Get them ready. The city will stand against us. So we will do as we like to them. They are worthier adversaries than we had realized, it seems, they are not as craven as we had thought, they understand the bright value of life. Idiots, he thought. Ten more days, some of them could have had. Ten more days of being alive. Ten more wonderful brilliant days of pain and grief and hate and feeling hurting weeping blood-soaked life. What would I have done, in their place? He thought: I don't know.

Ten thousand men drew up in lines before the bronze walls. Shadows gathered overhead. This is absurd. They cannot do a thing to harm us. We cannot do a thing to harm them. The walls were a barrier as vast as a mountain, as unbridgeable as a raging sea. They smelled cold, like a well-polished sword; as the day wore on they smelled hot like a forge and the air above them shimmered with rising heat. The gold and silver and marble domes and towers of the city behind them, like a city made of clouds in a child's bored daydreams. The eye saw tiny people at the windows, resting their arms on the froth of elegantly carved balconies, smoothing down their fine robes with jewel-encrusted hands, sipping wine from porcelain goblets, observing with baffled interest. What could they do, these invaders, prise the gates open with the point of a sarriss? Ride and ride their pretty horses round and round the circuit of the walls?

There were three women left alive from the last village they'd looted. Marith had them bound hand and foot and dragged by three horses round and round the circuit of the walls. No response. He imagined the people inside sipping their wine and wrinkling their noses, asking a servant to play the lyre until the screaming had died away. When the women's bodies were mostly coming apart he had them untied, stuck them up on stakes at the edge of his camp visible to the city beyond. Every carrion bird for the next hundred miles turned up shrieking and fighting over the remains. It got so noisy over the camp that he had a party of soldiers fight the birds off, cut the bodies down and bury them. Two soldiers ended up too badly wounded to fight.

They could have opened the gates, he thought. To stop it.

It got to noon. The sun overhead, blazing. Not a cloud in the blue-gold sky. The walls shimmered in the heat, seemed to sweat like flesh. The army stood and stank of sweat, tramping their feet, their knees and their shoulders aching, the long ash-wood shafts of their sarriss trembling from holding them so long, sweat coursing down inside their helmets blinding them. The horses were lathered and gasping, eyes wide and white, foam at their mouths and even blood.

The walls seemed to ripple in the heat. They looked like a great curtain of fire surrounding the city, an encircling ring of flame.

'Marith—' Kiana began, wiping sweat from her face. A jangle of horses' hooves: Thalia rode up beside him. White horse white gown white flowers, her face bronze dark her hair wild midnight black. Soothing. Her arms were bare, showing her scars. In her left hand she carried a knife.

'Marith,' Thalia said. She looked like a may tree in first blossom. Her eyes went huge and blue, looking down at the city before her. 'Marith. I . . . We . . . We could . . .' She took his hand, clutched it tightly. 'We don't have to . . . We could . . . I could . . .' She closed her eyes. 'Do it, then,' she said. 'Destroy it.'

Closed his own eyes. Opened them. Rode his horse forward down towards the great bronze walls of the city of Sorlost. No man knew who had built them. Perhaps, indeed, they had not been built at all. He stopped near to the Gate of the Evening, sealed and blank. Behind it, people must be waiting, soldiers of the Empire, guards in gold armour like the ones he had killed over and over, guards in black armour with blue flame racing down their sword blades. They must be afraid. They must be laughing at him, also, he thought. Ten thousand men in his mighty army! And here he sat, one man alone, at a gate raised by the gods before the world was born.

'*Hekykamena*,' he said quietly to the vast bronze walls before him. *Break*. And then he said, '*Tiamrekt*.'

Burn.

Did they not look like a ring of flame?

Like bronze in a crucible. Goldwork held in the jeweller's forge. And once, long ago, he had seen a master glassblower who had come to the court at Malth Elelane to show his wonders, glass cups, glass bangles, a glass figurine in the shape of a swan. He had blown a great bubble of glass for show, in the feasting hall, red glass, as delicate as a soap bubble, as wide as a man's arms could reach, the glass had been so hot, the craftsman's face had run with sweat. The man had played a game, a trick to amuse them, it had been summer and he had conjured up a cloud of yellow butterflies that had come dancing around the shining glass bubble, thinking it a flower, been burned to nothing; not even the ash was left, when they alighted on its beautiful lustrous surface.

* * *

Like breathing on a mirror. Breathe out and there's steam on the mirror. Your own face obscured. Funny thing for a little boy to do.

Liquid bronze. Flowing.

Even the men of his own army began to scream.

Chapter Forty-Five

Orhan Emmereth, adviser to the Emperor's Nithque, who once believed himself to be a man of wisdom
Sorlost

'He's melting the fucking walls! He's melting them! He's melting them! Melting them!' Until Orhan slapped Gallus's face, to make him shut up. The way he sometimes dreamed of slapping Dion.

'Great Tanis. Great Tanis. Great Tanis. Great Tanis.' Aris Ventuel the Lord of Empty Mirrors. His voice going on and on. 'What is he? What is he? Great Tanis. Mercy.'

'Do it. Give them everything. One in two of the people of the city. My wife's head on a plate. Do it. Do it. Anything. Everyone in Sorlost. Make him stop.' Selim Lochaiel. Whispering screaming whispering screaming rocking banging his head.

Orhan thought: he won't stop now. We all know that.

Everywhere, people were running. At the Maskers' Gate and the Gate of Laughing, people were trying to tear the gates open with their bare hands. Kill those around you, pile up their bodies before the walls, trample over them to escape. The frenzy devouring them. Remember people eager to kill their own children, when the plague came. Here are people casting all they love aside, trampling down husbands, wives, children, parents, in their desperation

409

to escape. The claustrophobia of dying. There is no way out. There is no way out. People fucking in the streets, uncaring, brother and sister, old lovers both long married, a man raping his young son. We do not care now for anything. Some small acts of kindness, a woman striking the man over and over, her companion dragging away the child, and a voice shouts to them, 'Why? Why? What difference will it make?' A girl carries her brother back away home, while their parents fight to die crushed in the mob against the sealed gate. A wine shop pours out bread and meat and wine for the beggars, so that they might die having had something good to eat. Two men meet and embrace and forgive some great terrible unforgivable deed each once did.

The Maskers' Gate cannot be opened. It is smeared with blood from trying. Fingers raw to the bone. Do not the people of Ae-Beyond-the-Waters have a story, somewhere, about a ship of death that will come sailing out of the north all made out of dead men's fingernails? Crowds begin to run screaming to where a single man sits on a white horse outside the walls and the walls are melting, flowing, mad with fear they hurl themselves into the flames.

'Open the gates,' Darath was screaming to Orhan. To someone. 'Let them out.'

Give the order. Orhan's mouth opening. But he cannot speak. It's all too late. In the Court of the Broken Knife they are raising up their godstones, laying out offerings, cutting each other's throats. Drinking themselves into a stupor. Roaring up the paean song to their god. In the Great Temple they are kneeling, praying, the Hymn to the Rising Sun stutters from dry throats. But had I agreed to his terms, Orhan thought, it would have been the same.

Orhan said, 'Get our soldiers drawn up. The palace guard. Anyone who can fight. Darath, are you coming?'

Gallus said, 'This is madness. You can't fight this.' All the wisdom of his profession as a bureaucrat.

'I'll come,' said Darath. Aris Ventuel. The gangly youth Mannath Caltren the Lord of Weeping.

Gallus the Chief Secretary and Selim Lochaiel did not come. 'My duty is here, with the Emperor,' Gallus said. 'Someone must be here, to die with him. How will they know how to find him again, Orhan? All the record of the time of his death will be lost. When he is reborn, how will they know who he is?'

He will die over and over, Orhan thought, in the next few days, if he truly is reborn. There will not be a baby or a pregnant woman left alive in Sorlost soon. The High Priestess will die, the Temple will be broken, there will be no one left to recognize Him. He will be reborn as a goatherder's child in the desert, grow up and live and die and be reborn in obscurity in the desert. He will be born a slave in the King of Death's kitchens, a captive toiling for the lowest of the Army of Amrath's infantrymen. Live and die in servitude again and again. I've done it, Orhan thought then. I've brought down the throne. I've ended a reign that has lasted a thousand years. What I hired the demon to do.

They had to fight their way through to the House of the East. Crowds around the palace, weeping, 'Go back to your homes,' Orhan shouted at them, 'shelter there. Please.' Bil was at the door, white and bloodless, her scars standing out from her drawn face. She looked old and dead, her face was an old woman's face with sunken lips and eyes, her teeth bared. Dion clutched at her skirts. Her arms clutched around him, the stumps of her hands digging into his chest. Janush was lurking in the shadows by the stairs, cramming the sleeve of his coat into his mouth to stop himself from breaking down in front of the boy.

'Orhan? Darath?' She said faintly, 'What is happening? No one will tell us.'

'The sky's full of fire,' Dion whispered. 'What's happening?'

'We must get armed,' Orhan said.

'I'll come,' Dion said. 'I'll help.'

'I can't do this,' said Darath.

'Yes you can.'

'God's knives, Orhan.'

The whole city smelled of hot metal now. Over the Gate of the West the sky was red and black.

'Look,' said Dion, pointing.

'I see it,' Orhan said. Not looking. I will be in it, soon, I don't want to see. I will walk into a furnace. You will look up thinking it is a fearful beautiful thing in the sky. I will die fighting a demon, Orhan thought, the King of Death who they say cannot die. It is . . . wondrous to me.

'No. Uncle Darath, look.'

Over the great central dome of the palace, shadows were gathering. Storm clouds over the sun. No – Orhan thought of washing his hands after killing a man, the blood spooling out into the water.

'What is it?' Dion asked.

Horror. That's what it is. 'I don't know,' said Orhan.

'It's a trick of the light, Dion,' said Darath. 'That's all.' The child did not believe him, not being stupid. But he had learnt things, being the heir to the House of the East, for he said nothing more about it, tried to help Orhan finish putting on his breastplate. Orhan lifted him and kissed him, and Darath kissed him too. Bil kissed them both at the doorway. She was trying not to weep, for Dion.

'Take care of her,' Orhan said to Janush the bondsman. 'When it comes. When it comes . . . kill Dion cleanly, Janush, don't let them . . . don't let them—' He could not speak what they were not to do. To say it would be to be struck dumb. One could not conceive of such things, once.

Once? Four years ago.

He thought: no, Orhan. People have always done these things. But you have not needed to know.

'Lady Emmereth and I have already agreed it,' Janush said. 'Dion, before her. Her, before me. But . . . not too soon. Let the boy play in the gardens a while.' He looked at the red and black sky, and said nothing more. Almost the last words Orhan would hear him speak. Good words, perhaps.

* * *

There were a few of them already assembled in the square facing onto the Gate of the Evening. The heat of the molten bronze was murderous. The air shimmered, one could see the heat eddies, drifts of heat as the walls fell away. One is used to heat, in the desert, the desert dwellers know the patterns in the way the heat moves and rises, can read the changes in the air as a map. *Hot dry air of the furnace, drawing out all of my waters, salt fingers sucking me dry. In her desiccation her stones drip perfume. In her desiccation I am entombed in ecstasies of rain. Curse you, and yet I will lie forever in your burning, my body wracked with the heat of your love.* The *Book of Sand.* The very image of the city in its death-throes. When one of the High Lords betrays the city, he and all his house down to the lowest slave are burned alive.

The bronze wall before them rippled. Moving. Flowing. It reminded Orhan of something he had once seen, he could not remember where, coloured silks moving in heat-breeze. It will be terrible beyond imagining, and it will be the wonder of my life. Ecstasy, to die consumed in such fire. I am the Lord of the Rising Sun, the Warden of the Eastern Marches, thought Orhan. I will die with honour at the last bathed in heat more terrible even than the desert sun. His hand linked into Darath's. Together, in fire.

The walls were falling. The air was filled with hot mist. It comes. It comes. The walls shimmered and they were a veil of golden silk, and they were not metal but fire, and through the fire the demon the King of Death came upon them. And he was as beautiful as the sun.

Chapter Forty-Six

Tobias, junior squad commander in the absurdly named 'Winged Blades' in the infantrymen under Lady Sabryya the Senior General of the Army of Amrath
Besieging Sorlost

You can't not look. You try to turn away before your eyes are burned from their sockets. No one is being harmed. But it's the most terrifying thing you've ever seen. The soldiers around are screaming. Gods know why they're screaming. He is Marith Altrersyr *Ansikanderakesis Amrakane*, we should be . . . kind of used to it, by now, and yes you say that and laugh and bloody laugh because those words don't have any meaning strung together like that, he is Marith Altrersyr *Ansikanderakesis Amrakane* destroying a lump of metal, that's all, no one's even dead yet. But you're screaming and everyone around you is screaming because it's a fucking huge thing that's been there since the world began. Some things are fixed, yeah? *As long ago as tomorrow, beneath the brazen walls of Sorlost.* They're solid fucking bronze. And he is a man, still, somehow, you tell yourself, a boy, and he is bringing them down burning fucking through them. They're just . . . gone. I mean . . . You know people are going to die here. But he's changing the fucking world here, right in front of you. So you scream and scream.

And then, when he's finished, when the walls that were raised by gods before the world was made have been evaporated into bronze steam blowing on the bloody wind, and then you're going in after him.

The walls fall away. Liquid bronze lapping in a pool on the yellow sand. In the void he has made in the walls, the boy sits his horse still, looking. His blood-clot cloak blows in the wind. His horse is crusted with drops of bronze, its body is jewelled with bronze. The air is filled with droplets of bronze, it's like a fog, it catches in your lungs, makes you gag and cough. The air is so hot you can feel your hair shrivelling. Chars your nostril hair off when you breathe in. The boy draws his sword and screams, roars a word you don't know but you recognize in the depths of your heart. He launches his horse forward through the breach. The thunder of its hooves makes the ground shake. You almost fall, because the ground shakes. You hurt from the heat. Your eyes are blinded, without the fire in the bronze walls the world is dark as night.

There are things crawling over the city, you see in the new cold dark. Then you're blind again, because fire from heaven itself has come down upon the city, burning it.

The order is given. And you're going in. The tramp of feet, you and your men, so very few of you. Through the breach in the wall where the King of Death is.

Chapter Forty-Seven

Orhan Emmereth
Sorlost

Flames.

Flames.

Flames.

Chapter Forty-Eight

Tobias, junior squad commander in the 'Winged Blades'
Besieging Sorlost

'Go. Go.'

His sword felt heavy as the whole world. They were jogging down the dead zone outside the walls. The ground beneath their feet was hot. Do you remember the beach, on the shore of the Sea of Tears, where you sat with Thalia, watched as she bathed her dainty feet? And the sand was warm, lovely to sit on, almost too hot underfoot? Gods and demons. Fuck and hells. The drums were beating. The trumpets rang. Silver fucking trumpets. Men on horses charging, some of the horses had silver bells on their harness, tinkling like little girls. The shadowbeasts were over them. They choked on liquid bronze and smoke. The horses were shrieking. They went down beneath the shadows with the horses gnashing their teeth.

'Go, lads,' Tobias said. 'Come on.' Feels like a pain in your heart, saying that. This is where you belong, yeah. Doing this. Don't give a flying fuck why or for what. 'Go. Now. Clews, you lazy fucker. Go.'

It's there. Gap in the bronze wall, the sides molten, running down like wax. Dripping on people going in through the breach, we're fucking wading through hot metal here, burning up as we go, blood cooling the ground.

'Go. Go.'

There's the breach. And there's no going back. Fire washes over the city burning their soldiers and the enemy soldiers; the boy's voice screams that word out, we all know what it means, deep in our hearts. The gap in the walls so narrow. You know what it looks like? It looks like the entrance to a slaughterhouse. Where they send the beasts in.

The cavalry in front of them went in. Their horses were already bleeding.

The infantrymen in front of them went in. Some of them were on fire. But they went in and went in.

This is fucking dream a fucking dream a fucking dream it's all Marith slumped in the wagon travelling across the desert, hatha dreams revenge fantasies.

There's a black shadow there. Once you go in, it's the end.

'Go. Clews, you lazy arse. Go.'

Through it like under a sword blade.

Flames.

Everything here is already dead. Mummified city everything dead.

Holds his sword loose in his hand doesn't need to aim it wield it. Not under Marith's spell, this isn't some blindness delusion like it was before. Honest. Not under Thalia's either, before you start on it, do many things just because for her but not this. She asked and he answered, but that's not to say it was out of anything as dumb as lust. But because, in the end, this is all any of it is. They go through the breach in the wall into a world of shadows and fire they're outnumbered a thousand to godsdamned one. His sword in his hand doesn't need him to think.

The boy screams and screams. There's shadow on the city's towers, spreading like wound-rot. They are very few people here facing them to fight. This is a death place. The killing ground after the battle has been fought, the morass of butchered flesh. This is not a battle. Everything here everything is long dead.

He swings his sword and someone is dead there. They are moving through the city and everything is waiting for them and everything is dead.

Chapter Forty-Nine

Orhan Emmereth, de facto commander of the defence of the city of Sorlost
Sorlost

Standing in the fire. He cannot turn away from it. He knows how to fight, just about. If he's dying, he can probably fight. They came pouring through the breach, above them shadows eating up the city, the sun is gone and the sky has gone out. A man died under his sword. A man was coming up at him, Orhan cried out because the man was bleeding from his eyes and his mouth, his body gleamed bronze. Covered and coated in bronze. The man's flesh was red raw. His fat melting running off him. He came at Orhan with a sword clasped in metal-coated hands, a roar came out of him breathing out blood. Orhan swung back, hands trembling. I cannot see this. Their swords clattered against each other, they were almost wounding each other, Orhan's feet were slipping in the man's blood.

The man fell back dead. Darath was there with blood on his sword and blood on his own face, his eyes round with terror. He was trying to say something, but his mouth moved without words coming out. A long low noise like Dion's baby cries. A man came at Darath. Not a man. An enemy. These are not men. An enemy came at Darath, lashing out sword blow and sword blow, one might think it cared that its comrade was dead. Darath tried to fight it, warding off the blows with his sword and his arms that were shielded by a padded coat. Orhan struck back, until suddenly there was an enemy on him also, a sword in his face all he could see or think, fighting it off. A pain, in his arm. Heat on his face as the sky itself burned the city above him. So hot his eyes stung. A gust of black smoke hit his face and the face of the enemy. Gasped and coughed fighting blinded, choking. I can't breathe. His body shaking in panic. A pain, on his face. Figures in the smoke, running. His eyes full of tears blurring them. Lash out. Cut out. The enemy's dead. Him and Darath. Running. They had had soldiers of their own here. Standing guard. Block the enemy's advance. All fled and gone. Six thousand men, the demon has in his army. This is the greatest city in the world, has never fallen, could never fall. Six thousand men could be swallowed up in the Grey Square before the Temple. Run. Flee. Hide.

Do as he asks and we will have ten days of grace, before he comes for us. Orhan thought: I would have given Dion's life for that. The streets were crawling darkness. Shadows flew overhead and the streets were filled with flame. We would have rebuilt this city in its glory. All my life, Orhan thought, all my life I dreamed of making Sorlost what it once might have been. And this is the end.

Horses, galloping through the streets. Their riders soaked through red, cutting things. Rally! Hold them! There, at a corner, a group of women with knives out, a street blade in his white silks, pressed up against white marble walls, fighting to defend something. So few of the enemy. But the enemy pushed them back, killed them. From the middle of the group a child began to wail. Orhan thought: we should have opened the gates. I should have ordered it. Remembered Darath shouting it to him. Let them run out into the desert and be hunted down slowly. Some few might get away, survive it all, live. The street before him disappeared in fire. Darath pulled him back, like pulling a man back from the edge of a great cliff. A curtain of fire. The bodies of the women and the street blade were gone as if they had never been. One might lie to comfort oneself, think that they had fled.

White light, and music. The shadows themselves flew up shrieking in fear.

A man on a white horse. Nothing more. He was riding through the street looking around him. Not fighting. His sword resting gently in his hand, his face moving looking left to right, almost quizzical. People swirling in the ruins, drifting, don't know what to do. He looks at them with weary interest. They see him. They kneel in the streets. They die.

'Orhan. Orhan.' Darath dragging him backwards. Darath knows. Sees. *You sold us to the fucking Altrersyr! What the fuck did they offer you? How can anything have been enough for that? You know what they fucking are. A thousand thousand years our enemies! Death and ruin! And you sold us to them!* You thought I was fucking him. You thought I was in love with him.

I'm so lost now I don't know any more. I hired him to kill the Emperor and the High Priestess. Did I do this? Did I want this?

The man on the white horse turned his head from left to right, looking. His eyes met Orhan's face.

'You,' he said in his soft young voice. 'Lord Emmereth.'

Darath stepped between them with his sword up.

'I offered you terms,' the soft voice said. There was confusion in it. As if he truly couldn't see why any of this should be. He rode his horse away from them into the fires. Darath dropped his sword. Clutched at Orhan.

Great creatures of shadows and darkness moved across the sky. Faceless and without limbs, maimed bodies, yet they bit and clawed at the city's buildings, they were translucent, shadow-things, reflections, yet where they touched stone broke beneath them. They swarmed together, broke apart, indistinct and formless, one and many, effluence of disease. They are despair, Orhan thought. The void in the centre of a man's heart. In the streets the soldiers of the enemy moved slowly. So few of them. Lost, overwhelmed, in the vastness of Sorlost. One breach in the wall at the Gate of the Evening, a handful of men scrambling in. In Fair Flowers, in the Gold Quarter and Yellow Birds Square, people could still be shopping, dozing, wandering undisturbed in the street deep in thought. They might look up, see the fire, see the darkness, wonder, shrug it off. They could fight, gather themselves, we are many, the enemy is so few. Take up arms. Save ourselves. Kill them all. Easily. But we do not kill them. We lie down and let ourselves be killed.

We're too weak, the way we are. One touch and we'll crumble to dust. The enemy sees us for what we are. The enemy can see no reason not to kill us. As I predicted we would and they would. But I don't understand, Orhan thought. I don't understand this. How can we be dying? How can they bring themselves to butcher us?

A man dies. A woman dies. A child dies. A man dies. A woman dies. A child dies. They are men, as we are. How can they bear this?

There is nothing but fire. Shadows devour the city down to its roots. In Fair Flowers or in Yellow Birds Square, a woman raises her head in confusion, looking wonderingly at the madness in the sky; she is like someone diseased, who does not yet know that she is sick, the world is ending for her, her death is close whispering, she steps out into the street to stare and her death is so close before her.

Six thousand enemy soldiers, and this the greatest city in Irlast. Running, dying, panic, the soldiers of the Emperor's army throw down swords that are sharp and could kill the enemy, strip off their armour that could protect them from the enemy's blades. Flabby. Weak. Fingers tearing at the gates, bodies choked against them, we can no longer open the gates to flee for the gates are choked with our own dead. We cannot remember how to open the gates. We have no mind left to save ourselves. The enemy kills us as if that is all there is.

423

Chapter Fifty

Tobias, junior squad commander in the 'Winged Blades'
Sacking Sorlost

Free as running water. Strolling through wide marble boulevards, killing people as and when. See a chap who looks like he should be dying? Stab him. He felt vast, a giant, wading through the people of Sorlost. Or they were small as animals, he was a farmer culling sheep.

Clews said, 'Over there.' Four Imperial soldiers and a handful of other random people holed up in a courtyard, managed to get a barricade up in front of them. Gods knew what they were trying to achieve. All the houses behind them were burning. A tower, rising dizzyingly high, cool blue tiles carved lintels, a shadowbeast crawling along it. Spreading and growing, flexing itself; the whole top of the tower came down in the courtyard in a roar of blue tiles and white dust.

'Come on then, lads,' Tobias ordered the squad. 'Come on. Get it done.' Butchered some people running away shrieking. Butchered a couple of people throwing themselves at his feet begging for mercy: 'King Marith! Something something something in Literan! King Marith! King—' Proper fight, briefly and enjoyably, with the Imperial soldiers, armed with long spears and shielded by barricades bristling like a thorn bush. Tobias and his squad of sword boys at a bit of a disadvantage, reachwise, refreshingly. Fight went on for more than ten heartbeats as a result. One clever chappy had a proper grasp of it, got the random people lobbing blue tiles at them. Bloody vicious things, wall tiles. You laugh, right, but a blue tile got an old bloke in the squad right in the face, blood gushing everywhere, that was him done.

'Fuckers.' Clews hacking at their spear points with his sword, yelling. Lorn, the bloke with the gold armour, beside him hacking almost got a spear point in the neck. Aura, one of the women in the squad, weaving herself through the twist of spears, cutting. Flesh wound to a spearman's arm, flesh wound to her face, the spear jerked at the pain of it, she got in and Clews got in, one man down dead. Knives and hands, the random people fighting with their hands, throwing the tiles, hammering at her. Another of the women in the squad, Senesa, killed two of them one two stab stab. Fewer and fewer of them. Spear shaft cut down to splinters. Senesa with a cut to her arm seriously taking them. Clews being a bit useless but he's trying, poor lad, all he wants is the cash for his dad's farm. The final soldier went down to Lorn's sword. People fighting on with a broken spear shaft and kitchen knives and a sword they can't use. Lorn got whacked in the cheek with the broken shaft spear, ooh, nasty, could get a splinter from that. Tobias got a wall tile in the face and it wasn't funny. Time to stop hanging around the back critically observing the squad, get it done. Went in hard at them. Two people dead. Easy. Quick. Neat. Starting to feel kind of impressed with himself. His arm feeling a bit shaky, his knee was a bugger still, but doing it. Proper beginning to get back in it.

They were all dead, all the people at the barricade. No, wait, one was down but alive, pretending, the sneaky fuck. 'Clews,' Tobias said, 'do it.'

'Do what?'

Aura pointed with her sword. 'Kill her.' The corpse whimpered and started trying to crawl away.

Clews did it smoothly. She had a pretty gold necklace on that he cut off once he'd cut her throat. 'Clean it up a bit, that's a couple of sheep for my dad, I reckon.'

'Could be, Clews, lad. Well done.' The price of gold would be plummeting, the kid'd be lucky to buy half a rat with it by dusk. Distant unknown islands in the Bitter Sea where the people lived on fish guts and they'd be turning their noses up at it by dusk tonight.

'This way, then,' Tobias said. 'Onwards.' Which meant backwards and wander around for a bit, taking down more random people, as the whole row of buildings in front of them went down in black fire in a rotting mass blocking the street. Shadows eating it. Crushing the stone to meaty shreds. Tobias went up to a block of masonry lying toppled before him, big column top, fancy carvings of seabeasts as carved by someone who'd never seen the sea. The stone looked strange. Smelled strange. Tobias touched it and it crumbled away, kind of like a clod of earth crumbling. Not into dust. Soft, yielding stuff.

A wide street, a running battle between horsemen of the Army of Amrath and Imperial soldiers, a proper lot of them, a proper battle, almost. Seemed a shame to get involved. Clews grabbed Tobias's arm and pointed. 'Look! Gods and demons, look!'

Marith, in the fighting, flushed and happy, literally just decapitated someone. The body actually did that thing where it stayed upright swaying around for a bit before it fell down. The head had ended up at Clews's feet, Tobias noticed then, which must be what had drawn the lad's attention to it.

'Hit my foot,' said Clews.

'I'm disappointed you didn't kick it back.'

A moment's darkness and a moment's blinding light. The shadows were dancing in the sky. People wailing in the streets driven mad with fear. Cowering in their houses, running out into the streets, wailing on and on, throwing themselves on the swords and the flames.

Some more brief resistance coming up ahead of them, up in the street in a pack, killing soldiers from the Army of Amrath. Twenty of them. Thirty, maybe. Not Imperial soldiers, but hard tough men. Hard faces. Armour. Swords. In the time it took his squad to get near, halt, think about it, Tobias saw two men go down from the squad of the Army of Amrath already fighting them. Four soldiers from the Army of Amrath already fighting them left now. Three. Two, maybe.

'Fucking kill them,' Lorn shouted, running at them.

Leg ached. Arm ached. Twenty-five against ten. 'Get after him,' Tobias yelled at the squad. Hack slash hack slash kick slash. Good, these boys. Properly knew how to wield a sword. Just not that good.

It was all really coming back now. Professional pride in the way he offed the next bloke at him. His squad were going through them easy. Clews took one and Senesa took one. Getting fun. Blood shit stink and his arm ached a bit and it was almost over. The guy in command of the enemy shouting something that must be Literan for 'Leg it, chaps, yeah?' Empty street full of dead men.

You really saw the difference, Tobias thought. Not having been in a fight recently, he could see it clearly, thinking about his squad and the Sorlostians they'd just been fighting. All the time spent hanging around the Army of Amrath, he'd got used to it; seeing them in action up close made him see it again. They were different, the soldiers of the Army of Amrath. Been fighting for so long, so hard, so fierce . . . It wasn't even that the people of Sorlost were mostly useless. These guys they'd been fighting, hard men, criminals and killers, he'd guess. But the men of the Army of Amrath were changed and different. As a wild beast is to something tamed.

When this is . . . over. Clews on his farm, talking with his dad, shearing sheep, bringing the harvest in. Aura bouncing a fat baby on her lap, ducking her head obedient to her husband.

'Fuckers!' Clews screamed. The blokes they'd just seen running off in panic were coming running back, more of them. Criminal gang, yeah. Obvious, from pulling a trick like that. Voice shouted in Literan: 'Paetyr's Men! No mercy! Kill them!'

'Form up!' Tobias yelled at his squad. 'Form up, hold steady. Wait.'

Thirty of them, maybe. At least. One of them had a fucking axe. Tobias stopped feeling huge and smug very quick.

They were oozing it, fighting. Brace. Keep together. Thirty men hitting them like a wave. Hack slash hack slash hack slash pray somewhere in the back of your head. The squad oozing blood and piss itself, now. Lorn in his fancy gold armour that he'd brought with him all the way from the White Isles, he went down quickly mouthing blood; the boy, the youngest one, Tobias could never remember his name which was shameful, he went down nasty, clutching his chest. Aura smiling and bloody and her face came open even through the helmet, her smile going on wide as wide across her whole face chin to ears. Fuckers. And this would be why I was never a one-in-the-lines soldier boy, Tobias thought.

Some horsemen came up, relieved them. Mauled the bastards up. A shadowbeast came down. Ripped with formless teeth and clawed formless wings.

'Get moving, lads,' Tobias shouted at the remains of the squad. 'Come on.'

Two of the blokes they'd been fighting turned out to be women. One of the blokes they'd been fighting turned out to have a pretty boy's face. Several of the horsemen dismounted, decided to take a nice little relaxing break.

'Come on, lads,' Tobias shouted to his squad. 'Give the blokes some privacy. Come on.'

Sick fuckers. Unnecessary. Dangerous, too. A couple of lads in the Free Company once started on this girl who had a pruning hook behind her back, and . . . ouch. Wince. Cross your legs. But way more trouble than it would be worth right here right now even hinting at suggesting at stopping them. 'Oi, wait your turn, mate,' a bloke shouted. 'Queue starts here, right. Where's your manners?' Senesa looked interested in watching but Tobias dragged her away.

'Come on. Keep out of the way here. More of them over there to kill.'

Chapter Fifty-One

My city. My home.

I follow the soldiers of my army in through the breach in the walls. The ground beneath us is hot and wet with metal. Setting into twisted shapes. Like someone has tipped over my jewellery box, necklaces and bracelets piled jumbled on the ground. All this, he has given me. My horse shifts and snorts, its hooves wounded by the heat. I ignore this. The men are half-ruined, and they ignore it.

Beyond there is nothing. Death. I wonder briefly where Marith is. Brychan beside me has his sword drawn, he is not happy that I have come here. Wanted me to stay safely in my tent.

'Take care, please, My Lady Queen,' he says.

'Of what?' I can only say to him.

I nudge the horse forward. Through the square beyond the Gate of the Evening, buildings rearing up blackened with smoke. Wide streets and narrow alleys. It comes to me suddenly with absurdity that I have no idea where in the city my Temple stands. I have never seen this square and these streets. This is my home and it is the most alien place in all Irlast to me. I need Marith to show me around. I only know the name of the gate itself because Marith told me it. I laugh aloud and Brychan stares at me.

'Come on,' I say to Brychan.

I look around me as we ride. High towers, fine houses with carved stonework thick and fretted. A magnolia tree is in flower, perfect, untouched, grotesque in these clouds of stinking smoke. It is familiar to me, all of this, in the strange way of a dream. I remember and I do not remember. A sheet of fire sweeps the magnolia tree away into nothing; a shadow rises, vast, the tower behind it falls with a crash. Like memories, the city is unmade and changed as I move through it. It strikes me suddenly, a thing I had never thought of: I was born here somewhere; I must have a mother and a father living somewhere here. Brothers. Sisters. I assume that they are or will be dead. I wonder what they would say if they saw me. Did they know that the High Priestess was the baby they handed over? Have they realized who I am? Marith talks so often of his family. Perhaps, I think, there is a woman here with my eyes, my skin . . .

'Which way, My Lady Queen?' Brychan asks. He looks around him nervously. The street is empty, two dead bodies are lying in the rubble in a doorway, I can hear the sound of fighting over to the left. A squad of my soldiers runs past me, disappears around a corner.

'Which way?' I also look around us. A shutter bangs upstairs in a house, I start and Brychan starts; a face appears in a window, mouth open, stares out and disappears. 'This way,' I say, nudging the horse on.

I should feel something. My Temple should ring in my mind, draw me on. I push the horse forward down the street. Brychan knows very well that I have no idea where we are going, of course he does.

'As long as it's not like it was at the Nimenest, My Lady Queen,' he says to me.

'It's bright daylight, and clear skies, and dry stone beneath our feet,' I say in reply. 'And we were safe then, weren't we?'

The street leads into a narrow courtyard, a drinking fountain in its centre. A foodshop with bread and meat scattered in a tumble of broken pottery. Someone has hung wet washing in a doorway: bright clothes flap in the smoke-wind, untouched. A man is face down in the fountain. The fighting is closer, we cross the courtyard into an alleyway, come out on a wide street where a handful of my soldiers are fighting a press of soldiers in gold armour crouched behind a barricade that blocks the street.

'We need to get away,' Brychan hisses.

'No. We stay.' I want to see it close.

'The queen!' one of my soldiers cries out. A noise from our enemy. They know me, then? Shouts and roars. The fighting redoubles, at the sight of me. Ugly dry hack of spears. I have heard so many songs describing the beauty of this moment, gleam of bronze, fury of men's hearts, killing music, sweet pleasure warmth. What all men live for. The joy of every human heart. I have never before seen anything of it so close. The words they sing – they themselves know, I assume, how absurd they are. Ugly stab of spears and swords, the dry rasp of the metal on metal, the horrible feel in my own skin when a blade cuts in. A dry feeling on my skin. They tell these lies about it, I think, watching them, because . . . I cannot say how and why they tell these lies about it without falling down laughing. Unless they are really so pitifully weak. One of my men falls backwards. He is all bloody in his belly. He will not have a quick death. One of the enemy dies, neat symmetry, to avenge him. Then another, another, another, because my men are the Army of Amrath the scourge of the world, the conquerors, the bloodletters, the plague-bringers, the despoilers of all that lives, the floodtide, the pestilence, thus our vengeance is great, thus we will win. Quickly we go onward, past the barricade, sweeping on down the street. In the houses people stare out, terrified; we ignore them, there is nothing they can do. A few ragged voices are already crying out in Literan and Pernish, 'Hail King Marith! Hail to the king!'

In the distance now I can see the dome of the Summer Palace that was hidden in the maze of streets. There are more of my soldiers here, and more of theirs. We still seem of course to be winning. The crash of the fighting flows around me. A group of enemy soldiers comes rushing toward us, Brychan has his sword on them, I turn my head away from them, I do not want to have to look at them as they die. They begin to weep with fear. I think that two of them kill themselves out of fear, before ever Brychan comes near them.

Tobias is there in the fighting. He looks happy. His face has a freshness to it I had not seen in him. Despite his armour he moves with more grace. I am glad that I thought of this for him. Does it surprise you, that I want him to be happy? I should hate him, curse him, for what he did to me. Oh, do not mistake me, I did hate him, certainly I have cursed him. But I think, with what I have, that I should be able to find it in myself to feel pity for him.

He sees me. Pretends he hasn't. I hear him roar at his men to redouble their fighting, or words to that effect. His sword is fast and fine in his hand, he holds his shoulders proud. His men follow him.

'Ride on,' I say to Brychan. He is looking better now also, having seen how safe I am.

The street opens into a wide square. I have never seen it, but I know it. The Court of the Fountain.

It is disappointing, compared to the poems and the pictures. A large square, handsome buildings around it, the fountain itself smaller than I had thought. Marith talks a great deal about this place: in his dreams, the fountain runs red first with blood and then with wine to welcome him. It is made of white marble, curls of stone, clots of stone like a tree in blossom; the water it sends up is clear as diamond, it is made to resemble a great waterfall. Which makes me laugh, for not one person in fifty who lives in Sorlost can have seen a waterfall.

Ah, my love, her hair, her slender feet as she dances,
Her eyes that look anywhere but at my face.
She moves like the waters of the fountain,
Rushes, falls,

I take her in my arms but I cannot hold her.

Marith liked to recite those lines to me, before I pointed out to him what they might be about.

The water of the fountain is tinted pink already, if not yet deep red. A woman's body is being pushed under and under by the weight of the water. Her hair bobs up and down. She didn't manage to escape, poor thing.

'They'll have to give it a good clean out, first,' says Brychan.

I should know where the Temple is, from here. This is the heart of my city, I should know. I have seen pictures . . . the Summer Palace is very near here. It is absurd I do not know.

This is . . . not my city. This place means nothing to me. The realization surprises me, then I am surprised I had to realize it.

'Thalia!'

Marith rides into the Court of the Fountain. Ryn Mathen and Kiana follow him, all three of them slick with blood. Marith is as covered in blood as my dead child. New born. He takes off his helmet, his skin beneath is clean of the blood so that his eyes look huge, his hair is soaked through with sweat. 'I'm so glad we came on you here,' he says happily. 'We can go up to the palace together, take it together.' He, too, has at last forgotten any fear for me. 'You should be there.'

'Not the palace, Marith. Not yet.'

He frowns. 'Why not?'

'The Temple, Marith.' Still I look about me, hoping I will suddenly know the way. 'First we must go there. That is what we need to set ourselves against, to conquer Sorlost.'

He says, 'I thought you wouldn't want to go there.' He laughs uneasily. 'I was about to send Ryn and Kiana to secure it for me.'

Ryn starts so much his horse bucks under him.

'I want to go there,' I say. The Great Chamber. The Small Chamber. The garden where they buried them. Only when it is done will I be able to go to the palace.

I remember him begging me to stay when he killed his mother and his brother. All night he sat in the hall where he had done it, with his sword in his hand. He sat in their blood, with their bodies at his feet. Screamed as loudly as Tiothlyn did as he died. I lay in our bedroom, in our bed with red hangings, I could hear the sea through the window, the gulls were shrieking all night. I covered my ears but through all of it I could hear his screams. I thought of Ausa my friend in the Temple, and the way that she had screamed when I cut her hands and her eyes. His screams that night, I think, were what made me certain that I could bring myself to marry him. The way he looked at me, in perfect human grief, once he had killed them, threw back his head and screamed that I had had to see it.

'Have they surrendered yet?' I ask Marith.

'Not yet. That was where we were going. To see if anyone is left who can surrender to us.'

'The Temple,' I say again. 'That is where it must be done. The palace is nothing. We will do it together, Marith,' I say to him. 'Side by side.'

A silence. He nods at Kiana. 'Get the palace secured. The Emperor . . .' He frowns then. The Emperor is a child of five. Though no one has said it aloud in my hearing. 'Don't tell me,' he says. Kiana nods back.

His eyes grow distant. Thinking. Something has come to him. A fear. And a relief.

There are a hundred songs of the king's sack of the Summer Palace of the Asekemlene Emperor of the Sekemleth Empire of the Eternal City of Sorlost the Golden. Marith does not like to hear any of them sung.

For him, also, the Temple is the right place.

'The Temple,' he says.

'So do you know how to get there from here?' I ask him. 'Or can you find someone to take us?'

So many years I lived within the Temple walls.

It is hard, it would seem, to wash the past away.

Chapter Fifty-Two

Orhan Emmereth, the last living defender of the city
The ruins of Sorlost

All of it was gone. All of it. Orhan fell back, and fell back, and fell back.

They were outnumbered, these scraps of an army, defeated, abandoned, they ate away the city, the soldiers of the Empire in their fine gold armour fell away before them. Pestilence and plague, they called themselves. They ate their enemies' bodies like the plague, yes. The soldiers of the Empire lay down and died before them. In places the streets ran ankle-deep with blood. The walls fell ruined in fire. They were not bronze but heaped sand. The men's swords corroded in their hands. Their bodies crumbled away to nothing.

Orhan fell back and fell back, rallying the soldiers, fall back, a fighting retreat, fall back, fall back. Darath beside him wounded, sweating, his sword weak in his hand.

'You should go,' Orhan told him. 'Go home. You're hurt.'

Darath only panted and shook his head. Didn't trust himself to speak.

'Go back. Go and guard Bil and Dion.'

Hiss through clenched teeth: 'No.' There was blood and spittle around Darath's lips.

'You can barely fight.' You never could. You should never have been here.

Hiss through clenched teeth: 'Doesn't matter. Does it?'

Two more of their men died. Swords in the air near them, and they died choking on blood. The ground trembled as a building fell. In the sky before them, a shadow came down. They fell back and they fell back. In places, the streets were so clogged with corpses they could not get past.

There is a point, Orhan thought, surely, when they will be unable to lift themselves for more killing? The swords in their hands will blunt. So the swords in their minds must blunt. At the last, surely, they must grow sated with killing.

I have killed, Orhan thought. That night in the palace, fighting the sellswords he had hired, fighting Tam Rhyl's men – excitement, and fear, and fury, and then . . . Weariness. Hunger. Thirst. The need to piss and shit. And finally something like boredom. Men grow bored of sex and drink and debauchery and rolling in gold thalers. I think I might know this. Men must grow bored of death.

The enemy drove the people before them, slaughtered them, the people of Sorlost died without a sword being raised. Just fell down and died, emptied, gutted, as the enemy came through the city streets. The sky was black. All around them the walls burned, the city was ringed with metal fire. Have you ever seen metal burn? It is . . . beautiful. The enemy did not become weary, or bored, or blunted. They slaughtered as the rain beats down on the desert soil, as the river runs down to the sea.

A crash, the earth shaking. A gap in the sky, with the walls lit behind it, a gap through which the fire showed bright. Then all was blotted out by a shadow huge and faceless, rising against the damage it had done.

'The House of Flowers,' Darath said. There was blood in his eyes. 'My house.' He sagged against Orhan's arm. Another of their men died, cut open. They fell back and fell back. Fighting retreat.

To what?

Orhan said, 'Darath: go back to the House of the East. Stay with Dion. Shelter.'

Darath almost spat at him. 'No.' Darath's teeth were chattering now. He looked at Orhan like he felt anger for having been made to unclench his mouth to speak. 'No. No. No. No.' Had to make himself stop saying it. Clench his mouth back shut, clutch his sword. The words stopped but his body shook.

The air smelled suddenly of incense. Sweet and soft through the filth. Fragrant as Darath's bedroom. Orhan stared through the rubble and found himself in the Street of the Drum Makers, which led to the Court of the Broken Knife.

There was a sound coming from the Court of the Broken Knife.

A woman was standing in the street holding out her arms. Even as they watched she fell to her knees, prostrated herself.

Beyond her, the square was filled with candles. Sacrifice offerings: milk, wine, meat, gold coins, animal blood. The statue was garlanded with so many flowers it was hidden beneath them. The broken knife in its hand jutted downwards, and the broken blade was sharp enough to kill. Its pointless burden raised to the sky. Orhan could not see its face.

The square was filled with people to overflowing. Kneeling, pressing each other for space. Begging the statue, imploring: look, behold, witness us here welcoming you, worshipping you, surrendering to you, spare us. Spare us! Praise him! Bodies jostling together for space, struggling, packed tight – yet there was no fighting, no arguing, the people gathered there tried to make room for each other, pressed up close and meek, very quickly the newcomers would become small and huddled, fit themselves into the crowd, in turn make way.

Some there were already injured. Orhan saw many of his soldiers there, still armed.

No one wept.

A flash of red fire caught on the roof of one of the buildings lining the square. Very quickly spread. The kneeling faces were cast in red from the fire. The flowers garlanding the statue bloomed red.

Enemy horsemen rode into the square from the Street of Water. They stopped, a line of them five abreast in the shelter of the street. The crowds spilled right down to the horses' hooves. The horsemen looked huge, compared to the people huddled beneath them. Sitting, kneeling, and the horsemen on their tall horses looked down at them.

A moan, from the square, and a cry of welcome.

The horsemen rode forward.

The statue watched; Orhan and Darath watched.

The people in the square flowed beneath horses' hooves. There was no other word for what happened there. The horses rode through them not like through men but as if they were crossing a stream. Children playing and splashing in a rain-flooded street. The people in the square lay before them. Did not move. Surrendered themselves to them. They died without a word, or they lay injured and uncaring, waiting for another horseman to bring his horse's hooves down on them. They were smeared and trampled. Iron-clad hooves reared up and crashed down into them. A child with her head smashed open. Her mother sat beside her, holding her dead hand, waiting. A man with his chest shattered, ribs jutting. A fine roan horse reared and came down, reared and came down, ground him away as a butcher grinds meat. The horse was gore to its withers. It wore a leather head covering that made its head look like a black skull. Its rider wore a helmet that covered his eyes. His teeth showed as he smiled, white in a face that was stained with smoke and blood. Spittle dripped from his mouth, like a dog.

All this time, Orhan and Darath and their few soldiers stood watching. Cannot look but cannot look away. Cannot move to fight or to flee. How can they bear it? Orhan tried to think. Tried to imagine that the soldiers of the Army of Amrath were not men. One of them pushed back his helmet, drank from a wineskin at his hip, fumbled in a purse on his belt to find a hunk of bread.

One of the Imperial soldiers in the square was still alive, trying to get up, his golden armour had shielded him. He got half to his feet, stumbling: Orhan had the sense that he did not know who or where he was. The enemy soldier eating bread gestured, lightly, still chewing with his mouth a little open. Another of them rode at the man, killed him. The first enemy soldier passed him the wineskin.

We have to get away, Orhan thought then. Brilliant flash of revelation: they'll come at us next and kill us! We're standing here, rooted here watching this impossible unreal thing, they'll ride over here to us, kill us. He dragged at Darath's arm, Darath too was paralysed with it, and the handful of soldiers beside them. The horsemen gazed over to them, uninterested. Had a piss, enjoyed a brief break.

Hide and get away and hide and hide and pray.

They began to run.

Chapter Fifty-Three

Tobias, acting senior squad commander in the 'Winged Blades'
Sacking Sorlost

Woooooo!!!!!!
  Kill!!!!!!!
  Kill!!!!!!!!

What he's been doing since he was a young man trying to find a way to scratch a living. The village dyer died and the village that depended on him to dye died with him. A joke that never got stale, for all he'd borrowed it from someone else. Weave cheap cloth for a pittance, remembering the good days when the merchants would sigh with pleasure over the cloth they wove. Or go away to do something else. Tobias went away to learn to kill people. Discovered he was good at it. Just like the weaving: if you've got a skill, be a crime to waste it.

Yeah, he feels guilt. I mean . . . obviously. What have this lot ever done to deserve any of this? Been born at the wrong time. Lived in the wrong part of the world. Been cruelly oppressed and ill-treated by a government that really hacked the wrong people off. He's fighting for a really bloody rubbish cause that he'd sooner drink literal goat's piss than profess to believing in, notice he's not shouting 'Hail King Marith' like the poor deluded fuckers he's leading on, but that's true professionalism for you, isn't it? He's good at this stuff. Too good to waste himself not doing it. Four years wandering around a wasteland of corpses doing nothing, telling himself he's not complicit in it, like that matters to anyone except himself.

It probably matters to the kid he's just disembowelled, to be fair to her. Girl might have . . . hidden in the pile of bleeding limbs that was her family and next-door neighbours, pretending to be dead . . . if he'd not swallowed any moral qualms he might have about doing this. Her mum might have had time to kill her peacefully before this particular squad of soldiers in the Army of Amrath got to them. Or, to really paint a good contrast here, her street might have been left completely untouched. Plenty of streets in Sorlost left completely untouched, her bad luck Tobias made a spur-of-the-moment decision to take his men down this one. A different squad commander might have gone left at the last corner, left her alone to grow up a healthy happy loyal subject of Marith Altrersyr King Ruin King of Death.

Look, you, another squad commander might have raped her and passed her on to his whole squad. He's a professional, yeah? We've already established that he doesn't do things like that. Can hardly stop a war, can he? One bloke, like. He did try. You know he did. Pissed out four years of his life on it. Small things, doing what he can, achievable targets: kid of six isn't gang-raped, dies fairly quickly. Be grateful.

Fairly quickly. Could have been quicker, yeah, maybe, okay, okay, yes, having your guts cut out maybe isn't the cleanest quickest nicest death. But this is war, right? They're all working at pace here . . . things happen like that, when you're pressed. Also, he's pretty certain Clews accidentally stepped on her head and finished her off, so it's not like he left her alive with her guts cut out, is it?

Look you. All these soldiers, these men women he's definitely seen soldiers that are definitely technically children in a strictly biological/temporal sense, all of them here from all over the world fighting like rabid beasts – they've got to live. Got to survive and earn money and eat. They love their family and their friends, they look up at the sky and appreciate the sunset, cry their eyes out when someone they care about dies, they're loyal to those around them, they like to do well at what they're employed to do, same as anyone does.

He killed someone that might well have been the kid's dad, and went on. They stopped for a breather in a bit, very nice little wine shop that reminded him . . . he'd been in a very bad mood about something? No . . . couldn't remember what it reminded him of. Meat and bread and wine and very good brandy. Weird coloured tiles all over the floor for playing some game nobody could for the life of them work out what. The lady innkeep and a random old bloke were lying dead on the tiles, for some reason the old bloke was wearing a woman's coat.

They started off again to kill people, if there was anyone left in the city to kill. Sorlost, it was pretty bloody obvious, had been taken good and hard.

Clews was beaming from ear to ear, cause he'd found a handful of gold coins on the floor of the wine shop and was sure he'd made enough to buy his dad's farm now.

Chapter Fifty-Four

Orhan Emmereth
The ruins of Sorlost

Running. Fleeing. Throws down his sword. Just run away and hide and pray. The city is ringed with fire. The sky is filled with shadows that bare their claws and their teeth. Dusk will fall in a few brief hours. He cannot think what it will be like here, when the dusk comes.

Home, he thinks. Back to my son. Die holding Darath's hand, looking at my son. This whole world we had is gone.

Chapter Fifty-Five

Marith Altrersyr, Conqueror of the World, whose deeds now exceed even those of his ancestor the first Amrath
His city of Sorlost

They made a street woman walk before the horses, show them the way. The Great Temple of Lord Tanis being one of the few places in Sorlost he had been careful to avoid going anywhere near. Although it seemed to him he might lead them to a firewine den instead. He tried to remember how much he'd paid the last time. Little enough he could have bought more of it, if he'd been left there, he could remember that. Really really nearly managed to drink himself to death.

The streets were almost empty now. Bodies, and ruined buildings; at the high pinnacles of the city's towers his shadowbeasts ate the hearts of those who had fled up and up. In the corners, the dark places, the best and worst of his men crouched and . . . did things. The air was getting thick with flies. Every fly in the desert, drawn back to Sorlost. Crows and carrion eaters. Pethe birds, larks, darting swallows, feasting on the flies that feasted on the dead. Hawks, to feast on the song birds. Jackals. Wild dogs. The creatures of the desert would glut themselves. The people of the desert, those who had not fought in his army, were picking their way forward, wide-eyed, to marvel and to feast. They would never have seen as many people in all their lives, some of them, as they would see here now dead.

He tried to see if he could recognize any of the streets. The Court of the Fountain he had known – but then he had known that anyway, before, from paintings and poems. The Four Corners, on the Street of the South. They'd got lost trying to find it, he remembered. *'Bloody hopeless, all of you.'* They'd got into a fight. Those pretty women who ran it, who'd smiled and flirted with him. And the armourer's shop, he thought. The feel of his hand closing around a sword hilt. The jeweller's shop, Landra, shouting, gold and gems scattered at her feet. Like the floor after the children Ti and Marith had taken their golden city, thrown their mother's jewels about. I can't remember where it was, what it looked like, thank the gods. But I should like to visit the Court of the Broken Knife again, he thought.

The city bowed down before him. Knelt, cowered, laid itself out for him. Like a lover lying back, waiting. No. Ha. Too kind to him. Like a beaten dog. He had read more about this city than any other place in all the world. All his life, he had dreamed of seeing it.

He tried to think to himself: there's Immish, a great and powerful country, very large; I can sack their cities, burn the Immish Forest, turn the waters of the river Immlane black with poisoned filth; they have great armies they will raise against me, strong well-fed men and swift horses, fine armour made by skilled ironsmiths. He had sworn once, hadn't he, to kill every living soul in Skerneheh and Reneneth? And there were still a few other places yet unconquered. Turain was shrieking out for his vengeance. Every stone, every roof tile, every bone in every child's body, the maggots crawling on the dead . . . Build my great monument to my glory on the southern shores of the Sea of Tears, where nobody will see it because nobody goes there: King of All Irlast! And Alleen Durith, he thought. Treacherous bastard. What I'll do to him. I'll need to sack Malth Tyrenae all over again. It was lucky, he thought, that

I lost my damned empire, I can indeed go round and round and conquer it all again.

There was the wine shop he had had a drink in before he killed Emit. Wasn't it? No, not the same place. That place had been bigger, brighter, cleaner, much nicer. He glanced over at Thalia, who sat very straight in the saddle, her eyes flicking around the street, staring. She had seen him studying the wine shop, was studying it too, curious, trying to understand something. She saw his attention move to her, blinked and looked back at him.

'What?'

They both laughed at nothing, shrugged. It all felt very strange.

'I sat there for a while,' she said. 'In the doorway there. I think. I remember the flowers growing by the door. The place was closed up. I didn't know what it was. I'd never seen a wine shop. Then a woman came and turned me off.'

Marith thought: we've both been kicked out of tavern doorways! Oh, I'm glad I know that.

Marith thought: you'd never seen a wine shop? Well, no, I suppose you wouldn't have . . . Gods.

'We're almost there,' Thalia said.

The woman guiding them led them left, then right. The troop of soldiers who followed them looked edgy; Thalia's guardsman Tal was muttering that their guide was betraying them, leading them into a trap. Narrow streets, stringing out the soldiers, even in Morr Town they would almost be classed as alleyways. Very few bodies here. Very little evidence of fighting. Because my men were afraid to come here, Marith thought.

'We're almost there,' Thalia said again.

They turned suddenly into a wide street paved in white marble. The buildings lining it were very grand, white marble like the flagstones, gilded and painted, some of them looked very old, the stone worn translucent as fingernails by a city's lifetime of weather and washing. Carved flowers, carved faces, blurred away with age. Down the centre of the street there was a long bed of yellow lilies. They were in bloom, every flower open, the petals heavy and huge.

446

Like thick strips of yellow skin. They looked too large for their stems, swollen up by something.

'The Street of Flowers,' Thalia said. 'It must be.'

They passed a pair of vast black gates in a high black wall, all carved into flowers, closed and surely sealed up forever, a gate into another world forever closed. The last time he came here, Marith thought, he would have been frightened of what might lie behind them. Black flames rose behind them now, and the hungry beating of his shadowbeasts' wings. A woman's voice briefly screamed. Like the walls of the city, the black walls shivered and hissed and began to burn as he rode past them.

'The House of Flowers,' Thalia said. 'From the *Song of the Red Year.*' She said, 'I hadn't really thought . . . it's a real place.' She said slowly, 'All of it, everything I read and was told about my city . . . it's a real place.'

Thus the Temple was just before them now. Behind the black fire where the house burned, Marith could see the towers and domes of the Summer Palace. Behind that, a wall of fire surrounded the city, red flames leapt from the bronze. The central dome of the palace sweated gold tears.

Could taste blood and raw alcohol in his mouth. Thought he was going to be sick or faint. Felt himself falling. Gritted teeth, half-crawling, bent under a weight. A man's face staring at him: the Yellow Emperor, the Asekemlene Emperor of the Sekemleth Empire of Sorlost, eternally reborn. In the man's face there was sorrow and pain at what he was doing. At what he was. Pity, almost. 'I'll kill you, then,' he had whispered. His words were red in the red filth. But he could . . . he could still have walked away.

Thank you, Thalia, he thought, for not wanting to go to the palace.

They rode on and rode on, this was a long street, the horses seemed to be going slowly. The lilies were beginning to wither, now, as they rode past them. Petals curling up, turning black.

'We must be almost there,' Marith said to the woman guiding them.

'Yes,' she said.

'You did not go there?' Thalia asked. 'When you were here before? Just to see it?'

'No.' What would have happened, Marith thought suddenly, if it had been Tobias's squad who had been sent to the Temple that night to kill her? It had never occurred to him before, that Skie might have sent him. But it might so easily have been.

Is there a god there? he thought. Does it – he – feel that I am coming for him, his enemy?

'The God is there,' said Thalia. She pushed her horse closer to his, reached out, brushed his hand. 'He will not harm you.'

The Street of Flowers opened out into a square. There before them was the Temple.

It was a square of black stone. That was all. Black steps leading up to a narrow closed door. A black box in which Thalia had lived the first twenty years of her life. He felt sickened, looking at it, thinking that. A charnel house, he thought. The waste of her life.

The square before it was filled with fighting. A seething mass of his men and enemy, struggling together, tearing bitter limbs. As Thalia had told him, this was the place he must destroy. The centre of Sorlost. Thalia had pulled her horse to a standstill, was staring at the Temple. Her right hand went to her stomach, then to her left arm where her skin was scarred and marked. 'After each sacrifice,' she had said to him long long ago, 'the High Priestess must cut herself, mingle her blood with the victim's blood.' He had already known. A little thing everyone knew about the cruelty of the death god of Sorlost and its child-killer priestess.

'That's what it looks like,' she said quietly. 'The Great Temple.'

The fighting swarmed around it. Soldiers of the Army of Amrath; enemy soldiers in gold armour and in black armour; the common people of Sorlost in silk and jewels and tatters, armed with kitchen knives. The last stand of the Sekemleth Empire here beneath the barren Temple walls. Marith drew his sword, cried out to his soldiers to rally to him. 'Stay here, at the edge of the square,' he said to Thalia. 'Take care of Brychan,' he almost said to her.

He waded into the fighting and took them apart beneath his sword. Endless numbers of them, dying. The last defenders of the city, they must be, howling out their last defiance, believing that their god could still save them. Your god kills children, he thought, your god wanted my love to kill for him, to shed her own blood. These poisonous insults you fling at me. Cut them down uncaring, they were not living beings to be thought about. The Grey Square is running with slaughter, the black stain on the flagstones was their blood that had been spilled here so deeply it had sunk down into stone from when the world began. The flagstones were scored and scorched by the strokes of his sword as he killed. His army drew back, watching, awed, as he alone killed everyone, everything. A river in spate, a flood channel in the desert surging in storm rain, the winds and the waves Ranene had called for him tearing themselves apart taking the world apart losing himself grinding the world into pain and ruin and nothing nothing beyond. The Grey Square was emptied of living. The flagstones were shattered, the bodies uncountable, rendered down to nothing, everything that had been in this place he wiped off the face of the world as if it had never been.

He was himself nothing. A sword, an act of butchery. Murderous revenge. But he felt her there watching, sitting on a white horse with diamonds at her throat and in her hair, dressed all in silver, she sat with wide cool eyes seeing these her people die. She had never before seen this place from the outside.

It ended. Everything everyone there was dead. It faded. He came back a little way into himself. He was tired. Aching. His horse moved slowly through the clogged flesh and blood. He rode back to where Thalia was waiting. Brychan beside her had seen him fight endless battles, Brychan's face was death-white, Brychan's whole body shook.

His soldiers knelt in wonder. Reminded again of what he was. He hoped very much that some of them had returned from Alleen

Durith's turncoat army. Remind them exactly what they'd almost set themselves against.

'Shall we go in, then?' Marith said to Thalia. He dismounted, she slid down from her horse beside him. Lifted her skirts to stop them trailing in the muck, had to walk carefully wading across the square.

'I fasted and sacrificed to keep these people alive,' Thalia said. 'Life for the living, death for those who need to die.'

'They made you kill children.' His voice sounded more savage than he'd meant.

'Not often.' She pointed. 'There's a child there.' They stepped carefully over the fallen body, arms thrown up to shield its face.

'And the things beyond either kept back,' Thalia said.

Marith laughed.

Wished he hadn't laughed.

Six steps, up to the door of the Temple. Black granite? Black marble? Worn down uneven by a city's lifetime of pious feet. Pockmarked, dimples in the stone like the dimples carved into some of the oldest of the godstones back home on Seneth. In winter sometimes village women would make offerings of beer and honey and human piss there. Ward off the winter cold. On the top step a flaw in the stone ran across the threshold, a white crack in the black stone. The door at the top of the steps was closed. It was made of dark wood, also very old, uncarved, crude. It was in shadow, after the bright light of the square; Marith had to squint to look at it. The wood had a rough loose grain to it. It reminded him of an old man's coarse-pored skin.

Thalia walked up the steps lightly and quickly. 'The door should be open,' she said. This should be the most momentous thing for her, coming back here. On the top step, before the door itself, she stopped; he thought that she had realized that. She said slowly, 'It is not locked. It should not be locked. You open it,' she said. Marith reached out, pushed.

Some trick of the afternoon light, a shadowbeast flitting over the square, a flicker of flames where a gilded mansion burned: a mark appeared very clear on the door, a long jagged slash in the wood. It is well-known, Marith thought, that there is a crack like claw-marks in the door of the Great Temple of the Golden City of Sorlost. The door opened, there was a darkness before them. A second closed door of darkness.

'It's a short corridor,' Thalia said. And then she paused, and said, 'Wait.' She bit her lip, the way she did sometimes when she was nervous.

Her light filled the corridor. Soft white light. Waking up in the morning in the middle of summer, long after the sun has risen, the day already warm.

They stood on the threshold of a short corridor. Plain black stone. Water-stained in places, cobwebs thick with dust. The same worn and pitted stone floor. Thalia let out a breath. It felt like nothing, like it should feel like so much more, as they walked down it.

And the chamber at the end . . .

There were a thousand people crammed into the Great Chamber. The priestesses moved among them in their silver and lapis masks. The place was so filled with candles. The walls were polished bronze, mirror-smooth, and their faces were reflected back and back. Thalia was bright as the candle flame. Marith saw himself shapeless, one of his shadowbeasts, with the red blaze of his blood-clot cloak. The priestesses themselves were skull-faces, turning to look at him. Grey desert rainclouds, his victims' smiling skulls.

Don't try to frighten me, god of child-killing. You have more blood on your hands than I do. My soldiers, Marith thought, kill for me willingly. Are rewarded for doing it. I pay them, god of child-killing. I pay them, and I give them pride in themselves, and I mourn them when they are dead. Look at them, god of child-killing. They will take all the wealth piled up here, and they will spend it, use it, do things. Been poor their whole lives and now they're rich as bloody kings.

'I want thirty men, with me,' Marith called back to the soldiers milling behind them. 'Then close the door, let no one out or in.'

He left it to his men to do it this time. He stood with Thalia, their backs resting against a warm bronze wall. Think how many swords and spear points one could get from the bronze here. Some of the people tried to beg his mercy, supplicate themselves to him. Some of them even tried to hurl themselves murderously at him. Two of the priestesses did, one of them a fat old woman with wrinkled hands like chicken legs. She came at him crying out in Literan, so fast and savage Marith could not understand her, threw herself at him.

'Ninia,' Thalia said softly. She bent, removed the mask from the dead woman's face. 'I hated her.' She looked around. 'I wonder if Samnel is here somewhere. Or Helase.'

'What was she saying?' Marith asked Thalia. Looking at the body in its grey robe, he realized why she had chosen to wear a silver dress.

She shook her head. 'Nothing.'

'It wasn't nothing.' There was a flush like shame in Thalia's face.

'She was reciting a verse from the *Hymn to the Rising Sun*,' Thalia said. '"*Look at the sun.*" That's what she said.' She tossed the priestess's silver mask away and a soldier grabbed it up. 'She hated me,' Thalia said.

The soldiers were spilling out across the Temple, disappearing down corridors to the sound of screams. It was almost done. 'Come on,' Thalia said. They approached one of the altars together. Divided off from the rest by a bar of iron, what Marith guessed must be the High Altar, where Thalia had knelt before the sacrifice. The candles crowning it had been overturned and extinguished. A single red glass lamp was still alight.

Thalia looked at it. Her hands went to her stomach. Her hands went to her throat.

'Great Tanis,' she said. 'Lord of Living and Dying.'

The lamp went out.

Chapter Fifty-Six

My Temple, I used to call it.

The body lying nearest to the High Altar is that of a woman. I will remember that forever until I die. A woman in a dress as brilliant as peacock feathers, her hair is black her skin is brown. The look on her face is peaceful. As though she were merely asleep.

My Temple.

'*You make things live. Keep the balance. You bring life to the living, and death to those who need to die. Which is not something anyone can say about many members of my family.*'

'*So that the living remain living, so that the dead may die. A good life and a good dying. And the things beyond either kept back.*'

'*Because of you, Thalia.*'

Chapter Fifty-Seven

Marith Altrersyr the Ansikanderakesis Amrakane, *the chosen of the Chosen of the God Great Tanis the Lord of Living and Dying, once hired to kill the Asekemlene Emperor of Sorlost*
The Great Temple of the God Great Tanis, Sorlost

There was a curtain behind the altar. Almost hidden behind its bulk. Dark cloth, metallic thread long tarnished away to black. Thalia stepped over the iron bar that ran around the High Altar, slipped past the altar, put her hand out.

'Thalia!' A great fear rose up in Marith. He ran forward to join her, his sword in his hand. This is not a good place.

'Cut it down,' Thalia said to him. Her eyes were huge and very deep blue.

A chattering of sound, from behind them. Marith whirled around. Laughed. On one of the altars a jewelled birdcage was still standing, somehow untouched in the shambles. Inside the cage was a tamas bird. It was old, its scarlet plumage faded to grey around its head.

'*Temene elenaneikth*,' the bird chattered. Which meant in Itheralik: '*Joy to you.*'

'It doesn't know what it's saying,' Thalia said. 'It recites what it is told, without understanding it.' She grasped the curtain. 'Cut it down.'

A yell. A soldier of the Army of Amrath ran out from a hidden doorway, dragging a woman in a grey robe. Long black hair fell loose down her back. So like Thalia's hair. There was a spreading patch of red on the robe, between her thighs.

Her arms ended in bandaged stumps. She had no hands. She shrieked in Literan, 'Spare me. Spare me. Great Tanis. Please. Please.'

'Ausa!' Thalia screamed.

The woman's head jerked up.

She had no eyes.

'Ausa,' Thalia said.

'My Lady Queen?' The soldier dragging the woman shoved the wretched thing towards them. He was too frightened to look at them. 'Do you . . . do you want her? My Lady Queen? I thought she was another woman from the Temple, that's all. I'm sorry, My Lady Queen, gods' truth, I thought she was, but if she's your friend, if you know her . . .'

'Please,' the woman moaned.

Thalia said, not looking at either of them, 'I don't want her, no.'

The soldier, confused, dragged the woman off.

Thalia turned back to the curtained doorway. 'Cut it down,' she said again. 'Please.' Marith's sword blade moved, almost without him thinking. Dust and fragments of tarnished metal thread. More cobwebs. The cloth was very heavy, hard to cut. Beyond the curtain there was a small room. Its walls and its floor and its ceiling were covered in gold. The light that flashed from it was blinding. A great gust of cold air seemed to rush at Marith, the golden light driving out the cold. Felt almost as though something was running past him, pushing past him, fleeing the light.

The God Lord Tanis the Lord of Living and Dying, weak and nothing beside the King of Death. Fleeing him. He almost saw it, he was sure.

A grief in him, quickly brushed away, that he had not seen it. A cry in his mind, quickly fading, his heart filled with sorrow as at a great and futile loss. So had Thalia cried, when the child—

Don't think of it. There is nothing here, I have driven it out. Weak, cruel thing. Itself a god of child-killing. Look what they made Thalia do for it. It has gone, afraid, cowering, banished before me.

There was the altar stone black against the gold. Every man in Irlast must have seen it in his mind, the black stone and the ropes and a woman's long-fingered hands reaching down. There beside it the bundle of cloth that contained the sacrifice knife. The altar stone and the floor were crusted deep with blood. The cloth around the knife was like a healer's rag. Or like the cloths they had used – they had used – gods, don't think of it.

I will dedicate myself tomorrow,
That I might see her close,
Hear her breathing, feel her skin,
My blood mingling with her bleeding,
Dying under her hand.

He had always known. But.

Squalid. And her beauty, and her splendour, and her light . . . And this, here, this obscenity . . . this is the cost of life.

Two men squatted in the far corners, behind the altar. Naked, also crusted with blood. Thin. Their hair lank and uncut. Their eyes were closed, hands up over their faces, blinded by the light. Grunting noises. If the woman outside had no hands and no eyes, they, he knew with absolute certainty, they had no tongues. Each held in his hands a long coil of rope. Beside the altar a child was crouching. A little girl. Her body was hunched up, curled up into herself. She had thin pale curly hair, thin flabby white legs. A white blank face. Her left arm was a mass of raw wounds.

He had always known. He had. Yes. She knew what he was. He knew what she had done. He was going to vomit. Black sand crunched in his teeth. He looked at Thalia, she did not see him, she did not see the child, she was looking at the altar. The chamber was so filled with light; in the light he saw that Thalia's hair was dry, thinning, there were dry lines around her eyes, her belly sagged from carrying his children that had not lived. Her hand went to her throat, where the skin was dry and her body was too thin. She turned, very slowly, took a long gasp of breath like a man who has been drowning, or like a man who has woken from a long terrible dream. 'Marith,' she said. 'Marith.'

A woman's scream, behind them somewhere off in the body of the Temple, and a child's scream, higher-pitched. Somewhere off beyond the Temple's walls a distant crash of a building falling. The child's hand went out, stealthily, to the knife in its bundle of rags. Marith's sword moved. Her hand dropped back. Huge child's eyes stared up at him. He in turn held out his scarred left hand, his right still clasping his sword, carefully carefully helped her up. Now he thought, he could remember her also, robed and bejewelled in a silver litter, her white face staring around at a world she had never before seen. Just the same expression on her face, he was certain, that Thalia had had when he first met her, the same glorious wonderous baffled astonishment at the world. The white face stared at him now with nothing but hatred.

'What should we . . . we . . . do with her?' he asked Thalia. Kill her, his heart said. Send her somewhere to be cared for, his heart said. She is like you are, his heart said. Pity her.

A scuffle. Grunting noise, 'Uh uh uh', something horrible trying to speak. One of the slaves had the knife in his hand, holding it oddly, a blinded witless dumb lump of flesh barely living trying to understand anything here, groping in the blinded remains of its human mind, this here that is happening is a bad thing a wrong thing. 'They sat in the Small Chamber, night and day, they carried the bodies out, they had nothing beyond that, I never even thought of them as alive,' Thalia had said once to him, and she had never spoken of it again. The slave moved the knife up and down. Trying to remember himself in the living world.

Sacred, God-touched, as the High Priestess was. That knife could kill me, Marith thought. The slave – the man, he thought – the man standing there with the knife could kill me.

And Thalia knew it, and Brychan, still loyally there behind her in the doorway to the Small Chamber, terrified, and the little girl High Priestess with the same eyes as his own.

Thalia said to the other slave, the one who had not moved or tried to speak, 'Kill him.'

Could almost ask whom she meant.

The two slave men fighting. They wrestled at each other, shoving, grunting, each trying to carry a dead body's weight. They grappled together for a long moment, then with a cry the man with the knife brought it down, slicing at the other's arm. The sexual obscenity of it. Two naked groping men. The man with the knife reeled backwards, his face contorted. The other leapt on him, he had the knife now, its blade flashing, stabbing out and down. The blade bit home into the soft hollow in the throat where the pulse beats. Blood sprayed up. A man lay dead on the floor in the blood-muck; a man stood over him with the knife raised, staring, as if he suspected a trick.

The child High Priestess in her turn screamed, 'Kill them!'

The man with the knife did not move.

Distant crash of a building falling. Woman's shriek. A little girl of eight, crying. The slave man cut his own throat with the sacrifice knife.

Something's coming. Shadows. Sorrow. Death.

We can't go on, the way we are. And yes, that does mean blood.

The little girl High Priestess crumpled at his feet in a child's sobs. Thalia said, awkward, 'Find someone. To take care of her. Sissley, her name is. Sissaleena.'

A shuffling, fidgeting; a soldier in the Army of Amrath came forward, a woman, blood all over from the killing here but she took the girl's hands in her hands, led her off. Gods only knew to what.

'Take care of her,' Thalia cried out. 'She is a child. Nothing more.'

'I am the High Priestess of Great Tanis Who Rules All Things,' the child shrieked in a high thin terrified voice.

They walked out of the Temple together hand in hand. Stopped on the top of the six worn black steps. The crack in the stone ran beneath Marith's feet. The city was ringed with fire still, where the walls were burning. In the square, in the streets, his soldiers picked over the last of the dead and the dying, their arms piled high with loot. The Summer Palace, the Imperial Palace of the Asekemlene Emperor of the Sekemleth Empire of the Eternal City of Sorlost, was burning now also. Again. The people of the city, those few still living, knelt to them, kissed them embraced them showered them with gifts. Through the wreckage of the Grey Square, tiptoeing through the slaughter, a man in fine silk robes made his way towards them, stopped at the foot of the steps to prostrate himself in the city's blood. Grey Square was filled with their soldiers, rejoicing. The paean rang out, their names, shouts of 'King and Queen! Eltheia and Amrath!' Behind them, the door to the Temple slammed shut in a breath of wind. A cracking sound. The dark wood of the Temple door torn with claws.

Looked up and saw black fire. Coloured stars. Broken glass. There was a dream there once, he thought, in the glass falling. But I've done now what Amrath Himself could not do.

Chapter Fifty-Eight

Orhan
The ruins of Sorlost

It was dark before the soldiers came for them. Bil was weeping, stunned, Dion finally asleep on her lap, his hair damp with sweat, tears staining his face. They had put out every lamp and candle, dismissed any servant who had not already fled. Two had gone: a boy from the kitchens, who had taken two cook's knives with him tucked in his belt, 'You should have taken me out to fight, my Lord Emmereth,' his face said to Orhan, 'I would not have run away back here like a coward'; one of Bil's serving girls, hoping for things, dreaming of things. All the rest stayed with them. The household of the Lord of the Rising Sun, his people: they barricaded themselves into the breakfast room that opened onto the east garden, one wall a trellis of white jasmine. The beautiful furniture, the pearwood table, the chairs with their ivory backs and gilt legs, they piled against the doors as a barricade. Why that room, Orhan could not say. Some vague thought perhaps of Janush's words about Dion playing in the garden. Here they could feel the living air, see green leaves. Bil had already arranged, before Orhan and Darath returned, the order in which they would kill each other when the soldiers of the Army of Amrath came.

The soldiers had come in at the Gate of the Evening, this is the House of the East: we have a little time still, Orhan thought. Thank Great Tanis the Lord of Living and Dying that Felling Street is plain and narrow, that the gates of my house are tatty and old.

'They are as tall as giants,' one of Bil's serving girls would say to no one, 'they eat human flesh, their spears are taller than the city's walls.'

'Stop,' Janush the bondsman would say, looking at Dion sobbing in his mother's lap, his eyes blank with fear. He could understand everything, his huge child's eyes would move to the speaker's face and then to the doorway, as if they were coming now. But he had lost all power of speech. A little time would pass, one of the servants would start up again crying, running mad for the door then running back, clapping their hands over their mouth. 'They are as tall as giants and they have no mercy,' one of them would say. 'They take their enemies' heads as trophies. Build them into towers of skulls.' It grew dark: they sat in the cool green breakfast room with all the lamps and the candles extinguished, waiting. The dusk seemed to come very early, because the sky was so dark with smoke. For the first time in all the history of Sorlost, dusk came and the twilight bell did not ring.

The ferfews sang and darted among the trees of the garden. The jasmine was in bloom and smelled very strong. In the breakfast room with its wall of jasmine, the smell of smoke and blood almost did not reach. The sounds almost did not reach. The soldiers seemed to be a long time coming: 'You should be offended,' said Darath, trying to magic it all away, 'that they don't think your house worth gutting like they did mine.' Bil laughed at him in the mad way of someone grieving beyond reason: 'Even the army of the demon,' said Darath, 'must have heard that the Lord of the Rising Sun is poor. Or did you come to some arrangement with him, Orhan, when you paid him and fucked him and begged him to sack our city if only he'd let you look at his cock?' Bil laughed and laughed, Orhan laughed also. Pathetic kind of magic: if it is ridiculous, it cannot be true. Just once, the sky through the jasmine leaves flashed white and silver, a flash like lightning that left them all blinking, was that my mind or my eyes?

'The palace,' said Darath. 'The palace has been destroyed.'

It was only a little while after that that the soldiers came for them. A crash of someone hammering on the door, a crash of the door being broken down. A voice shouted in Pernish, 'Lord Emmereth! Come out!' In the dark of the breakfast room Orhan could feel the faces turning to the door, waiting.

'Lord Emmereth!' the voice shouted. 'Lord Vorley!'

'If you don't come out,' a second voice shouted, 'we will burn the house down around you.' It was hard to understand what it was saying, between the accent and the absurdity of the words.

Back to the traitor's death, thought Orhan. He felt all the faces watching him. Too frightened to make a sound, all of them; he could not speak for the sword blade was already at his throat cutting, I wonder what it feels like, really feels like, to die? He thought: hadn't we agreed to kill Dion and the women, before they came? And that too had seemed the rational thing to do. Tried to move his hand to his own sword on the floor beside him. Dion, and then Bil, and then the women. And then Darath, if he had the time for it before they came, if Darath let him do it, which he would. At the same time, stabbing each other, eyes on each other, left hand gripping left hand. Orhan thought: my blood and Darath's blood.

You have to do it now, Orhan. Before they come. You still have time. He could feel the sword. See the sword, in the darkness. All their fear lighting up the blade. He could feel them all watching him.

'Lord Emmereth! Lord Vorley! Come out!'

They won't come. If they come, they won't kill us. If they do come, which they won't, they'll leave us alone. They won't fire the house. It's full of valuable things. This cannot be. This cannot cannot be.

We still have an eternity of time, Orhan thought, before they find us here. There's still the entrance hallway, the dining room, the courtyard with the fountain . . .

They won't come. They can't be.

The silence broke: one of the servant girls let out a scream. Dion, in Bil's arms, joined her in a scream. Darath and Janush and Bil cried out together, 'Stop. Dion. Stop.' Tramp of footsteps, shoving at the doors, the doors smashed against the table and the chairs they had piled against them. The girl screamed on. Dion screamed on. Unable to bear it, wanting the soldiers to come and find them, get it over with. The peace of death. Or they screamed because they still believed that something would hear them. In the dark Orhan saw Janush's arm move. The girl's scream cut off in a raw ragged choke.

Crash against the doors. The furniture piled against them shook. Orhan took up his sword. Bil, seeing it or feeling it, cried, 'No. Please. I can't bear you to do it.' Dion in her arms fell silent, but Orhan could hear his breath rasping out.

'Lord Emmereth, Lord Vorley,' the voice shouted in Pernish. 'Surrender yourselves.'

Darath was on his feet, scrabbling at the furniture barricading the doors closed. A shriek of the gold table legs on the stone floor. Set Orhan's teeth on edge. They were blinded by torchlight. There were the soldiers of the Army of Amrath in the doorway, shoving their way in, the table legs shrieked on the stone, absurdist death song. A gilt chair tumbled to the ground and a soldier from the Army of Amrath kicked it away and swore. Glorious domestic elegance of a city's end.

Darath was standing with his sword in his hand. Darath said, 'If you touch the women and the child, we will kill you.'

One of the servant girls was already dead in a pool of blood. It spread glossily across the stone floor, trickled towards Janush's legs. Janush held the dead girl's hand in one hand, the knife he had killed her with in the other. Pointless cruelty and mercy both. Dion was crouched in Bil's lap, his eyes glassy, his hair gummed to his forehead with sweat. He looked like he was dying from fever. He croaked and whimpered, twitched in Bil's arms; she held him, stroked his forehead, he did not notice.

Orhan too got to his feet. His sword was lying so close to him. He should have done it hours ago. Why had he not done it? 'Make it quick,' Orhan said. 'Please.'

'I'll make it however I like to do it.' There were men there in expensive armour, handsome and heroic, red plumes on their helmets. But the speaker was an old man with a battered face, poorly dressed, his armour barely fitting him. His voice had the accent of Immish. That struck Orhan as somehow worse than anything, having been pleading with an Immishman so recently to help him.

'You, Lord Vorley,' the Immishman said. 'Come here.' He jerked his sword, pointing to the doorway. 'Outside. And you must be Lord Emmereth. Outside too. And you can put that sword down, Lord Vorley.'

'Make it quick,' Orhan said in Immish. 'Please.' Darath's sword clattered on the stone floor. Dion's eyes closed, his body jerked in Bil's arms at the noise.

'Now,' the Immishman said. 'Move. Or I won't make it quick for anyone.'

Orhan looked at the boy's face. Try to remember. Try. The thin silky limbs just starting to grow strong, the bones of his arms like bird's wings, the plump-thin goat kid's legs. The smell of his hair. The howls and shrieks that filled the house when they made him let them wash it, 'help, help, Mummyyyyyyyyy'.

The Immishman must have seen something in the way he looked. Said roughly, 'Your son, it is? Your wife?' Orhan nodded. 'Look, you. Look—' Pause. The Immishman said, 'Look, right, we've got orders, and we have to keep them. But . . . you come quietly, both of you, I promise you—' Pause. 'I'd say I'd let them go,' the Immishman said roughly. 'But I can't. And there's no point. But, look, I promise you—' Pause. 'Look, right, whatever happens – I bloody swear to you – I'll make it quick.'

'Orhan,' Bil cried out. Just once. Orhan walked out through the doorway and Darath walked out. They clutched hands tight together. One of the servant girls screamed, they could hear it so loudly through the doors. One of the kitchen boys screamed. The man with the red plumes marched out with them, and five soldiers of the Army of Amrath with dried blood still covering their armour and their swords.

Just like that. The doors closed behind them, and there was one more scream, and a sound that might have been Dion. It was quick, yes. Behind the door there in that pleasant room his son was dead, they were all dead.

Chapter Fifty-Nine

Outside in the streets it was a slaughterhouse. Soldiers strolled through the wide streets laughing, the city's deathlight glinting on their armour so very much like the lamp light had glinted on the jewels of women promenading in the cool night after a fine day's pleasure in Sorlost. Laughter and song and shouting from the wine shops and the brothels; in a courtyard by a drinking fountain a boy was dancing to the rhythm of handclaps; outside a tavern two men were fighting with knives and fists. Close your ears to the language, the death words: you could be walking the streets on any night in the eternal summer of the golden city of Sorlost. The sky was green now from the ring of fire around the city where the walls burned. But even that, Orhan thought, could be a wonder worker's illusion, a trick for a party. Setting the city apart from the world, ringing it with fire, hiding it with enchantments. Green sparks like fireworks; beyond the circuit of the walls liquid metal would be flowing out over the sand. The people of the desert would look on in wonder, asking each other what new marvel had come down to engulf Sorlost.

There was a column of fire, also, where the palace had stood. White, and very brilliant. The flames there were almost clear, like diamonds. Their route led them nearer: figures dancing past them, maimed by the darkness, too many arms, too many leering mouths, bonfires of corpses cast their shadows back and back. Orhan saw that the light from the palace cast no shadows, was not reflected on the men's faces or on the stone of house walls. Ragged men danced past them whirling the bodies of murdered children, held tenderly in their scarred arms. A pack of street children ran past shouting in triumph. They carried severed heads. The soldiers marched them down the Street of Flowers and they had to wade through a river of blood and tears and semen.

'Where are we going?' Darath asked. 'He's burned the palace, the stupid fool.'

The blood was coming from Grey Square. The stones there must be sodden with human blood, Orhan thought. The guilt of every man who had tried to shape the fate of a city, lapping at the kerbstones, flowing down in long glittering curves. Grey Square was carpeted in human bodies. Hacked and dismembered, crushed half to nothing, limbs and faces and human offal nuzzling together, embracing, endless ways in which human bodies could fit and not fit.

The Great Temple seemed to float above the killing. It rippled, in the green firelight, it seemed to change colour, to glint in the light. It should be black as midnight, sucking in the darkness. It crawled in the darkness like snakes. It had been covered and hung all over with raw flayed human skin.

The doorway to the Temple stood open. Laughter and music were coming from inside. The soldiers surrounding them walked on through the square without a thought. Orhan clutched Darath's hand so tightly. If we survive, Orhan thought, if we survive this, we'll never be able to touch each other, all I'll see if I touch him is this obscenity laid out here, dead hands clutching dead opened wounds, these men who do not notice it. I killed someone and then shortly after that I fucked Darath, he thought.

He walked with Darath over the carpet of bodies, treading like treading in wet sand, slippery, they had to hold each other, step over bodies thrown down, scrambling over them. Crack of bones. The hard-soft yield of flesh. Most of the bodies here were unarmed.

A cascade of blood ran down the steps of the Great Temple. White petals floated in the surface.

Dreams of beauty: cool murmur of water, the night-flowering jasmine blooms; we light the lamps, drink wine to blur our vision, whisper together in an arbour of green rose leaves. An artifice of desire I have spun here for you. Even the God might be jealous.

It is beautiful, Orhan thought.

The door stood open. The crack in the wood of the door stood out clear. The dark passageway beyond was a short dirty corridor. The soldiers led them on, splashing through the blood.

'Great Tanis,' Darath was whispering. 'Dear Lord, Great Tanis, have mercy.'

God dwells in His house of waters.

God is not here. Never was here.

There was nothing here but death, Orhan thought. Ever. Those people kneeling in worship in the Court of the Broken Knife, worshipping the demon – long ago, we should all have joined them. *Seserenthelae aus perhalish*: night comes, we survive. The most pitiful obvious delusion. Even if we sacrificed every man woman and child in the city, Orhan thought, we could have found no other end.

The Great Chamber blazed with candles. A thaler's worth of candles, he had once burned here. Like the white fire consuming the palace, the candles cast no shadows. Yet shadows moved on the walls, bared their teeth at him as he passed. The black floor was dry and clean of blood.

The High Altar had been overturned. It was broken into rubble. A stone block broken down, no different to a house being brought down to rebuild. The curtain covering the entrance to the Small Chamber was missing; despite it all, Orhan strained to see what was beyond it, felt Darath do likewise. Every child in Sorlost had thought once about dedicating themselves there.

Before the Small Chamber the High Priestess's bronze chair and the Emperor's gold chair had been set up. They were flanked by gold candlesticks, the largest and finest in the Great Chamber. The flames of the candles burned blue.

Finally he must look at the figures seated on the chairs. Tried to turn his eyes on them; his eyes slipped away, could not look.

'Lord Emmereth,' the soft voice said. He could not look. He could not but look.

He saw Dion's body, the throat cut ear to ear; Bil's body, her maimed arms thrown out towards Dion, her beautiful hair again clotted with blood. The Immishman had lied, they had both been despoiled. He could not say the true word for it in his mind. Tam Rhyl, as he tortured him, grunting, maggot-white, saw his own face as he tortured Tam. Darath cursing him. Darath ordering his own brother to poison March Verneth, and Darath's face after his brother had left. Dion playing in the east gardens, running his hands beneath the spray of the fountain there, blowing his ivory flute. All the people of the city, going about their business.

All those things he saw, in the face of the woman who sat on the bronze chair before the entrance to the Small Chamber.

It was indeed the High Priestess Thalia. He remembered her enthroned on the day of her dedication. She had grown old, since then.

Marith Altrersyr beside her looked almost a child. Very weary. Porcelain white, with the hatha scars standing out harshly. He looked as if he was dying in great pain. He was a young man with terror and horror in his eyes. He was nothing, a writhing mass of shadows without shape.

I killed every member of your household. There was no need for the soft voice to say it. *Are you satisfied?*

The High Priestess Thalia beside him raised her hand, gestured at someone behind him. The way she had once held the knife, welcoming the newly living, giving peace to the waiting dead. A stirring in the air behind them. A shifting, a sound of metal and cloth and footsteps. A terrified silent gasp of breath. Other people were coming forward. They were not under guard.

Mannath Caltren the young Lord of Tears, his hand wrapped

around Leada Verneth's arm. Aris Ventuel the Lord of Empty Mirrors, who threw the best parties in Sorlost. Celyse, her son Symdle behind her but not her husband. Selim Lochaiel the Lord of the Moon's Light was not there. Neither was old Eloise Verneth. Neither was Mannelin Aviced, Bil's father. Thank Great Tanis, Orhan thought, that Mannelin was not living to know that his daughter and his grandson were dead.

They knelt. The demon coughed, very politely. They went down flat on their faces, lower than any of them would ever have prostrated themselves for their Emperor. Orhan and Darath went down flat.

'You are prostrate before the *Ansikanderakesis Amrakane*, the King of All Irlast, the World Conqueror, the King of Death, the King of Ruin, the dragonlord, the demon kin, Amrath Returned to Us, the new god, the only man in all the history of the world to have conquered your city of Sorlost,' a voice proclaimed. Orhan's face pressed down into the floor of the Temple, seeing dark depths in the black stone. He knew the voice very well. Chief Secretary Gallus.

They lay there prostrate for a long time, before there was a rustle from the two seated figures and Gallus said, 'You may rise to your knees.'

Creak of bones, rattle of jewellery, a little puff of breath from Darath.

'You are blessed, to be left alive to prostrate yourselves,' Gallus proclaimed. Orhan squinted over at him: he was standing beside the demon's chair, his silk coat immaculate, a little smudge of blood on his left cheek. 'Thank Him,' Gallus continued. 'Thank Him for sparing you.' Perhaps, if one tried, one might find something other than blank contentment in his voice.

Celyse began it. 'Hail to the king!' in every language she could think of. No one could say she was not practised in it. Harsh vulgarity, bred over the years as their city rotted, no different from their own absurd game of an Empire and an Emperor: a boy with eyes like wound scars, a woman with grief written hard on her

470

face, trying trying to pretend to vast matchless glories, to be the wonder of the world, trying trying to pretend this was a great meaningful thing. Swap your Immish occupation for occupation by the Altrersyr demon. See how it goes. All the same in the end.

A parade of the demon's soldiers came down the Great Chamber. Still coated and dripping with blood. At their head, a young man with dark hair armed in the style of Chathe, whom Orhan guessed must be the famous Lord Mathen, and a young woman leaning heavily on crutches, who must be the equally famous Lady Sabryya. Behind them, the little figure of the Asekemlene Emperor in his black, his yellow silk crown still around his head.

Gallus seemed astonished to see the Emperor alive. A silent murmuring from the High Lords and Ladies of the Sekemleth Empire.

The child had the same fevered emptiness that Dion had had in Bil's arms. Flushed, exhausted, all reason wept out of him. 'I am begging you to,' the Emperor said haltingly in Pernish. 'Spare. My people. Begging. Gifts.' He said in Literan, 'They said, they said.'

The demon said, 'Well, then. Here we are. Shall we get it done?'

Queen Thalia shifted in her bronze chair. Orhan thought: I wonder what they have done with the High Priestess Sissaleena? Killed her, I suppose, he thought. Lord Mathen moved towards the Emperor.

'Wait.' The demon said, 'One of them should do it, I think. Lord Emmereth should do it.' He said to Orhan, 'Well, then, Lord Emmereth? What you hired me to do. Go on.' Queen Thalia sat very still now. The sleeve of her dress had fallen back, showing the scars on her arm.

Orhan got to his feet. Took a step forward, bowed his head low to the king on his throne. Lord Mathen put a sword in his hand.

This isn't real. None of this.

I'll make it quick, he thought. Lord Mathen, Lady Sabryya: perhaps they would not make it quick. The Emperor still didn't understand what was happening: 'Begging,' he kept saying in Pernish and Literan. Orhan went up to him. There, at the last, the Emperor knew and understood. Orhan saw that he knew what a terrible thing it is to die.

As the Immishman had cut Dion's throat. Felt the blade on the boy's skin. The Immishman had lied, when he said it was quick.

Orhan untied the yellow silk cloth from the boy's dead curls. Darath will hate me forever. Darath will never be able to think of me without sickness engulfing him. I don't know myself why I am doing this. A cheap shoddy palace coup, he thought. In two years or ten or twenty they'll find a boy born roughly at the right time, claim he's our rightful Emperor, people will fight and die to try to crown him. The God knows all things. The demon here will reign over us in glory, or ride off to battle and never come back, or drink himself to death in six months.

Whatever comes after, I've done it. I've brought down the throne. I've ended a reign that has lasted a thousand years. As every pathetic backroom plotter says.

He raised the thin band of yellow silk. Approached his king on the gold chair. Bowed, straightened, bound the cloth around the demon's head. Red-black curls. A boy's wide frightened eyes, pleading with him.

Orhan turned to the soldiers of the Army of Amrath, the High Lords of Sorlost, the Great High Nobles of the *Ansikanderakesis Amrakane*'s dazzling empire.

'Behold Him! Worship Him! Praise Him! The King of Death! The King of Shadows! The Lord of the World! The Conqueror of the Sekemleth Empire of the Eternal City of Sorlost!'

The decaying heart of a decayed empire. It is only fitting that I should crown him, Orhan thought.

PART SEVEN

THE WARMTH OF
HER LIGHT

Chapter Sixty

Tobias, senior squad commander in the 'Winged Blades'
The King's City of Sorlost

Had a long wallow in the steam room, a swim in the warm pool, another turn in the steam room. There was a cold plunge, which sounded tempting when you were out in the hot dust taking your turn on watch duty. A special pool lined in green tiles where the water was so salty you floated, you literally couldn't sink if you tried. The whole thing was underground, dug out of the earth, the rock walls dripped with cool water, it dripped from the ceiling and made you think of tears, natch. There were shafts cut to let in the light, overgrown with green stuff; greenish light came down in long blades. The ceiling was tiled to look like the morning sky. The walls were tiled to look like a forest. The floor was tiled to look like damp green grass.

His fingers were getting all wrinkled up. Had to go on duty soonish. Tobias towelled the worst of the sweat from his face, had another rinse off in the warm pool, a bath girl rubbed him down all over – all over – with rose oil. Lounged around for a bit, another girl brought him a cup of wine and some fruit and bread. His leg didn't hurt. His ribs didn't hurt. Even his arm where King Marith had stabbed him didn't hurt as bad.

When he'd dressed, Tobias went up and out to his barracks. His squad was billeted in a merchant's house just off the Court of Spices. It had a lovely little private garden, with an orchard of almond trees and peach trees and a fountain. The windows of the mess room looked out on it. They were sleeping two to a room, in real beds with real cushions, the frame of Clews's bed was inlaid with what was generally agreed to be real ivory. They'd diced for that bed, Clews had won. There were twenty of them now in his squad in the Blades, spread across this house and the house next to it, six servants between them to look after them, couple of wives and lovers lodged in rooms round about. Clews had a man he saw sometimes, seemed happy as Larry, had sent a box brimming over with gold back to his family on the Whites. Tobias had visited a brothel twice with some of the others. The first girl had been fair and milky and yellow-haired, the second dark bronze.

He got himself all sorted for duty. Senesa, whom he'd promoted to his second-in-command, bawled at the men to get a move on. The squad trooped out into the Court of Spices to form up. Twenty men, women and children, bright their armour, bright their faces, bright the swords they held. Sleek look to them, he thought proudly, glossy hair and faces of soldiers well-fed and well-trained. The new ones, the Sorlostians and the Immish lads that had started arriving to sign up, they had a nice dash to them; the old hands were rock solid, all of them. The Court of Spices itself had seen better days, even before the Army of Amrath had sacked it. They had to form up in neat rows around gaping holes in the paving stones and random piles of rubble and ash; from the smell, there were still some bodies under there somewhere. But the remaining buildings were pretty fine and grand, as befitted a spice market. Lots of carved flowers, gilded frescoes of forests exploding with beasts and birds. Cinnamon trees, clove trees, creeping ammalene vines, fields of purple saffron. They'd found a painting of Mr Spice Merchant and Mrs Spice Merchant and their two little spice merchants on a wall in their lodgings: looked at them sometimes, all of them, trying to remember if they'd killed them in the sack.

'Right, lads,' Tobias told his squad. 'Get yourselves drawn up smart and listen.' More squads of Blades trooping in, forming up: point of pride, after a lifetime's soldiering, after everything, that his lot were first in the square formed up every time. As is always the case with soldiers, they all somehow knew his history, Tobias the bastard-hard sellsword who'd once been squad commander to the king.

'Right, lads. You, Maran, yes, you, get that spear straight. I said straight. Gods and demons, boy.' The offender, a Sorlostian who dreamed of being a poet like his namesake [Maran: that's the bloke who nods! Dirty poet Maran something, knew it would come back to me!], the offender Maran shuffled the spear shaft. 'Right. Thank you, Maran. Right, lads. Lady Sabryya's coming to inspect us all tomorrow, right, check we're all ready and up to scratch. So we're going to show her how well we're up to scratch.' Damned sight more pleasing on the eye as a commander than old Skie, was Lady Sabryya. And damned good at her job. Tobias gestured at a fresco behind him. 'Then, if she's satisfied, which she will be, a little bird told me the Blades are going to be in the advance guard. Maun, lads. They say the air there positively smells of spices. Diamonds big as your fist lying about in the earth to be gathered up. The women go about topless. Soon as the rest of the Immish troops come in, we're marching. And us lot, the Winged Blades, we're going to be right in at the front for the kill.'

A cheer from his squad. The other squads forming up cheered with them.

They had roll call, inspection, paraded around the Court of Spices up the Street of Bones and Longing around down the Gold Quarter and Fair Flowers back through Bird Street to where they began. Lots of cheering from the six and a half surviving civilian inhabitants of Sorlost.

'Fancy a beer?' Tobias asked Clews. He'd arranged to meet Rovi and Naillil in that wine shop the Star. It was still something of a shambles (sic), a month, a whole frigging month, and the new owners still hadn't got the door fixed, but it had been the first wine shop to start selling proper Immish beer. The one with the yellow flowers over the door sold an approximation of that White Isles herby stuff. Best avoided any time of day or night. '*His throbbing spear, his throbbing blade, Whole cities lie wet at his feet, Death! Death! just bloody listen to yourselves, lads, it isn't the cities that are gagging to have something thrust into them here, I think maybe, Death!*'

'I'm meeting Carinos later,' Clews said. 'I'll come for a bit. Carinos is going to come with me, he says, when we march. Follow the army. We've talked about it.'

'That's great, Clews, lad. I'm happy for you.' Really was. They wandered on down a wide street that had been over half cleared of rubble, so the death stink here wasn't quite so bad. A wide detour to avoid the Court of the Broken Knife that stank worse than anywhere else in Irlast. Cleared and cleaned, the flagstones scoured with sulphur, but nothing could get the smell out. The statue of the king there . . . And the dead horse hung up there wasn't really adding to the atmosphere in the place. Took the long route past the House of Glass, where the insanely rich inhabitants burned incense day and night. The square outside its gates must be the most popular gathering place in Sorlost.

'You know,' Clews said, 'Carinos has got a sister. Widowed. He and I were wondering . . .'

The wine shop was crowded. Rovi was there already, had found a table at the back. Hadn't bought a drink, the miserly bugger. Tobias bought a jug of Immish Gold and a plate of candied apples. Poured out three cups.

'To the king,' Clews said, raising his cup. People said it before they fucked someone, now. People said it as they came fucking someone. Women said it as they gave birth.

'To the king,' said Rovi in his dead rasping voice.

'To the king. Yeah.' Closed his eyes to savour the taste. Best beer in the bloody world. They'd be marching on Immish soon enough, he'd reckon, go through Maun and Medana like through butter and then on up. Immish! Turain, for vengeance! Polle Island! Those little lumps of rock off the Medana coast! Ae-Beyond-the-Waters, even, maybe, and he'd finally get to see what Alxine's homeland had looked like and whether it really existed and whether they really did worship a giant man-eating squid thing. All those big trees, in the Forest of Maun, for making boats. The stars! The moon! The sun!

'You met her, then? Carinos's sister? When you say widowed . . . she got kids?'

Naillil came into the wine shop, looked around, she had this look on her face like she was hoping so desperately he was there and so on edge that he'd not have turned up. Her cheeks were flushed with excitement.

'You heard?' said Naillil. She waved away Tobias trying to pour her a drink. 'Lenae told me this morning.' Naillil bent her head closer. 'Not common knowledge outside the court yet. You have to promise you won't tell. But . . . the king's regent in Illyr, Lord Stanis—'

'Lord Stansel,' said Tobias.

'Lord Stansel, yes. Whatever he's called. There are letters from him. Here, in Sorlost. Chief Secretary Gallus had them.' Listen to her, Tobias thought. Chief Secretary Gallus! Friends with one of the queen's women, thinks she's someone herself. Where's that rough clever woman who cursed him for killing children? 'Lord Stansel was conspiring against the king,' Naillil said with a breath. 'Plotting with Lord Erith to kill the king. Remember Lord Erith? In Arunmen? A year, at least, it had been going on.'

Exchanged glances with Rovi. Had to laugh. All the boy's dear beloved friends. Anyone left in Irlast who hasn't shafted him or been shafted by him – come and line up.

'The king sent soldiers to kill Lord Stansel,' said Naillil. 'But . . .' She lowered her voice, stared at them wide-eyed. 'A messenger arrived last night. The fortress collapsed. Ethalden, the king's tower. The whole top of it collapsed, killed him.' She sat back, looked at them in triumph. 'The tower collapsed on him.

479

Lord Stansel was plotting against the king with Lord Erith, and the king's very fortress fell on him. Crushed him to dust. Not a single bone of him was left intact.'

!!!!!!

'Fuck,' said Tobias.

'Fuck,' said Clews.

'It's true,' said Naillil.

Rovi, who had fought against the king in Illyr in the ruins of the previous fortress of Ethalden, and who should have died there, gave a dead smile, coughed his dead laugh.

'"The *Ansikanderakesis Amrakane* punishes all who think to betray him",' Naillil said. 'That's what Lenae says the court's saying. The building itself knew. The monument to his glory, his triumph. The stones of it couldn't bear the guilt.' She rolled her eyes. Kind of rolled her eyes. Kind of believed it.

The building was jerry-built on a swamp of rotting bodies. Boy can't keep his tower up, fnarr fnarr, brewer's droop wink wink nudge nudge etc etc. But even then he gets all the bloody luck.

'The men the king sent never got there to do it,' said Naillil. 'It happened before the king knew anything. While the king was still in the mountains.'

Outside in the street someone started shouting something about glory and triumph and praise the king. News was obviously spreading. Several drinkers scurried out to see what was going on. Those that weren't blatantly straining themselves to listen in to Naillil.

'Shame about the fortress, though,' said Clews after a while. 'Always wanted to see that.'

'It's all right,' said Naillil. 'The king's not upset at all. He was going to rebuild Ethalden anyway, Lenae says. Remake it all in the gold from the Summer Palace dome.' Naillil said, 'They'll be a big feast day, to celebrate. Lenae says Lord Vorley is in charge of arranging it.'

Eager smile from Clews: 'The same Lord Vorley who organized the victory feast?'

* * *

480

It turned into quite a long session, as the news got out, what with everyone and his dog wanting to talk about it and have a drink to celebrate it and repeat it. Clews slopped off to meet his bloke already half-cut. Naillil was popular, seeing as she knew things. Sort of. 'My friend who attends the queen.' 'My friend, who heard it from a woman who heard it from a man who was there when the letters were shown to the king.' So in the end it was Tobias and Rovi, sitting in the back of the wine shop with an empty jug and an empty plate and four empty cups.

'I remember you,' said Rovi. 'On the battlefield, in Illyr. In the ruins of the first fortress. Amrath's fortress. The real one.'

The real one? No, I know what you mean, Rovi, man. 'I didn't fight at Ethalden, Rovi. You can't remember me.'

Rovi said in his dead voice, 'You never fought, no. I remember you there when we'd lost. You, and a woman with her face burned, and the other woman you were with, with the yellow hair. The one that wasn't really a woman at all.

'I was trying to get close to him myself,' said Rovi in his dead voice. 'I'd sworn on my parents' grave to kill him. I got close to him. In the end, right at the end, we'd lost, they were butchering us, his soldiers were drinking and celebrating, off guard. I crawled along in the ruins of Ethalden, a knife in my hands, I got really close to him. He was with his friends, they were all drunk and laughing, didn't notice me. I could feel it, his death, inside me. I got so bloody close. And when I woke up, alive, I thought . . .'

Longest speech Tobias had ever heard from Rovi. Dry gasping dead voice cracked in Rovi's throat. 'Doesn't matter,' Rovi said. 'Not now. Four years,' Rovi said, 'I've been following him. Hoping to kill him.' Rovi got up. Walked off, went out into the city night through the doorway that was still broken from the sack.

Parade the next morning, all dressed up with their armour polished to mirrors, red cloaks flapping in the dusty warm excuse for a breeze. All of them dozy and hungover, after celebrating all night that, uh, a big big tower had fallen down crushing some people to death. Lady Sabryya was understanding, didn't push them, looked like she might have been up all night celebrating herself. I should imagine, Tobias thought, that a lot of people in the court were celebrating mighty hard last night that a traitor is dead. Had it confirmed, at the end, that their lot were going to be some of the first heading off south to Medana and Maun. Everyone cheered their heads off, then marched back to their lodgings to get some kip.

'Carinos is definitely coming,' said Clews happily. 'Thinking about signing up, in fact.'

'I'm glad for you, Clews. Really I am.'

'His sister . . .'

'Never mind, lad. Don't need a woman.' Tried to leer. 'There'll be those topless girls in Maun, yeah?'

'That's almost certainly not true,' said Senesa.

'I made it up,' said Tobias. 'Obviously. Your bloke know what he'll need for a desert march, Clews? Whatever he says, tell him he's wrong and tell him to bring what I say he'll need. And we'll need to start getting ourselves packed up.'

'Wait, wait,' said Senesa. 'We're leaving before the celebration feast? Say it's not so.'

'The king doesn't exactly stint on celebration feasts, does he? There'll be another celebration feast soon, I should think. Lots of villages to sack.'

'Also your liver will thank you,' said Clews.

Thus three days later, at dawn, on the first day of the month called in Pernish *Bahak*, the month of the lilac, in Literan *Sorerethae*, the month of rest, the Winged Blades marched out of the Golden City of Sorlost, heading east into the rising sun. For many miles the ground they marched on was coated in bronze, the great bronze walls that had burned and melted at the king's command. It ran like lace over the dun and yellow desert, the yellow-grey rocks and the scrubby yellow-brown thorns. Flashed in the waking light. In places, where the land rose up in hillocks, there were clumps of ragged delft grass putting out pink flowers, islands of living things. In the hollows, the bronze was deep and smooth like forest pools. At noon they stopped for a breather in the shadow of a big red rock. There was a stream, dirty with goat shit, and some little rocks to sit on. This early out, they had clean water with them, and cold meat, and bread. Pack horses for the equipment and the tents. If you looked back, a few black jagged ruins were still visible, just, on the horizon; then they went on over the slope of a hill and the city was gone. A village with fields and fruit trees, where the people came out to stare at them as though they had never before seen armed men. They pitched their tents by a waterhole, the first night out, there were thorn trees thick with berries that Senesa said were poisonous, the noise of insects was very loud. Big green beetles that blundered into the tents with a thudding almost like raindrops, fell to the ground in a buzz of wings. All around them the campfires of the Army of Amrath shone like the proverbial stars. Above them, the real stars blazed down. The Dragon's Mouth. The White Lady. The Dog.

A good star, the Dog, Tobias thought.

'How long until we get there, you think?' Clews asked.

'Gods, I don't know. Does it matter?'

They weren't going to Maun. He'd noticed that five paces out of what had until recently been the Maskers' Gate. They were going north-east. Towards Immish. His home country.

Be nice to die on home soil. Turn on the blokes around me, all unsuspecting and innocent, raise my sword, 'Death to the invaders! Resist the murderer the right sick little bastard the King of Death!' chop chop hack stab and go down dead neat. How many years I got left in me . . . ? A good soldier's death and my bones left unburied in my native soil, gnawed on by my native dogs.

Or, on the more pessimistic side, I know my way around Alborn to loot it, know the lingo to ask people where their valuables are hidden, know some chaps in Alborn I'd be more than happy to see get whacked.

'When we get there, right, when we get there, I'm going to eat a really big big steak . . .'

'Topless women! Diamonds growing out of the ground!'

'Oh, I'm going to kill some people! Just watch me!'

'Oi, gods, watch it! Look where you're waving that.'

Senesa was bollocking one of them for not cleaning the saucepan properly. One of the new lads from Sorlost had wandered off to look up at the stars, sad look on his face like he was missing his mum. Two of them were arguing over who cheated who first in a game of dice.

'Ten to one, right, sad-sack there starts blubbing for his comfort blanket by next Lanethday.'

'Lanethday? He'll be blubbing for it by tomorrow night. And for gods' sake don't trust him to make a pot of tea. He can't boil a pot of water, that one.'

I'm sorry, Raeta, Tobias thought. Look, Raeta, Landra, if you're lucky, if you're really lucky, I'll die in the front rank in the first fight. Good quick clean man's death. What you want and I want. For the best, I know. A bloody kindness, he thought, and almost wept.

'I'll take last watch,' he told his lads. Crawled into his tent, went to sleep to the sound of them.

Chapter Sixty-One

Marith Altrersyr, Lord of the World, King of All Irlast,
Conqueror of the Sekemleth Empire, **Ansikanderakesis**
Amrakane, *Amrath Returned to Us, King Ruin, King of*
Shadows, King of Dust, King of Death
His Empire

'Pethe birds,' said Thalia. 'The brown ones.'

'Pethe. It means . . . What does it mean?'

Thalia thought. 'I don't know. That's just their name. Pethe birds.'

Marith settled his head onto her shoulder. She stiffened, very briefly. Put her arm around him, began to stroke his hair.

'I thought you knew everything about Sorlost?' said Thalia.

'Not the wildlife. That's not of much importance in war, really, is it?' He felt himself beginning to doze off. Delicious feeling of warm coming sleep tugging at him. Flowing into him. '"*In the garden, by the water, where the birds sing*" . . . I'd always imagined they were prettier. White, maybe. Or gold. I'll cancel that . . . whatever it was I had to do this afternoon. Stay here. Have a rest.'

Felt her stiffen again.

'I didn't sleep well.' Woken up in the dark, had to have a couple of cups of wine in the end before he could get back to sleep.

'The green ones, in the evening, they're ferfews?' he asked.

'Yes.'

'I knew that.' Closed his eyes, let his languor roll over him. They were sitting in the garden of the Great Temple, closed off from the city by a high black stone wall. There was only one door in and out of the garden: if he ordered it shut and guarded, they could be almost properly alone. The flowers grew very lush here, there were lilac trees and peach trees, a pool with fat gold fish. A very tranquil, peaceful place.

'It was sacred to the God Lord Tanis,' Thalia said, 'of course it is a peaceful place.'

'What?' he had asked her, when they first came out into the garden – when she first showed him the garden – the way she looked at the green grass thick and rich beneath the lilac trees. She had only shaken her head. 'I loved coming here,' she said, 'when I lived here before.' He had ordered cushions to be set out, for them to rest on in the hot afternoon in the shade of fruit trees and birds' wings, as all the poets said.

They slept at night in the bedchamber she had once slept in. The palace having been burned up in a column of white flame. It was here or Ryn Mathen's wretched tent. And I am their god now, he told himself. Fitting and right. A small, not unpleasant room, a window looking out over the gardens; he had stared wide at the sky from the window, thinking with wonder that this had been her whole world once not so long ago. They had slept in his chambers in Malth Salene, in the bed he had shared with Carin. All across Irlast, they had slept in palaces where the last man to sleep there had died at his command. It is no different, he told himself.

From a little room hidden away at the very back of the Temple they had brought out a silver box filled with squares of painted wood. It was in his treasury, beautiful, valuable, old and precious, no different from any other of his beautiful precious looted things.

'The little girls, all the other girls who were dedicated to the Temple, all of them but you, they drew the lot and they were killed?' He had arranged the lots in a long pattern, staring down at them, shuffling them. So many black and white and green and yellow. One red. He didn't know why he thought of it now. Talking about the different coloured birds, perhaps. Or looking at the green grass beneath the lilac trees.

'Yes.' Her hands had strayed over them. Almost touched. Not quite. She had drawn her hand back. 'No. If a child drew a yellow lot, she became a priestess. Like Helase, Ausa – they spent their whole lives here, lighting candles, taking offerings.'

'She must have been seventy years old, that one who . . . Seventy years old. At least. And all she did her whole life was light candles in one room?'

A strange little indrawn breath. 'I suppose so, yes.' He felt her body stiffen. He could feel her breath frozen, a kind of cold come over her in the soft garden heat.

'What's wrong?' Gods, he thought, why did I start talking about that, her past? Shall I talk again about our dead children? Tell her I know she cries over it in the night when she thinks I'm asleep and I pretend she's asleep? Ryn Mathen whispers I should put her away, he has a sister, he says suddenly, good child-bearing hips . . . King and Queen of All The World, and we can't get a child like the peasants in the fields can.

'Nothing's wrong,' Thalia said. She smiled. 'Nothing. I'm glad we came back here. I'd forgotten how beautiful this garden was. Look at the sun.'

'Hmm?'

She kissed his face, got up. 'You stay here, then, have a rest. I have things to do.'

'Yes. Yes. I have things to do too. I know.' Planning, preparing, logistics, subordinates, supply lines, his head bent pouring over maps . . . All these soldiers, all these places. Petitions and letters and messages from all over his empire. I lost a battle, stumbled alone in the barren darkness, believing myself almost dead. And my empire has gone on quite happily, unaware of it. I really should have killed every single one of them, he thought now. Remember that, when I have to go around and kill them all again. There is a petition from the people of Morr Town regarding their trading rights with Illyr, My Lord King *Ansikanderakesis Amrakane*. One of your tax collectors in Ith has absconded with six months' of taxes, My Lord King *Ansikanderakesis Amrakane*. There may be the beginnings of another outbreak of deeping fever in southern Chathe, My Lord King *Ansikanderakesis Amrakane*. Alleen Durith has crowned himself King of Irlast, he is claiming that you are dead, My Lord King *Ansikanderakesis Amrakane*. The final structure and hierarchy of the new infantry division still needs to be signed off, My Lord *Ansikanderakesis Amrakane*. You need to make a decision about what is being done with the ruins of the Summer Palace, you said you'd have it yesterday, My Lord King *Ansikanderakesis Amrakane*. You still need to sign the condolence letter to Lord Fiolt's widow, My Lord King *Ansikanderakesis Amrakane*. On and on. There's rumours, My Lord King *Ansikanderakesis Amrakane*, that Cen Elora and Immier might be threatening rebellion. We need more money for your new temple in the ruins of the Summer Palace, my Lord King *Ansikanderakesis Amrakane*. The tailor wants to know, My Lord King *Ansikanderakesis Amrakane*, if you're happy with your new cloak.

But a great wash of warm peace came over him. The green of the leaves and the blue of the sky were soft as silk sheets. 'If you'd drawn yellow,' he said sleepily towards Thalia as she went out, 'you'd have lit candles and done nothing else.'

Thalia turned back to look at him. 'And gathered flowers and sung hymns. Yes.'

He yawned, looked at the flowers. 'Probably not that bad a life.' The hidden guards on duty opened the door for her into the King's Palace as though it was magic opening it and she was gone to do her queenly things.

'They buried the sacrifice dead under the trees here,' he said aloud to the silent garden. 'She thinks I don't know.' So many of them the bones were layered deep. Piled up, all the dead bodies, running down and down, men women children all cut open, some by his wife's hand. The earth beneath the tree must be miles deep with them, bones and flesh entangled so deep into its depths. The trees grow up beautiful and perfumed, rich and green and strong. It's such a fucking obvious metaphor it hurts. Lilac smells of sex.

There was so much business to attend to. But Marith Altrersyr the World Conqueror, the new god, the only man in all the history of the world to sack the city of Sorlost, stretched out on silk cushions in the shade of a lilac tree in the gardens of his new palace and went to sleep in quiet peace.

He slept till almost evening, woke to the falling shadows blinking and confused. In the Tem – in the King's Palace, the windows were all lit. It is a shame that the mage glass in the Summer Palace was all broken when I set light to it, Marith thought.

There was a celebration of some kind again tonight in the Great Chamber. He should get himself dressed, he thought, I wonder what Thalia will wear tonight? She was looking very well, although she had had to cut her hair shorter, after the desert winds had ravaged it. Her new serving woman, this women Lenae, had found her a man who called himself a doctor, who had brought her a potion to drink. 'So now there is no danger that I will conceive again,' she said. 'It's for the best,' she said. 'We should accept it.' She had held out her arms to him last night, hot sweat scent of her, licking salt off her body, the fish-yeast-flower-birth scent of her sex. Marks on her stomach, where the skin had stretched to hold their child, silver scar-folds. I know what that reminds me of. The scars on her arm were worse, from being out in the dry heat and the desert sand and the desert sun. The celebration for the death of Yanis Stansel, that was it, what the party tonight was for. I was half-dead in the wilds, defeated, my army wiped out, and on the other side of the world my will is done, my enemies are cast down, the glory of my empire shines on. My triumph, my glory. So great I am, such a king, such a conqueror; death comes while I myself need do nothing. Her body, her eyes, her arms that clutched at him. They had fucked and fucked and fucked and she'd enjoyed it more than she had for, maybe, gods, years. *After me is only death*. Later he'd had to go and drink wine to get back to sleep.

Thus the party, later:
  'Hail to the king!'
  'Glory to the king!'
  'Triumph! Triumph to the king!'
His cloak stank and his brooch felt rough at his shoulder. The servant had scratched her finger on the pin fastening it.

The Great Lords of his empire sat in what had until recently been the Great Chamber of the Great Temple and was now the King's Hall. The floor was scored in places, if one looked closely, where they had scrubbed off the blood. Traces of slave women's fingernails: get down on your knees, scratch it off with your hands if you must. The doorway was open, through the entrance corridor lights flickered, long tables set out in the Grey Square for the soldiers of the Army of Amrath, loaded with food and drink. The lowliest soldier would eat off gold plates and drink from crystal goblets, as the beggars of Sorlost were said to do and very obviously did not. They would be coming to reface the Grey Square and the Temple in red porphyry soon. That was one of the things he should have seen to that afternoon. In the King's Hall the diners reclined on low couches of sweetwood and red samite. Each wore a crown of gold flowers, garlands of white lilies and darkest red-black roses hung around their necks. But they ate the same food off the same plates as the army, drank the same wine from the same cups.

'Glory to the king!' They would never stop cheering him. The glitter of their costume was almost too much for his eyes, the sound rang too loudly off the bronze walls. He hesitated, standing in the stairwell to go in to them, shook his head trying to clear it. Stumbled, because of shaking his head. It was a very long walk down the aptly named Great Chamber, to stand in the doorway and accept his troops' acclaim, to go back right to the end to the Small Chamber, where their couches were set, king and queen's, all made of solid gold. The Emperor's throne behind the couches, ugly gold chair, the gold all crimped where the palace had burned around it, taken thirty men to shift it. Fixed his eyes on the brimming cup waiting for him. Nod and smile, nod and smile, the lords and ladies of his empire applauding him, rustle of silk, flash of jewels, feathers, perfumes, a man with a coat embroidered in every colour of the rainbow, patterns moving in the thread, a woman with mirrors on her gown reflecting his face back at him. Smile and nod. Keep looking at them. He stumbled, caught Thalia's hand, his fingers brushed against the lace sleeve of her dress. There's Ryn Mathen, he looks tired, now Osen's dead and he's so very very important, he's still smarting after the woman Lenae turned him down with a slap on his cheek. Some Sorlostian noblewoman in red satin trying to cosy up to Ryn, red is the Altrersyr colour, she shouldn't be wearing red. Lord Vorley, who arranged all this, understandably on edge. Lord Emmereth, still looking like a walking corpse, clinging onto Lord Vorley like Lord Vorley will die too if he lets go for a moment, I shouldn't make them come to these things, either of them, it's too cruel to them both, leave them in peace. Alis Nymen: everyone else betrayed me, all of my friends, Valim, Alleen, Yanis; watch him, watch him. Secretary Gallus: chiselling little petty bureaucrat, sucks up to power whoever holds it, I hate him, doesn't everyone hate him?

Got to his couch, sank down, drank. Kiana Sabryya got to her feet. A wince of pain, quickly hidden. Sorlost was famous for its doctors – a shame no one had told his men that, as they went through the city killing everyone. Try the chap who burned Thalia's womb out, Kiana. He might help you. Or better not.

'My Lords and Ladies of the Empire of Amrath Returned to Us,' Kiana called to them. Sweet happy delighted false silence. Faces all fake joyful lit up. Another hilarious drinking game one could play was to down a cup every time anyone looked something like that.

491

'We are gathered to celebrate a triumph over the *Ansikanderakesis Amrakane*'s enemies,' Kiana said.

We are in-bloody-deed. Oh yes. Marith stood up. Knocked the table, his cup went over in a pool of green. Thought I'd finished that. 'A building collapsed. That's all. A building collapsed. How proud I am.' Thalia's hand reached for him, then dropped back. He said, 'Fuck off.' Kiana started, stared around her panicked, looking for help. Lord Vorley, glimpsed through the doorway into the Great Chamber, looked like he'd shat himself. Lord Emmereth next to him was crying with fear. 'Fuck off.'

It was so silent, almost a weight of it. Hippocras dripped off the ivory table onto the floor. Like sweat. Thalia said, very quietly, 'Marith. Stop.' He stumbled out of the Small Chamber, the bronze walls of the Great Chamber staring at him, reflecting him. All the terrified faces, drained of colour like dead men bled out. Carin's face had looked like that, all drained and shocked, all the blood run out, shocked frightened white lips. At the little door up to his bedchamber, as the door slammed behind him, he heard a woman's cracked terrified laugh.

He flung himself on the bed. She had slept here, after she had killed children for her god. *Because of you, Thalia. Because you keep life and death balanced. Those who need death dying, those who need life being born.* Five years, she'd slept here after killing them. One morning he had found a tiny smear of old blood on one of the sheets, from the arm of a High Priestess where she cut herself after the sacrifice. From Thalia's arm, perhaps. He had been too revolted to speak of it to the servants. Pretend it was a trick of the light. He ran over to the window, the night air was pleasant but in the garden beyond were all the bones of her dead. He could smell them, taste them. The leaves on the lilac trees rustled in the wind.

There was a jug of water on a table near the bedside. Poured himself a cup. There was ice in it: 'The servants bring fresh jugs of water every hour to keep the ice from melting, have you noticed?' Kiana had said in astonishment only yesterday. He crunched one in his mouth. It reminded him of crunching icicles with Ti in the winter back home.

Thalia had followed him up. She said, 'What are you doing? Marith? All those people down there, waiting—'

'I don't know.' A memory of something he had been thinking about earlier: 'I'm going out.'

'Going out?' She said after a pause, 'I'll come with you.'

'I want to go alone. No. Yes, please, come.'

She brushed her hands down her dress. Pale pink silk, almost perfectly sheer, a collar of diamonds from her throat to her breasts. Opened her mouth to say something, stopped. 'Everything will be in confusion,' Thalia said, 'down there. The Great Lords and Ladies of the Empire, scrambling to leave the palace with any dignity. Poor Lord Vorley. He worked so hard on it. Brychan will follow us, I should think. Shall I send him away?'

'No.' Marith gestured Brychan over, the man came out from the shadows guilty and relieved, his hand still resting carefully on his sword hilt.

'I want you to take us to the place they are keeping the wounded,' Marith said.

'My Lord King . . . That would not . . . Are you certain, My Lord King?'

It was at Thalia that Brychan was looking. She had flinched when he said it, but she said quickly, 'Yes.' She said, 'Bring me my cloak, Brychan. And one for the king. Put your sword away.'

A long walk, to a storehouse beside one of the lesser gates. Dark in the darkness. The smell came up the street to meet them, and a sound from inside, there were no windows and the door was barred and the sound clawed its way out of the stonework. The street around was empty, every house shattered, no lights. No one would live here, even the beggars. Rats and beetles ran in the street. And flies. Many flies. Over the roof of the sickhouse a shadowbeast curled, licking shapeless paws in its faceless mouth. Here is my house and my people and my temple, Marith thought.

'Here,' said Brychan. 'In there, My Lord King. If you're sure

493

. . . But please, My Lord King, My Lady Queen . . . Don't go in there . . .'

'Have you ever been in there?' Thalia said to him. Brychan shook his head. The door was unbolted, slid open. No one was guarding it. No one was watching it.

There stood Thalia, beautiful, in her dress that was pale silk nakedness, dripping jewels, honey and wine on her breath. The dying lay on the bare stone floor in rows like the rows of his sarriss men, writhing with fever the sweat dripping off them in salt pools, shivering clutching at the flagstones with cold, their lips blue their fingertips blue. Two men lay together, clutching each other, tight embraced and their bodies were rotting together, black meat oozing together so that one could not tell where one began and the other ended, and they had no beginning and no end now, the two of them, one circle of flesh with four mad eyes staring, staring. An arm thrashed against the floor striking it bruised and bloodied from the flagstones. Striking striking it, a drumbeat, 'It sounds like horses' hooves galloping,' Thalia whispered, 'make it stop, Marith,' she clutched at him shaking on her feet. The man had no face, he did not move except that his one arm beat against the stone floor so that it bled.

'Peace,' Marith tried to say to him. This lump of flesh. 'Peace. You were a hero of my armies.' They moved away down the ranks of dying men, a few faces turned, could almost see them, mould growing over eyes over mouths, bodies corroding away in fungal patterns into the flagstones. Shapeless lumps of flesh without arms or legs. A few of them he recognized. From Arunmen to Turain to Elarne to Sorlost they had trailed along in the carts with the baggage, hanging on beyond life and death. Through victory and defeat. There still the old woman who tended them, grey as their wounds, herself shapeless, walking among them offering water, wiping away their sweat. 'My son. Be at peace now, my son.' Her voice crooned it to nothing rambling on at nothing. Like the Temple slaves of the Small Chamber, she had forgotten anything but this place.

'Will any of them survive?' Thalia asked.

'A few of them, perhaps, My Lady Queen,' said Brychan after a time, when Marith did not speak. 'No,' Brychan said then.

The bright glory, the killing, the joy, sweet pleasure in it, the triumph, the certainty of my own immortality in that. The towers of skulls raised to my victory, the bodies of my enemies trampled into a slurry of flesh and rot. These are not real things. Not living things. These men are not real men. When Thalia was killing a child in her Temple, she didn't think it was a real child, that was really alive, and would be really dead. When I fight my battles – I don't really, deep down, I don't really think it's real people, being alive and then being dead. Because that would be absurd. Real people. Being dead. Killing them.

I open my eyes wide and I think I see it, I claim to be King of Death, knowing it all, understanding it, death is truth, all else beyond death is a lie. But it's impossible that people die.

Thalia stood and looked at them and shivered. Her silk dress was like the film over their wounds, like the cauls of her dead babies, like the fat that stretches over their innards as they spill out fragrant with their rot. Her dress is like the mould blooming on their bodies her jewels are like their crusted matted stinking pus. She writhes in ecstasy like the maggots that consume them still living. The tendrils of her hair are like gangrene. He loves her and adores her so much.

'Death to those who need to die,' Thalia whispered.

Her light rose around her. The sickhouse was filled with her light. Marith's eyes were dazzled and blind. Her light as black darkness, her body a pillar of radiant bronze. Her light alone killed them, scouring the sickhouse clean. The light faded and king and queen stood together in an empty place filled with bleached corpses, dried out, made clean.

'That was a good thing,' Thalia said. 'A reason to have come back.'

They could not look at each other, afterwards, until they were back in the Temple, drank wine together, lay silent fingers entwined listening for each to speak. Trying to fall asleep in the High Priestess's bed.

'Why did you come back, Thalia?'

She murmured half-asleep: 'I am their queen.' A pause. She said half-asleep, 'And of course I wanted to see you again, Marith.'

Chapter Sixty-Two

Another month passed. Marith drew up his war plans: ride hard at the Immish, kill them. There was definitely an outbreak of deeping fever in southern Chathe, there was definitely a rebellion in Immier, a tax collector on the White Isles had also run off with six months' worth of tax. Alleen Durith had occupied the city of Gaeth, set himself up as king there; the people of Gaeth had thrown him out again. Work on the temple on the site of the Summer Palace was running three times over budget already. The word 'pethel', as in 'pethe bird', Chief Secretary Gallus turned out to know somehow, was probably Aeish in origin, meant 'brown bird'. Marith hated his new cloak. On the third day of the month called in Literan *Janusthest*, the month of remembering, in Pernish *Ammak*, the month of the earth, the Army of Amrath gathered in Sorlost to march out.

The advance columns had left stores of grain and water, to help the main body of troops in the desert. They would be well on their way now. Must have realized by now where they were marching to. Even the most unobservant and ignorant. Marith thought: I swore I'd raze Reneneth to the ground. That gives me some faint sense of purpose to this. They saw me hungover and self-pitying, the shameless bastards. Deserve everything they get.

The columns lined up in the Grey Square – still not rebuilt in red porphyry – all the fierce old hands from before Turain; the new ones from Chathe and the desert villages who knew now the pleasures and rewards of their work; a new muster from Illyr and the White Isles, mere eager children; one in two of every surviving inhabitant of Sorlost. The people of Sorlost had seen butchery and murder, lost everything. Thus a great wisdom had come upon them. Marith and Thalia stood on the steps of the Temple to receive them, watch them file out past.

It would very soon be Sun's Height and the Feast of Amrath's Birth Day. Celebrate in the ruins of Reneneth, treat any survivors to another glimpse of Marith Altrersyr with a hangover, roast their flesh and drink their blood and grind their bones for bread. 'And we will be King and Queen of Immish by Sunreturn,' Marith said to Thalia. 'I think you'll like Alborn. It's not as grand as Sorlost, of course, but very fine in its own way, I'm told. We can celebrate Sunreturn in the tower where the Great Council meets.'

'Year's Heart, it's called,' Thalia said. Then she said, 'I will look forward to seeing it, yes.'

'Yes.'

'All cities look the same,' said Thalia, 'after we have sacked them.' A troop of sarriss men marched into the square, the great spears as tall as pine trees perfectly aligned. Acclaimed their king. Marched out towards the Maskers' Gate. A troop of Sorlostian swordsmen followed, a rabble after the old guard, but eager. Marith took a sip of iced wine. They had to have chosen the hottest day yet, to march out. The swordsmen acclaimed their king. Marched out towards the Maskers' Gate. The White Isles horsemen a little while later were at least just about worth watching. If so shockingly frighteningly young. More horsemen, more sarriss men, more swordsmen; an eternity of bronze helmets, bronze armour, every face turned to him parading past him with the same words written in their eyes. On and on and on. Red banners, curled leather crisped with gold, standards topped with human heads. Some of them wore armour of human skin now, tanned peaty-brown, soft, they said, beneath the bronze plates. If he had died in Turain, they would now be marching past another king, with the same hunger in every face.

He took Thalia's hand. 'I'm glad you came back to me. Thank you, for coming back to me.' She stiffened, and relaxed, and smiled at him.

Another troop of sarriss men filed past them. A troop of swordsmen from Immish, poor bastards, a few of them also must guess. It might be best to dispose of them quietly, out in the desert, there were a lot of them. His luck wouldn't hold forever: there must come a time when a troop of soldiers would refuse an order to kill their own kin. One might hope. Ryn Mathen came out of the Temple behind them, to tell them that everything was ready, it was time they themselves rode out. The beautiful horse Ryn had given him; and a matched one had been found for Thalia now, a gelding to his stallion but so similar it was almost comic, the great war horse and the smaller one beside it, pure white with red ribbons in their manes, gold and silver trappings, the cheekpieces, the nodding headdresses, the black-red saddle clothes, the high arched gilded hooves. Marith helped Thalia up, though she barely needed it. She made her horse rear, as he liked to do, laughed with him. At the Gate of Dust Celyse Amdelle went down on her face before them, so close Marith could have trampled her beneath his horse's hooves simply by nudging his horse forward a pace.

'Glory to you, My Lord King,' Lady Amdelle said when she was up on her knees again. Then all the honorifics. The woman must have been practising, to get them all in the right order without stumbling. There were so many of them now a man might fall asleep before he reached the end. Can you down a drink for every one of your titles, Marith? Honestly, no, even I couldn't do that. 'Conquer, be victorious, bring all the world of men beneath your rule,' Lady Amdelle finished, making a gesture of encompassing with her hands, her fingers curling smooth as polished wood.

Marith said, 'To you, Lady Amdelle, I entrust the city of Sorlost, the jewel of my empire. The lives of all who live here I entrust to you.' The first of all of the nobles of the Sekemleth Empire to do

him homage as king, so eager to do it, so bright-faced to kneel
and praise him. She'd do it well. She went down on her face again,
murmuring further pleasantries. A great shimmer of gold and
jewels, as all the other nobles of Sorlost prostrated themselves
behind her to see him off. Oh, they would be rejoicing in the city
streets tonight. He glimpsed Lord Emmereth at the back of the
crowd beside Lord Vorley, when they came up out of their protes-
tations the man was dazed with wonder that the demon was leaving
them and Lord Vorley was still alive in his arms. Lord Emmereth
was whispering something to Lord Vorley, thinking the king
couldn't see. Let us pretend I can lip read, that Lord Emmereth's
telling Lord Vorley he loves him. Two men, so close in age, so
devoted to each other: gods, Marith thought, please let it work
for them, let them be happy together. But Thalia had seen him
watching them, and he needed to get on.

In the dead place beyond the circuit of the walls he made the
horse sacrifice, stood sticky with blood as they raised the corpse
up. Beneath his feet the ground crunched with melted bronze. His
skull towers stretched away to the horizon, squatting over the
ancient burial grounds of the people of Sorlost. A great patch of
newly disturbed earth where his own dead were tumbled; the beasts
of the desert came at night, clawed down to get at the soft meat.
There, too, he had sacrificed a horse. They had not stripped some
of the bodies: he thought of men in future years coming to dig
there as the beasts did, mining the bronze and the iron, the jewellery of silver and gold.

He gazed over at the city he had conquered. Ragged people
cheered from the windows of every house. Kiana Sabryya shouted
an order, a trumpet sounded, the men began to march.

To the endless ringing of silver trumpets and the slow steady
beat of war drums, beneath their banners of human skin and
human bones and human grief, the Army of Amrath marched out
into the desert, towards Immish, taking the path that Marith had
once taken with Tobias, when he had been a man like any other,
before it had all been done and too late. Horses in the desert, grey

and blind, their hooves beating, the sand made the sky darken, blocked out the light of the sun.

'Do you regret any of it?' Thalia said that evening in their tent. Even more splendid than the last one, so glorious its fittings they needed their own wagon train to transport them. The exterior walls were dusted with crushed rubies. The sleeping chamber was lined with the skin of goats cut from the womb three days off birthing. The bed was whale bone and gold.

'Do I regret any of what?'

She sipped her wine. 'Never mind. Nothing.'

'I . . .' He thought, closed his eyes, said slowly, 'I regret . . . some things. Yes.'

They were silent a little, listening to each other's breathing. 'I should like to see the sea again,' said Thalia. 'The winter trees against the sky. I am glad I got to see Sorlost again.'

'I should like to see the White Isles again,' said Marith. 'The hills all dark with cloud shadow, the rivers running down, the silver water, the green grass. Smell the first autumn frost. And the smell the air has, the change in the light, the first morning suddenly when you know spring is coming.' The desert is so bleakly changeless, he thought.

They rolled into Reneneth grim and determined, the first charge against the town walls coinciding with the first rays of the morning sun. The sky flamed pink, the dawn was in the men's eyes, blinding, a great bank of clouds massed in the west behind them so that as the defenders of Reneneth looked out at him it must seem still to be black night over his camp. The advanced guard had got the whole thing set and ready, burned out every surrounding farm and field; the people of Reneneth were hungry, frightened, wretched – and had been years before a single soldier from the Army of Amrath appeared in view. The rotting buildings, houses sinking into the dry earth, brickwork crumbling. Thin cattle, thin-faced children. The fires they burned to bake their bread in

Reneneth were made of cattle shit. The water in the wells was greenish, stinking, gave his men the gripe. Grey worn-out eyes stared over the walls at Marith. They can't remember me, they can't, he thought, they couldn't have known who I was. A sick man stumbling in bonds behind a horse, muttering curses. He was dressed now in silk and velvet, crowned in silver, his new cloak shimmering spun bronze. I swore that Reneneth would burn, that I would kill every person that lived there, that I would kill the beasts in the fields, the rats in the walls. The pleasure of it. Killing. The most beautiful thing in the world. Go through it hacking them down, taking them to pieces, rending their lives down to fat and broken bone. Trample them. Piss and puke and dance and sing. The ram began to pound against the gates of Reneneth with the breaking morning, heaving itself thrusting in out in out, gleaming red with flayed skins. On the walls the defenders cried out in terror. Tried to let off arrows while their hands shook. Scaling ladders up against the walls, his men swarming up them. They looked like beetles climbing up in their armour. Helmets making their heads like insects. Like a dog running with fleas. Ryn Mathen, dear eager man, first up the first ladder, a knife clenched in his teeth.

The ram broke through the gates with the wood splintering. Rotten. It bulged and gave and ripped. Marith tasted meat-rot, smelled pus. The way it gave, creaking, rotten . . . Reminded him . . . His men roared with delight, pushing forward, too many almost to get through the break in the gates. Marith spurred his horse, rode in through the current of his army. The gilded hooves trampled his men's blood and the enemy's blood. On the walls above Ryn waved, cheering, a sword in each hand dripping. A man in silk robes went down on his knees in the filth before Marith, babbling: 'The town surrenders, My Lord King, the town surrenders unconditionally, if we had known, if we had known you were coming, My Lord King, My Lord King—' Marith killed him with one stroke of his sword. Rode on in. So here we go again, we must start getting bored with this soon, you'd have thought, it's getting kind of hard sometimes to know where we go from here really, don't you think? Endless repetition. Kill kill kill tediously unvaryingly unendlingly kill kill kill kill kill. There's a girl of five screaming: kill her. There's a big chap with a thing he must use for breaking up rocks, there's a boy with a meat cleaver, there's a woman with a hammer, there's a woman with a baby clutched to her breast: kill them. There's a pregnant woman, one up even from the woman with the baby, there's an old old man who's obviously blind, there's a starving curly-haired beggar child with a withered leg: kill them. Wait, look, how about a pregnant woman with a child and a crippled old grandfather trying to protect her, and his troops will torture them slowly slice them up despoil them dismember them? That too much? Oh, and there's a strong tough man dripping in the Army of Amrath's blood, laying around him with a sword, rippling muscles bulging biceps, standing wide to show his muscular firm strong thighs and arse: spare him, let him live, enlist him. He'll be grateful for it when he finds someone else's rosy-cheeked children to chop up into little bits. Thus one more town falls the same way as all the others, people die and suffer the same way they do every moment of every day everywhere we're not looking, and we go on. I hear there's a village two days' march onwards, we can gut that, then there's another town, then a village, then another village, then another town. Death and joy! Gods, it's boring by now, yes it is.

That night Marith lay with Thalia in their red tent. So great were the flames from Reneneth that the night was red, her skin was bathed red. Sweat ran down her body, outside in the dark the screams of women rang. What else can I do? Nothing. Do I regret any of it? No. Of course not. Shouts and song and bright laughter. His men were dizzy with happiness. Thalia's eyes were cold, she was stiff beneath him. She turned her face away from him, and then she clutched at him. She shut her eyes tightly as she fucked him.

'I swore I'd sack it,' he said. 'Remember?'

She said after a long time, 'Yes.' Her body smelled like miscarrying. The red light made her look like raw chopped meat. Through the leather that dripped their sweat like wounds he could just make out the words of a filthy song about him.

Chapter Sixty-Three

The village two days' march away.

The town beyond that.

Chapter Sixty-Four

The desert made a last stand north of Reneneth, reared up dry and barren before finally giving way to the Immish plain, rolling green that would be soft beneath the horses' feet. The advance guard had reached the Immish Forest, burned it. The Immish army was reported to be forming up in Alborn, marching south to engage them. A single letter was sent from the Immish Great Council: *We are ready for you, betrayer. Do not think that we are not.* Piss on them.

'Come riding with me tomorrow morning, Marith,' Thalia said that evening. There was something in her eyes. 'We'll be in the grasslands soon. It will be too late.'

Too late? 'I'm sure we'll come back to the desert once we've conquered Immish.' Round and round and round Irlast, killing.

She frowned at him. 'Please?'

'Oh, all right. If you really want.'

They gave orders to be woken before dawn. Rode out south to watch the sun come up. Kicked their horses and went fast, the horses matched neck and neck. Fast so that neither of them could think. Up over the brow of a yellow and dun hill, away from the camp where the air was clear, the ground here was stony, the stones rang and shifted under the sound of the horses' hooves as they ran. Birds had followed the army out into the desert, they

506

watched them wheel in the sky black lace fragments, listened to them sing. 'Pethe birds,' said Marith. '"Brown bird" birds. Gorging themselves on the flies that follow the men.'

Thalia said, 'The army's filth will be fertilizing the desert.'

'Really? I suppose it will.' All that pink delft grass. Meadows of it. People will come here, till the soil, grow wheat. New villages, towns, cities. In five years' time or in ten or in twenty the Army of Amrath will come back here, burn the fields burn the houses kill them. The desert sand will be black with ash. The army's filth will fertilize it.

The sun's rays caught the slope of a hill off to the south before them, lit it up golden. Heavy metallic light. The valley below it was deep shadow. The shadows there seemed to move. Feel them. Hear them. Call them.

Thalia said, 'Marith.'

They looked at the desert stretching away before them. Dismounted, turned back to look north over towards the army camp. Their tent glowed in the very centre of it. All very small and neat, like his toy soldiers and toy fortresses. Campfires burning. Tiny little flashes that might be armour. Twinkling. The Fire Star was still shining in the west. The King's Star. The great green slope of a hillside, the stone outcrops jutting up through it, clawing their way out to the light, the rain has come down making them shine like mage glass. So steep we have to go up it crawling, digging our fingers into sweet soft earth, staining our hands fresh green. She's beside me. Or Carin's beside me. Or Tiothlyn. Just the two of us, we'll scramble to the top, stand in the damp air, the world will spread itself before us, the high hills running on and on to the sea, the valleys rich in cattle and wheat. A shaft of sunlight will break through the grey sky, fall over a village in the green distance, light up the roofs of the houses where the people live in peace. Cloud shadows will run over the fields. The clouds will come down, cut off the world, we'll be alone there in the cloud mist. We'll clasp hands, swear our loyalty until death. 'Just you. Only you. That is enough.' But in my heart I want the clouds to lift so that I can see it all, the world spread out before me, staring away to the world's end.

There are so many things, Marith thought, that I should like to see again.

Thalia took his maimed left hand in her scarred left hand. 'In the Mountains of Pain, Marith – by the shore of the Sea of the Tears – I thought – After us there is nothing. But we – we can walk away, Marith. All we have to do is to walk away. We have food and water in the saddlebags. And gold. There are streams in the desert, going south. We have crossed it before. We can cross it again. And when we get to the coast, we can find a ship.'

She looked around her at the blazing sunshine yellow desert. Laughed. '*Seserenthelae aus perhalish*. Night comes, we survive.' The hope in her face. She said, 'We can learn other things, Marith. We can be other things. We can live in peace. We dreamed of living alone together in peace, once.'

Her eyes were blue as summer. Wide and huge as the sky and the sea. Beautiful. She's so beautiful, he thought. 'I should have done it when I first came back to you,' she said. 'I would have done it. I wanted to. But I wanted to see us made glorious again.'

She said, her voice very low, 'I wanted to see the Temple fall. I wanted to return to being a queen. I am glad that I saw the Temple falling. I wanted . . .' She shook her head. 'It is more difficult than it would seem, to wash all of these things away from me, I think.' And she laughed at a joke that he did not understand. 'Or perhaps they deserved it. Perhaps it was a good thing to destroy the Temple. Perhaps Sorlost was dying anyway, and we merely hastened it. Who can tell?' She said, 'It doesn't matter. It's done. But we can leave it all behind, Marith.'

His heart leapt. Ah, gods. I knew it. From the first moment she came back to me. From the first moment I first saw her, he thought, in Sorlost, her light, the hope in her, I knew then what she would one day do. She is so strong, he thought. She can do this. She left her god behind her, her Temple, her glory as a priestess, she can bring this too to an end. But look at all of this around us. Everything that we have, we are, everything we've made together. Crowns of silver, thrones of gold, the world kneeling subject before us.

'Don't,' he cried out. 'Don't do this, Thalia.' His voice cracked, saying it. The army, the massed ranks of his soldiers, the grain wagons, the weaponsmiths, the cities, the slaves, the servants, the lords and ladies of his court . . .' Thalia! Don't do this.'

'I should have done it a long time ago.' He heard in her voice: *I should have killed you long ago, Marith. I am better than you are. I know you, and I should have killed you.* She said, angry with him, 'Come with me, Marith. It's so easy. Just walk away.'

'My army—' He stretched out his arms towards them. 'Our army, Thalia.'

Her face shone, radiant, brilliant. The scent of flowers. The scent of desert rain. The scent of snow. The two of them, together, not wanting, not needing. Riding through green summer woodland. Reading by the fireside. Sitting beneath an apple tree.

'I can't. Don't do this. Please. I am a king, Thalia. A king.'

'You can leave it behind,' Thalia said. In her eyes his face was reflected, the shadows writhed in his eyes, ate at him. The scars opening up in him. Kill and kill and kill, don't stop, don't let it end.

'I am a king,' he said. The shadows screamed. Wept and raged for him. Her face shone. She should have done it before, when she first came back to him, yes. Left him the last things of his dreams.

'*Athela*,' Thalia called to the yellow dust of the desert.

Come.

It came down over them, blotted out the light. Beat of its wings.

The red dragon of the Empty Peaks had told him that he had driven it mad, when he had spoken to it. 'You killed my son,' it had said to him. 'Do you think I care about your son?' he had said back to it.

Its body was a deep grey in which all the colours of the world flickered. Its wings were the red of old wounds. Its eyes were the green of trees and leaves. It circled over the desert hills, over the dark valley, over the Army of Amrath so low they could almost reach up and touch it.

A dragon. Of course a dragon. There are dragons in the desert, said the old maps of old empire; this is an age of wonders, over and over, summon them and they will come to you. He had tamed this dragon, bent it to his will, broken it. It circled over and over his army, staring, it did not speak because it could not speak, it could not think. And he was Marith Altrersyr, dragonlord, dragon kin. Marith reached up his hands towards it. '*Lanla*,' Marith whispered to it. *Heal. Be made well.*

It ignored him, circling, its heat raising the smell of singed hair and warm bronze. It felt like standing at rest in a warm breeze. It screamed out the one word '*Ynkykgen*.' Repeated it out again and again. '*Ynkykgen. Ynkykgen. Ynkykgen.*' The only word he had left it able to think or to say or to be.

I will kill.

Its fire took his army. He watched the flames wash them away. They were just waking, stumbling out of their tents, rekindling the cookfires for their breakfast and morning tea. A blacksmith was reshoeing an officer's horse before the day's marching. Children awake since before dawn in the excitement of everything played together in the dust. Kiana would be massaging her injured legs, soothing them with oils. Ryn would be fucking his acrobat. They were drowned in fire, sinking in fire, wallowed in the fire of their death. They stretched and reached for it, enjoying it, luxuriating in the wonder of the end. 'He was killed fighting a dragon. A dragon killed him.' It is like to becoming a god. All men dream of wonders. All men dream of death.

They had brought him to this. They must have known, all of them, that it would end in their deaths.

'Thalia!' Marith cried out clutching her. In Illyr you banished the demon. In Sorlost you turned your eyes on me and gave me hope. Make it go away. Take it away. Thalia! The men of his army were streaming out across the desert, black things small as toys running. His great new red war tent began to burn, all that wealth and splendour, he could have told them not to bother with it. That, more than the soldiers dying, made him understand what she had done. The soldiers were fleeing scattered. I wonder if Kiana is still alive, Marith thought, or Ryn? And Alleen, crowning himself King of Ith. But I want to be king, he thought, I want to be king, I thought you wanted to be queen, Thalia, stop this, what have you done? She, too, she was frightened now, she was filled with fear, she knew that she had been wrong. Marith drew his sword Joy, ran down the slope of the hill towards his distant camp crying out to his men to rally, to the dragon to stop. '*Denakt*,' he screamed at the dragon. '*Denakt, Tiameneket. Ansikanderakesis teime temet ansikysaram.*' *Leave, dragon. Your king commands you.* 'Thalia, what have you done?'

It was mad and wild, and it would not obey him. In the fury of its killing, it had no understanding left. It ran free of all things. They are like me, Marith thought, the dragons. Death things.

It saw him. Its head came around, it wheeled in the air as the birds had. It was grey as iron. Its wings were the same red-black as his hair. Amrath died fighting a dragon. Amrath is a story, a tale told by firelight when the wine had gone around. Do you think you are greater than Amrath, little Altrersyr boy?

Thalia screamed in grief or in horror. The dragon's fire washed over him, took him. He was swimming in flame. His blade was hacking at it, cutting through the fire, shaping it, parting it. Once, in Sorlost, when he was still a man, he had watched a mage shape fire with a twist of a hand. Black fire, burning. Blue fire washing over a woman's face as she wept. His own statue, heaving to the sky its pointless burden, running with flame. The dragon fire flowed away from him, parted, as a child parts a trickle of rainwater with a blade of grass. You see? I am still a king, I will not give this up, wondrous the power that I have. I can destroy a dragon. I have conquered the world. I can save my army, kill the dragon, how great shall be my glory, how measureless my renown. I'll make you a cloak of dragon skin, Thalia my love, seat you on a throne of dragon bones. I'll build my monument in the Mountains of the Heart, my palace on the southern shore of the Sea of Tears. I'll slaughter every living thing in Irlast, I'll cross the Bitter Sea and put every man, woman and child in Ae-Beyond-the-Waters to the sword. I can do it all.

The sword Joy bit deep into the dragon's jaws. Blood spurted out burning the ground. The dragon's tail lashed the earth making it tremble, making Marith sway on his feet. Its claws bit into the sand. A worm, he thought. A stupid dumb beast. Any last fear he might have had of it fled away. His sword came up again to meet it. Rainbows brilliant on the blade, dancing on the ground around him. Rainbows dancing on its scales. It breathed its fire and the flames were soft and warm on his face, soothing like the warmth of Thalia's hands on him. The fire ebbed away. Faded like mist. He drove his sword in. The scales and the flesh of the neck. His sword was so small, compared to it. Swaying on his feet, this huge thing coming at him, facing down so close to him. And him killing it, like a man with a knife cutting open a great bull. And he was so small, and it was so huge, and in a few strokes of his blade it would be gone and dead. Its blood ran down the slope of the hillside, onto the bodies of his men, the blood smoked on the blade of his sword. Oh my army, you who fought and died and lived for me, you who would follow me forever, my companions, oh you who trusted me, who loved me and placed your lives in my hands . . . you see? You see? Didn't I promise you death? Death and ruin and killing without end? You want it! All of you! Rotting flesh, my army, men marching who are a long time dead. Purged in fire now, we can still go on. On and on, never ending. On and on and on. You see, Thalia, you see? There is nothing else. All that I can do is kill. It drew back up into the blue sky, vomiting fire over his army, it was dying, it was afraid. The Army of Amrath staggered together, he could hear their cries, the wails of the dying, the weeping and mourning of those that survived. But you wanted this. Death and death and death! On and on! In Sorlost his statue stood in the Court of the Broken Knife, had stood since the world began, waiting for him, raising aloft in useless triumph his glory and his guilt and his shame.

The dragon came back down towards him. Wounded jaws open, dripping blood and flame. He was running in fire. It was nothing real, it was all he could see. Its claws reached into him, opening him, breaking him, opening up bones and meat. *My heart, is it?* His heart his entrails the depths of his body opened. Teeth long as sword blades burrowing into his stinking flesh. His sword in turn digging into it. Pounding and tearing at it. Obscene. Comic. His body falling away in fragments. Its body falling away shredded. Its fire and its poison, its body arched over him. Stabbed up at it, his sword blade caught it, the sword Joy hissing. It screamed so loud he could see its screaming. The fire and the blood searing his eyes and he was blind.

Thalia. Thalia. Help me. He could not speak. His mouth like his eyes was eaten away. The ruby in his sword Joy's hilt was melted. The runes on its blade were melted away. His bloody cloak was burned to nothing. The brooch that Thalia had given him was smashed and gone.

There is nothing outside of himself. He thought: I don't want to die. I'm so afraid, Thalia.

The dragon's body lay crushing him. Its wings moved, very weakly. It made a gasping noise deep inside itself. Marith drove the hilt of the sword Joy deeper into its belly. It drove its talons deeper into his flesh. Bodies running together.

It, too, was afraid of death.

All the cities broken, all the lives thrown down into dust. All the sacrifices the world had made for him. He thought: I'm so afraid. I'm so afraid. I thought I couldn't die. I thought – I thought – she'll come back to me, save me. Someone will come. My mother, my father, Carin, someone. They'll come.

It wasn't my fault. My men, my soldiers – I tried – I wanted it to end – I wanted the world to be a wondrous place.

There's a blaze of light, and his body screams. There's no peace in dying, he thinks. None. I wanted – I thought – Ti – Carin – Thalia—

Please—

Chapter Sixty-Five

Landra Relast, the murderer
The White Isles

Morr Town was almost rebuilt. Like the fire had never happened. The dead had been buried. The injured had died, or had been tended back to something like health. Some would be scarred for life, burned, bereaved, left destitute. Such things happened. The townspeople looked at the fire's victims with pity, and then went on. They celebrated Sun's Height and the feast of Amrath's birthday; their thoughts turned towards the coming harvest; the days stretched long and sweet.

No one concerned themselves with the woman Lan, lodged in an inn by the harbour. She did not much concern herself with the town. She had been there ten days when the innkeep had shown her his great story: a silver brooch in the shape of a bird, fine work in the Ithish style with garnets for eyes, that the then Prince Marith had traded for a cup of drink one night. 'He didn't have a penny to his name,' the innkeep said, 'the king his father had taken it all from him. He was near crying. I took pity on him.' Landra had settled into the inn by then, got used to the feel of it. She had thought about leaving and finding somewhere else.

She had developed a kind of routine: walk down to the harbour to watch the ships coming in; walk up to the market square to listen for traders' gossip; walk up to the gates of Malth Elelane to watch the soldiers there; walk back to her inn to sit listening to the drinkers in the common room. She would learn nothing of interest. She watched white-haired Ithish merchants unload copper ore for smelting into bronze swords; watched boatloads of soldiers sail off south to a chorus of cheers and sobbing. She had thought to wish the bronze to shatter, flawed; the ships to sink in a storm with all hands; those that cheered and waved off the soldiers to fall sick. Her heart leapt at it, the last cruel killing strength within her. But she had not in the end wished for these things.

Landra Relast, who had nothing. She was consumed and empty, and there was nothing. Not even hatred. Not even grief. The *gestmet* and the *gabeleth* were spent and gone; a dog howling over a grave until its throat is dried, no sound is left it, the dust chokes it. All the strength of her hate she had poured out to break dead bones into dust. She thought of drowning herself. Went so far as to walk out of the town to the rocks of Morren Head, her pockets filled with grey stones. The waves had broken on the cliff with a hiss like voices calling that were the dead of Morr Town and the dead of Ethalden, a drowned sailor with a black beard, a woman who had died when she could have made a choice to die or to live as a slave. Landra had walked back, sat in the inn's common room as the evening fell, eaten bread and hot stew; there was a singer in the common room that night, a tall young man with a weak voice but a beautiful face.

'Going to be a fine morning,' the innkeep said to her as she came down the stairs from her bedchamber the next morning.

'Yes.' He tried to be friendly with her, she had been here for weeks now. And yes, sunlight came in through the windows, fell in bright bars through the cracks in the door, she had watched the water sparkle from her bedchamber window.

'You'll be staying a while longer?' He was fishing for more money from her, paid in advance.

'I think so.' If I had drowned myself, she thought, he would be delighted to claim all of my things. The gold ring, her father's ring, he would have snatched up joyfully, sold it with a song in him.

Today she went to the market place first. For a change in her routine, that was the reason, she told herself, the only reason she went up the streets with her back to the shining sea.

Every day the walk up from the harbour seemed harder, her legs seemed to get heavier, her body heavy as stone. Her legs were getting swollen like her hands. But her hair was growing back, she had noticed that morning. Thick yellow curls tight on her head. When she had put out her hand to feel them, astonished, they had felt fur soft. I am turning into a beast creature, she thought. Truly a *gestmet*, as Raeta had been. Unless that old healer woman's magic has finally worked. In the bottom of her pack she still had the stick that Ali the Healer had given her, with the charm in it.

More prosaically, she thought: I will need to buy a comb and oil to wash my hair with, I suppose. Hence the market first.

'It suits you,' she imagined Tobias saying.

Slaves and silks and gold and silver in the market place, but she had to search for a hair comb. Unless she wanted one made of gold with hair still caught in the teeth. The people shopping had the pinched look she saw everywhere on the White Isles, drifting abstractedly between the traders' stalls. If she no longer wished death on them, they were already weary of death.

'Silk cloth from Cen Andae!'

'White jade from Balkash! Amber from Arunmen! Amber such as was worn by the old Queens of Tarboran!'

At the edge of the market, she found a stall selling what she wanted. 'How much is this?' A cheap-looking thing. The stallholder had a collection of objects spread on a tattered cloth on the ground.

A good feeling, to need such a thing again.

'One in silver,' the stallholder said.

'One in silver?' It was carved from the shinbone of a cow. Any of her father's men could have carved her one themselves.

'And how much is a loaf of bread now?' the stallholder said.

The price of her room and her food was going up, Landra thought. And the one thing that was not being sold in abundance here was anything to eat. Yet she had seen a ship setting out only yesterday for Immish, laden down with grain, its owner seeing it off fat and expensively dressed.

'One in silver,' the stallholder said. Landra paid her. Took the comb. In an alleyway looked around to see that she was alone, ran it through her hair. She went next to an inn in the market square to listen to the talk. The cup of beer she bought, she noticed now she was thinking about it, was expensive also. She thought of the fields burned and sown with salt and ashes, Marith shouting and his men echoing after him: 'Burn it! Destroy it!' The rivers running poisoned. Great forests hacked down for firewood. Soldiers grumbling for their dinner, hungry after a long day's march or another battle. Soldiers' cookfires numberless as the stars, scattered all across Irlast.

The spoils of conquest to the White Isles! she thought.

The inn was crowded, as always. As always, there was nothing said of any interest to her. People would gossip about distant battles, far away and impossible to imagine and quickly washed over with local matters, a sister remarrying beneath her, a son making a success in his trade, a neighbour's child falling sick.

'Old Lord Ronaen is dead,' a man would say to his companion.

'No? That was quick? Unexpected?'

'You could say that.'

'Ah. Yes.'

'Yes.'

'And, hmm, his daughter . . . she'll be off to the wars now, I suppose?'

'I won't bet against it.'

And Landra would start up, thinking, feeling, voices whispering inside her heart, vengeance, vengeance, I am his death, kill them. But the men would move to talking of a mutual friend of theirs whom old Lord Ronaen had once been friends with, and then onto the friend's son who had been a wastrel and a trial to his father but was now a fine young man a credit to his kin. 'If the wars end . . .' they would say, wearily, as one might hope for an end to winter rains. And Landra would sink back in her chair, sip her beer, silence the *gabeleth* the death voices, trying to feel something.

Another ship went out that evening, loaded with well-forged bronze weapons and ardent young men. Briefly, even, she thought of trying to join it. Find Tobias. Find someone. I will go to Malth Salene, she thought, as she thought every day, I never buried them, never said goodbye.

She thought suddenly: I never told them how sorry I was.

She thought suddenly: What would Marith have done if I had asked him to forgive me for the things I did to him?

The ship slipped away into the evening sea leaving its white wake. None of them sailing off to war will ever come back. She thought suddenly: Eltheia, merciful one, be kind, bring them back here to their family's embraces; let them win glory in the far corners of the world, be proud, settle themselves in peace to grow old somewhere. Eltheia, you grew old, you saw your son grow to manhood. Always the world is ending for someone. But some, she thought, some must be kind even as the world ends. And suddenly after the hatred a warmth filled her. A memory of happiness.

'I'll be leaving,' Landra said, 'tomorrow, early. If I could buy some bread and some beer, for my journey?'

The poor innkeep, who had thought to keep her forever, paying out silver without a thought to the cost. 'Tomorrow?'

'Early, as I said.'

'Ah?'

She went past him, reluctant to end up drawn on anything. It felt strange, she thought, talking to him. Now it was said, she thought, it could not be unsaid, she could not change her mind and stay. Up in her room she packed up her few things; most of her possessions, such as they were, already lay at the bottom of her pack. Her father's ring, gold, stamped with a design of a winged horse; it had been too big for her to wear, and now her fingers were too swollen, the knuckles puffed and heavy, she had seen the innkeep wince at them, and the weight of it on her skin would be painful. A spindle carved of horsebone, it had been chipped before she was given it, in the long journey across the Wastes with Raeta and Tobias it had somehow been broken almost in half, was as raw as her skin in the place where the break was. A scrap of cloth, faded to grey, little more than a loose collection of thread. She squeezed the cloth tightly in her hand.

When she left the inn the next morning she left her hair uncovered. Close tight curls: there was a mirror hanging in the common room, an ancient thing of polished silver, splendid with crystal flowers around its edging if one ignored the marks where someone had hacked at it with what might have been an axe; there were still traces of plaster on the back that came from the walls of Malth Tyrenae itself, the innkeep said. The most precious thing he owned, after the brooch that had belonged to the king. In its watery depths Landra saw her hair looked almost like a lamb's fleece, or a mass of yellow spring flowers crowning her head. She set out quickly, forcing her aching legs to go fast, up the street inland towards the Thealeth Gate. She stopped once, to gaze up at the gates of Malth Elelane that she had once thought would be her home.

'Make him promise to do it, Carin. Make him swear it.'

'I'll try.' The pale eyes so like her own eyes, unable to meet her face.

'You will.' Her father's voice. 'And the other thing. He must swear to it all, Carin.'

'I said I'll try,' Carin says. A trumpet sounds from below, a summons to the hall for a state audience, they leave off their plotting, go down together, the tall strong Lord of Third Isle and his fine strong children, how much many of the lesser lords must envy him. In the hall Marith will disgrace himself, turn up barely able to stand, the king's guards have had to drag him out of a tavern, in front of all the court the king his father will scream at him in what she thinks then is shame and hatred but what she now understands is guilt and grief. 'You're no son of mine. You disgust me,' the king will rant. The queen his stepmother will wring her hands. Her own father's face will smile in bitter triumph, even as Carin weeps.

Landra walked on more slowly. The *gabeleth* and the *gestmet*, all the dead of Illyr and the White Isles. A dog howling over the grave of its own heart.

She went through the gates out into Thealan Vale. The corn was high and pale gold as her hair, studded with red poppies and blue cornflowers. A breeze made the ripe ears dance. Green stuff had softened the burial mound of King Illyn on the Hill of Altrersys. She went on and there were elder trees growing up very close to the Heale river, heavy with blossom like new milk, smelling like a child's breath. A cart went by her, oxen kicking up the dust of the roadway, carrying a great load of wood. She crossed the king's bridge over the Heale, soft yellow stone carved with beast-heads, Marith's grandfather Nevethlyn had had it repaired and strengthened, before he sailed off to die in Illyr. After the bridge the road divided running east and north and west. A gibbet hung at the crossroads, black with flies; someone had made an offering beneath it, left the skull of a bird in the hope of health or coin. On the other side of the road across from it, a godstone seemed to envy the dead its gift. Landra went west at the crossroads, the poorest of the roadways, badly made with deep cracked ruts from the timber carts. The forest had come up close to the road, before. Now the earth was raw, nettles growing up, sawdust patches, tree stumps. Further off, where the trees were still thick and green, she could hear the thud of an axe.

The road ran down back to the coast, narrowed to a horse track. In places she stood almost on the edge of the sea. It was warm, she slept out in the open, in the shelter of an ash tree, in the morning it rained blurring the boundary between the land and the water, she walked enjoying the feel of the rain soaking into her hair. The feel of her body drying off, damp clothes and damp earth, as the sun came out. In three days' walking the land became wilder, gorse and heather moorland in which bees drowsed. Yellow and purple, and the grey of the rocks, and the blue of the sky, and the clear blue of the sparkling sea. The ache in her legs raged at her; her hands were sore and swollen, looked like bad meat. She walked on faster. She was almost there.

There was something in her pocket, caught in the lining. A little grey stone, small as a fingernail. It must have been left from when she had thought of drowning herself. It had a hole running through it, clogged with broken shell and dark sand. Wards against the powers of dark, the fisherfolk thought them. She rolled it in her hand, it felt pleasantly rough against her hot rough skin. Made her skin feel very dry. She thought about keeping it, but threw it away into the yellow gorse.

A goat bleated, appeared scrabbling over the crest of the hill above her, two white kids following it. She walked on until the roofs of the village appeared below her, where the path wound down and inland. She had to go down, the path dipping to cross a stream tumbling away to the sea in a little waterfall, a cairn of stones beneath a hawthorn tree beside it to mark it a sacred place, she should have kept the stone, placed it there, she thought, though the cairn had a tumbled, weather-worn, abandoned look; the path went up again steeply, she had to scramble over rocks; a place where a great mass of vegetation had sprung up, the path almost blocked, more stunted hawthorn trees closing around it in a tunnel, a tumble of stones all overgrown with honeysuckle where a cottage must once have been. Then very suddenly she was on scrubby wind-cropped turf, soft underfoot, an outcrop of stone like a huge version of the stream's cairn; she was standing above a cove where the sea broke with a hiss on black shingle and the path ran inland to the village or on along the cliff towards the next point. The horizon ended there ahead of her with a steep slope of gorse and heather and bracken, another rock outcrop black against the skyline. A hawk hung above the stones and was gone in a dark flash. On the other side of the headland there would be another stream running down, and then a little cottage, low to the shore, where an old woman who was a god lived. Or had lived.

'Ru?' She called it nervously. The cottage was quiet, the windows dark. The garden looked very overgrown, a mass of nettles in which butterflies flitted, brambles humped over what had been the garden wall. But smoke rose from the smoke hole in the roof.

'Ru?'

A goat bleated, behind the cottage, up on the moorland. She's dead and gone, Landra thought. She's found her seal skin, gone back into the sea.

A bent figure came up the path from the seashore. Thin, crumpled, brittle as driftwood. Her skin had a grey tinge to it. Her hair was very thin showing a grey crusted scalp.

'Lan?'

A great scream of seabirds, gulls wheeling over the figure, almost mobbing it. Its arms beat upward, driving them off.

'Ru!'

The woman held up her hands to Landra. Grey skin. Grey as stones. Grey as a seal's pelt. Her fingers were clutched together. Changing back into a seal's limbs.

'Lan, girl.' Rheumy eyes, black as pebbles. Seal eyes in a woman's face. 'Come in, then,' Ru said, 'make some tea, will you, Lan?'

Landra followed Ru into the cottage. The door stuck; Ru had to shove at it, hard enough that her paddle-like hands shook.

'Where's the girl who came to look after you?'

'Gone.' Run off, the moment Lan left her with Ru, doubtless. Foolish, Lan: be thankful she left Ru with a roof over her head. Inside, the cottage stank of fish. The furniture was all still there, the thick long housewife's table, the bed, the chair by the hearth with the spinning wheel and the wool basket beside it where Ru had taught Lan to spin. Everything was covered in grease and dust.

'She found my skin,' said Ru. 'Her and her brother, they searched the stones behind the house, and they found it. I asked her not to, like I asked you. But I couldn't go back,' said Ru. 'I couldn't go back to the sea. Not now, like this.' She drank her tea, smiled at Lan. 'Sit down here, Lan, girl, get out that spindle I gave you, and I'll teach you to spin.'

Landra the *gabeleth* the *gestmet* the bitter hating dead held out her ruined hands, swollen, clumsy, red and puffy as rotted meat. 'My hands are too damaged to spin thread, Ru. And the spindle you gave me is broken.'

Chapter Sixty-Six

Orhan Emmereth the Lord of the Rising Sun, the Dweller in the House of the East, the Nithque to the Ever Living Emperor and the Undying City, the Emperor's True Counsellor and Friend

The City of Sorlost the Golden, the Eternal, the Undying, the decaying heart of the mummified remnant of the Sekemleth Empire the Yellow Empire the Empire of the Rising Sun's Light

Chief Secretary Gallus and Orhan between them run the Empire, write carefully in gold ink in a thick new Treasury ledger that is certainly not bound in human skin. The question of rebuilding the guard house at the Maskers' Gate at least is now resolved, the gate having been destroyed. As is the question of rebuilding the Imperial Army, there being no one left in the Empire to defend. The balance of trade has improved, nothing travelling in equalling nothing travelling out. And the poor live in hovels of sweetwood and marble and onyx and melted bronze. In twenty years, or thirty, or fifty, Orhan pretends, there might be something to show for all his efforts. He has certainly been able to strip things down to the roots and start again. He'll probably have to kill Chief Secretary Gallus soon. Before Chief Secretary Gallus kills him.

The Asekemlene Emperor is a child again, like the last one and the one before that. It took thirty men to move the Emperor's throne back from the Great Temple to the ruins of the Summer Palace. The High Priestess recognized the child as the Asekemlene Emperor when one of the thirty men fell down dead from exhaustion in front of him.

Of the remaining twenty-nine men, well over half of them are now either dead or fucked off. Excuse the undignified language, so unlike Orhan's usual civil turn of phrase. No other term is fitting, however, when you watch the population of your city decline before your eyes day by day. It would be nice to be able to order the gates shut, keep the bastards from fucking off into the desert. If. It would have been nicer to have been able to order the gates shut a year ago, keep the plague out. If.

The city's population would be still smaller, were it not for the wretches that stumble out of the desert, running away from war or famine or plague or all three at once and other things. An accursed death-worshipping wasteland in the desert is a blessing, a wonder, a promised home, when you've nowhere else to go and everything you've ever loved is dead. They beg the Emperor's Nithque to let them stay and sometimes, sometimes, if he's feeling generous, he agrees. Chief Secretary Gallus warns against it; the Emperor, Orhan suspects, will warn against it too if he lives long enough to learn to talk. Can't have people thinking the Sekemleth Empire is soft and weak.

Though perhaps the Emperor will have other things on his mind to worry about, if he lives long enough. The Emperor has a palace with five habitable rooms including the famous bathhouse. The Emperor has an empire that runs from the ruined palace to three feet beyond the line of the ruined city wall. The Emperor has a Nithque who doesn't sleep at night without dreaming of his murdered wife and murdered child and murdered sister, winces and shakes dripping cold sweat at the memory-sound of his sword blade cutting the previous Emperor's throat and his sister's throat.

All day every day Orhan starts up, hearing that sound. Darath puts his arms around him, when he's there with him, holds him, tells him it's fine, killing Celyse was a necessary thing to do. It probably was a necessary thing to do. 'It's all right,' Darath tells him. 'It's all right, Orhan. Believe me.'

Darath? Oh, Darath's there beside him like any old married couple, they live together in the ruins of the House of Flowers, Darath keeps the house, stays at home, reassures Orhan, puts his arms around Orhan when he wakes screaming at night. In his secret heart Orhan knows that one day Darath himself will break under his own guilt and grief and suffering that he never speaks about, that being Orhan's strength is a crushing weight that will one day prove too much. Until then, what can either of them do but carry on and carry on.

They go to the Temple together every week to offer flowers, beg for something. Though many in Sorlost now worship the Death God in His statue in the Court of the Broken Knife.

Chapter Sixty-Seven

Tobias, senior squad commander in the 'Winged Blades' in the Army of Queen Kiana the True Heir to the God Marith Altrersyr the True Ruler of All Irlast
Besieging the city of Arunmen. Again. Three bloody times, now, it's been besieged. No, wait, tell a lie, four

Killed by a dragon! Gods, he'd wet himself laughing when he heard. Cried a bit, too, maybe. Stupid boy. But it's bloody great now. He can fight and kill and sack and plunder, and know he isn't doing it for that degenerate diseased poisonous little shit. All the kings looking to hire good old hard old soldiers. Work for a bit, defect, get a pay rise from your last boss's sworn mortal enemy, work for a bit, defect, get a pay rise, work for a bit. Quids bloody in. Only a shame Rate and Alxine aren't here to see it.

'*She pays how much, Queen Kiana? No! No. Get out of it.*'

'*No word of a lie. And King Alleen . . . rumour going round he'll pay double that, if we come over to him again, he's that bloody desperate since King Ryn took Immier off him.*'

'*King Ryn? What's he paying?*'

'*He's not paying anything. He's dead. Lord Cauvanh of Immish killed him. Lord Cauvanh now . . . he pays so little he might as well be paying his soldiers in goat shit, doesn't exactly lead from the front, either, that one. But he knows what he's bloody doing. Hasn't lost a single bloody battle yet.'*

The Blades don't rape and they don't torture. Which is rare now. So piss off with it. Not the greatest job in the world, in all confidence and honesty, shit stinks, wet leather stinks, his legs ache and his back aches and he's got a shiny new wound to the face. Always another twenty men queuing up behind, though, every time a vacancy in the Blades comes up.

Good lads.

Regrets? Hells, yeah. Just a few. What have I got to hope for, now, he thinks at night, except a crap death? In a different life, maybe . . . Tobias, son, husband, father, maker of beautiful things. But the village dyer died, and the village died with him, and the gods know and Marith Altrersyr knew the world's a cruel place.

Chapter Sixty-Eight

I do not remember his face now, or the sound of his voice when he spoke to me. I do not need him. He was not a good man. He deserved what came to him. I cannot remember, now, why it was that I cared for him.

But I did think that he would come with me.

On the other side of the world, in Ae-Beyond-the-Waters, which may or may not be a real place, there is a house that looks out over the shining sea into the east. A woman lives there alone. She walks on the beach, stands staring out at the horizon, rides in the hills, goes out on the rocks of the headland to watch the waves, visits the village to buy meat and fish and bread. Talks to the village women of little things. Her hair is turning grey now; she can feel old age drawing its fingers across her back. A memory might come to her sometimes of terror and glory. What it felt like to be the most terrible and most glorious power in all the world. Memories to break her heart with grieving. Memories to make her smile. Memories to make her cold with shame. Her life is pointless, in the way most human lives are pointless. Dull quiet peace, hope, memory, her life going on and on. She wakes each morning with the sun on her face.

* * *

She has in her house a bag of gold thalers, a bag of diamonds, a bag of rubies, a bag of dragon's teeth. She is the Chosen of Great Tanis the Lord of Living and Dying, she is the Queen of the World, she is Eltheia Returned to Us.

Perhaps it is easy for her to live in peace.

Chapter Sixty-Nine

The young woman stands on the headland, listens with closed eyes to the sea. She's come out here to make him have to walk to find her. Put it off.

His footsteps scrunch on the turf behind her. It's wild here, right out on the edge, where the cliff tumbles down into the sea. In a few years' time he will be buried here, out on the cliffs at the edge, she will weep bitter tears of guilt over his grave, promise him she'll avenge him, curse herself, curse their father, curse him. A bee buzzes too close to her, she shakes her head and her yellow hair blows in the sea wind.

'He's agreed to it. All of it,' her brother says.

She turns. It's done.

'He promised me,' her brother says. 'Swore it. On his sword and on his name.' He looks uncomfortable, shifts his eyes away from her. There's a dirty stain on his jacket, his clothes are crumpled and smell of sweat. He's getting heavy in the face. Hasn't slept.

'Held a bottle to his lips, told him you'd pour it into him if he agreed, did you?' she says. She was the one who made him do this. She shouldn't be angry with him. It's all getting out of control. 'Made him beg?'

'Not quite,' her brother says. His face crumples up with pain as he speaks.

A disturbance in the water, just where the waves break on the rocks. A seal, a very large one, raising its dog head, seems almost to be staring at them. It's too far away to see us, she thinks. It dives. Comes back up and it's got something in its mouth. An eel. It wrestles, fighting the eel, biting at it. The waves break over it, washing it white. Carin rubs at his eyes. He's started doing that recently. It irritates her. She's beginning to guess what it is. 'You'll have a wonderful wedding night, I'm sure,' he says.

'That's years away.' The Altrersyr lie, she thinks. Desperate.

'It can't be years away, Landra,' her brother says. 'Are you stupid? It has to be soon. Before his father finds some way to get him out of it.' Her brother says savagely, hatefully, to her, to himself, 'Before he drinks himself to death. Joy to the bride, Landra,' her brother says. 'Start planning your wedding dress.'

'We'll rule the White Isles!' she shouts back. The seal is still wrestling with its prey, can't get its jaws around it to hold it. Her shout makes a gull start up, sweeping out over the cliff over the sea with a shriek. She shivers.

'How wonderful.'

It will be, she thinks. Yes. She thinks of her mother, fussing over how the household is run, bending her head to their father in servitude, doing as she is bid.

'I'll take him out to celebrate the betrothal, then,' her brother says. 'Thank him. Tell him how delighted you are. Start prodding him on how and when.'

Shut up, she thinks. Stop. She tries to look for the seal. It's gone. Just the gulls.

'He won't do it,' she says. She frowns. 'You're lying. No one would agree to do that, not to their own father. Not even him.'

'Not even him?' Her brother says, 'Gods, Landra, why do you hate him suddenly?'

'I don't hate him.' It's his fault, she thinks. Somehow. He should have seen through them. Said no. Pushed them away. How can he go along with this, his own ruin, if he's not vile and poison and only worth her hate? 'I want to marry him, don't I?' she says.

'He loves me,' her brother says then. 'He told me that. He loves me.' The gulls scream. Twist in the air. Dark shapes. The seal resurfaces, dog head staring, pebble wet black eyes. Too far away to see her brother's face. Her brother says, 'He says he doesn't want anything else in the world, not the throne, not a crown, not eternal glory, not anything, apart from to love me.'

'The Altrersyr lie,' she spits out. She wants to shake him. But Carin says fiercely, 'He's not lying,' and she knows that's true for now at least.

Acknowledgements

There are more people to thank with every book:

Once again once again, this book was only possible because of my agent, Ian Drury, and my editors Vicky Leech, Jack Renninson and Natasha Bardon at HarperVoyager and Brit Hvide at Orbit. Between them, they have changed my life. I cannot express my gratitude to them.

Michael R Fletcher is the best writing friend and collaborator I could wish for, also his books rock.

Adrian Collins at Grimdark Magazine is too good for this world. Grimdark Magazine itself is brilliant. The Grimdark Magazine team are very cool.

Steven Erickson, Christian Cameron, Mark Lawrence, Lucy Hounsom, Deborah A Wolf, James A Moore, Anna Stephens, Sam Hawk, Jen Williams, Micah Yongo, Steve Poore, Joanna Hall, Adrian Tchaikovsky, Peter McLean, Andy Remic, Luke Scull, John Gwynne . . . the list of authors whom I admire and am privileged to know is wonderfully long.

Leona Henry. Jo Fletcher. Michael Evans, Laura M Hughes and Kareem Mahfouz at The Fantasy Hive. Petros and everyone at BookNest.eu. Bethan Hindmarch. Thomas James Clews, who really did like the porridge. James Allen Razor – thinking about you and Stacey. Team Grimbold Books, not very grim in person but bold indeed. The Fantasy Inn crew. Alex Khlopenko at Three Crows Magazine. Red Star Reviews. Coffee Archives. The Speculative Kitchen. Book Wol, who makes of drinks worthy of Marith. The facebookers of the Second Apocalypse. The Fantasy Writers' Bar. Everyone at GDWR, my spiritual home.

Julian, Gareth, Jo and everyone else at PP, for being understanding. It's <possible> a few lines of this thing were written when I should have been doing briefing, yes.

Sophie E Tallis, for the map.

Dejan Delic, Stas Borodin and Quint Von Cannon, for the pictures.

Allen Stroud and Karen Fishwick. Kate Buyers. Kate Dalton.

Judith Katz.

My family.

Everyone who reads my books.